I0614695

UPTON ARMS

A Retirement Home for Supernaturals

UPTON ARMS

A Retirement Home for
Supernaturals

SCOTT CRAVEN

UPTON ARMS
A Retirement Home for Supernaturals

CITY OWL PRESS
www.cityowlpress.com

Cover Design by Butchikhongruot. All stock photos licensed appropriately.

Edited by Danielle DeVor.

For information on subsidiary rights, please contact the publisher at info@cityowlpress.com.

Print Edition ISBN: 978-1-64898-474-7

Digital Edition ISBN: 978-1-64898-473-0

Printed in the United States of America

 CITY OWL PRESS
Escape Your World ◆ Get Lost in Ours

ALSO BY SCOTT CRAVEN

Dead Jed Trilogy

Dead Jed: Adventures of A Middle School Zombie

Dead Jed 2: Dawn of the Jed

Dead Jed 3: Return of the Jed

To my aging friends and loved ones, especially those who have accepted and embraced its inevitable changes. Don't worry, Melissa, you'll come around.

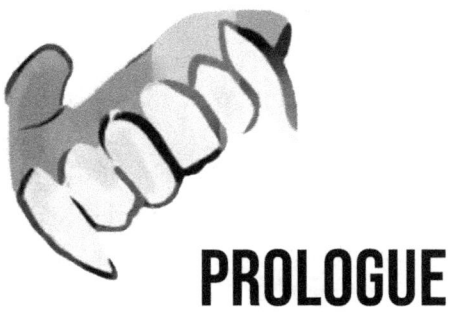

PROLOGUE

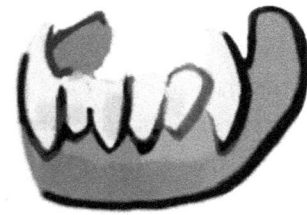

FIVE YEARS AGO

AFTER MORE THAN six centuries of predatory dominance, it had come to this.

Cargo pants.

The vampire hadn't been this depressed since the Great Famine, which mortals called the Black Plague.

Yet here Vlad was, outside a Chili's, wearing pants with far too many pockets, the majority of which were empty. His hunting skills had deteriorated to a point where camouflage, rather than a fangs-out assault, was his best option.

There had been a time when this particular all-you-can-slay buffet would fly well below Vlad's radar. Inside was the bland and tepid blood of those who spent weekends watching sports, washing cars, and screaming at kids. In a different era, he'd hunted only gourmet meals provided by the smart and the strong. Their fighting spirits enhanced their flavor, like sipping wine of an exquisite vintage.

That was long ago and far away. For reasons hinging on both his abilities and morals (more the former than the latter, if Vlad was honest with himself), his diet consisted of small mammals, from squirrels and chipmunks to the occasional feral cat. He avoided raccoons due to their feisty nature and the cuts they left behind, now that even flesh wounds took days instead of seconds to heal.

Still, Vlad needed a cheat day every few months, if for nothing more than to give him a reason to keep living. The centuries had taken their toll, and he had to make a few lifestyle adjustments to his aging body and powers when it came to enjoying a human dish.

But a Chili's? Now he knew how seniors felt joining those tours adapted to people with walkers. This was the vampire version.

If he had to be here, Vlad was going to make the most of it.

An hour before, he had donned his Ordinary Guy costume of blue oxford shirt, khaki pants, and loafers. It was one of the few times Vlad was thankful vampires didn't cast reflections, though he remained curious as to what he looked like (not to mention how handy it would be to see himself when shaving).

Though the sun had set an hour before, the heat and humidity slapped Vlad's face as soon as he exited his apartment in a rundown duplex. At least it was biologically impossible to break a sweat, since his skin was either cool or flaming, based on the presence of UV light beamed directly from the sun.

He walked the half mile without once looking skyward, bored more than a century ago with the planets and stars locked to the only world he knew. Soon he was outside Chili's, where he was a lion visiting a watering hole filled with lumbering, dull-witted, and often intoxicated wildebeests. Vlad headed straight to the bar, the vampire deli counter. Casting about for the weakest in the herd, his eyes settled on the out-of-shape, forlorn gentleman sitting at the end. From the Crocs to the plaid shirt tucked into cargo shorts, the outfit screamed, "Prey here, get your prey here!"

No need to open the menu, Vlad knew what he wanted. He nudged into a narrow gap and put his elbows on a wood surface that had likely absorbed a thousand spilled Bud Lights. He ordered just that, not wanting to upset the flock. Vlad pretended to take a sip every few minutes, figuring the patrons were oblivious to their surroundings and wouldn't notice the always-full beer in front of him. He glanced down the bar every now and then, realizing he was definitely in the mood for Mexican (assuming, wrongly, his catch of the day was from Mexico).

The vampire settled into what he called "Brad mode," that genial guy who blends into the background to the point he fades away, sip by faux sip. Vlad liked to think it was related to his (dwindling) power to hypnotize, but in honest moments realized it was because he was just another poorly dressed white guy at America's most generic bar.

Vlad glanced over just in time to see his mark lay a twenty on the bar and push away. Vlad followed, maintaining a hunting distance of forty feet. He pushed through the front door just in time to see his dinner round the corner. The vampire hustled, hoping his target had parked his car away from the halo of lights in the parking lot. If this spot didn't work out, there were other hunting grounds, starting with the Applebee's just down to the street, then the Olive Garden, and ultimately the Red Lobster, in descending order of decent meals. As he rounded the corner, Vlad's thoughts drifted to the last, hoping he wouldn't be stuck there because he was not in the mood for fish—

WHAP! Two bodies collided, and Vlad reluctantly pushed away his dinner because nothing was more awkward than bumping into prey.

"Excuse me," Vlad muttered, eyes down. He wanted to add a quick apology, but the hand squeezing his throat made it impossible to talk.

"I can smell the vampire on you," his (not) supper growled, tightening his grip..

Vlad caught a whiff of something too, an earthy scent behind the cheap cologne. *Werewolf,* Vlad thought. He'd dealt with them before. He was no match physically, not anymore, but he had other ways to deal with this unexpected encounter. Vlad gripped his foe's wrist, met the wolf's stare, boring down deep—

"Seriously?" the man said, digging his nails (bordering on claws) into Vlad's throat. "You think you can pull that hypno-vampire bullshit on me? I should go full-on wolf and tear you apart, except this is my favorite Chili's, and I don't want to burn bridges." The truth, as Vlad would learn in the coming days, was that this particular predator hadn't achieved full-on wolf in years, lucky to achieve Goldendoodle and rarely getting past a member of the rodent family.

At this point, however, Vlad felt at the wolf's mercy. He tapped his assailant's arm, motioning that he'd like to speak. Fingers loosened just enough for Vlad to stutter a clumsy apology to a meal starting to give him heartburn.

The werewolf released Vlad with a look the vampire had never been the recipient of—one of pity.

"Dude, I get it," the man sighed. "It doesn't get much lower than hunting at Chili's. Unless it's at Applebee's." He paused, seeing the defeated expression on Vlad's face. "Oh man, you were going there next, weren't you? Please don't tell me Red Lobster is on that list."

All Vlad could do was nod.

The man stepped back, analyzing Vlad in the dim light. "I'd say, five hundred and sixty-one years old? Give or take a decade."

"That's oddly specific," Vlad ventured, because he wasn't quite sure himself.

"The wrinkles, the liver spots, the creaky joints. Well, I'm guessing about the joints, though there was a time I could have heard them."

Vlad shook his head. "You're not far off. It's just that I stopped counting a long time ago. When I hit two hundred, I had a few friends over for an epic party that eventually led to a pretty horrific mural in Bucharest. There might even be a museum about it now. Since then, birthdays are just more math."

"I get it. My talents aren't what they used to be. I had no idea what I was going to do if you'd gone for my carotid."

Vlad shook his head, lips curling into something resembling a smile. "You were bluffing."

"I was indeed. Good thing because that saved us the spectacle of two ancient dudes slapping each other before collapsing in exhaustion."

"In a Chili's parking lot, adding insult to injury."

The man laughed and stuck out a hand with its stunted claws. "Luis. Sorry about starting to turn. Awkward, right?"

"Vlad," the vampire said, gripping the meaty half-paw. "Nice to meet a fellow supernatural. Don't run across too many these days."

"Dying breed. Literally."

"The night is young even if we're not. Care to join me for some fun? There's a place not far from here that offers a younger, much fresher clientele with an ABV high enough to give you a nice buzz."

With that, two creatures of the night hopped into a rideshare to a prey-bearing watering hole teeming with pretty. The TGI Friday's was bulging at the waistline with potential, a land of milk, honey, and cargo shorts. Settling in at the bar, the two ordered pastel drinks as camouflage and surveyed the menu that packed the seats. Vlad couldn't quite settle on what to have until Luis offered to do the bulk of the hunting.

"You mean give it to me on a silver platter," the vampire grinned.

"Yes. But don't say 'silver.' It's like mentioning 'cross' to a vampire."

"'Kryptonite' to Superman."

"'Subpoena' to any politician."

The two were still laughing when they chose a boisterous and inebriated twenty-something hipster off the late-night menu, a happy meal indeed. Once the sky had changed from black to deep purple and brightening every minute, they stood in front of Vlad's apartment.

"I'd invite you in but..." Vlad paused, unsure where to go.

"No worries. I'm not your type and frankly, you're not mine. No offense."

"None whatsoever."

Luis gave the duplex a once-over and shook his head. "You live in this dump?"

"Now I'm going to take offense," Vlad said. "Yeah, this is where I live. Not nearly as nice as a castle, but that was centuries ago."

"I have a suggestion if you have a little time."

"Sure." Vlad gestured to the eastern glow. "As long as it won't take more than a few minutes. I burst into a fireball at sunrise."

Luis scribbled something on the back of a Chili's napkin and shoved it into the vampire's hand. "Come by Upton Arms some evening. Head to Building C and ask for Worley. She'll take care of the rest."

Vlad had about a thousand questions, but held onto them when Luis pointed out how unhealthy it was to smoke. "Which is what your forehead is doing right now."

———

A week and seven rodent meals later, Vlad had nothing to lose. Little did he know it would be the start of a beautiful friendship.

Until he met a particularly cranky rainbowchaser bent on taking the gold right out of the golden years.

ONE

IT GLEAMED LIKE A JEWEL, a thing so precious that it had no business being inside a decrepit industrial building with so little security. Yet now it was about to be his, this treasure bringing out the bloodlust Vlad hadn't felt in far too many years.

His heart quickened as he readied himself to pounce, imagining the taste of the crimson liquid that pulsed with life under translucent skin. Vlad felt his once-dormant fangs slide into place as he widened his jaws until the click of dislocation let him know he was ready. His victim, meanwhile, remained oblivious to the clear and present danger presented by an apex predator.

At least that's how it played out in Vlad's mind until he couldn't figure out the cap and get the damn pouch open.

"Need help with that?" came a voice that didn't sound helpful at all, especially since the offer was bookended by a low chuckle.

Vlad looked his companion up and down, noting the uneven eyes and ragged patches of sparse fur that blemished the face. "Like you're the one who should be laughing," Vlad said. "You look like what happens when a wolf and a possum mate inside a reactor core."

"Fuck you and the bat you rode in on," Luis glared. "Oh wait, you rode in on an Uber."

Vlad ignored the werewolf's trash talk, having had the "wings vs. all fours" debate too many times when it came to transformations. Instead, the vampire focused on the task, and the pint-sized pouch, at hand. "Damn, this thing must have one of those caps, you know the kind?"

"Child-resistant?" Luis grinned, his face approaching its gruff, hairless normalcy. "Or maybe it's not that complex. Just vampire resistant."

When workers would watch the tape a few hours later, not long after discovering the break-in and theft at the blood-donation center, they would see a disfigured, perhaps homeless man talking to himself as a blood pouch floated nearby. Instead of informing police, management ordered the tape destroyed for fear of being accused of digital manipulation. An enterprising (and only) member of the security team made a copy as well as a few extra bucks peddling it to shows that included "inexplicable" and "paranormal" in their titles. It was soon taken down when viewers complained it exploited a housing-disenfranchised man of atypical features.

But for now, Vlad and Luis were oblivious to the cameras, as well as the threat they posed. Vlad focused on opening the pouch of blood, and Luis on getting back to appearing as an ordinary man rather than one suffering from mange.

"You know, at any time I could slice it open with my fangs," Vlad said, flipping the pouch in his pale, long-fingered hands. "I choose not to because it could get messy."

"I know for a fact you haven't had a fang-on in a very long time. Otherwise, we wouldn't be at a blood bank during non-business hours to make a withdrawal."

Vlad could only groan, knowing that even if he could see himself in a mirror, he wouldn't want to. He cut a majestic figure in the day, over six feet tall when the average size was a foot less. Thin but not skinny, the first thing people noticed were his piercing blue eyes set in perfect, milky skin. Jet-black hair, once swept back past his collar, was more salt than pepper, more mop than mane. Lines outlined his mouth and eyes, and the three creases along his forehead were threatening to multiply. It was even worse below the neck when a chest that demanded V-neck shirts was sallow and non-threatening.

Time also had taken its toll on his slightly shorter lupine companion. Luis had made sure to show photos of his younger self, the one with a barrel chest and sloping shoulders. With deep-set eyes over a sharp nose and broad chin, Luis could easily have been taken for a linebacker. His ponytail was gray, his face jowlsy, and while he had a dad bod, he did not rock it.

The problem at this point was that Vlad's hunger was inversely proportional to his dexterity, thus finding the opening to the blood pouch was like discovering the entrance to a secret Egyptian tomb.

"You realize the pouch is not designed for straws," Luis wagged his head in shame. "I'd suggest packing up what fits in the cooler and getting back home where you can enjoy it in peace and relative quiet. Besides, at this rate, we'll be here to sunup, and you know how that plays with your complexion, setting it on fire an all."

Vlad hated to admit it, but Luis was right. Messing with the pouch only made him hangrier, and while they were both pretty sure they hadn't raised any alarms (they had), it was time to go.

"Fine, but make sure you're getting those with the latest expiration dates," Vlad said, tossing the pouch back into the large, blood-packed refrigerator. He and Luis reached toward the back of the orderly rows, grabbing blood guaranteed fresh for two weeks. A minute later, Luis shut the cooler now heavy with several months of Sweet Neck-tar (Vlad's term and no one else's).

Getting out was a lot easier than getting in, their entrance requiring Luis to turn into a small creature that looked vole-like, only more awkward. Had Luis still been capable of wolf-man with the requisite strength, it would have been easier to tear off the security screen blocking the back window. Neither one of them had that kind of strength, not anymore. Not for decades.

Instead, Luis snuck through various ducts and unlocked the necessary doors, progressing slowly to make sure there were no cameras or silent alarms (there were). Then again, who monitors a blood bank? (The owners do.)

Vlad was much appreciative, knowing how long it took Luis to rebound back to man. They each grabbed a handle and headed toward the exit when they heard the front door open, followed by shuffling footsteps.

"I thought you said there were no alarms?" Vlad sneered.

"None that I noticed," Luis shrugged.

"So much for your finely tuned wolf senses."

"If you remember, I wasn't a wolf. And if you had any idea how sore I'm going to be tomorrow, you wouldn't be giving me—"

"Hold on." Vlad lowered the cooler as a flashlight beam danced at the end of the hall.

"Fuck me." Luis spun his head around. "We need to find another way."

Another way? Vlad thought. *Are you joking?* There was a time he could have taken on ten men leaving with nothing but a full stomach. Had it come to this, running from a couple of rent-a-cops? Yet even as his heart commanded him to attack, his brain (and face it, his body) told him a retreat was in order.

"*Was* there another way?" Vlad spun in a complete circle, hoping Luis had a clue where they might be in the blood-lab maze.

"No idea, but I suggest we reverse course—"

"Hold on there!" a voice screamed at the end of the hall as the flashlight beam found the culprits. Luis froze instinctively.

Vlad shielded his eyes but could not make out the figure behind the beam. He was pretty sure of two things, however. There was just one man, and his voice suggested his age was long past "I'm going to kick your ass" prime.

"What in the heck have you got there?" He aimed the light at the cooler. In the reflected glare, Vlad saw a man so close to his expiration date, he'd be half-off in the potential victims bin. The problem wasn't the guard himself, but the mess he and Luis might leave behind. The man bent at the waist, eyes in a tight squint. "Is that a cooler?"

"Could you put down the light?" Vlad felt a fang break the surface, happy he still had it in him but wary of following through since whoever was on the other end of the flashlight was likely no threat. "We're not here to hurt anyone."

"Why would you want to hurt me?" The man lowered the beam to reveal a tactical vest with pockets, loops, and clips designed to hold any manner of weapon, both lethal and nonlethal. The body wearing the impressive display of might was definitely nonlethal. Vlad judged him to be in his mid-eighties, maybe five feet five with the vest weighing more than he did.

"Because we broke in?" Luis wondered aloud.

"You broke in to hurt me?"

"No, we broke in to…" Luis looked at the cooler, Vlad knowing there was no way his slow-witted friend had a reasonable explanation in mind. "Actually, we didn't break in at all, we took a wrong turn—"

"Now hold on," the guard interrupted, patting himself as if to put out a fire. He searched six pockets before producing his phone, flipping the screen toward the vampire and werewolf. "I know you broke in, says so right here on my app. I'll read it to you." He turned the phone back around. "'Break-in at 1939 Hawthorne.' Came in at 1:19 a.m. That was about a half-hour ago."

"Took your time," Vlad couldn't help muttering.

"Had I known it was a dang blood bank, I would've taken my time," the guard retorted, his hearing of a quality that surprised the two of them. "Now what's in the cooler?"

As Vlad searched for a plausible lie, he asked the guard his name.

"It's uh…George." He patted his pockets again.

Looking for ID to double check, Vlad thought. "Well, George," Luis purred, putting Vlad on alert because nothing good came when his friend flashed his lupine side. "The cooler is full of blood. Obviously."

Vlad shot Luis a look that screamed, "Don't make me kill George," a possible outcome now that the werewolf had come clean.

Luis continued without missing a beat. "It's a delivery. From the drive today. The one by the, uh…"

"Girl Scouts," Vlad chimed in. "They are just so darned helpful when it comes to getting people to bleed."

George stopped patting his vest pockets. "Good, because I have no idea where my Taser is. Let me show you where storage is."

The guard pushed past Vlad and Luis. "I was afraid you were trying to steal blood, and boy would I get in trouble for letting that happen. But who steals blood? Follow me, I'll help you put it away. Sooner we get it done, sooner I can get home."

As Luis began to follow George, Vlad grabbed the werewolf's shoulder and pulled him close. "What are you doing? Let's go. This guy can't stop us."

"Exactly. You know what happens after that? He gets fired and has to live on the street because if he's working at his age, it's not by choice."

Luis had a point. With shoulders slumped, Vlad grabbed his half of the cooler and followed George back to storage, where the pouches were (re)placed.

Back at the front entrance, George let out a big yawn as he locked up. "Not to be rude, but I got a semi-warm bed waiting for me at Upton Arms, so good night gentlemen."

Luis and Vlad exchanged shocked looks. Upton Arms? That's where they lived.

"George," Luis scratched his head. "Are you, um, enhanced?"

"Rather personal," George perked up. "And while I'm flattered, neither one of you are my type, even if I could still get it up."

Five minutes later, with George long gone, a vampire and a werewolf were still laughing out loud in front of a blood bank.

"Guess he's in the normal ward, filled with those with penchants for heart disease and pickleball." Vlad wiped tears from his eyes.

"You think?" Luis shot back. "Let's give him another five minutes to beat us home. I know we came up short on blood, but damn if this wasn't a night."

Back at the retirement home, Vlad raided the community fridge for the five-pound brick of ground beef he kept there for emergencies, squeezing it for every last drop. Still hungry, he headed back to his room and couldn't help but conjure images of himself as a young man, a fearless creature of the night. As usual, he didn't just wonder when his body might finally surrender to the ages, he hoped for it like a metaphorical stake through the heart.

Little did he know that stake was on its way.

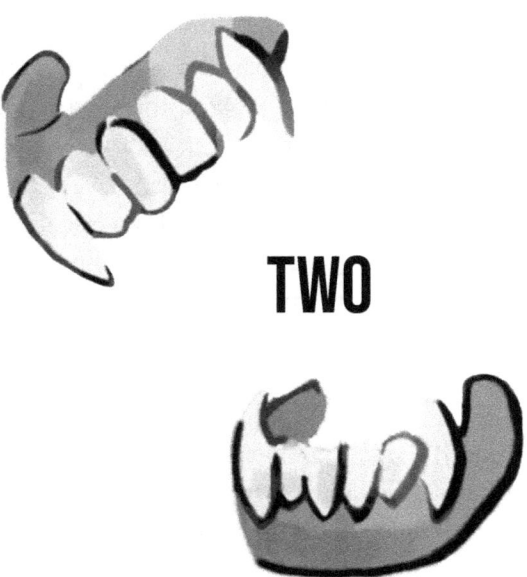

TWO

"DAMN, people, can you keep it down, trying to get a little sleep here!"

A rumpled, now-ravenous Vlad stood in his doorway, staring down the hallway toward the community room where a TV blared amid shouts. He scratched himself absent-mindedly, sharp fingernails nearly cutting through the pale blue boxers that held onto his thin frame for dear life.

He shuffled toward the door at the end of the hall that was propped open by a ceramic urn whose ashen resident was believed to linger spiritually (though Vlad refused to believe in an afterlife, especially one used to explain faulty plumbing and uneven shelves). The cursed glare of daylight spilled through the opening, and amid the several voices bouncing off the walls, one stood out. It was Patrick, resident loudmouth, whose big voice could never compensate for his small body, not that he could be convinced otherwise.

Such was life at Upton Arms. Vlad had had no idea such a retirement home existed for the allegedly immortal, or that one was even required. Immortals relying on assisted living was like Republicans voting for tax increases. It just didn't exist.

Yet here they were, a ragged assortment of beings who were very mortal indeed, but with expiration dates far exceeding that of the misguided majority who thought anyone who lived past one hundred was a miracle (though more of a curse based on their appearances and abilities, Vlad assumed). Upton Arms harbored those who had come to grips with their age-related shortcomings, from arthritic zombies barely able to lurch, to witches plagued with misspellings.

No more than a half-century ago, Vlad would have scoffed at such a home, and particularly his need for one. During the ensuing years, he came to the slow realization that immortality was a broken promise. Being a creature of the night didn't cheat death, it simply postponed it several centuries. "Late-onset mortality," as Luis liked to call it.

Thinking back on the day he met Upton Arms' unofficial ambassador, Vlad was grateful indeed for the werewolf's ability to spot creatures whose dwindling supernatural abilities made survival difficult in the mortal world. The werewolf often fetched the no-longer-abled, and as pleased as Vlad was when he coined the pun, Luis made it clear there was a day such quips would have led to severe wounds. That time was long past, but Vlad respected the sentiment.

Vlad had since settled in among legendary, mythic, or "imaginary" creatures dependent more on aspirin and stool softeners than their abilities to make it through each day. It was a pleasant place, one where Vlad could see himself live out his days, however many were left.

Patrick's continued screams shattered the pleasant reminiscing.

"Everyone just needs to shut the fuck up now because they are about to reveal what crawled up there," Patrick cried as the final minutes of his favorite TV show *What Crawled Up There?* ticked away. "I got twenty says it's an insect."

"The size of that dude?" Beatrice pointed at the screen from the second row, her thin frame taking up most of a couch stained beyond most people's comfort level. "I'm going with gerbil."

"No fucking way, crone." Patrick peeked back at Beatrice, making a lewd gesture with his fist. "If you'd paid any attention, you'd know it was just Gerbils Week."

At that moment, a wriggling and soiled gerbil appeared on screen, off-screen medical personnel chattering away about how it may have gotten there as the patient had been less than forthcoming.

"That's twenty, 'chaun," Beatrice leaned over Patrick's recliner, sticking her palm under his nose. "Pay up before I fire my cauldron and wish you nothing but toil and trouble."

"Fuck you crone," Patrick slapped away the offending hand, squirming deeper into the front-row-center recliner that nearly swallowed him. "We didn't shake on it."

Vlad could only chuckle as he watched the scene unfold in the only way it could. Patrick was a tiny nuisance of a man who spent most of his days in Upton Arms' community room, a space featuring a handful of vending machines, a ping-pong table and carpeting that, like most of the residents, was long past its expiration date. What drew most people was the TV, a relic built long before streaming shows and LED-powered screens. It was mounted on the far wall like a trophy of a past best forgotten, lord and master over a few rows of chairs and couches boasting upholstery from the shag-carpet era.

Beatrice, a witch of questionable talents, was his constant foil. The two were a regular presence in the community room, a place by Vlad's estimates was avoided by ninety percent of the resident monsters, cryptids, and fantastical creatures that, on the whole, weren't believed to exist and thus remained invisible to the outside world.

"What's on the tube?" came a familiar voice to Vlad's right.

The vampire shrugged. "Something about stuff that crawls somewhere. But the better show is—"

"Oh, I know," Luis stood with hands on his hips and a look of boredom on his face. "I always drop by when the screaming starts."

Beatrice rose and stood in front of Patrick, aiming a well-manicured finger at the leprechaun. "Produce the cash now or you're going to be the face of Unlucky Charms," Beatrice demanded.

"Of all the things I've got in my pants, you chose the one thing that's staying right where it is," Patrick yelled back, twenty decibels louder and two octaves higher.

It went on like that for a few minutes before Patrick noted the next program, *Unsolved Proctological Mysteries*, had started. "I'll give you ten just to shut up," he spat, the witch holding out her hand. "Jesus, woman, like I carry cash around this place. Come by my room later."

"Fine," the witch blurted, turning on her chunky two-inch heels and stalking off.

Luis shook his head, disappointed. "Not that I approve of witch-on-leprechaun violence," he said, "but I was expecting some physical contact."

Vlad agreed. "Especially when trying to pry cash from Patrick. No way is Beatrice going to see that ten."

"She may have a spell in mind. Then again, remember what happened when she tried to cast an anti-fairy barrier around the gnomes' weekly poker game?"

Vlad did indeed. Instead of repelling the obnoxious sprites and their foul-smelling fairy dust, the spell simply made the fairies visible, revealing them to be hideous and far more numerous than anyone thought. It was like shining a black light on hotel sheets and seeing bodily fluids lit up like neon. As with vampires, it's better to keep that stuff in the dark.

He watched Luis saunter toward the ping-pong table where a mummy faced off against an eight-foot golem. The only loser was the maintenance crew, if only Upton Arms had had a maintenance crew. One side of the table was spattered with mud, the golem losing bits with each stroke. The other side was layered with dust and sand flying from the mummy's frayed bandages. The mummy moaned each time the ball flew past him, putting his paddle on the table before slow-limping to retrieve it. The golem wasn't much faster, so anyone waiting for the table had to have the patience of Job (who was not a resident of Upton Arms despite the rumors).

Where else could a vampire not only blend in, but be so inconsequential? Even better, or so he was promised by management when he moved in, was how Upton Arms was protected by various spells, rendering it invisible to a public that, for the most part, didn't believe in the inhabitants anyway. As stated in Section Twelve, Paragraph Three, "Upton Arms has been substantially Boy Wizarded, rendering it unseen to those lacking requisite abilities and/or supernatural DNA."

Vlad was sold, happy to live off the grid from the most fervent conspiracy theorists who refused to believe he didn't exist.

But for now, he'd settle for some much-needed sleep, the reason he came to the community room in the first place. Initially roused by

Patrick's incomprehensible shouting at the TV, Vlad now listened to the leprechaun screaming at yet another inanimate object, this time the vending machine that dispensed snacks meant to fuel obesity and premature deaths.

"You drop those pork nuggets, or I will truly fuck you up," Patrick threatened, pausing to see if the machine would capitulate to the threats of a man one-quarter its size. "Swear to god I will reach up your dispensing hole and deliver such wrath that—"

"Patrick!" Vlad slammed the side of the machine to get the leprechaun's attention. "Can't a vampire get a little shuteye?"

The leprechaun's hand froze in mid-strike as he made a slow and deliberate turn toward Vlad. "I don't know, you fluid-seeking simp. Can you? The real question is, do I care? And I fucking do not."

The leprechaun refocused his ire on the machine, but Vlad wasn't done.

"Patrick, if you don't shut up, I'm going to not only find your pot of gold but shove it so far up your ass you're going to be shitting rainbows for weeks." He smacked the machine again for emphasis.

When Patrick's eyes lit up in surprise, Vlad assumed it was partially out of fear. Instead, the little man reached into the machine and extracted his fried treasure, the vampire's well-aimed strike prodding loose the sought-after snack bag. Patrick waggled the nuggets in Vlad's direction. "Fuck off. You couldn't find my pot of gold with turn-based directions from Siri. But you could sure as hell find my ass, I'll bet. Still, thanks for the nuggets. Makes you good for something around here. I'll call you the next time a vending machine tries to fuck me."

The dozen or so in attendance didn't seem to notice the argument. A furry gentleman wearing a University of Oregon ballcap and (so it was said) size sixty-seven shoes strolled toward the soda machine, his long arms swinging like a pair of pendulums. The witches playing pinochle didn't seem to notice, though Vlad was definitely getting bad vibes from the trolls, whose eyes glared at him from above their laptops (and how in the hell were they the only ones to get wi-fi?).

Vlad summoned everything he had and psychically drilled into Patrick's mind, searching for that switch that would turn the leprechaun into his slave. A few hundred years ago, mind control required focus and willpower. Nowadays, Vlad tried to convince himself that minds weren't worth controlling even if he could. Besides, Facebook and X beat him to it.

After a few seconds of roaming the vast wasteland that was Patrick's mind, Vlad came away with nothing but a headache and the sort of resignation that had become more common in old age. He could hide neither from his antagonist.

Vlad put his back to the machine and rubbed his temples, realizing too late Patrick would interpret his posture as a sign of weakness.

As predictable as winter weather at the North Pole, Patrick took advantage.

Before Vlad could come back with something clever, Patrick stepped in front of him and, with his non-nugget-holding hand, grabbed his crotch and made several unseemly thrusts. "I know how vampires must suck to live, so you can try this any time. But you're probably past your bedtime, you casket-dwelling dick."

As Vlad mentally ticked the "Definitely homophobic" box on his Patrick checklist, he heard a few snickers from the back of the room. Trolls, probably, always feeding on the humiliation of others. Vlad smoothed his shirt and tugged on his sleeves as if preparing a clever retort, but Patrick wasn't done.

"No amount of preening is going to shed the indignities of someone who lives off the bodily fluids of others." Patrick turned toward his audience, speaking louder than necessary. "That is if you're able to open the sippy pouches that now make up your meals."

Even as he wondered just how Patrick knew about that particular humiliation—no way Luis would share it, one of the many who despised the leprechaun—Vlad heard the snickers turned to laughs. A few cursed princes high-fived one another with their frog hands. Fairies flitted over the ping-pong table throwing out streaks of glowing pixie dust. Within seconds, those plumes formed the letters "B-U-R-N," and the high-pitched squeals indicated just how pleased the fairies were with their aerodynamic addition to the conversation.

The skywriting encouraged Patrick further. He leaped off the recliner and stepped toward Vlad, standing stiff and straight as if he were six feet tall instead of three. "Speaking of 'burn,' that's a pretty embarrassing

Achilles' heel, right? You come in here strutting and spouting as if you own the joint, yet if someone opened so much as a single curtain, you'd violate one of our most important rules."

Patrick paused, his audience leaning forward.

"Smoking's not allowed!"

The room erupted in chortles and guffaws. Even the ogres joined in, a typically sullen bunch who never got over the "No mindless clubbing of residents including other ogres" policy.

Vlad took a deep breath, trying not to take the bait. This was Patrick's specialty, goading others to do something unseemly, like hurling small objects through windows (explaining the community rule prohibiting leprechaun-based defenestration, a regulation Vlad found odd until he got to know Patrick).

"Nothing to say, oh prince of the night?" Patrick poked Vlad's knee. "No? Then maybe it's time to go back to the dark shadows from whence you came, you supernatural disappointment."

Vlad's heart involuntarily quickened, black dots forming along the edge of his vision. Fangs clicked into place. He was going into hunting mode and was already past the point of no return.

Before he knew what was happening, Vlad bent—no, swooped— toward Patrick, the vampire's face inches from the leprechaun's vulnerable throat. Instinctively, Vlad hissed, long and loud, a warning to his prey that it was about to have its life drained one swallow at a time.

Only Vlad felt something shoot out of his mouth, that something landing at Patrick's feet.

It was small, white, and serrated. His tongue explored the gap along his gums, confirming the worst. The only thing to be drained here was his dignity.

Vlad reached for the errant incisor but was beaten by a tiny hand.

"Well, well, well, look what we have here," Patrick held up the tooth for all to see. "Of all the fairies here, none of them are of the Tooth family, a shame because this would be worth at least five bucks, am I right?"

Vlad froze like a vampire in ultraviolet light, seeing no way out of this ridiculous situation. The incisor would grow back, he'd lost hundreds over the centuries. But those had been embedded in bone or muscle, gone in the throes of feasting passion. He'd never spit one out, until today. All he'd wanted to do was get some sleep. Was that too much to ask?

Patrick wasn't done, shoving the tooth into his pocket. "Vlad," he spread his arms theatrically. "'Fangs for the memory."

Laughter was interrupted by a gruff voice at the back of the room. "Can everybody just please shut up and let the few of us trying to sleep do just that," Luis marched into the center of the room, arms bristling with fur.

Vlad eyed his friend; the vampire mortified that Luis felt he had to come to the defense. Vlad shook his head. "Luis, trust me, I got this."

"Oh, I know you do," Luis agreed, pointing a single claw at the vampire. "That's why I'm here. As president of our community association, I'm here to make sure you neither maim, injure nor dismember another resident regardless how any rational person would consider the act reasonable, if not preferable. In other words, Vlad, fangs off the little person."

Patrick took a step forward, his mocking expression in full force. "Wolfboy, you have *got* to be shitting me."

"Not me," Luis swiveled toward the leprechaun, aiming a slightly longer claw toward Patrick. "But give Vlad half a chance, and you might be taking up valuable space in his digestive tract."

No one knew at the time that the only thing about to go to shit was Upton Arms itself, thanks to Patrick. And there would not be a rainbow in sight.

THREE

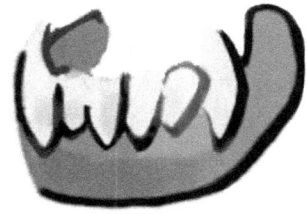

"SEVEN-ZIP GENTLEMAN, AND THAT'S A SKUNK."

Luis felt the hairs on the back of his neck sprout. He could let himself turn and take out his frustrations on his ping-pong teammate, but there were two problems with the imagined scenario. First, Luis knew he'd probably only get as far as were-possum. Secondly, even if he achieved werewolf and tore off his partner's arms, Darnell would just snap them back in again. That was the problem with teaming up with zombies and their pathetic athletic skills. You can't win, and you can't kill them because they're already dead.

"That went by so quickly we have time for a rematch," Henry remarked, flipping his paddle to imply his talents extended to juggling, ignoring his fumble, causing it to clatter to the floor. "Several in fact."

Henry wasn't a bad guy, a shapeshifter whose powers were so depleted he couldn't even change into a younger version of himself. Though hundreds of years old, Henry appeared to be in his mid-fifties with a baby face, narrow forehead, and unkempt mop of salt-and-pepper hair. He looked like a guy voted "Most Likely to Blend In," not a terrible thing when you could change into almost anybody, which Henry could no longer pull off. Yet Luis fumed, not just at the loss but at things in general. He wasn't even sure why. It was as if there was an undercurrent of tension at Upton Arms, something he couldn't put a claw on.

"Fuck off, Henry," Luis said, flinging his paddle with its shredded rubber face onto the table. "Too bad you can't change into something that isn't such a douchebag."

"And too bad you can't change into something that isn't so shitty at ping-pong," Henry taunted, retrieving the paddle so he could bounce the ball rhythmically, an easier task. "Or into anything that didn't suck at everything."

Luis's eyes bored into Henry as the shifter wandered off, knowing it was a bad idea to get between a couple of supernaturals, even those whose powers had bottomed out. Luis took a breath, told himself to calm down. That Henry would come at him like that was uncharacteristic of the shapeshifter he knew, a man whose company he frequently enjoyed.

Until this second.

"That may be true, Henry," Luis said in a measured tone. "But at least when I change, it's not into some of the most inconsequential people to have walked the earth."

A low blow, Luis knew, but on target. Henry winced, reminded that he was a pathetic shadow of his former self. He'd confided to a handful of others that his shapeshifting talents had narrowed to mimicking those in the Kardashian orbit, perhaps due to their ubiquitous presence in the pop culture landscape. Gossip being what it was, the revelation soon was known throughout Upton Arms, spreading faster than anything ending in "-itis."

Breasts began to stretch Henry's pastel-blue polo shirt, a byproduct of the shapeshifter's stress. Before it was clear which Kardashian was on its way to Henry's body, he turned on his heel and scampered out as fairies placed their bets (Khloe was the favorite).

"Henry!" Luis called out, waving his paddle in the air. "Please, I'm sorry. Henry!"

It was too late. Luis ignored the neon yellow "Asshole" floating over the table, hating that he gave the fairies reason to display their dickish nature.

A voice whispered in his ear. "Uncool Luis."

"Fuck you, Ralph," Luis responded instinctively, tossing the paddle on the table. The invisible man was always inserting himself into uncomfortable situations, aided by the fact no one had any idea he was there.

Ralph was right, of course. It was uncool. Luis had retaliated against basic trash talk with a precision-guided insult fired by the drone of callousness. What was wrong with him?

The vibe also contributed to tempers as short as Patrick's inseam. Arguments were sparked by incomplete jigsaw puzzles, clothes left too long in the dryer, and microwaving salmon in the common kitchen (seen more as an attack than ignorance). While such tensions would result in little more than the shaking of fists at a typical retirement home, confrontations could lead to damage, injury or, in the case of a particular oracle who said she could summon the Grim Reaper, death. (The only power she was known for, however, was summoning farts that could clear the room, which encouraged everyone to stay on her good side.)

It was the first time the werewolf felt uneasy within the comfortable confines of Upton Arms. Not that he ever thought he'd need such a place. It wasn't all that long ago—or maybe it was—that Luis was the Alpha, leading a small pack comprised of Cuban immigrants looking to create a new life (if not more than a few livestock deaths) in America. He'd even discovered he could change into a werewolf at will, lunar cycle be damned. He struck out on his own, determined to fit into a world that often rejected his kind (his Latino self more than his werewolf self). The more resistance he met, the more likely he was to go wolf, leading to aching joints, a stiff back, and a monthly clothing bill.

His addiction to lupine powers nearly destroyed Luis. His body crumbled under the weight of dependency, unable to tolerate frequent transformations that demanded bone, muscle, and sinew to grow and stretch in a matter of minutes. Each transformation took more time than the one before, as did recovery. Skin winkled and drooped, a paunch developing as if to take up the slack. Once an intimidating six-foot-two, the mirror reflected his reality of a five-foot-nine guy with a dad bod.

The end as Luis knew it came on a self-pitying bender of domesticated fowl. After being kicked out by his latest girlfriend—relationships had been the only source of his income—he stumbled across a backyard chicken coop. As if to prove he still had it, though on a modest scale, Luis returned that night under a three-quarters moon. He transformed under the pale light and tore into the flock, feasting upon blood and raw flesh. Or so he thought. A few days later at a local watering hole, he heard a woman complain about a skinny, largely toothless mongrel that had gotten into her coop and injured two of her chickens. "Started to go after it with a broom until it started whimpering in a way to break your heart," she said. "Gave him a few beef jerky treats before he took off."

That explained the non-chicken aftertaste when Luis woke up the next day in the alley where he shared a lean-to with another unhoused individual.

It wasn't long before his roommate kicked him out of the makeshift shelter ("I don't want to spend any more time smelling whatever it was that died in your pants," she said.) From then on, he was a lone werewolf, preferring a solitary life where he didn't have to meet anyone's expectations. He spent random nights transforming into creatures unrecognizable by nature, scaring feral cats, raccoons, and other creatures battling for scraps.

Then, on an unseasonably warm April night, Luis stumbled across the city's most dangerous playground, its ranking based on its syringe-to-swing ratio. Any parent bringing their kids would immediately show on the radar of Child Protective Services. Shortly before midnight, Luis noticed a crumbling castle spire, the perfect lofty perch for someone who'd hit rock bottom.

Sun and vandals had conspired to fade and splinter the plastic tower's façade. Luis was sure it hosted far more addicts than kids, thus an appropriate place to crash(land) for a night. Or two. All he had to do was cross a flimsy plastic bridge and scramble up a child-sized spiral staircase. A cozy niche, indeed, as long as he didn't wake up at the bottom of the steep slide leading off the tower. That was a metaphor for life he could do without.

Luis traipsed across the burning sand, pausing with each step to look for needles or glass shards reflecting the pale moonlight. His dollar-store sandals, the footwear of choice thanks to transformations that could shred shoes, didn't offer the kind of protection one needed in a minefield of sharp objects. He hopped to the top step of a three-step staircase before starting across the bridge.

"STOP!" a voice thundered from below. "The other side you shall not see, lest you answer these riddles three."

Luis froze. He peered over the edge to the sand two feet below. Nothing.

"What the fuck?" he muttered, then louder. "Who's there?" No answer. "Hello?" Pause. "Fine, fuck you." Luis took another step, support chains rattling.

The voice again, this time with a conversational, almost pleading, tone. "What was it about 'The other side you shall not see, lest you answer these riddles three' did you not understand? It's pretty straightforward."

Something shuffled below. Luis took out his phone and shined its light under the bridge. All he saw were the remnants of a shattered beer bottle and what appeared to be cat feces.

Something shifted in the shadows and Luis turned the beam toward it, the light catching a small, hunched figure, its (his?) head sporting hair in thick, matted clumps. Brawny, furry arms and legs poked from a stout torso wrapped in what appeared to be a badly tailored hotel robe. It reminded Luis of something he'd turned into a few weeks ago after several highballs on a moonless night.

"What the fuck you staring at?" the thing rumbled, partially emerging into the light and shielding its eyes. "Get that magical light out of my eyes, adventurer." The creature said, its face gnarled with a bad case of warts.

"Who...what...are you?" Luis wondered aloud, ignoring the creature's request. "And what are you doing under playground bridge?"

"Who the fuck do you think I am?" the creature snapped, hurling a bit of sand in Luis's direction. "Ruminate a bit. I'm short but could still tear you in half if I wanted. I live under a bridge. I ask people three clever, rather ingenious riddles to prove themselves worthy of passing. Any guesses, Einstein?"

"If I remember my folklore correctly, I'd say bridge troll," Luis pondered, rubbing his chin. "But to call this a bridge is pretty generous."

"A bridge is a bridge, no matter how small." A pause. "Great, now you got me talking like Dr. fucking Seuss."

"Look, I don't care who you are or why you're here, but we're done." Luis took another step when a stubby-fingered hand shot from below, grabbing his ankle.

"Riddles three first, asshole."

"I don't think so," the werewolf argued, lifting his leg. Or at least tried to lift it. The hand remained like a steel manacle. Luis winced when that cuff tightened. "OK, OK, give me the riddles, geez."

"The first," the troll pronounced solemnly, releasing Luis's ankle. "One look at my face and you know what time it is. What am I?"

"Is this a trick question?"

"It is not a question. It's a riddle, one so devious as to cause—"

"A clock."

"Did you say a clock?"

"I did."

There was a long pause before the scratchy voice returned. "That would be, you know, not it. The true answer I vow and will reveal to you now."

"Yes?"

"A, um, watch. Yes, a watch."

"Same thing," Luis retorted.

"You're saying a watch is a clock?"

"A form of clock, absolutely." Luis glowered at the troll, revealing his "I'm about to go wolf on your ass" expression, though it was a complete bluff.

The troll folded. "When you put it that way…" The troll cleared his throat. "Number two. It has lots of eyes but cannot see. What is it?"

Luis knew this one from his childhood. "A potato."

"Nope," the troll said firmly, crossing his arms. "A cave full of bats."

"That's stupid. And wrong."

"*You're* stupid and wrong. Have you never heard the saying, 'Blind as a bat'?"

Luis shook his head, trying to wrap his head around such an inane conversation. "Bats can see, just not very well. Here, I'll prove it." The werewolf pulled out his phone and tapped the screen a few times and handed it to the troll, who scanned it for several minutes before handing it back.

"I am not sure how or why your magical slab knows so much about bats..." the troll trailed off again. "Never mind, for my third question is truly diabolical."

"I hope so because the first two have been lame."

"If only you knew me in my youth. My riddles were known to turn brains inside out. I lost count of the quests that ended with brave seekers being flung off bridges."

"I'm sure," Luis agreed, hoping it didn't sound as patronizing as it was.

"Don't patronize me. That just makes me want to give you a real brain buster, a puzzle with a side of enigma."

Luis was about to correct the saying but this had already gone on too long. He waited quietly for the third riddle.

"Here it is," the troll began.

Silence.

Luis waited, tapping his foot with impatience. "Go on," he prodded.

"Don't you know a dramatic pause when you hear one? It's like you've never been asked riddles three by a bridge troll before."

Silence.

"Oh, a dramatic pause in return," the troll applauded lightly. "Well done. Last riddle: What's in *your* wallet?"

Luis was pretty sure the riddle was more a slogan but answered. "Three bucks, a dollar-off coupon at Stan's Sandwich Stand, and a punch card giving me my next car wash free, if only I still had a car."

"I'll take your word for it. You may pass to the Forbidden Tower."

"Forbidden?"

"If you knew what happened up there just a few hours ago, you wouldn't question that."

Equipped with that valuable bit of insider knowledge, Luis changed his bedtime plans. "Mind some company?" he said, moving to join the troll.

"This is a one-troll bridge," was the answer.

"Good thing I'm not a troll, nor is this really a bridge."

"You know why this is a bridge? Because a troll lives under it. Case closed, wolf-boy."

"You knew I was a wolf?"

"Of course. I'm the bridge troll, not the village idiot."

"I'll take your word for it." Luis hesitated, wondering how in the hell this creature knew his secret. He was far too tired to ask, and to find a better place to sleep. He curled up next to a merry-go-round held together by rust and determination. Sleep came quickly, limbs twitching as the wolf in his dreams took down a grizzly bear before cracking a cold one and browsing Lupine Love, a dating app that existed only in his mind.

Finding the perfect match, he swiped right. The woman on the screen reached out and pushed his shoulder. "We need to leave," she insisted, giving him another shove. "No fucking joke, man, time to get a move on."

"What?" Luis opened his eyes, then closed them since they were not ready for so much sunlight.

Hands wedged themselves under Luis's shoulders and lifted him into a sit.

Sand. He was sitting on sand.

The playground, the troll. It all came back. And he was sore as hell.

He opened his eyes, quickly raising his hands to block the rising sun. He looked around, saw the merry-go-round, the tower, the troll.

"Let's go, hombre," the troll insisted, slipping his hand under Luis's armpits as he had any hope of lifting the werewolf. "People tend to call the police when they see trolls, especially when those trolls are not under a bridge."

"It's not a bridge," Luis said, pushing the troll away.

"At this point, I don't give fuck all what you call it. We just need to be gone." The troll nodded past the merry-go-round. Luis twisted around to see two—no, three—cop cars and several officers talking to a group of twenty-somethings in the process of emptying their pockets. "Drug bust," the troll explained. "In a minute or so, those officers of the realm are going to search the Forbidden Tower for substances forbade by authorities. They will see us and will find our presence very suspicious. Especially yours given your current look."

"What?" Luis was offended until he discovered his clothes were in shreds, but his sandals in fine form. He wasn't sure what was more disappointing, experiencing a werewolf version of a wet dream or having one of his best transformations in years and not being aware of it.

The two stumbled out of the park, the troll leading the way. "I know a sewer not far from here. I use it to travel between the many bridges I call home."

Luis looked at him quizzically.

"Long story," the troll muttered. "Let's just say when you live under a bridge five feet long and two feet high, you're easily spotted."

"What about a freeway underpass or something?" Even in bringing up the obvious, Luis wondered why he cared at all.

"Good spots all belong to troll millennials. Just because they're only a thousand years old, they think they rule the goddamned planet."

The troll pulled Luis into some shrubs as a car went by.

"Anyway, we need to get out of here before we attract attention, which is what a troll and an elderly man wearing shredded clothes tend to do."

"Fuck me," Luis blurted, now down to one set of clothes and a pair of mismatched Crocs. "I appreciate the help, but I'm not very good with sewers." He held out his hand. "Luis, by the way."

"Tony. Before you leave, mind if pose one more riddle?"

"Shoot."

"I'm an aging, unhoused werewolf with performance issues. Where do I go?"

"Uh…"

The troll put his hand in his pocket and withdrew a crisp white business card, handing it to Luis. "Trust me on this," he said before trotting off.

The werewolf looked at the card. "Upton Arms: An Active Lifestyle Home for the Supernaturally Enhanced." Below that was an address and phone number.

"Active lifestyle home?" Luis knew that was code for old folks' home, and he'd be damned if he was ready to give up.

He would change his mind two days later when, after an intimate night with a bottle of tequila, he woke up in the wolf habitat with an angry alpha staring at him.

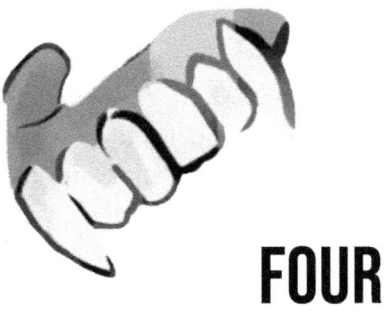

FOUR

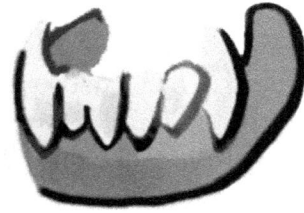

"WHY CAN'T we ever get a signal in here?" Vlad noted with exasperation as he sought a signal strong enough for just one bar on his phone. "I mean, never. You'd think one would sneak in every once in a while."

Nim shrugged his shoulders. "Just the way it is," he gurgled before walking off, leaving a trail of wet footprints.

All Vlad knew about Nim was that he was some sort of Vietnamese water spirit who haunted the dreams of the wicked. Now all he did was haunt the waking hours of the cleaning staff—or would, if there was a cleaning staff.

Vlad wandered the community room with his phone in the air, desperately seeking a sign of digital life so he could download the next dozen levels of *Cookie Diner 3: The (Chocolate) Chips are Down*. He needed to add another stove and expand his counter to serve more customers. But once again, no damn signal. And the Wi-Fi was non-existent, thanks to the cheap bastards who owned Upton Arms. Probably some hedge fund trying to squeeze out the last few bucks of an unwise investment. The only thing worse than no signal was the smell, where mold and mildew battled constantly for custody. It was a draw.

Though his eyes were glued to the screen, Vlad effortlessly slalomed among furniture that could have been older than he was, having memorized a layout that rarely changed. He settled for a quiet spot next to one of the vending machines, the one filled largely with rice cakes and protein shakes and thus the least used. (Vlad loved how shakes were marketed to seniors on the go, though most residents were seniors on the pause.)

A handful of seats were occupied, since it was 11:17 p.m., the middle of the night by Upton Arms' standards. Only those who had trouble sleeping were up at a late hour, almost three hours past the customary bedtime.

The vampire sensed his personal space about to be invaded at the same time Luis sidled up to him, nodding to the table where cards flew by themselves.

"There was a time I would have joined them," Luis offered, nodding to the game in progress. "But no one cheats more than fairies. I probably would, too, if I were small, enchanted, and fast." At that moment, the table flipped over, cards whirling in a vortex before exploding in all directions. "And there it is," Luis nodded. "Probably a sprite not willing to put up with all the bullshit."

"Fairies are such dicks," Vlad sighed, intoning what was likely Upton Arms' most common phrase.

"Biggest ones here, symbolically speaking," the werewolf pointed out.

"What the fuck is going on here?" Patrick roared from the recliner that had until a second ago appeared to be unoccupied. The leprechaun hopped off and pointed toward the cloud of glitter floating over the upturned table. "You little fucks need to keep your shit together or I swear to God …"

Vlad wasn't sure what sort of age-related failings required fairies to need a retirement home, but it probably had to do with extreme-onset crankiness. The fact they brought out the worst in everyone was bearable knowing they nearly drove Patrick crazy.

"And what the fuck are you smiling at, bloodsucker?" Patrick screamed from across the room. "Used tampons for dessert tonight?"

If Patrick could be counted on for anything, it was spite and crudeness.

"Yes, Patrick, that's exactly it, you got me," Vlad shrugged, having learned to pick his battles carefully. And any battle that started with "used tampon" was not worth fighting.

Patrick approached, Vlad going to his resting "aw shit" face.

"Everything OK, Vlad?" Patrick probed, getting a little too close since the leprechaun's sense of personal space was in proportion to his stature. "Can't help but notice you seem to be lost. Do you know where you are?"

Vlad sighed. "All too well."

"Something wrong?"

"No signal. Again."

"Maybe that's your signal to go to bed. No, wait, isn't this dinnertime? Shouldn't you be out hunting your usual prey? Or is it too late for short buses to be out?"

Vlad resisted the urge to snap Patrick's neck. First, he wasn't sure he had the strength or energy. Secondly, a dead Patrick broke one of Upton's unwritten rules—don't kill where you live.

"Yes, Patrick, my bedtime isn't for hours yet. So, I was hoping to get a signal, download an app or two and kill some time."

"Time is about the only thing you can kill nowadays, eh?"

It crossed Vlad's mind that some rules, like necks, were meant to be broken. Proprietors of Upton Arms would likely frown on such acts, not because of any concern for the victim, but that it would well be the first of many dominoes to fall. A string of deaths would not be tolerated in a home promoting active lifestyles (emphasis on "life").

"Good one," Vlad growled, stifling the urge to flash his incisors, which was behavior unbecoming of a vampire in polite society. "Good thing I'm not interested in a midnight snack. Or, in your case, a nibble."

"Is that a threat? For a guy whose life is just one fangless task after another, you talk pretty big."

Vlad again longed for the sixteenth century when getting rid of such a man was as easy as dumping him in a river brimming with sewage (as most rivers were). Ah, for the days when the only official cause of death was death. Thanks to DNA and strictly enforced water-quality standards, getting rid of a body was much more difficult. Not impossible, just a huge hassle.

"Of course, Patrick, sometimes I forget how you're nothing more than the house pet," the vampire smiled wryly. "And about as dangerous. But perhaps you could be of some help."

Vlad gave Patrick his best "I vahnt to drink your blood" stare, arching his eyebrows and pressing his lips together. Rather than crumble under the vampire's menacing power, Patrick reached out to give a reassuring squeeze to the vampire's knee, the one place he could reach comfortably.

"I know that look," Patrick said in a voice that both soothed and grated at the same time. "I think I may have some milk of magnesia. We can mix it in with a little Type O, your favorite. Would that help?"

Once upon a time, such a remark would result in fangs buried deep into the offender and the horse he rode in on, literally. Vlad had long since tamed his anger and appetite, aided by the fact he was in no shape to conquer the world, not even a three-foot-tall piece of it. He also hated to admit he'd grown comfortable at Upton Arms.

"What I really need," Vlad insisted, putting his phone in the air for emphasis, "is dependable cell service. You can find gold at the end of a rainbow, so it should be pretty easy to find a decent signal."

Patrick scoffed. "Well, if life isn't just one insurmountable object after another. Maybe you should be happy you have a place to stay with what little rent you're paying."

Had Vlad not been so angry about the technological shortcomings of Upton Arms, he may well have asked Patrick just how he knew about rent amounts.

Instead, the vampire brought down the phone and maintained a calm voice. "I sure pay enough for management to arrange a bar or two. Not too much to ask."

Patrick stepped back and took a deep bow. "Well, I didn't know I was in the presence of royalty, forgive me if Upton Arms has not met all of your personal needs."

Patrick turned and Vlad detected a little jig as the leprechaun walked away. Despite the vampire's best efforts, fangs broke through the gumline. He ran his tongue over his old friends, remembering what it was like to feel no guilt while on a killing spree. Instead, he took a deep breath, counted to ten, then twenty, and flicked off his phone. He watched dully as Patrick settled into his front-and-center recliner and turned on *Name that Growth.*

"I can name it in three photos," the leprechaun screamed at the TV. "No, two photos. Two!"

Vlad stalked back to his room. It was time for a stiff drink—B-positive—and a little chat with Luis.

Vlad knew of only one way to bring Patrick to his knees, even if his diminutive height made that particular position hard to notice. It was time to get him out in public, since Patrick mixed with people like the Road Runner and Wile E. Coyote, and he was the hapless latter. He needed comeuppance to put him in his place.

Besides, the residents were always up for a field trip, especially if there was alcohol and an opportunity to use their talents in ways that wouldn't result in them trending on X. Vlad would also have to convince Luis to go along, since the vampire would need to tap the Upton Arms Entertainment Fund to financially support this jaunt to Revengeville.

Then Vlad remembered what he'd seen when rummaging through Luis's closet looking for a pastel blue dress shirt that had gotten mixed in with the werewolf's laundry (no one hesitated to empty out a dryer as soon as it buzzed, leaving still-damp clothing on the folding tables). Vlad had spotted a pair of red and tan shoes almost too hideous to wear in the light of day. They could only be one thing.

Bowling shoes.

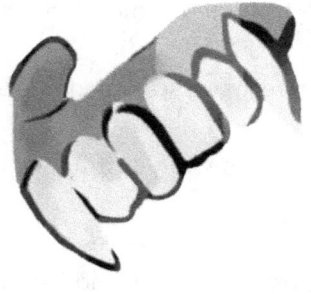

FIVE

THE NEXT EVENING, a little man in bright green was the center of attention as he hurled a series of profanities that begged all bowlers within hearing distance to wonder about the benefits of language.

"Why the hell did you invite Patrick?" Luis argued, nudging Vlad as the two stood two lanes over, hoping few would connect them to the angry man in green. "This happens every time. The guy cannot take adversity, even when wearing rented shoes."

"What the hell do shoes have to do with it?" Vlad countered, lifting his left foot to admire his well-fitting though temporary footwear..

"Nothing, I just like the thought of that nasty little man in shoes worn by thousands of others, not to mention the indignity of stuffing the toes with tissues to make them fit."

Vlad glanced toward Patrick who was hurling more f-bombs than bowling balls, thus attracting far more attention than was healthy. The vampire was most concerned with the birthday party on lanes nine through thirteen. According to the banner, the dozens of kids were celebrating Jenny and her completion of seven years as a human. Why anyone would celebrate a notable occasion in a place that smelled of beer and feet, Vlad had no clue. A thin haze of smoke clung to the ceiling, no doubt a remnant of days when cigarettes were encouraged in a fruitless way to make bowling seem cool.

There was a tap on his shoulder. Vlad turned, and his field of vision was filled with a chest that stretched a dark blue shirt to its breaking point. Catching his eye to the right was a red shield that read "Ricky D's Bowl and Lube," the business offering half-off games with every oil change. Upton Arms was a regular client (though not for much longer, it appeared).

Vlad tilted his head back to take in the rest of the man who would be a threatening presence even to a vampire at the height of his power. A thick neck led to a sharp chin, flat nose, and narrow eyes, topped by a creased forehead and black bristled hair. Vlad wondered if Upton accepted giants, but by the man's look, he would be more interested in destroying the retirement home than living there.

Vlad instinctively took a step back, what with a body that had just swapped out a twelve-pound ball for a ten-pounder. "Can I help you?" he said tentatively, his chin angled toward the ceiling.

"You need to control your friend over there," the giant grunted, jerking a thumb toward Patrick. "If you don't, I will. And you will finally find out if the little man can fly. Hint: He can't."

Vlad knew that little was more humiliating to the leprechaun than being hoisted like a toddler. Unfortunately, such a move would bring too much attention to their group, which included a werewolf, a witch, a leprechaun, a shapeshifter, and a zombie. Besides, as soon as Patrick made his first attempt to roll a ball roughly twenty percent of his weight, let alone knock down a pin or two, ample derision would be accomplished.

Vlad needed to counterattack in a way that would not lead to significant injury.

"Speaking of flight," Vlad said, crossing his arms and throwing back his shoulders, "how do you think little-person abuse would fly on social media?"

The giant looked down his nose at the vampire. "Just know that I'm watching," he grumbled, stalking off. Vlad sighed, another disaster averted. Not that there hadn't already been some hiccups.

Just a few frames in, the vampire noticed one of the balls in the return rack contained a disembodied hand, with thumb and two fingers stuffed tightly into the holes. He pried it off gently, making sure to lift the fingers intact, then returned it to Darnell, the zombie looking surprised before shaking his head very, very slowly.

"Are you serious right now?" Vlad said, trying to keep his voice down. "Whose hand would it be?"

When Darnell put his arms out in a "beats me" pose, Vlad pointed to the zombie's right stump. While it was impossible to read the expressions of the undead, Vlad was pretty sure Darnell looked sheepish as he snapped the hand back on. The vampire wasn't sure of the (very handy) mechanics of reattaching one's limbs, but there was always an unmistakable click, like the locking of LEGO blocks. That was followed by a squishing sound, which Vlad assumed was the various tendons and ligaments reaching out to embrace their lost companion. Vlad had once inquired about the process, but the conversation didn't get past, "Rrr-arr-mmnn."

Elsewhere, Beatrice was in the midst of a perfect game, Vlad was sure the witch was casting whatever bowling-related spells she had in her hex bag. And based on the way Henry the shapeshifter pulled his balls to the right yet tallied one strike after another, it was clear he'd employed the services of Ralph, the invisible man rarely invited to such outings since no one could find him.

Still, the outing went much better than anticipated. Smiles and laughter were the dominant forms of expression. Something about bowling brought out the best in those who were otherwise easily irritated.

Until Mt. Patrick erupted. The fiery little leprechaun spewed forth molten invectives burning the ears of every man, woman, and birthday-celebrating child in the place.

Patrick had, for the most part, kept his anger in his pants for the first game. He broke one hundred thanks to bumpers that kept his balls out of the gutter. Overcome with unearned confidence, he ordered bumpers removed for the next game. With each roll, as pins stood defiant, Patrick's voice grew louder and his language more colorful. By the fourth frame, he insisted on being allowed as many balls as it took to knock down all pins.

"The two-ball rule is bullshit," he screamed. "The only thing that should be limited to two balls is my fucking nutsack, because if you added a third, I'd never be able to zip up."

Moms clapped their hands over the children's ears, but Patrick was far from finished.

"This is fucking bowling, a piece of shit activity that no one takes seriously," he whined, peeling off his shoes and tossing them halfway down the lane. "It's an excuse to keep busy between beers, and only losers aren't drunk by the third frame. So, give me as many goddamn balls as I need to knock down every fucking pin that dares to stand against my leprechaun might."

The use of the "L" word in public first grabbed Vlad's attention, followed soon by Beatrice shouting, "You tell'em, you gold-stealing, rainbow-chasing magical Irish fuck!"

That resulted in another visit from the giant. The third, and what would be final, visit was hardly a lucky charm. Patrick, emboldened by the attention he was getting, upped his antics. With a heavier ball in hand, he walked over to the birthday party and plopped it into the center of the cake. After rolling it back and forth until nothing was left but pink and white pudding, the leprechaun ran his finger over the ball, sucking the dollop he'd gathered in a suggestive, almost obscene way.

"There's your fucking show," Patrick declared with a bow. "Be sure to click like and subscribe, and follow me at 'You can all go fuck yourselves.' Have a nice day."

To no one's surprise, the giant reappeared.

"Sir," he told Vlad in a voice not at all polite, "it is one thing to flaunt the sacred rules of bowling. But rolling a ball through a little girl's cake…"

The giant had no words to express his disgust, so Vlad (regrettably, based on the reaction) added, "The frosting on top?"

A hand far too large than any hand should need to be gripped Vlad's neck. "You remove him, or I do. Oh, one more thing."

Vlad braced for impact, knowing the giant's hand was likely balled into a fist, but no blow was forthcoming.

"Your van?" the giant said, his tone unnervingly soft. "It needs a cabin filter. The one you have is filthy."

Vlad quickly agreed to the new filter as well as a transmission flush and tire rotation. With that, he went to look for Patrick. He found him outside the arcade with the strangest and most surprising look on the leprechaun's face. Little did Vlad know the danger behind that look.

SIX

A FEW HOURS later and back at Upton Arms, Vlad and Luis huddled near the vending machines, the vampire relating the story he still had trouble digesting, like medium-well steaks.

"A smile?" Luis shook his head. "You sure Patrick wasn't suffering from temporary rictus? Because Patrick smiling is about as believable as seeing Bigfoot in a podiatrist's waiting room." He twisted his neck and said over his shoulder, "No offense, Bigfoot."

"The name's Chet." The towering beast shoving a crumpled dollar into a soda machine that refused to accept it. "And offense taken. You'd think in this day and age, we're past characterizing people by atypical biological features." He snatched the dollar and stalked away, Yeti-like.

"I swear." Vlad lifted two fingers as if the Boy Scout pledge still meant anything. He shifted in the recliner to face Luis. "A grin big enough to cause scarring."

"And you couldn't hear what they were saying. Only that Patrick appeared oddly polite."

"Not just polite. Almost deferential."

Vlad went over the previous evening's scene in his head, an encounter that had put an odd spin on bowling night. With festivities winding down, the vampire had watched as Patrick shook hands with two men, one middle-aged (and very handsome with smooth ebony skin) man in a wheelchair, and the other, a full-bearded elderly, too pale gentleman dressed smartly in a tailored suit. Knowing Patrick's ability for finding aging supernatural creatures in need of assistance, he thought the man might be Santa Claus, what with the snow-white hair and beard. But everyone knew Santa didn't exist.

After a few minutes, the younger man spun on his wheels and went on his way. Patrick positively beamed as he led the older man back to Upton Arms' bowling party, where everyone met this incredibly charming man with one of the strangest powers Vlad would ever see.

Patrick made introductions. "This is Todd, a good friend." The next few seconds were still unclear when the leprechaun turned to the gentleman and whispered something that made the visitor smile.

Vlad did not read lips well, but he could have sworn Patrick added, "And savior."

Small talk ensued, and Todd would make it clear he was comfortable among life's extracurricular creations, as when he helped Darnell remove his rental shoes, the zombie losing his left foot in the process. An unfazed Todd plucked the foot from the shoe and slipped it back on Darnell's ankle like Prince Charming guiding Cinderella's foot into the glass slipper.

Besides an almost supernatural ability to charm others, what was it about Todd that earned him an invitation to the island of misfit toys?

Yet even Vlad's cautious eye, one honed over centuries by looking for signs a village was about to turn on him (like a surge in wooden stake sales), spotted nothing out of the ordinary save for Todd's friendly demeanor.

Which made Vlad extremely suspicious.

Todd even joined them for a last game, exhibiting better than average bowling skills thanks to an exceptional curve. He wasn't perfect. As if he knew the exact score needed to impress you yet keep from being a dick who took the game way too seriously.

If Todd did belong among them, he would put the "normal" in paranormal.

Until the last frame.

Todd faced a seven-ten split, impossible to pick up for anyone who doesn't arrive with their own ball in a custom-made duffel bag (which also puts them in "kind of a dick" territory).

As Todd stepped up, his ball almost glowing red, Vlad imagined he'd do what ninety-nine-point-nine percent of bowlers do, aim at either the right or left pin, then bowl right between them.

"Todd," Beatrice called from the scorer's table, "you pick this up and the last round is on me."

A safe bet, Vlad knew, made even safer because he'd seen Beatrice put "free drink" spells on many a server.

"Really?" Todd lifted a battered ruby-red ball from the rack. "Well then, that makes it very interesting."

"Hold on there, Toddster." Patrick tugged on Todd's perfectly pressed slacks that miraculously maintained their shape through aggressive bowling.

"Yes, Patrick?" Todd intoned sweetly.

"Rookie mistake to try to clip the outside of the seven, sending to the ten. Instead, hit the seven on the right with enough force to bounce it off the wall, turning it into a spinning projectile to knock that ten on its fucking ass. I mean, fuck that ten!"

"Fuck that ten!" a fairly large crowd of elderly bowlers echoed.

"Where the hell did these people come from?" Vlad breathed to Luis.

"No idea," the werewolf answered, perplexed. "Such is the mysterious power of Todd."

Todd turned to the many who had gathered behind him and announced in a voice that shook the rafters, "I have my own technique, one I hope you'll enjoy."

Todd hefted the ball to chest level and faced the impossible split. He took three steps, winching his arm back and propelling it forth. The ball shot down the alley with none of Todd's characteristic spin.

Mere feet from the target, the ball certainly doomed to failure, there was a sharp "crack!" as it split in half. The left portion shattered the seven, the right destroyed the ten.

Beatrice leaped to her feet. "Holy Moses!"

"Hardly." Todd's voice was soft, almost deferential "But in the right ballpark."

Vlad wondered, even now, if anyone else had heard that. While the vampire's sense of hearing wasn't as sharp as it used to be, it was more superior to that of a mortal.

He couldn't get Todd out of his head, which was why Vlad was back in the community room a few hours after they'd arrived home in one piece (save for Darnell, who returned a few toes short). Nothing chased away deep thoughts like a few episodes of *Blind Date Weddings*, followed by *Divorces Everyone Saw Coming*.

He was surprised and thankful to find Luis, allowing him to sift through the strange events of the night before.

"The fact Patrick liked Todd so much was weird enough," Luis chuckled. "I was ready to write it off too, as much as I would have sworn Patrick's leprechaun talents were limited to hating everyone."

"But that bowling thing." Vlad's eyes widened once again, still in awe from the split that picked up the split.

"Yeah, that bowling thing. That was incredible. When we got home, I Googled 'Creatures with super bowling powers.' All that came up was some dude named Earl Anthony, and he died in 2001."

"I assume that was *a* power, not *the* power."

"Yeah, that makes sense. Still, who wastes supernatural abilities on bowling? And since we're getting all private detective here, what was up with the guy in the wheelchair you told me about?"

Vlad shook his head. "Maybe it's innocent. Maybe Todd is just an old friend Patrick ran into, just like he told us."

"That would assume Patrick has any friends, let alone someone from the past," Luis countered. "You know what's easier to picture? Darnell as a Harvard student."

"Mmmrrrr," Darnell moaned, likely in protest.

Seconds ago, the zombie was softly bouncing against a vending machine, the sleep-walking dead. It was a common sight, and no one paid attention to Darnell's nocturnal habits.

"Sorry Darnell, no offense," Luis clapped the zombie on the back, gently so that nothing would fall off.

"Mmm-mm," Darnell replied.

"Sounds like he doesn't accept your apology," Vlad said as if well-versed in Zombie.

"No, we're cool. Right, Darnell?"

"Rrr."

"See?" Luis gave Darnell another pat as if making a point.

Vlad pushed himself out of the recliner, still restless in his thoughts. Something wasn't right about Todd or Patrick or the guy in the wheelchair. But what?

Luis saw the troubled look in his friend's eyes. "Remember, you were the one that wanted to go bowling."

"Thanks for the input, Señor Downer. If you haven't realized it by now, hindsight is everyone's superpower."

Lost in thought, Vlad plucked the only remaining pool cue from the rack, a warped bit of wood that had far outlived its usefulness. No matter since there were only a handful of billiard balls that could be found in the pockets of the threadbare pool table.

As he absent-mindedly twirled the cue, a thought came to Vlad out of the blue, and he shared it with Luis. "The voice. So authoritative"

Luis perked up and nodded. "It was a perfect mix of Morgan Freeman and James Earl Jones, with a dash of James Mason. Exactly the kind of voice you'd expect if it ordered you to make tracks to a certain burning bush, or maybe build an ark."

"What? No. Come on, that's ridiculous."

"Is it? Remember what he called that last shot?"

"Yup, and it made perfect sense, in a really corny way."

"He has the look too. The guy has held up well for being around since the beginning of time."

"That's because he's only been around since the beginning of the last seventy years or so." Vlad tossed the cue on the table, unsure if Luis was really going there.

"I wouldn't write it off so quickly. There are things on this earth beyond explanation. Like why someone hasn't killed Patrick yet, cut his body into even tinier pieces and packed him into a certain cereal."

Luis was right, anything was possible in a world where the supernatural was as real as the natural. But even if it was God, what the hell was he doing at Ricky D's Bowl and Lube? Why did he show such interest in a bunch of aging, allegedly nonexistent creatures?

And why would he be friends with Patrick?

"I know, but there was one more thing," Vlad said, laying the cue stick on the table. "On the way out, Todd said he was happy to 'finally' meet me and that he wanted to do me a favor."

"Oh really, and what did God say he'd do for you? If he brought your dick back to life, it was a wasted effort around here."

Vlad again went through it in his mind, just to make sure it happened just as he saw it. Everyone cheered Todd's shot, Beatrice mumbling something to the server, the server returning with a tray heavy with plastic cups of beer.

"He handed me a beer," Vlad recalled. "But first, he dipped his pinky in and gave it a quick stir. He said, 'That should be more to your liking.'"

Luis laughed and rubbed his chin thoughtfully. "Man, I thought water into wine was a good trick. But beer into blood, not bad. And a waste of a perfectly good brew, if you ask me."

Maybe Luis was right. It hardly came off like a parlor trick.

But then Vlad remembered the taste of that blood, like drinking from the veins of an angel.

"I knew you'd love it," Todd whispered to Vlad. "Just one of the many things I know about you and the rest of the—interesting—residents of Upton Arms. I just hope there's room for one more."

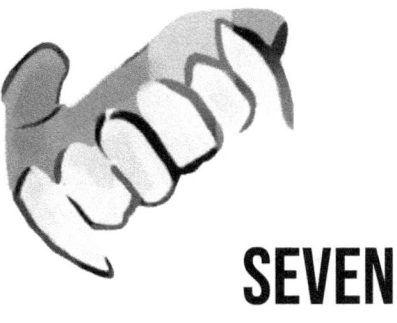

SEVEN

LUIS COULDN'T REMEMBER when he'd seen the community room this full, especially with the TV off.

The last time a board meeting attracted a crowd, Patrick was on trial, accused of a myriad of rules violations, from declaring squatters' rights on the best recliner to the far more serious charge of kidnapping (the TV remote was found safe the next day, tucked between the cushions of a recliner searchers swore they had checked the day before). When Patrick called for a special meeting of residents to vote on his fate, Luis was shocked when the show of hands was in favor of acquittal. The margin was just one vote, and little could be done when someone pointed out that Patrick was in possession of Darnell's arm. Luis merely credited the luck of the Irish and had forgotten all about it.

But now another issue had captured the attention of residents, one involving Todd and his miracle splitting of the bowling ball. This vote would have far more impact than the waging of fines against a selfish leprechaun.

Luis had always felt fortunate to live in an active lifestyle home that allowed residents to enact change based on personal agendas. It was the basis of democracy itself. Start with a selfish idea, add a bit of mob mentality, and pretty soon one of the vending machines is filled with the kind of gluten-free shit that everyone hates, save for the person who demanded it.

While most residents pulled off various paranormal tricks to duck a three-year term on the Upton Arms board of residents—Ralph the invisible man was particularly hard to pin down, if in fact he still lived there as no one had seen levitating dishes and cups recently—Luis embraced his role as president.

His first act —"Sweep Out Sunday" —was among his best, and it also let people know he wasn't afraid to shake things up. Each Sunday, those of a species that enjoyed devouring decayed flesh were free to enjoy the buffet of spoiled food that awaited inside the community refrigerators. A few witches were upset, claiming ghouls gulped down potions that were fresh from the cauldron. Ghouls said they only picked out the putrid bits, like infected eyes and entrails that had turned. Once the ghouls had stated their case, no one wanted to ever think about it again.

Luis became known as the president of making life not as much of a living hell. He pushed an agenda focusing on entertainment. During his tenure, he'd doubled the number of usable decks of cards to four and had successfully restored the games Battleship, Mouse Trap, and Clue to a functional condition either through the discovery of missing pieces or creation of replacements.

Luis had once considered his greatest accomplishment to be the budgetary juggling required to add Monopoly to the gaming arsenal. Only Patrick complained it was the "My Little Pony" edition, launching into a homophobic rant at the last board meeting that earned him a censure, and stern looks from the wee folk for weaponizing, and certainly misusing the term "fairy."

Yet even the addition of Monopoly paled in comparison to the creation of the Upton Arms Entertainment Fund, a bit of petty cash to cover sporadic outings. In digging through the books, Luis found Upton's monthly cut of vending machine proceeds were going to the Tot Shop. His investigation revealed Patrick used the money for a subscription box of clothing, answering the question no one asked— "Where does a small man get such adorable vests?" Now the vending machine money was spent on trips to museums or zoos or theaters. Even bowling.

Without cash from the machines, such outings would be impossible. The most pressing concern remained Upton Arms' finances, as there was barely enough money to pay monthly bills, let alone unclog the drain in the shared kitchen. Early on, he'd tried to contact the owners to figure out what could be done, but a confusing paper trial led to what appeared to be a company registered in Dublin, with no phone number or website. The only thing each filing had in common was a signature—Lawster McLegalton, clearly a fake name. Luis was surprised authorities would accept such a ridiculous name without checking.

Luis could have raised a fuss, perhaps even gone to a lawyer himself, but given the makeup of Upton Arms' residents, it was all for the best. Still, if the home's finances didn't improve soon, the future would be dim.

The werewolf took his seat at the table and faced the large crowd, happy he'd taken the time to set up forty more seats than usual, which totaled forty seats (attendance was notoriously sparse).

He'd been aware of the buzz about this meeting, but was still shocked to see every chair occupied, with others standing to the sides.

Vlad sat quietly in the back. He told Luis he was going to watch from the sidelines, happy to let the community decide just who Todd was, and if he was a good fit for Upton Arms. But Luis was sure fear had a lot to do with Vlad's decision because if Todd were God, the vampire (and so many other supernatural creatures, including Luis) would be held accountable.

Luis couldn't worry about that now. He pounded the soup ladle on the plastic card table, resulting in a hollow, non-authoritative thud. There was no room in the budget for an item as luxurious as a gavel.

"Everyone, please, eyes up here," Luis announced to no effect. "If we can all quiet down, we can get down to business, but first we need everyone's attention."

Luis focused on Patrick, who sat front and center while holding the TV remote like a scepter. He had no trouble overhearing the leprechaun's conversation, that squeaky voice rising above the fray.

"You know we're missing *Emergency Room Extractions*, right?" Patrick mentioned to the pair of bridge trolls sitting behind him. "Tonight's theme was small mammals. God, these fucking votes. As far as I'm concerned, Todd's in, and I will personally piss on anyone who votes no."

There was a time when new residents did not require community approval. That changed after people started complaining about the trolls, who snuck into rooms, hid under beds, and popped out to ask riddles three every time residents tried to get to the bathroom. When informed beds were not bridges, the trolls responded, "They are but a bridge from night to day." When told that was absolute bullshit, the trolls posted vile comments on the Facebook pages of those foolish enough to friend them.

Patrick finally relented on a screening process, though at first his focus was on a potential resident's ability to pay rather than any bothersome qualities they'd bring with them. That changed when a Bogeymen kept jumping out of Patrick's closet at a frequency far more irritating than scary.

"We need to control our borders if we're to protect our lifestyle," Patrick had testified before the board in an effort to evict the startling species, a first step to keep out those who did not fit in. "We can't just allow in everyone who thinks they belong. Otherwise, you're opening yourselves to various undesirables. You really want nymphs in here stealing your partners with their siren song? And we know if mermaids want to come here, they're going to insist on pools and hot tubs. Do you really want to pay for that?"

The vote was unanimous. Finding a group worse off than you was always a morale booster. Mob mentality remained undefeated against logic.

Still, only once had the community failed to approve an application of residency.

Harold the Dogboy was neither dog nor boy (and probably not even Harold, but no one had proven that), he was merely a floppy-eared elderly man who preferred bushes and fire hydrants to toilets, a habit that eventually led to a very short trial period. "You don't piss into the wind or on Beatrice's petunias," Luis pronounced as Harold was led out on a leash.

All in all, Luis disliked anyone having a say when it came to evaluating potential neighbors. Especially when it came to someone who may or may not be a deity.

Not just a deity. The deity.

Luis took a big breath and got down to business, hoping to capture just enough attention from the humming crowd to get something done.

"Please, the faster we get going, the faster we can get out of here." He turned his head toward Patrick, the leprechaun's smirk daring Luis to gain control over the masses. "Or just go ahead and watch whatever mind-sucking show you think might be better than actually paying attention."

Patrick jumped out of his seat, making him even shorter. He pointed a tiny, gnarled index finger at Luis, who instantly regretted mentioning TV. There was one thing Patrick hated more than people making fun of his height, and that was people making fun of his favorite shows, especially those involving the most debasing situations.

"Mind-sucking?" Patrick bellowed. "*Emergency Room Extractions* is a fucking medical show and if you watched, maybe you'd be able to extract Vlad's dick from your ass once in a while. Or do you just wait until the moon is full when you get your wolf period?"

"Luis, you're not going to take that from a sawed-off pot-o-gold-chasing dickweed, are you?" The voice came from Luis's left, but no one was there.

"Ralph?" He waved at the empty space, hitting what felt like an ample torso queried.

"Watch it," came the disembodied voice. "And yes, present for now, but not for much longer. You know how little patience I have."

Beatrice chimed in, offering to cast a spell imprisoning Patrick in the TV shows he cherished. It was all talk, Luis knew, since the witch didn't even have the power to vanquish her own arthritis. But the thought was nice.

Noise rose throughout the community room. The natives were getting restless and that was never a good thing. Curses would be thrown, shapes would be shifted, and empty threats would be traded. There might even be a few minor skirmishes, resulting in nothing other than sore muscles the next morning.

Patrick raised the TV remote control, his finger poised over the "On" button. It was the ultimate threat, a move that reminded Luis of who had all the power. The leprechaun had agreed to this meeting because, as he told Luis, "It's the kind of bullshit formality that makes it appear everyone has a voice." But when it came to these meetings, Patrick's fuse matched his height.

Luis slammed the ladle once, twice, a third time. "As soon as I have your attention, we can begin."

The din continued and a trio of mummies at the back stood with a groan. They shuffled sideways toward the door, each with one arm raised in stereotypical horror-film fashion. Luis wasn't worried as it would take them several minutes to exit, but it meant breaking out the vacuum to clean up the ancient dust being shed. It was time to assert himself.

"WILL EVERYONE SIT THE FUCK DOWN AND SHUT THE FUCK UP!"

Heads swiveled toward Luis, save for the zombie noggin that toppled due to the quick movement. Luis waited the few seconds needed for his friends to replace it.

"Please, let's get started. For God's sake."

At that moment, a bright light from the back of the room forced Luis to put up his left hand and shield his eyes. The light was followed by a thunderous boom, as if a lightning bolt had just struck someone dead. Patrick, Luis hoped.

"Sorry," grumbled the elderly man standing in the doorway. "Thought it was one of those doors with the hydraulic opener. Gave it quite a push."

"Just turn off those damn emergency lights." Patrick shielded his eyes, squinting toward the back.

"Ah, I thought it was the button that operated the door," the man said. "That's what you get for thinking you're all-knowing."

The light flicked off and illumination returned to normal. Still, thought Luis, it was quite an entrance.

The werewolf immediately recognized Todd in all his glory. He wore a well-tailored white suit and red tie. Luis noticed Todd had trimmed his beard for a more contemporary look, though it gave off a Colonel Sanders vibe.

A week ago, he'd filed paperwork to become a resident. Well, at least according to Patrick, who usually showed little interest in such details.

Yet it was Patrick who gave Todd's application to Luis, asking the werewolf to schedule the meeting for necessary resident approval. It was the first time the leprechaun urged a "yes" vote for anyone, including a time he voted against his own cousin. "He's part elf," Patrick had explained. "A damned half-breed baking cookies or some shit."

In delivering Todd's paperwork, Patrick ordered Luis to expedite approval, a first. Luis assumed two things—Todd's annoying habits did not rise to "microwaving fish in the shared kitchen" levels, and that he was rich.

When Luis pointed out how many boxes Todd had left blank on the application, including last name and previous address, Patrick paid no attention. Then there was "Occupation," where everyone put, "Retired."

Todd had jotted, "Chairman, omni science," or at least that's what Luis assumed. There appeared to be no space between "omni" and "science."

All that went through Luis's mind when the mysterious new applicant suddenly appeared, crashing their meeting. It made things very uncomfortable and was the main reason residents-to-be were never invited. Hard to vote behind people's backs when they were facing you.

Todd stepped into the room and offered a warm "Good evening, all," greeting that gave Luis an embarrassing tingle inside. Todd flicked his lapel as if brushing off a bit of lint, but Luis got the feeling not even an ounce of detritus would dare invade the visitor's personal space.

The potential resident strolled in confidently, looking left and right with a smile that didn't budge. Luis couldn't shake the feeling they were being judged by the interloper, which certainly would fit the MO of who he suspected this to be.

No, that was impossible. First, he wasn't sure God existed. Secondly, would the most powerful being in the universe choose such a stereotypical look? He could be a hipster with a manbun, or a goth girl, or a precocious eight-year-old. Though Luis was unfamiliar with the Bible, he was pretty sure it did not include a complete description of the world's most powerful badass—or giver of unending love, whatever your belief.

Luis leaned toward badass, especially with all that vengeful Old Testament shit going down. War, sacrifices, stoning. He was aware God let up in the New Testament, allowing Jesus to spread the love. But still.

An odd sound broke the uncomfortable silence. As Luis noticed all eyes on him, he realized he'd burst out laughing at the preposterousness of his thoughts. He was losing it. Truly losing it.

The good news, he finally had the attention of the group. Even Patrick was silent, and Luis was thankful there would be a brief ceasefire in the carpet f-bombing.

The bad news, he couldn't start the meeting with its subject in their midst.

The visitor broke the silence. "I'm not interrupting anything, am I? I thought I heard my name."

Luis thought back, certain no one had mentioned Todd. And if someone had, how could he have heard it?

"I'm sorry, but to be honest, we don't know your full name," Luis said sheepishly. "Your paperwork was rather lacking in detail."

"Well, I must be the one to apologize. My presence must be a bit awkward then, yes?"

"What do you mean?" Luis feigned ignorance. It's not as if they posted a meeting notice that said, "Next meeting, 7 p.m., thumbs up or down on resident who may or may not be omniscient."

But if he were omniscient, he'd know exactly what they were doing. *Jesus, there, I go again,* Luis thought, immediately regretting the addition of Jesus into the inner conversation.

Todd stepped up to the card table, not taking his eyes off Luis. "While many here know me, perhaps I should formally introduce myself to everyone, including you." He extended his arm.

Luis stood, wondering if he was prepared to touch the hand of Todd. "Of course I am, he's just a man," Luis tried to convince himself.

"Excuse me?" Todd posed, hand still extended. "I didn't quite catch that."

Luis was sure he hadn't said that aloud. Or had he?

"Sorry, nothing."

The second Luis's hand gripped Todd's, it felt as if he'd dipped it into a bucket of warm wax. The soothing feeling flowed up his arm, caressed his shoulders and flooded his body with, with...

Comfort and joy? Yes, that was it. Cares floated away. If this is what heroin felt like, Luis understood why there were such things as addicts.

"I'm assuming I can have my hand back at some point."

Did Todd say something? He did, something about returning a hand, only it wasn't Darnell, who would mean it in a literal sense. Last thing he remembered was reaching out and...Todd. It was Todd's hand. When Luis returned to reality, he saw dozens of eyes locked on him, each pair with arched eyebrows suggesting something untoward had occurred. Had it?

Releasing his grip, Luis apologized, again, adding, "That was some trick."

"Trick? Not sure what you mean. Did I make something disappear?"

Indeed he had, vanishing most of Luis's doubts as to whether the applicant should join the merry band of misfits.

"That is a good trick then, isn't it?"

Luis knew he hadn't said that out loud. He always kept his opinion to himself when it came to new residents, sharing them only when the time was right—in a public forum, where gossip was meant to be voiced.

"I'm not sure I know what you mean," Luis said, refusing to believe anyone could, or would want to peek into minds.

"Of course not," Todd said.

"By the way, I didn't catch your last name."

"Last name? Why, I've never given it any thought."

"Going to be honest, when it comes to going by first name only, 'Todd' really isn't in the same league as Bono. Or Slash. Or even Cher." *But it is as pretentious*, Luis thought.

"Yes, I suppose, and I am hardly pretentious," Todd implored, pulling long, elegant fingers through his well-groomed beard. "My last name is, let's see...Frakes."

"Frakes?"

"Yes."

"Todd Frakes."

"Of course."

"Oh, for God's sakes."

"Precisely."

He couldn't possibly think...Luis thought. There is just no way in hell... He cannot be the almighty.

Because if he was, Luis knew, life as they knew it was over. There was only one reason an omniscient being known for peace, love, and goodwill would be among the world's most infamous creatures. And it sure wasn't to bless them.

EIGHT

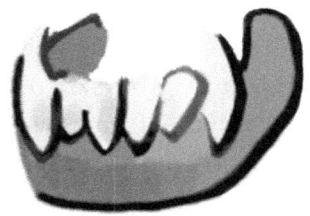

LUIS WASN'T sure if Todd was misguided, cocky, or both. But the werewolf knew he was far from rubber-stamping this particular potential resident, no matter how it would incur leprechaun wrath.

Patrick, of course, wasted little time making his opinion clear.

"Whomsoever has any objections, let them speak now so I know who they are and can wring their fucking necks and we can finish this meeting before *Colonoscopy Nightmares* begins."

A hand shot up, but Luis recognized when a goblin was shooing away a swarm of fairies. Fairies loved to mess with the goblins, something about an ancient rivalry. Luis ignored them and turned to the leprechaun. "Patrick?"

"Yeah?"

"Not the way we handle the membership process."

"Really? Because we've been dicking around for, what, at least ten minutes now."

"Not surprising from someone whose attention span matches his height."

As soon as Luis said it, he knew he'd gone too far. The leprechaun made a surprisingly agile leap toward the werewolf, but still failed to clear the card table which collapsed under Patrick's weight. Fortunately for Luis, he'd backed away just in time to avoid considerable damage to his knees.

The crowd applauded the unseemly stunt, though Luis wasn't sure if it was for the attempt at athleticism, or its spectacular failure involving one so short-tempered.

As the claps receded, Luis couldn't help but notice the one figure at the back who didn't react at all. Vlad stood with the scowl on his face speaking louder than words (of which there would be none during this meeting, Luis knew). The vampire had made it clear he was not on Team Todd, believing the newcomer to be hiding something other than a frustrating smugness. Luis stared at Vlad, taking in the slim jet-black tailored suit his friend always wore, an outfit that only emphasized his pallor. Though he couldn't see them, Luis knew shiny black size-twelve wingtips finished the look. When Vlad slicked back his dark hair, as he often did, anyone who saw him would almost be convinced vampires do exist. Luis didn't blink as he met Vlad's eyes, daring the vampire to involve himself in something bigger than himself. Just as the werewolf had anticipated, Vlad turned on his heel and stalked out, just as Patrick lifted himself to his size—three feet.

"You pug-faced hound," Patrick said, jabbing the air with a stubby index finger. "Next full moon, I'm going to call animal control to put your mongrel ass in dog jail where you'll spend the next few months being some pit bull's bitch."

Todd, who had taken a seat in front as Patrick spoke on his behalf, patted the leprechaun as one would a lapdog.

"Nice character reference, Todd," Luis said, not as upset with Patrick's launch as it was the landing. Luis chalked up the card table as a complete loss with no room in the budget for a replacement.

The werewolf picked up the remains of the table, expecting it to weigh a bit more than it did. Then he noticed the opposite corner levitating.

"Thanks Ralph," Luis nodded.

"Don't mention it," came the voice from the opposite side.

The two walked the pieces to side of the room, setting them next to a trash can, its odor a cry to be emptied. Either that or fairies had taken up residence, and they were a filthy bunch. Luis started to return to his seat when something gripped his bicep, holding him in place. He heard Ralph's faint voice.

"Hang on a sec. I've got a few concerns."

"We should get back to the meeting," Luis insisted. Looking back to the front of the room, he saw Todd attempting to calm a wildly gesticulating Patrick. "On the other hand, what's on your mind?"

"This Todd guy." Ralph released his grip on Luis. "I've heard some interesting things."

"How so?"

"Enough so that at this point, I'm not sure I can give him my vote."

Luis had been pleasantly surprised when Ralph agreed to serve on the board a year ago. Since then, Luis knew well the disadvantages of working with someone you can't see. For most meetings, Ralph either was present and quiet, or not there. The second was typically true.

"What exactly have you heard?" Luis said to the empty space he assumed Ralph occupied.

"That Todd is special with some amazing powers," Ralph observed from the empty space opposite of where Luis was looking. The werewolf hated that. "Telekinesis, mind-reading, generating a sense of positive self-esteem in others. And he's not afraid to use them, even if he's just bowling. That seems such an abuse of power."

"Well, I wouldn't…"

"One more thing. A siren told me Todd could really be God."

Luis sighed, ignoring the imps now looking at him. They giggled, no doubt thinking their mischievous "voices in my head" potion had everything to do with this phantom conversation. Everyone at Upton Arms had learned long ago to toss any beverage left unattended for more than a few minutes, giving imps ample time to spike it with any number of disagreeable elixirs. This was why Luis tossed his Coke before the meeting and after he returned from the bathroom.

"Ralph, sirens lie," an exasperated Luis whispered. "It's what they do, besides luring men to their deaths."

"I know, but with everything else I've heard, I'm not ready to vote one way or another. So, I'm abstaining for now. And I'm heading out to drink. Heavily. Because this is getting too serious."

"But I need you for a quorum," Luis begged.

"And I'm not going to rubber-stamp a guy who can be extremely dangerous."

"Not asking you to rubber-stamp anything, let's just keep an open mind and hear him out."

"Jesus, Luis, do you even hear yourself? Quit being everyone's lap dog."

"What did you say?" Luis felt the hairs on the back of his neck start to rise.

"You heard me. I know you're trying to make this shithole less of a shithole, but some changes aren't for the better. And this is one of them. You need to…" Ralph paused for emphasis … "stay…your ground."

Claws crept from beneath Luis's nails at the sound of a dog-related command. Still, Ralph had a point. If nothing else, Luis wanted to make everyone's life at Upton Arms a better one. Hell, he brought more than half of them here. They were his responsibility. What choice did he have?

A whisper in his ear. "And stow the claws. Remember, you can't mangle what you can't see."

Luis caught himself, stopping his inner wolf (or whatever angry mammal might be lurking inside) from revealing itself. It was fruitless to argue with Ralph who, being invisible, always had the last word. Besides, what kind of example would he set by disemboweling a fellow board member?

"Now that we're all better here," Ralph went on, "what about the rest of the board? Mothman?"

"Cocooning."

"And that wraith? What's-her-name."

"Forfeited her seat when she tried to eat Darnell's brain."

"Damn, you're screwed, and I'm gone. You never saw me."

"No shit," Luis muttered, returning to his seat at the front of the room. At least Todd had managed to control Patrick enough to get the leprechaun back in his chair, even as Patrick shot daggers at Luis as if the werewolf had taken a dump at the end of the rainbow.

"If everyone can settle down for just a minute," Luis raised his voice over the low rumble of indistinct conversations. He wished he had his soup ladle and something to pound it on.

The din continued.

"People, if we quiet down, we can wrap this up."

It got louder.

"Did he really crack a bowling ball in half just to pick up a split?" someone mentioned.

"I heard he turned the vampire's beer into blood," came another voice.

"Can he make me feel better about myself?" That originated from the back, probably a ghoul. Which meant the answer was, "No."

Luis held out his hands, lowering them slowly to indicate silence was requested. A futile gesture.

A figure suddenly appeared next to him. Todd. Either Luis wasn't paying attention or Todd teleported from his recliner. Luis went with teleportation, a better fit with his current faith.

Todd slowly raised his arms slightly above his shoulders and boomed, "Let there be light!" in a voice that made Luis, if not everyone else, believe in miracles.

The room fell silent, all eyes on Todd.

"'Let there be light?'" Luis arched his eyebrows, wondering if he'd heard that cliché correctly.

"Yeah," Todd affirmed, throwing a nod to the crowd. "Just seems to work when you need to go back and start from the beginning. And to get attention."

The werewolf couldn't argue. The audience sat in rapt silence, even after Todd lowered his arms and sat back down.

Luis was about to raise his arms in a similar way to get eyes on him, but now it just seemed silly. Instead, he went on as if a potential deity were not in the same room. "As you know this was your chance to get to know Todd, have him say a few words. Then, as we always do when new people apply for residency, the board would ask for a show of hands when it comes to who approves of the potential new neighbor."

Several hands began to rise as if slowly inflated with helium.

"No, please, not while the applicant is still here," Luis went on, the arms lowering. Being mystical creatures was no excuse for bad manners.

"Just one problem," he continued. "We don't have enough board members, at least as far as I know..." Luis looked left and right, muttering Ralph's name. No answer. "Right, so not enough board members, as I said. That means we must postpone our decision indefinitely." Luis tensed for imminent leprechaun impact, but relaxed as Todd rose, motioning to Patrick to stay seated while intoning, "Bless you and keep you."

An odd thing to say at the end of a community meeting, Luis thought, *but it worked*. Everyone quietly filed out. Soon, only Luis, Todd, and Patrick remained.

"Another time then." Todd turned to Patrick. "I'll be in touch."

"When?" Patrick blurted in a way-too-anxious voice.

"Soon, I hope."

Todd disappeared, but not like most people who hurry away. His vanishing occurred between "Soon" and "I hope," with a flash of light in between.

"Fuck, fuck, fuck it all," Patrick stammered, gripping Luis's wrist. "We need to talk because the shit just took a hard turn toward the fan. "

"What are you talking about?" Luis snatched his arm back.

"My room. An hour. Bring Vlad."

"Why?"

"Honest to Todd, I don't know. But Vlad needs to be there."

Luis ignored what he assumed was Patrick's slip of the tongue. He had no clue that one day, he'd see it in a new light.

If only it had been the one at the end of the tunnel rather than the one at the end of life.

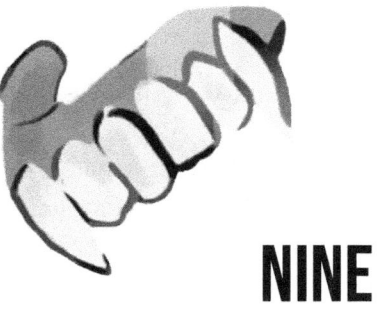

NINE

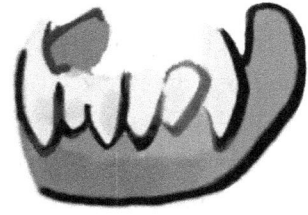

AS A LIFETIME MEMBER of the vampire club, Vlad knew what sucked. And this certainly did.

The California king bed was roughly the size of Vlad's room, yet it fit comfortably inside Patrick's place with plenty of room for an overstuffed leather couch and massage chair.

Then there was the full-size refrigerator when residents weren't even allowed a porta-fridge. And the killer wasn't the fifty-five-inch TV bolted to the wall. It was that it was showing a soccer match available only on a streaming channel.

The son-of-a-bitch had high-speed internet!

No wonder Patrick refused to have visitors. His room was the Gulliver in the Lilliput kingdom.

"Jesus, Patrick," Vlad whined as he struggled to take it all in. "Overcompensate much?"

Patrick made a show of cupping his pal around his ear. "What was that?" He bellowed over the drone of the massage chair, its back rollers massaging the top of the leprechaun's scalp. "Not that hearing you would be worth turning this off."

Vlad couldn't see how the chair could be of any value to a body occupying roughly twenty percent of its surface area and out of reach for most of its massaging benefits.

"Fine, I'll take my leave," Vlad huffed. "The less time in your company the better."

The vampire cast one last lingering look at what had to be the presidential suite at Upton Arms, with its stately oak and mahogany furniture. Too bad it was occupied by the Secretary of Dickishness.

Vlad turned and put his hand on the doorknob, which he couldn't help but notice was a wonderful antique bronze and connected to an electronic deadbolt. Vlad's room came with a push-button lock and sliding chain, elements right out of the Design School of Cheap Motels You Stop at When You Run Out of Gas on a Stormy Night.

"Relax, Vlad, just fucking with you," Patrick confessed, punching the chair's remote and stopping the infernal buzz of relaxation-inducing machinery. Juggling remotes, he switched off the soccer game as well. "No wonder you can't survive a little sunlight with such thin skin."

Vlad could only shake his head noting the oak coffee table in front of the couch, as well as the pair of dark mahogany nightstands on either side of the bed. The fanciest bit of furniture in his own room was a set of wood veneer tray tables, yet Patrick had somehow managed to afford furnishings that were worthy of the coasters stacked on the nightstand. The vampire had a million questions, most of them having to do with unwarranted entitlement, when there was a knock at the door interrupted a train of thought heading toward Anger-Management Station.

"Get that, would you?" It was more order than question pointed aimlessly. "I mean, being you're standing right by the door and all."

Luis entered and soon wore the same look of amazement that Vlad wore when he'd stepped in.

"Holy shit, Patrick, did you find a way to squeeze out a few wishes from that dried up old genie?" Luis's head swiveled about, feeling like a farmer seeing New York City for the first time. "Because he told me I couldn't wish for anything, only hope. I did and since I'm still living here, you know how that turned out."

Vlad waited patiently for Luis's look of awe to turn to one of anger, assuming his friend would come to the same realization. He mentally ticked down—three, two, one…

And there it was as Luis's mouth dropped and eyebrows furrowed.

"You son of a bitch," the werewolf grunted. "I thought that pot-of-gold stuff was horseshit. Yet here you are, living off the proceeds and pissing rainbows up everyone's ass. And coasters too. Coasters!"

Patrick climbed off the massage chair, hopped on his bed, and made the long journey across the mattress to go nose-to-nose with Luis.

"Everything in here was earned with hard work and know-how," the leprechaun insisted, wagging a finger inches from of the werewolf's nose. "While you were chasing women and orphans on the moors, I was building a fucking empire. What you see is a very small part of that."

Luis smiled wryly. "Speaking of small parts—"

"Enough already," Vlad interrupted. "Patrick, why the hell are we here? Assuming it wasn't to reveal a standard of living far above everyone else." Vlad shot a look at Luis. "And no comments about height or the lack of it, please."

"Fine," Luis spat. "Let's just get to it."

Patrick leapt off the bed and returned to the massage chair as Vlad and Luis took seats on opposite ends of the couch. Luis rubbed the armrest. "Real leather?" he asked no one, knowing the answer.

"Let's be clear about one thing," Patrick said, brushing aside Luis's arm before picking up the chair's remote control. His thumb jabbed at one of the buttons, the chair responding with a low hum. "Ah, that's the stuff. Right there. It's all about good vibes. And you guys are sending out all the wrong ones."

Vlad crossed his arms. "Meaning?"

"Meaning you, Luis, need to get your shit together as the so-called president of this so-called community," the leprechaun emphasized. "And since you never do anything without being backed up by your righthand butt-boy here, I need to make something very clear to the both of you."

There was a quick rap on the door before it opened. A well-groomed gentleman in gray slacks and checkered dress shirt pushed his way in, the wheelchair thumping slightly over the threshold.

Vlad recognized him from the bowling alley. He'd been talking to

Patrick and Todd in a way that suggested he'd known each for quite a while.

"Ah, there you are, finally," Patrick said, more an announcement than a greeting. "Hope you don't mind if I don't get up."

"As long as you don't mind me doing the same," the man retorted, swiveling adeptly to shut the door behind him.

He pushed into the room, stopping opposite the coffee table from Luis and Vlad, who each stood.

"This is Lawster," Patrick gestured to the stranger. "My attorney. And Lawster, these miscreants are Luis and Vlad, chosen based on your request."

Lawster proffered his hand, ignored for the moment by all those in attendance. "Lawster McLegalton, so very nice to meet you. Patrick has told me very little about you, which is fortunate based on his general ill feelings toward people as a whole."

"Lawster...McLegalton?" Vlad said, brushing a lint off his sleeve. "Seems more a label than a name."

Lawster tipped back, meeting Vlad's stare. "As I understand it, you're a vampire. Hardly one to cast stones in the glass house of unimaginative monikers. But yes, Lawster McLegalton, long story not worth getting into here."

Had Vlad been able to see himself in the mirror, he would have seen an elderly, slack-jawed vampire with a pair of fangs poking slightly from blood-red gums. He was in fight-or-fright mode, wondering if he should kill or intimidate this intruder who knew his most valued secret. Ot maybe he should direct his building anger toward the leprechaun who had made plenty of mistakes since the vampire had known him— personally vouching for that swamp monster as a tenant, for example. Guy continuously tracked in fetid water causing a stench that lasted a month after his eviction—but allowing a norm into their protected space exceeded the boundaries.

Patrick sat up and shut off the recliner, a move that drew all eyes to him. "I see that look, Vlad, but just tuck those fangs back in your pants. I've known Lawster a very long time. He's proven his loyalty many times over. Besides, you should relate, one bloodsucker to another."

Vlad felt his fangs slide back into place even as he remained doubtful, tentatively offering his hand to Lawster, who gave it a vigorous shake.

Luis did the same. "I'm Luis, and yes, I'd very much like to get into the story behind your name. It seems familiar and—"

"Muzzle it, dogboy," Patrick interrupted, continuing quickly before Luis could react to words designed to irritate. "We have more important things to discuss, so put a leash on your curiosity and shut the fuck up. Lawster, you were saying?"

The lawyer pushed himself to the center of the room, a rare space unoccupied by expensive furniture. "Patrick tells me you two are in a decent position to help us with a little predicament. How much has he shared about the situation?"

Before Luis or Vlad could answer, the leprechaun interjected. "Thought I'd leave that to you, Lawster, as much as I hate thinking about it, let alone talking about it."

Vlad and Luis leaned forward. This couldn't be good.

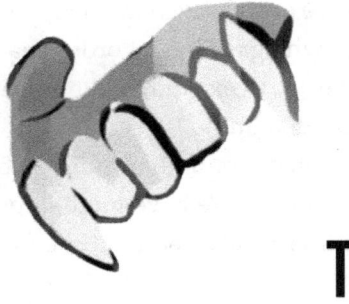

TEN

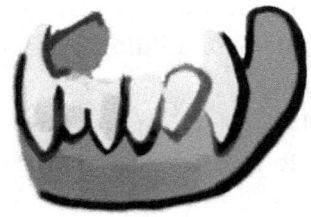

"YOU'RE TELLING us Patrick owns this place," Vlad reflected, rubbing his chin.

"Yes," Lawster affirmed. "And the real Upton Arms, the one out front built for the mortals."

"The real Upton? The building facing the street, the nice one with stucco not worn down to the chicken wire."

"Right, with the putting green and pool and pickleball courts. For people who are in their eighties rather than their two-hundred-and-eighties, or whatever it is you live to. *That* Upton was needed for zoning and permits, since I was pretty sure the city wouldn't grant a variance for fictional creatures. Yet not so fictional, as it turns out."

Vlad nodded, imagining how neighbors might feel if they knew they lived next to supernatural people who could consider them victims as much as neighbors. Block parties would be out of the question. "And Patrick owns both?"

"Technically speaking, Upton Arms is owned by GTFO Enterprises, a wholly owned LLC registered through a very complicated network of shell corporations connected to one Patrick O'Shaughnessy."

Vlad could guess what GTFO stood for. "So, he's our landlord and has been for years."

"Exactly."

It made sense now. The rundown community room. The slow Wi-Fi. Even the pastries put out every December 25, courtesy of management.

"The Christmas Danishes," Vlad brought up. "Day old?"

"Weeks," Patrick interjected. "Not that I heard any complaints."

"Tell me then," Vlad said, ignoring the leprechaun and pointing at the lawyer. "How can the stingiest man on the planet be so broke to the point that Upton Arms is hanging on by a thread?"

"Let's just say it was a wardrobe malfunction. You want to hear the story?"

"I think that would be a good idea."

By the time Lawster finished, Vlad felt like throwing himself into a sunbeam (not that it would kill him, he knew from past experience, but it was the thought that counted).

According to Lawster, Patrick stood out (in a figurative sense only) at an investment conference almost thirty years earlier. Even as the financial industry reeled from the bursting of the dot-com bubble, Patrick encouraged further investment in the online sector. He spoke of a future world where people would tire of friendships requiring people to go out of their way to meet up every now and then, if not perform favors for the sake of maintaining a civil society. Those same people would also be too lazy to get off their asses to shop or eat or go to work or even deposit a check. "Down deep," Patrick had said during his pro-online presentation, "people can't stand the presence of people. And that is going to change the world." Lawster recalled being one of the few who applauded, Patrick shooting him the finger on his way off stage.

The lawyer wasn't all that surprised when, several years later, he received a job offer from Patrick. Though he was taken aback by Patrick's reasoning, telling Lawster that "with a cripple representing me, they'll never see the financial ass-fucking I'm about to give them coming."

As Patrick built a small fortune on the sorts of companies that banked on people's inherent unwillingness to connect with the world, he was besieged by entrepreneurs looking for seed money for apps. Despite Lawster's misgivings (and outright warnings), Patrick invested in a series of losers, from Diaper Dan's Toddler Tracker (the device's batteries often leaked, though the screams made it easy to track any toddler) to

Mansplainer ("Simple answers to stupid questions so you can finally enjoy a beer in peace").

Patrick's fortune dwindled to the point where he resorted to asking Mansplainer for help. "How can I make more money?" When Mansplainer answered, "If only you hadn't quit your job after having kids," the childless Patrick nodded, wondering why such an insightful app had only been downloaded twenty-seven times.

"That says so much about Patrick," Vlad interjected.

"Thinking the exact same thing," Luis added.

"Right?" Lawster piled on. "Now if you don't mind, we get to the mess that is sharts."

At some point, Patrick crossed paths with a multi-millionaire who'd made his fortune in clothing design, a man known in the fashion business as the Tagless Titan.

The second Vlad heard that moniker, Vlad felt the blood drain from his body faster than the way he used to pound down a quick waif before sunrise. How long had it been since he'd heard "Tagless Titan?" Not long enough.

As Lawster went on, Vlad struggled to listen. "He not only recognized the value of underwear that had no tag, but discovered the process to imprint size and laundry instructions directly on the fabric, as if that makes him such kind of genius. But apparently it did because he got a cut of every tagless item sold, from briefs to polo shirts."

Despite the success, the Tagless Titan couldn't find anyone to invest in his next brilliant design, shorts featuring master works of art. He was ready with an entire line of shorts imprinted with Monet, Degas, and Picasso. Even contemporary artists were represented, including Pollack, de Kooning, and Murakami.

That's when a desperate Patrick threw in, based on the Titan's past success. He even had a clever name for shorts with art.

As Lawster got to that part of the story, the leprechaun groaned but remained otherwise silent.

Luis stared incredulously at the attorney. "And he had no idea what sharts were? "Seriously?"

"Apparently not. Nor did he listen to those who counseled him otherwise. Patrick can be pretty stubborn."

"We've noticed. Like when he watches, *Surprisingly Short Hospice Stays*, tends to remind people around here of their own mortality challenges."

"Uh, right. But it wasn't just the marketing that stained the brand. Turned out the Tagless Titan didn't bother to obtain licensing, as if artists would be proud to see their works on the asses of every Walmart shopper across America."

Another groan from the massage chair.

"As a result, Patrick is the majority owner of tens of thousands of sharts inside a New Jersey warehouse that he can neither sell nor, because of a lack of funds, destroy."

"Wait, if the Tagless Titan was so rich, why did he need Patrick?" Luis offered.

"People like the Tagless Titan are rich because they gamble with other people's money, never their own," Lawster related.

Vlad knew that better than anyone. But instead of delving into memories that would only force him to relive the pain, the vampire pushed them away to focus on Lawster, his concerns deepening about the presence of an outsider. And just why was he droning on about Patrick's dire financial straits? It wasn't like Vlad had the funds or desire to help.

Until Lawster arrived at the kicker.

"Before my client took it in the sharts, he invested heavily in this place." Lawster gestured grandly. "Upton Arms, where the not-as-immortal-as-they-thought live out their lives quietly when not taking field trips to bowling alleys."

Vlad stiffened his spine, rising to his full height, though his stature was not nearly as intimidating as it was a century ago. "Patrick may vouch for you, but I take that as seriously as his promise to stop using the community fridge as a magic box of free food."

"The fairies swore that was true," Patrick smirked. Vlad didn't know who the bigger dicks were, fairies of leprechauns. Nah, it was fairies.

The vampire ignored the crack and shot a look at Lawster that screamed, "I will bleed you faster than an overeager phlebotomist ten minutes late for her lunch break."

"Just how long have you known about us?" Vlad wondered. "And who else does?"

"Now don't get your fangs in an uproar," Lawster suggested in a way he did not feel the least bit menaced, aggravating Vlad even further. "I've known for quite a while and, as you know, your secret has been safe or an army of Buffys and other vampire slayers would have descended by now."

Vlad exchanged a wary glance with Luis. He knew they could take care of this particular problem here and now. Disposal of the body would be simple, and one of the ghouls had a birthday coming up. Two birds, one lawyerly stone.

But killing a man in a wheelchair was so unseemly. Like taking blood from a baby (not that such a thing had ever appealed to Vlad; he was a vampire, not a monster).

"Hold the fangs and claws, please," Patrick piped up. "Lawster has not just been representing me for years—keeping this place afloat, mind you—but he's also a friend. He's even helped Beatrice sell the kinds of potions that aren't exactly open to clinical trials. And do you have any idea how much Darnell rents for during *Walking Dead* conventions?"

Vlad sat back down slowly and reluctantly; his eyes glued to Lawster. He waited a bit to see what happened, but with no end to the standoff, he asked the question on the tip of his tongue since he entered Patrick's room.

"Why," he said, looking at Patrick, then Lawster, then back to Patrick, "would I care what happens to a conned leprechaun?"

"Lepre-conned, so to speak," Lawster noted to another groan from Patrick. "If you're not concerned with the future of Upton Arms, which is on the brink of foreclosure, perhaps you might be interested in the Tagless Titan himself?"

There was that name again. Vlad knew there was no escaping it. "Victor Breeze."

Lawster nodded. "You know him." A statement more than a question.

"We have a history." A history that broke Vlad's heart more than any wooden stake could.

ELEVEN

IT HAD BEEN at least six years since Vlad had seen Victor Breeze, aka Vic the Dick, aka the man that brightened Vlad's life like the sun, burning the vampire worse than any solar rays could.

Even as Vlad's sex drive had slowly wound down over the last century, there was something about the elegant Breeze that pushed Vlad from neutral back into first gear (and soon into overdrive). Victor's look, his money, and certainly his power was quite the aphrodisiac for a vampire who hadn't been intrigued by sex for at least ten years.

Not that it mattered to Vlad, whose lifespan confounded attempts to remain interested in sex with either gender. His true pleasure came from his palate rather than his penis, a fine, gently writhing meal always brought him to orgasm. Part of that was due to the rarity of such occasions, Vlad having long given up the types of suppers that left bodies in a string of trash bins in dark alleys. Though the food was always good, the ambience left something to be desired. He swore off Dumpster-dining, relying on late-night withdrawals from blood banks as well as the occasional small-plate samplings offered by those into that sort of thing.

Yet it was a craving for tapas that drove Vlad back to one of the clubs appealing precisely to those who found sexual gratification through donating blood to those happy to take it orally, preferably through minor flesh wounds. Vlad gave little thought to the vampire fetish. Anything was fair game between consenting adults, be it having sex dressed as two adorably cute animals or having their throats sucked. As Vlad sat patiently at the bar nursing a cocktail even worse than the music, it wasn't long before a woman sat beside him and placed her hand on his knee.

He scented pineapple and clove. Type B-positive, aged slightly more than seventy years. The vessel was nice enough, most lines smoothed by whatever creams and elixirs women used these days. Best yet, the heart was strong, providing a well-flowing tap as well as decent odds of survivability.

Yes, she'd do. The vintage was a bit older than he was accustomed to, but the rarity would make up for it.

He slid next to her. "May I buy you a drink?" he cooed, shifting his leg to provide her easier access.

"No," she said, nodding toward the VIP section. "But my husband would like to buy you one."

It was a humble beginning to an intense though doomed affair. For six months, Vlad appeared nightly at Breeze's front door for various adventures that involved almost every toy a millionaire takes for granted. If they weren't cruising the harbor in Breeze's yacht, they were aboard his private jet for a quick trip to whatever destination appealed to them at the moment.

Breeze never questioned Vlad's adamancy that he be back before sunrise. The vampire had various cover stories ready but was never asked to supply them. With that kind of trust, Vlad found himself falling into a very comfortable relationship filled with the kind of luxury appointments he'd not had since the seventeenth century when he fell in with English royalty that happened to be between wars.

With each rendezvous, Vlad knew he was digging his proverbial grave even deeper. Like every mortal, Victor came with an expiration date. Each kiss, each languid night in bed, each whisper of love eternal would only make the inevitable departure that much more painful. How many times had Vlad rushed home, the sun peeking over the horizon and shooting its flaming daggers toward him, his skin burning not due to daylight but from their last embrace? Even as he dragged his body into bed, he swore he would give up a relationship that would destroy him. When he awoke, Vlad was ready to surrender to his passion rather than his logic.

Vlad knew it was doomed yet still wasn't prepared for the way it ended.

One night, a nurse answered the door, directing Vlad upstairs. As he trudged up the stairs, Vlad heard the distinctive beep of a heart monitor.

Light framed the last door on the right, the master bedroom. Vlad's mood sank as he approached. How many times had he put himself through this? Too often in the beginning when he ignored the disadvantages of immortality (or what he'd assumed at the time to be immortality).

People whined about putting down a series of dogs through a lifetime. Vlad wanted them to imagine outliving everyone important to you over several lifetimes, without the convenience of dropping them at a strip mall storefront to be put down. No, you had to be there to the bitter end, nature taking its own damn time to erase this precious life from the face of the earth.

Vlad poked his head in, knowing what he'd see.

"Vlad," Victor greeted. "Hope you didn't have your heart set on Vegas. Thought maybe we'd stay in."

"Sure, I see you're tied up," Vlad smiled.

Tubes snaked from various dangling plastic bags and metal tanks, tethering Victor to a life no one deserved. He struggled to sit up a little higher on the stack of pillows, gesturing Vlad to come closer.

As he approached, Victor seemed to melt right in front of him. The body Vlad had gotten to know so well lay under covers, its outline lost among the layers, disappearing into the bed below Victor's chest.

The vampire knew what he was looking at. Victor had maybe a month of agony left.

Vlad could leave right now and never come back. He didn't sign up for this. It was just for fun anyway, a delightful sideshow that proved an entertaining distraction. A reason to get out of the coffin each night.

Vlad felt himself sitting. Taking Victor's still hand, squeezing.

"When?" Vlad whispered.

"Three nights ago."

"Why didn't you call?"

"Wasn't sure we had that type of relationship. I could ask you for a ride to the airport. But to hang out right after a stroke? That's up there with helping someone move."

The stroke was the tip of the medical iceberg. Heart disease and high blood pressure performed a deathly duet. His diabetes had worsened, and the most vital organs refused to work full-time. When they did work, Victor mentioned with a smile, they complained about it.

"Like every millennial I've ever met," he said with disdain. "Little fuckers."

Victor hid the condition from Vlad for fear his late-life, wife-approved fling would be over. He buried the truth under every questionable medication his greedy doctors were happy to provide. The man once brimming with life now was propped up by a steady cocktail of prescriptions that patched everything just enough to keep the *S.S. Victor Breeze* afloat. But now he was taking on way too much water and would soon slip beneath the waves.

"God, you are such a dick," Vlad muttered.

"Right? Vic the Dick. I was probably three the first time I heard it. Comes with the name. Like Vlad the Bad, or Mad, or Sad. Right?"

"Sometimes all three."

Victor reached over with the arm that still responded to commands and grabbed Vlad's wrist.

"You can help me now. You can be Vlad the, well, I don't have anything that rhymes that makes sense. But you can save me. Vlad the Savior."

"I'll do anything, just name it." To this point, Vlad figured Victor was talking about a metaphorical save, maybe ensuring his fortune goes to a worthy charity (blood donations briefly came to mind), or write an inspiring eulogy to lionize a man who had plenty of faults.

"I know who you are," Victor confided. "What you are."

No, it wasn't possible. Save for the few times he awoke to find interlopers armed with mallets and sharpened stakes (why did they always linger past sunset, Vlad often wondered), his secret was safe.

Vlad broke Victor's grip. "Of course, you know who I am, what I am. We've spent a lot of time together these last months. I know who you are too. What you are."

Victor's chin dropped to his chest. The sound of a ticking clock filled the room, each click a step closer to a future Vlad was only just now beginning to dread.

It was several minutes before Victor lifted his head. "I'm sorry, I can't do this dance anymore. It's last call and life's bartender is about to kick me out."

Words tumbled forth, ones Vlad struggled to make sense of. For years, Victor had been looking for cures to the incurable. He used his vast resources to track down everything from homeopathic remedies to alternative treatments. Reiki. Acupuncture. Then further down the rabbit hole to witchcraft and voodoo.

Damned if he didn't come across an honest-to-goodness vampire.

Victor planted his finger on his lover's chest. "Even your name. I'm pretty sure the only people named Vlad are Russian dictators and vampires. And I have it on good authority you're not a Russian dictator. You knew what that meant? You were the key to my immortality."

For almost two hours, Victor argued and threatened and cajoled. No matter how many times Vlad refused, Victor came back with fresh arguments.

There was a time Vlad could turn others into vampires, but that time came to an end more than a century ago. It was one of those powers that deteriorated with age, like hypnotizing the weak-willed to do his bidding. He'd hated reaching the point where he had to pay people to mow his lawn and clean his house.

In the end, it was guilt that killed the beast inside him.

"Do you love me?" This was Victor's last stand.

Vlad had known that answer since their second date. "Yes, deeply."

"Then try. I know there are no guarantees, but if it's one shot in a million, please take it."

Victor stared at his lifeless hand, the one Vlad was holding again. His eyes bored in on it, as if willing it to move.

Vlad felt a twitch. And another.

"I want to live, Vlad. Please let me live."

It was true Victor desired Vlad more than anything else. But it wasn't about love. It had never been about love. It was all about the power over life and death.

What Victor didn't realize was who held that power. He was about to find out.

TWELVE

"YEAH, I KNOW VICTOR BREEZE," Vlad rumbled, brushing his hands along the front of his shirt as if wiping away memories that deserved to live forever in the darkest pits of his mind. "But how did you know that?"

Lawster winked. "I know the stuff I need to know."

Vlad wasn't sure what made him angrier, that this lawyer had a supernatural ability to take advantage of others, or that Patrick invited a member of the magically unendowed inside the walls of Upton Arms.

The vampire rethought the consequences of killing a man who couldn't put up much of a fight. Clearly no one would miss another shyster, but Patrick would give Vlad endless grief for the cleaning required to get Lawster out of the carpet and drapes, if lawyer stains even came out.

Vlad also held onto the regret that came with the deaths of many victims who fell so easily as he adjusted to his new life during the early years so many centuries ago.

Dark Ages indeed.

"Don't even think it," Patrick waved his arm dismissively. "There's not enough bleach in the world to clean up attorney."

Luis leaned toward Vlad and slapped his friend's knee. "Patrick is right. And it would be a waste of good bleach."

"Fine," Vlad pouted. "Lawster, might you have a business card?"

"Yes, of course." He pulled out his wallet and laid a crimson rectangle on the table. Vlad snatched it and gave it a good look. He noted the address and phone number, shaking his head when he saw the motto at the bottom.

"'A free-wheeling attorney,'" Vlad read aloud. "Really?"

"That tagline is figurative and literal, making it a winner," Lawster argued. "Embrace who you are."

Noting Vlad's glare, he added, "Except, you know, maybe not this instant. Because I have something very important to tell all of you."

Vlad made a show of slipping the card into his pocket, giving it a gentle pat as if to say to the attorney, "I know where you work."

"So why are we here?" Luis said impatiently. "Other than to soak in the grandeur that is Patrick's not-so-humble abode."

"I worked for everything I've got," Patrick said, fondling the massage chair's remote control.

"And that makes this fair?" Luis challenged, puffing his chest. "You've got your own refrigerator while I have a tough time finding room in the community fridge for my leftovers. Which doesn't matter anyway because my stuff is always stolen."

"You should label it."

"I do fucking label it, and I know goddamned well the fairies can read no matter what they tell me."

Lawster perked up. "Fairies are such dicks."

Heads nodded in unison.

"Look, this isn't about who has the biggest whatever," Patrick insisted.

"Good thing for you," Luis retorted.

Lawster spun in a tight circle, getting everyone's attention. "You guys need to get your shit together and listen to what I have to say, or in a few months, Upton Arms is going to be Out-on-Your-Ass Arms."

The room quieted. Vlad focused on Lawster because the only thing worse than being an aging vampire was being an aging, homeless vampire. "Go ahead."

"Thank you. First thing I need to make clear is that you have two options, each with inherent problems."

"Problems?"

"Only in that the first option may require a certain amount of deception on our part."

"Deceptive my ass," Patrick growled, his voice the same pitch as the hum of the massage chair, which he'd flipped back on. "Breeze owes me. I just want to reclaim what's rightfully mine."

Lawster nodded. "Exactly, and the only way to do that might require a little breaking, a little entering."

Vlad placed his hands on his knees, his head down. "No, no, no. You're talking about burglary. A felony."

"Well," Lawster said with a deceptive languidness to his voice. "It's a gray area. In a way. Patrick, might you explain?"

Patrick lifted the armrest and stabbed a button within, the chair silent once again. "I happen to know that Victor was working on some secret project, something even bigger than tagless underwear if you can even imagine. He was going to unveil it right before the Christmas shopping season knowing that people would go absolutely apeshit and make him rich all over again. Then there's all the money Breeze supposedly buried. Oh, and the gold he allegedly hid. But all that pales in comparison to whatever fashion breakthrough he invented. That's the real prize."

Vlad looked up and let out an exasperated sigh as if he were in the dark, which he usually was. But this time, it was figurative. "And you know this how?"

Before Patrick answered, Lawster held up his hand. "We just know. Just like we know how Victor kept safe from prying eyes. Our sources are impeccable. The less you know the better."

Even before Vlad realized he was speaking, he blurted, "And the second option?"

"Rather tenuous." Lawster met Vlad's gaze and took a deep breath. "You all met Todd and know he's got various powers to easily qualify for residency. But he was more than a possible new occupant. He was a potential investor, one with enough cash to keep this place open for eternity. You remember eternity, right? It's what you all thought you'd live for."

Christ, Vlad thought, *lawyers could be bigger dicks than fairies.*

Lawster held up his hand, his thumb and forefinger millimeters apart. "One problem. He's this close to calling the whole thing off."

"Why?" Vlad shrugged.

"'Bad vibes' is all he told me. I was shocked given how well it went at the bowling alley. He felt welcome, almost a part of the family. But he said he felt an uncomfortable amount of negativity at the board meeting."

Everyone looked at Vlad.

"What?" The vampire pointed his palms skyward and shrugged his shoulders. "I just watched. Didn't say a word."

Patrick sat up, shaking his finger at Vlad. "You didn't say a word because you didn't have to. You sat back there like a shining beacon of 'fuck you,' then took off without a word. Your skepticism was blinding."

"That's true, Vlad," Luis confessed. "You were like a mental vampire draining all the energy out of the room."

"Hold on," Vlad said, his palms now turned out. "I'm not the bad guy here."

"Not what I see," Patrick muttered. "You're the only one with the kind of minimum daily nutritional requirements that often result in fatalities."

"You little shit, how dare—"

Vlad felt an iron grip on his bicep. He looked at the black hand grasping his upper arm, its knuckles whitening under the strength being employed to restrain the vampire.

"It wasn't just you," Lawster said, slightly relaxing his grip. "Are we clear on that? Because you know how tough it would be to get leprechaun out of leather."

Vlad shut his eyes, imagining the tension flowing out of him, a red river of stress that then swirled around Patrick, suffocating the little man. As he envisioned Patrick drawing his last breath, Vlad took a deep breath and opened his eyes. "We're clear. I'm fine."

Luis looked from Vlad to Lawster. "If not only our resident skeptic, then who?"

Lawster rolled a few feet back, returning Vlad's personal space.

"From what I've been told, a certain invisible man was in attendance. And then he wasn't, which meant a vote couldn't be taken."

Vlad glanced at Luis. "Ralph? Is he talking about Ralph?"

Luis nodded. "Yeah, but how did Todd know? Kind of goes against the whole point of being invisible."

Something thunked against the side of Vlad's head, a slab of black plastic that now lay between the vampire's feet. It was a small remote control. Too small for the TV. The massage chair? Vlad massaged his temple, recalled what Lawster said about getting leprechaun out of leather.

"Jesus, you guys are a bunch of fucktards," Patrick said. "Of course he knew Ralph was there. Nothing gets by him."

"He's right about that," Lawster agreed. "I've seen that for myself."

The attorney explained how, several weeks ago, Todd reached out to Lawster to find out more about Upton Arms. Todd knew the attorney represented the home's owner and wanted to discuss an investment. "He knew everything about the place, despite all the paperwork I filed to bury Upton Arms deep in red tape. Sherlock Holmes couldn't have deduced ownership, yet Todd knew it all."

"Because Todd knows all," Patrick interjected. "Nothing else to it." The way he and Lawster exchanged knowing glances did not escape Vlad's watchful eyes.

He didn't need his centuries-honed vampire senses to know the two were covering something up, but he wanted to hear the rest of the story. He filed this bit of information away should he need it later, happy again for that business card.

Lawster went on to describe a meeting at a park on the edge of town, a park not on any digital map so the two relied on Todd's precise directions. When they arrived, it wasn't the abject silence that grabbed their attention as much as it was the stripes of dazzling color arching down from a cloudless sky.

Patrick put a fist in the air. "It was a fucking rainbow! Dazzling. Fresh from a unicorn's ass."

Knowing a sign when they saw one, Lawster continued, the pair walking over a berm and there was Todd, grinning beside a tremendous black kettle and the end of a stunted arc of color.

It wasn't long before the three shook on a deal that would make Todd a silent partner of Upton Arms, contingent on his residency at Upton Arms. "Want to keep an eye on my investment," he explained, and no one at that particular meeting was about to argue. Not with a fabled treasure within their grasp.

To seal it, Todd snagged a gold coin from the kettle full of them and handed it to Patrick, at which point the kettle disappeared.

Luis raised his hand tentatively as if in high school biology. "You didn't ask for a few credentials when it came to qualifications?"

"He was waiting at the end of a fucking rainbow with a pot of fucking gold!" Patrick stormed. "You kidding me? Credentials? You're a moron, you know that?"

"I'm just saying we don't know anything about this guy."

Patrick produced a gold coin and twirled it between his thumb and forefinger. "This enough for you?"

Luis sighed in surrender. "That's pretty impressive. Between the rainbow, gold, and mad bowling skills, he's in as far as I'm concerned."

With those facts in evidence, Vlad was able to fill in the rest of the story on his own. Patrick was sure he had a sweet deal to save his own personal kingdom only to have Todd later come down with a serious case of cold feet. Perhaps the vampire had indeed played a part, supplying the ice. But why would Todd care so much about the opinion of one vampire? Or want to invest in a place best forgotten?

Luis stood and began to pace, the lupine in him acting up whenever he got nervous. "OK, Mr. McLegalton, now that our financial lord and savior has disappeared, and we're left with a bagful of debt rather than a pot of gold, what do we do? Assuming you have ideas as Upton Arms' attorney at large."

Luis looked at Patrick. "Or, should I say, attorney at—"

"No, you shouldn't," Vlad cut in, staving off a leprechaun-launched nuclear f-bombing. "Lawster, this has been a lovely chat, but right now all I'm holding is a big bag of I-don't-give-a-shit."

"I know," Lawster turned his gaze away from the vampire. "Which is why it's time to come back to Victor Breeze."

Reaching into a briefcase strapped to his chair, he pulled out a folded newspaper and tossed it onto the coffee table. Vlad, Luis, and Patrick gathered around and looked at the ad circled in red.

Luis leaned in closely, absorbing the text. "No fucking way."

A broad smile creased Patrick's face. "Yes, fucking way."

Vlad said nothing, trying to take it all in.

The werewolf put a hand on his friend's shoulder. "Vlad, you OK? You look like you've seen a ghost."

Patrick chuffed. "That's how he always looks."

Yet Vlad did feel as if he'd seen a ghost, one that had been haunting his past for quite a while.

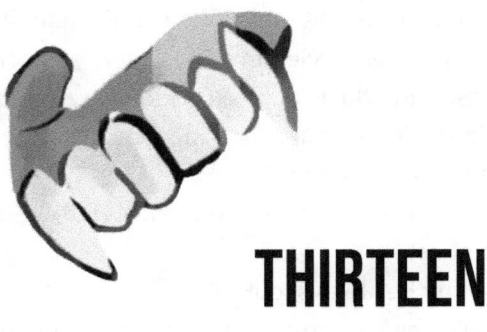

THIRTEEN

IN THE GLOOM of his darkened apartment, Vlad stared at the newspaper and ignored the persistent knocking at his door. He was trying to wrap his centuries-old mind around what was right there in black and white. He'd long ago accepted the inevitability of it all, but the fact it finally happened took his breath away. Why hadn't someone called him? Had they already had the funeral? Would he have been welcome?

The knock became louder, more urgent, followed by Luis's muffled voice. "Vlad, everything OK?"

No, it wasn't. Vlad watched his hand reach toward the door. Long white fingers wrapped around the knob. His wrist twisting, arm pulling the door inward.

Luis pushed past Vlad, the vampire tottering before collapsing in bed. The werewolf sat down beside him. "I'll take that as a 'No, everything is not OK.'"

Vlad placed the back of his hand against his forehead as if in a soap opera. He held a dramatic pause before uttering, "I didn't know he was dead."

"Victor Breeze? Why would you?"

The story he'd locked inside spilled forth. Vlad shared the condensed version of the love affair, reluctantly at first. But it felt good after a while, unburdening himself of the shame that came with providing aid to a man who didn't deserve it.

Luis listened silently as Vlad described what had occurred after Victor had begged for his life. How, with a fingernail, the vampire opened a small slit on his own wrist. The way Victor bent forward with the quickness of a hungry teenager seizing the last piece of pizza, his lips feeling like sandpaper on Vlad's skin.

Victor supped for just a second. Or perhaps a minute. Maybe an hour. It didn't matter anymore. When Vlad left, he knew he'd never return. He wasn't even sure if his anger stemmed from capitulating to Victor's demands, or how he'd misled his lover into believing it would make a difference. Or was it a lie? Vlad had no idea what effect his blood might have, though he'd come to doubt its power to unlock immortality. He'd disproven so many other vampire myths over the centuries. He despised crosses, not because they harmed him, but because they so rarely went with the décor. He laughed at those who wore garlic to fend off vampires, because it did more to keep friends and loved ones away than someone determined to feast. Nor had he ever wanted to turn someone into a vampire, out of love or simply a need for companionship. At first, it was about selfishness, not wanting to share these gifts with anyone. Later, it was about kindness, not wanting anyone to be saddled with this curse.

Even now, as he learned Victor had lived long past the perceived expiration date, Vlad wondered if his blood had played a role in Victor's longevity, or it was more the man's access to the best medicine money could buy.

Not that Vlad cared. Or so he tried to convince himself.

Vlad glanced at the clock. 4:07. AM or PM? He had no idea how much time had passed since Lawster had warned them what was in store for Upton Arms if certain measures weren't taken. All Vlad knew or felt was exhaustion.

His blackout curtains made sure no hint of sunlight came through the window. Once Lawster had finished with a scheme far too crazy to even discuss, the vampire returned to his room and collapsed—until his friend came knocking.

"Breeze was a real piece of work," Luis muttered, not understanding at all what Vlad had just revealed. "Seems to me you'd be pretty happy he's sucking dirt."

"More complicated than that," Vlad confessed, rolling away from his friend. "Which is why there is no way I'm going back to his house."

Vlad tried not to blame Lawster. The attorney had no idea Victor Breeze was not a man to trifle with, even in death. He'd been very suspicious of anyone who had nothing to contribute to his own personal gain, a legacy that likely continued among his heirs. No one would steal from Victor Breeze, during his life or after his death. Not only was Vlad unwilling to participate, but he knew it would be a mistake to involve creatures long past their prime.

No matter that on its face, the scheme was simple enough. With Victor's recent passing, his latest wife (Breeze didn't so much marry as manage a partner-exchange program) was conducting an estate sale, opening the house to anyone with cash and no discerning taste in furnishings, a lucrative combination.

Lawster informed them he had on good authority news that Victor was working on a fabric-based invention that would be even more successful than the one that made him the Tagless Titan. His not-so-untimely death meant the idea was still out there, waiting for the right entrepreneur.

Better yet, Lawster pointed out, an estate sale provided the perfect opportunity to stroll right in, eliminating the "breaking" part of "breaking and entering." But "entering" would not be enough, not with the various security measures likely to be in place as unwashed masses were invited inside the lofty Breeze estate.

Vlad was having none of it, as he now explained to Luis. "Nothing for me in that house but bitter memories and overwhelming regret. Besides, we have no idea what the invention is, whether he even kept it as his house, or what we'd do if we found it. It's not worth considering."

"Sorry," Luis choked.

"For what?"

"This." Luis pushed himself off the bed and flipped on a light that cast a yellow glow, bringing Vlad's room into focus. Not that there was anything worth looking at. A bed, a chest, a chair, and a table between four bare walls. No TV, music player, or computer. Not even a coffin, for cliché's sake.

"Really?" Vlad said, blinking as his eyes slowly adjusted to the brightness.

"It's like Todd would say. Let there be light."

"No, not this again."

"Yes, this again. And you brought it on yourself. If we don't go the Victor Breeze way, then we go the Todd way. In Todd we trust."

Vlad stifled a laugh. They'd all seen the parting of the bowling ball, a true miracle in a land of beer and shoe disinfectant. He wasn't sure he believed the tale of the partial rainbow because Patrick could have produced that gold coin any number of ways. But it was clear Todd had powers Vlad had never seen.

"Hear me out for a minute," Luis implored, standing up. "You and I both know Todd is the most powerful and persuasive thing to hit this place since the new microwave in the community kitchen."

"You mean the previously owned microwave with built-in fish odor."

"Anything that can cook a burrito in less than a minute can smell like fairy farts as far I'm concerned."

"I'll agree Todd's powers exceed that of a well-used microwave oven. Now will you please leave me in peace?"

"One more thing." Luis dug into his back pocket for his phone. He tapped the screen and tossed it to Vlad, who made no effort to catch it as it thunked against his chest.

"I see your vampire reflexes are at their peak," Luis grinned.

"And I see your powers of being a were-douche are at a peak."

"Jesus, Vlad." Luis perched again on the bed next to Vlad, retrieved his phone, and tapped the screen a few more times. "As you may know or not—"

"Or care."

"—or care, I record our Upton Arms meetings. I finally got around to listening to it. So here, let me cue it up to the right spot."

"Don't bother. Just tell me what you found, though I'm happy to guess. Todd's voice doesn't show up."

Luis stopped tapping and slipped the phone back in his pocket. "So much for the element of surprise. How did you know?"

"On the scale of supernatural powers, it's about as impressive as having your DNA affected by the lunar cycle. In other words, *meh*."

"Really? Because I happen to think the ability to fundamentally change your human DNA into wolf DNA is pretty cool. Especially if you can change even when there isn't a full moon. Like, 'Hey, it's a half-moon, and I'm going full-on predator just because I feel like it.'"

Vlad shook his head. "Maybe if you could transform into a powerful carnivore rather than something a six-year-old would keep as a pet."

"I know this Breeze stuff has really messed you up," Luis spat. "But I'm not going to stick around just to be attacked by a vampire whose blood comes from sippy pouches."

Vlad rubbed his eyes, wanting only to go to sleep. But his friend was right. He not only sucked his blood from sippy pouches, but pouches he needed help to acquire (and sometimes to open, if he was completely honest). "Sorry," he relented.

"Sorry my ass." Luis let his eyes wander around the sparse room. "No wonder you don't believe. You don't even believe in yourself. Look at this place. You've given up. The mere fact you sleep on something from The Mattress Shack instead of Coffin Castle says a lot."

"Coffin Castle?"

"You know what I mean."

Vlad did, the exhaustion returned. He was tired of the discussion since he'd figured out a long time ago God didn't exist, though he realized his theology no longer strayed outside the "a true God would not allow so many bad things happening to good people" argument. Even if God was a passive spectator letting the free will flow, that was just as bad. As far as Vlad was concerned, he was done watching what life kept dishing out. He determined his own fate, not some cloud-based mystic who should've spent far more than six days creating this mess.

Luis reached for the door, twisting the knob just as there was a sharp rapping. The door opened to reveal Patrick, fist poised in mid-knock. Pushing past Luis, he hopped on Vlad's bed and stared down at the vampire.

"Pull up your big-boy fangs, Beatrice needs you."

Vlad bolted upright because he didn't think have to think twice when it came to helping Beatrice, one (if not the only) genuinely good souls in all of Upton Arms.

Had he known why he was being summoned, he would have shooed everyone out and returned to the darkness, the only thing that understood him.

FOURTEEN

BEATRICE HAD ALWAYS BEEN THIN, her wrinkle-free coffee-colored skin stretched tight on a frame that would be prized by any Jazzercise enthusiast (the last physical exercise attempted by Beatrice, who preferred weight maintenance by potion control). She was a constant presence in the common room, whether she was knitting colorful sweaters for Brownies (for which the helpful sprites were appreciative, given their very name was due to their drab wardrobe), or experimenting with what the witch called "Knock that shit off" hex bags, used to keep the fairies in check.

Vlad hovered over Beatrice, his heart racing from anxiety (or, more likely, the brief run between rooms, not that the vampire would accept that depressing reality). He noted how thin she was, more so than usual. Her carotid artery pulsed slowly (sensually) under tissue-paper skin. Delicate veins laced each arm, and Vlad was sure if he touched them, they would shrivel under the slightest pressure. She lay still, eyes closed, blanket pulled up to her chest.

Vlad noted something else. A scent of lilac, with a bit of clove just underneath. And yes, there it was, a touch of sulfur.

Vlad looked at Patrick, standing on a stool at the foot of Beatrice's bed.

"She cast a spell recently, didn't she?"

Patrick nodded, staying silent as his eyes remained riveted on Beatrice.

Vlad put his hand on Beatrice's forehead because it seemed like the right thing to do. The witch was burning up, alarming Vlad until he remembered that because his body temperature was a steady seventy degrees, everyone was burning up.

Luis also put his hand on the witch's forehead. "She's on fire."

"No shit," Patrick fumed. "You can tell all that without a fancy thermometer. Aren't you a walking-talking WebMD."

"Fine Patrick, just tell us why we're here." Luis's voice contained the kind of sharp claws he longed to summon at will, Vlad knew. He'd have to keep a close eye on his friend so the situation didn't get worse.

"I don't know why you're here, you full-moon mongrel. I asked for Vlad, so why don't you just trot out of here and practice getting on your fur suit? Maybe learn how to transform past schnauzer."

Sure enough, hairs began to curl along Luis's forearms. Vlad was well aware the werewolf couldn't control the transformation when he was angry, and he just might turn into a schnauzer as a self-fulfilling prophecy. Or worse, a goldendoodle. Vlad loved goldendoodles, and if he started petting Luis, it would put a real crimp in their relationship.

"I'm here for Beatrice, not you," Luis said, starting to scratch behind his ears. "If anyone should leave it's you, you half-pint hobbit."

Oh shit, Luis went there, Vlad thought. Patrick hated the H-word, and not solely because *Lord of the Rings* made more money in one day than all the *Leprechaun* movies put together. The vampire knew he had to act fast, deflect the attention.

He hissed.

It was such a stereotype, the angry vampire threatening victims with a hiss. As if strength and power were not as favorable as pushing air through a small gap between tongue and palate. It was the vampire equivalent of a tantrum, some humiliating Christopher Lee shit that had no business being done outside a soundstage.

It was so debasing.

But in this case, effective.

"Did you just hiss?" Patrick's eyes widened.

"Seriously, Vlad?" Luis chimed in.

"Man, that's some crazy Christopher Lee shit there," the leprechaun added for effect.

The last time Vlad was so ashamed to be a vampire, he was cruising the hobo buffet served by the Depression. But at least his unfortunate behavior got their attention.

"Luis," Vlad turned to his friend, putting a hand Luis's chest to reassure him. "Can you just give us a few minutes?"

Luis, scratching his stomach and realizing his body was heading to a bad place, left the room without a word. The door clicked behind him.

Silence. Blessed silence. Even Patrick was uncharacteristically quiet, letting Vlad know just how dire things were.

He breathed deeply, focusing on Beatrice's carotid, willing it to continue its weak pulse. Normally, the sight would get him in the mood, a kind of vampire porn. Two things stopped him: he genuinely liked Beatrice, and at his age, he suffered from bouts of enamel dysfunction.

Beatrice was kinder than most witches Vlad had met. She was full of bluster but often put the needs of others in front of her own. Now and then Vlad caught her performing simple magic tricks for Upton's more elderly residents, like making coins disappear or pulling cards from thin air. Perhaps her powers were such that at one time, she could truly levitate herself, or saw someone in half and put them back together. These days, Beatrice needed help to pull off such effects. The invisible Ralph would lift her into the air, and Darnell often agreed to be halved as long as Beatrice promised to knit him back together stitches necessary when such large swathes of flesh and bone were involved. If the witch was ashamed to need assistance as her powers dwindled, she didn't show it.

Her room reflected the Beatrice who didn't take herself too seriously. Witch and warlock knickknacks filled the shelves, making her about the easiest person to shop for when it came to her birthday. As Vlad took it in, he wished he'd taken more time to get to know Beatrice a little better.

"So, Patrick," Vlad exhaled. "What happened? And why am I here? Because you need a doctor, not a vampire."

"That's where you're wrong." Patrick placed a palm on Beatrice's cheek and, to Vlad's surprise, kept it there. "I do need a vampire. But I have to settle for you."

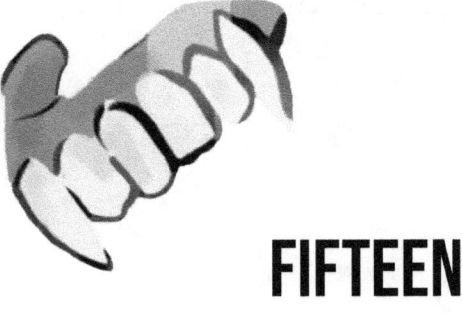

FIFTEEN

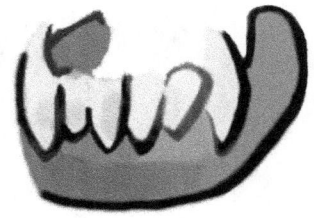

VLAD SETTLED ONTO THE BED, noting how Beatrice's eyes flickered when he took her hand. He suspected the reason he was called, but was still surprised when Patrick made a request Vlad would happily perform if he'd been able to. The leprechaun was in a lot of pain, so Vlad knew he had to be patient when he broke down the differences between real and fictional vampires. Not that all the patience in the world would avoid the shitstorm of leprechaun fury once Patrick learned the truth. And it would not be magically delicious.

Vlad thought about being upfront, something along the lines of, "Vampires rarely if ever beget other vampires since it would lead to the exponential growth of a certain demographic reliant on hemoglobin, and what a terrible world that would be." Or he could take a more personal approach, admitting that he'd never turned anyone into a practitioner of the bloodsucking arts, which was absolutely true. As far as he knew.

Instead, Vlad went with the obvious choice.

He perched on the bed and touched Beatrice's forehead, more to find the right words than gauge the witch's (still rising) temperature. Best thing to do now was stall. He looked at Patrick, who stood atop a chair peering expectantly at the vampire across the bed. "Let's start with what happened. My guess is a spell. What was she casting, Patrick?"

"Fuck-all about the spell, bucko," Patrick screamed, the chair wobbling beneath him. "You do what I asked you and forever hold your fucking peace."

So much for stalling.

Even if Vlad could do what Patrick demanded, why in the hell would he? There was a time where he enjoyed being the most powerful man in town, feasting on blood as well as the palpable fear that hung sweetly in the air. It made it difficult to keep friends, as he inevitably drained them, but it allowed him to throw the best parties because no one turned down invitations from the person believed to be the village death merchant. If a few partygoers never made it home, such was the price of growing up in the Dark Ages. When it came to the all-you-can-drink buffets, Vlad was the first (and only) person in line. Just the way he liked it.

That wasn't always true.

Vlad dug up memories he longed to keep buried, those rare occasions when he wanted to bestow immortality. He had formed a handful of close relationships during his life, knowing it was just another ill-fated coupling that would end in heartbreak. Depression was a natural occurrence in a life when the only sure thing was taxes, not death.

He remembered the years when he dedicated himself to creating a lifelong companion. Vlad brought them to the edge of death, the flow of blood slowing to a trickle. That's when he felt a spark of energy travel up his spine, the powerful jolt of a dozen orgasms. He could almost see a life force brimming from his own soul, threatening to break containment and bursting into the cooling body he held. Each time it was too much, that energy flinging him away as if nature itself knew what he was trying to do. Or Vlad pushed himself away, knowing he was about to bestow more curse than gift. He was not God, after all. He had no right to damn anyone to eternal life.

Not that there was such a thing, Vlad had since discovered.

When Victor Breeze made it clear his relationship with Vlad was based solely on the probability of a death-resistant life, the vampire knew he'd never feel that spark of energy should he try to grant his lover's wish. Nor did he have any desire to fulfill such a selfish wish.

Vlad wasn't sure what might happen if he made a sincere attempt with Beatrice. He cared about her, she was a dear friend. He wanted her to make it through this, but at what cost?

He toyed with the idea of doing exactly what Patrick asked, being sure to pull back before any vampire-making was consummated, then feigning ignorance as to why it had no effect.

Vlad noted Beatrice's pulse getting fainter. He had to at least convince Patrick to call a doctor. No, what was he thinking? Any physician arriving at Upton Arms probably wouldn't get past the zombie bouncing off a vending machine, let alone know how to treat a witch likely suffering from spiritual dehydration.

"Patrick," Vlad stuttered, removing his hand from the witch's forehead. "I'm not sure you understand—"

"What I understand," Patrick leaned forward precariously, "is how you can start sinking those pearly whites into Beatrice's neck, real gentle like. Start sharing a little bit of that life force someone saw fit to give you. Time to pay it forward, even if it means readjusting my biological clock to the nocturnal side."

Vlad stood and made his way around the bed. Even as he reached toward Patrick, he couldn't believe he simply wanted to console Upton Arms' five-time winner of the Prick of the Year award. Vlad was a vampire, not a monster.

The leprechaun, however, responded in a way to solidify a sixth year.

"Don't you fucking touch me, you vein-seeking missile," Patrick said with an eerie calm. "I did not ask you here to get touchy-feely. You need to do what I asked and not go all vadge-pire."

Vlad knew that no matter how much proof he had for the vampires-can't-make-vampires theory, Patrick would never buy it. Beatrice was the leprechaun's only pot of gold, and he would do anything to keep it safe at the end of his personal rainbow. Vlad wasn't sure Beatrice would be OK with that, because Patrick's feelings for the witch looked to be way past the friend zone.

All Vlad had left was his honesty, his least effective weapon when it came to Patrick.

"I'm not the Henry Ford of vampires," Vlad sighed, retreating to the other side of the bed. "I can't churn them out on an assembly line."

"Beatrice isn't good enough to be a vampire. Is that what you're saying?"

Patrick 1, Honesty 0.

"Vampires can't pass on their conditions as if they were hand-me-downs. I can no more turn Beatrice into a vampire than I can make you the least bit tolerable."

Patrick clamped his hands to the side of his head. "I can't hear this shite right now. All I know is you're a vampire and vampires beget vampires, and she needs to be a fucking vampire right this minute so she can damn well live!"

Vlad longed for days when he could mesmerize Patrick and be done with it. Send the little man into a mental abyss for a few hours as Vlad figured out a decent solution. His current state forced him to deal with the situation. Maybe there was an alternative.

Luis, forgive me for what I'm about to do, Vlad thought. "You know," Vlad tapped his chin, "werewolves have been known to transfer certain characteristics to their surviving victims. What about Luis?"

"What about that flea-bitten mongrel? He's probably out chasing cats." The leprechaun suddenly hunched his shoulders and stared at Vlad with eyes narrowed, the vampire's suggestion dawning on Patrick. "If you think for one second I'd allow that fucking were-rat to put his lips on Beatrice to make her into something that transforms based on moonbeams or some such shit—"

"No, no, bad idea, I get it." Besides, if Vlad couldn't make vampires, no way could a mere werewolf duplicate itself.

Vlad sensed Beatrice fading away. Her pulse was down to a flicker. He wondered what happened, what spell was so important that she had to spend nearly all of her life force on it.

Patrick seemed to have come to the same conclusion, jumping on the bed and striding toward Vlad, Beatrice bouncing with each step.

The leprechaun but his nose an inch from the vampire's unnaturally smooth chin.

"So you're as worthless as the rest of them," he cried. "I live with a bunch of people who have no clue about death, from delivering it to being threatened by it. But when it comes to sharing this so-called gift, the entire world can just fuck off, is that it?"

Vlad blinked twice, hard, to make sure he wasn't seeing things. But no, there it was. A tiny bit of water, glistening in the corner of Patrick's left eye.

The actual beginning of a tear. Vlad almost expected to see smoke as signs of a deep emotion came in contact with the leprechaun.

"Patrick, if I could I would, I'd go down on her right now." Didn't quite come out right. "You know, to make her a vampire. But that's—"

"Then do it. Do it right fucking now. Just please SAVE MY WIFE!"

What?

Vlad, too stunned to speak, looked at Patrick. Then to Beatrice. Back to Patrick.

The reality set in. Patrick and Beatrice, husband and wife. Sure, why not? Stranger things have happened.

No, stranger things have not happened. But at least it explained Patrick's behavior.

"Save her! Save her, damn you!"

Maybe, Vlad thought, he might have something inside him that could give Beatrice a few more hours, at least to figure out what was going on. Maybe convince Patrick to call a doctor, even with the risks that would bring to every resident.

Or maybe, just this once, it was meant to be.

The vampire leaned toward Beatrice's neck, ready to plunge his incisors into familiar, inviting territory.

"God help me," he muttered.

He hovered for a moment, feeling his fangs snap into place, when he heard a knock at the door.

SIXTEEN

"AM I INTERRUPTING?"

Dressed in crisp white shirt, brown tasseled loafers and pleated khakis, Todd strode in more stylishly than he was dressed.

A surprised Vlad hovered over Beatrice, his lips inches from the witch's throat, a vampire frozen in the headlights.

"Seems early for dinner," Todd continued, his gaze piercing the vampire. "Nor is this a dish I'd recommend off the menu here. Surely there is something more appropriate than witch, and one with little life force left."

Patrick hopped off the chair, standing chin to shin with the visitor. "Todd, please, Todd. Help her. Heal her. Please."

Vlad straightened and stepped back as Todd leaned in for a closer look at his "patient." Todd placed his right hand on Beatrice's forehead and softly grunted. He left hand hovered over the witch's waist, then ran up her body to her neck as if scanning for something.

Now he's a human MRI machine, Vlad thought. *Is there anything he can't do?*

Todd cleared his throat. "Yes," he said. "As I thought."

"What?" Patrick stammered. "You can you fix, I mean heal, her?"

"It's not good, I'm afraid, but I've seen worse." Todd put the chair aside and pulled the sheet up to Beatrice's shoulders, smoothing it out. "She suffered blunt-force trauma to the soul, likely the result of doing something against her better judgment. Perhaps out of love, not that it makes any difference." Todd turned toward Patrick. "You wouldn't know anything about the cause, would you?"

"Course not," Patrick answered too quickly.

"How did you come to that diagnosis, Todd?" Vlad challenged, crossing his arms because it seemed the right thing to do to maintain a position of authority. "Or should I call you Dr. Todd, mystical healer?"

"Vlad, you never disappoint," Todd chuckled, switching his gaze from Patrick to the vampire. Vlad met it head-on, wishing there were some truth in Luis's unwarranted faith that Todd was a supreme being, since the almighty sure could come in handy right now.

Vlad, however, was sure this was no omniscient being ready to retire and start collecting a faith-based pension, thus leaving the few billion stockholders in Humanity Inc. to look for a new CEO. He was Todd Frakes, emperor of the misguided, because of one simple fact.

There was no such thing as God.

Vlad was a firm believer early in life, since not believing in God had terrible consequences in fifteenth-century Europe. The Inquisition left marks, so Vlad was happy to admit the existence of a supreme being without having to be tortured. He preferred a way toward grace that did not involve noticeable scars.

When the age of reason dawned, so did Vlad's doubts in a heavenly force guiding humanity. For too long, he'd blamed God for everything that was wrong with immortality, including what was necessary for extending it. Vlad had long forgotten the number of times he'd cursed the Creator as fangs sank deeply into unwilling throats, his own eagerly taking in sustenance as life fled his victims. By the time he'd arrived in America, drawn by the camouflage offered by the Civil War (so much bloodshed, so little time to think about causes), Vlad had decided it was much easier to discount the existence of God than rage against it. It brought him the little peace he had desired.

"Todd, you just going to stand there?" Vlad protested. "Or get to healing?"

Patrick eased around Todd and placed his hand on Beatrice's. "Can you do that, Todd? I'll do anything. Even give you a ten percent discount on your rent. For the first month. And twenty percent off your security deposit."

Two things struck Vlad, the first being how Patrick truly loved Beatrice since he was willing to lose money in the deal. The second was that Patrick apparently had made a unilateral decision to allow Todd to live at Upton Arms, a move that, if not against the covenants and restrictions, violated the tradition of requiring a vote.

Todd grasped Patrick under the shoulders and put him on the floor, a move that was at the top of the leprechaun's very long list of "Shit Most Likely to Lead to an Ass-Kicking."

Vlad braced for it, the Biblical tide of curse words about to crash over the white cliffs of Todd, eroding his calm demeanor and revealing sharp creases of anger and frustration.

Any second now, Vlad thought, wondering what new profanities would emerge in Patrick's tirade.

But...nothing. Silence. Patrick stared at Todd...reverently?...waiting for an answer.

"Happy to help," Todd smiled, patting his stomach as if he were a jolly old elf rather than divinity.

The leprechaun nodded, neck bones creaking with the foreign movement.

"I'm going to leave you two alone to figure this out." Vlad eased himself around Todd, only no matter which way he stepped, Todd continued to be in the way. Before the vampire could figure out what was going on, an gruff voice rang out.

"No."

Vlad's chin dropped, because it wasn't Todd. It was Patrick, who was pointing at the vampire.

"Stay," ordered the Patrick-notPatrick. "It's best that way."

Vlad stopped, an odd sensation building in his chest. An anxiousness built within as if he hadn't fed in days.

Just as quickly as it started, it began to fade. He could feel it drain, as if someone had pulled a plug from the bottom of his heart. The last of it vanished with a spasm in his gut.

Had he been forced to explain the feeling, Vlad would have described it as a tug, a brief pull on his soul.

If he had a soul. And he most certainly did not.

"Maybe I will stay," Vlad heard himself say. "For a bit."

"Very good." Todd stepped past Vlad and Patrick to the chair he'd put aside. He carried it to the foot of the bed and eased himself into it. He placed an arm on each of the rests, leaned back and set his feet slightly more than a shoulder-width apart.

"First, let me assure everyone I've seen much worse, souls that appeared to have been in a head-on wreck due to questionable moral decisions. Mostly in Washington DC around election time." Todd stared at Patrick. "Now, tell me what happened."

"It was a spell," Patrick murmured in a voice that seemed ten miles away. "One that stretched her limits."

"Were you aware of that?"

Here they come, Vlad thought. The lies Patrick stacks one upon the other to protect himself at all costs.

"Yes...I was. Aware."

For the very first time, Vlad actually considered that Todd was at least somewhat godlike, given that he could make Patrick tell the truth.

"What was this spell?" Todd arched his fingers. "Precisely."

Patrick took a deep breath, wiped away a tear. "Money. We needed money. I mean..." he trailed off.

"You needed money," Vlad completed, disgusted and yet slightly comforted to see the old Patrick, because the new loving-and-kind-husband Patrick was messing with his world.

"It's my fault," Patrick cried, seeming to snap out of his fugue. "I hate myself, I really do. I never should've let Beatrice make that kind of sacrifice. Not for anyone, especially her husband. But I was desperate. When the board postponed the vote...when there was a chance you wouldn't the investment, we'd counted on it and..."

Vlad still struggled with this unlikely witch-leprechaun pairing. What could anyone possibly find in Patrick to love, let alone sign legally binding documents to affirm the relationship? The world was rife with odd marriage pairings, but cynicism and ignorance led Vlad to believe most of them involved young, gorgeous girls and offshore bank accounts. Size definitely mattered when it came to stacks of money.

Todd tapped his fingers on the aluminum armrest. "You're telling me she risked corrupting her soul for money?"

"No, not for money," Patrick shot back. "She risked corrupting her soul for *me*."

Even as Vlad lost what little respect he had for Patrick, he couldn't help but envy the bastard. There was not one person in the vampire's life —present or ancient past—that would have made such a sacrifice for him. And the one man he thought capable of just that, of putting Vlad first, hadn't been interested in who he was. Just what he was.

"Good, good." Todd leaned forward and pushed himself out of the chair with a soft grunt. "That's all I needed to know. Now, if you don't mind, I need you both to step outside and allow me to work my, well, let's just say it's magic, shall we? So much easier to accept."

Vlad stared at Todd, wondering what the healer/mystic/fraud had up his sleeve. Before he knew it, Patrick had grabbed his hand and dragged him into the hallway.

SEVENTEEN

VLAD LISTENED MORE PATIENTLY than was warranted as Patrick went into full pointing-finger mode to address the financial plight of Upton Arms. Never mind that his ailing wife was just on the other side of the door, attended to by a likely charlatan.

"People here can't fucking deal with something so ordinary as aging," Patrick paced the hallway, whining solidly between turns. "OK, so you have to get up in the middle of the night to take a piss. Use the toilet for chrissakes. You know how hard it is to get troll urine out of carpets? Fucking impossible, then the whole room smells like stale wet fairy."

Vlad found himself nodding. Nothing cleared a room like the scent of moldy fairy.

The leprechaun then aimed his wrath to a handful of werewolves known for imbibing heavily during the full moon. Terrible things happened when mixing alcohol with transformation, resulting in thousands of dollars in damage, from stained furniture to clawed mattresses. "I don't care who or what they maul as long as it ain't here," Patrick ranted, spun, then ranted some more. "I thought canines knew not to shit where they ate."

(Vlad refrained from asking the obvious, fearing the answer would have him sympathetic to Patrick's cause. It was one thing to cause some damage when returning to a primal state, but indoor defecation was inexcusable regardless of biological state).

The leprechaun noted how items frequently disappeared from communal areas, no matter that it was the kind of crap adored only by women named Edith or Agnes. Taken were fake flowers, mass-produced art, and even porcelain figures featuring wide-eyed kids posed in creepy adult poses.

"There was a reason I bought the kind of crap no one would ever want to steal," Patrick lamented. "I underestimated the taste around there, that's for sure."

Patrick swore he spent several thousand dollars on alarm systems and surveillance cameras, spending another thousand or so ripping them out when he received the first monthly bill. Not before, however, the system revealed a couch floating out the front door.

"Evicted every single invisible person at Upton," Patrick droned on. "You know how you can tell if an invisible person obeys an eviction order? Here's a hint. You fucking can't."

The biggest financial blow involved a pixie sucked into an intake vent when the air conditioning kicked on. There was no insurance on the place—"that one company may save me fifteen percent in fifteen minutes, but none of its policies covers ogre-related damage" —and Patrick faced immense bills due to pixie injuries.

"Did you know how expensive the pixie medical care system is? Healthcare isn't based on size, that's for sure. Then I had to spend a shit-ton for sprite-safe air filters, which need a very pricey pixie-repellant charm."

Vlad knew a little something about pixies, and it sounded like they pulled one over on Patrick.

It struck Vlad how the leprechaun relied on perceived slights to keep his wits about him as Beatrice balanced between life and death. If that's what it took for Patrick to stay sane as his wife hovered between life and death, so be it.

The vampire tuned out Patrick's relentless ravings, including the unreliability of using a mystical orb for important financial decisions ("I'm not so sure the 8 Ball was magical at all") or how the magic beans he purchased just created a gardening nightmare. Then he said something that finally got Vlad's attention.

"You know what really fucked me? The balloon payment. It seemed so far off when I bought the place. I thought Upton Arms would be a fucking gold mine. Instead, it's stripped-mine me own pockets, boy-o. No matter how I tried to get people to pay up, all I got were curses and, not coincidentally, rashes in places I can't reach. I even tried a GoFundMe page, with none of those fucking sob stories that are so irritating. I made it straight and to the point. 'Give me money because I need it.' Not one donation."

Patrick stopped mid-step, hanging his head in what Vlad might have assumed was shame if he didn't know the leprechaun better.

"That's it, the whole sad story. An unfortunate series of events."

"Wait," Vlad said. "Isn't that the name of—"

"Shut up." Patrick gripped the handle to Beatrice's room and immediately pulled away, blowing on his fingers. "Fuck all, that hurts." Vlad saw a bright red stripe glowing across the leprechaun's palm, precisely the width of the handle.

"I'll say this for Todd, that's some interesting powers he's got, right?" Patrick flapped his scorched hand. "Scary powerful. But with great power comes a great financial standing, his dividend portfolio alone...I mean, if I cared about such things. And I don't."

"You do," Vlad said with surprising sincerity. "Very much so."

The vampire thought back to the conversation with Lawster, the call from Todd unexpectedly, and the (alleged) pot of gold at the end of the rainbow. He wondered about the offer to invest in a failing retirement home, which no responsible financier would ever make. Especially not one supposedly all-knowing.

"It was complete bullshit." Vlad knelt in front of Patrick and grabbed the leprechaun's injured hand, giving it a squeeze that would have been reassuring under different circumstances.

"Boy-o, fuck," Patrick warned as he squirmed in the vampire's viselike grip. "Let go before I—"

"Before you what, Patrick?" Vlad added a little more pressure. "Push Todd to move in, make all these improvements to show him what a successful business you run, have Lawster introduce him to books that are more cooked than you're about to be if you don't come clean?"

"Jesus fuck a duck, no, not at all."

Vlad tightened his grip until he felt tiny bones rub together.

"Goddamnit, let me go you bat-fucking buffoon—"

Another squeeze.

"OK, let me go and I'll tell you!"

Vlad released the appendage, now in worse shape than it was just a few moments ago.

"The truth, Patrick," Vlad demanded, smiling not just because he forced Patrick to fold, but that he still had that killer instinct without having to actually murder someone.

As the leprechaun massaged his ailing hand, Vlad thought about Todd's wealth. If the apparent faith healer were truly rich, it might help Vlad convince everyone the man was a fraud. After all, the truly gifted preferred life in the shadows, careful to hide talents that would cast a spotlight. Grifters, however, made a living of that same spotlight, which attracted the gullible like moths.

A thought occurred, one that would have long before now if Vlad was at the top of his game. "How do you know so much about Todd? Why do you think he's rich? It's not like he took that pot of gold out of his savings account." Or that the gold existed at all.

"Because his lawyer told me so," Patrick squeaked.

"Lawster." Vlad leaned against the wall, knowing he was correct without Patrick's confirmation.

"It wasn't so much a call out of the blue as Lawster putting two of his clients together," Patrick confessed. "Todd didn't want to invest. He just wanted to move in. Needed to know how I could make that happen."

"You gave him the same answer you have for everything. Money."

"Of course. That's what it takes to run this place, you know."

Vlad pushed off the wall and stretched, thrusting his arms overhead and listening to the cracks marching along his spine. Patrick stepped back when the vampire grabbed the small shoulder with a strong but not painful grip. "Don't make this about us, because it's always about you."

"All I know is that I quoted a move-in price ten times the usual, and

Lawster says fine. Just like that. Doesn't even call Todd. Then I'm kicking myself for not charging him twenty or thirty times more."

This, Vlad thought, *puts a different spin on things.* Todd was hardly some random applicant who stumbled across Upton Arms and wanted in, affording him the kind of care and protection required by supernatural beings. He'd probably had his eye on the place for, well, weeks? Months? So desperate to get in, money was no object.

Unfortunately for Todd, it was not simply a matter of cash. He also had to get board approval, a tricky step that could make a man take drastic measures. Perhaps by making someone deathly ill only to appear at the last second to save her. That's just the kind of miracle that might sway the more reticent board members. (Not Ralph, Vlad knew, who was an asshole and would continue to be an asshole in the face of any miracle that did not allow him to savor some sort of schadenfreude).

Vlad released his grip, prompting Patrick to rub his shoulder with his non-burned hand. No doubt seeking to avoid further injury, the leprechaun went on without being threatened. "When Todd moved in, I'd make my own move. Throw him a welcome party like nothing he'd ever seen."

"Because no one has ever seen such a party. At least not at Upton Arms."

"No one at Upton is worth a party, especially privileged, pasty-faced parasites who…" The rest of the sentence died on Patrick's lips, no doubt an attempt to cut his losses. "Anyway, Todd was worth it. I'd break out the brand-name cereal and Fruit Roll-Ups, make sure everyone availed themselves to the finest processed meats and cheeses. Treat him like a king. And in a few months, I'd explain a once-in-a-lifetime opportunity to invest in a retirement home like no other. And Todd would bite because I was hoping that among all those powers, none involved common financial sense."

Vlad cleared his throat, ready to point out a man like Todd did not get where he was without being smart with money. Instead, he allowed Patrick to go on.

"Then the board gets involved and this whole plan goes up in a big puff of fucking stupidity." Patrick moaned. "And now where is this guy we shunned? Trying to save my wife. You think his heart is in it?"

"I do. I do indeed."

It was, in fact, time to find out.

EIGHTEEN

"EVEN BEFORE I could open the door, Todd appears in the doorway, like a magic trick," Vlad recalled, shaking his head at the scene from a few days ago. "He's wearing this goofy smile and telling us everything was fine. Patrick pushes by me and jumps on the bed as if he's a kid waking up Mom for Mother's Day, giving her a big hug. It was sweet and creepy at the same time."

"Beatrice snapped out of it just like that?" Luis challenged, ripping the sodden napkin around the base of his sweating beer glass. The werewolf demanded to know all the details of Beatrice's apparent resurrection, and Vlad thought it the perfect excuse to get out of Upton for a few hours in a way that did not involve a random death. It was nice to relax at a bar among strangers who didn't interest him, least of all as a meal.

"It wasn't 'just like that,'" Vlad countered, taking another sip of his Bloody Mary, an aptly named drink as it was spiked with the vampire's own concoction snuck into the bar under his jacket. "She was a little groggy, probably wondering why a tiny man was clinging to her neck. Only a few minutes passed before she was back to her old self and asking me if I might give her some time alone with Patrick and Todd."

"Those were her exact words?"

"Actually, she wondered how I'd missed the sign prohibiting creatures who required the bodily fluids of others to survive, then something about how it was a good thing she'd gone through menopause decades ago so I wouldn't be tempted by feminine leakage. She was quite rude."

"How very like Beatrice that is." Luis drained his way-too-light beer with a final swig. Another appeared in front of him, but it wasn't Todd's magic, just bartender Chet's excellent service.

"No kidding. But a few hours later she apologized, said she wasn't good with near-death experiences." The vampire swirled the contents of his half-full glass. He set it down, watching the filmy coating slide slowly into the rich red liquid below

Vlad rubbed his temples, the exhaustion sinking in and leaving him with just enough energy to drink. He was trying to process that Patrick and Beatrice were leprechaun and wife, let alone how a still-unresolved debt likely threatened his place of residence. Throw in the death of Victor Breeze and rumors of certain residents planning a very ill-advised home invasion, and life had become quite complicated.

But tonight was dedicated to a discussion of The Touch, or at least that's how Beatrice described it to the few people who cared to listen as she planted herself in the community room spreading the gospel of her miraculous recovery. In a dramatic telling of the tale, the witch described how she swirled around a black void as if water circling a drain. She felt a pull toward that void, thinking death itself had latched onto her soul. Suddenly there was a pinpoint of light that grew, giving her hope. Before long, Todd hovered over her, a golden aura shimmering about his body. He placed his index finger on her forehead, and a bolt of "energy and love, maybe even some orgasm" coursed through her. Next thing she knew, she was being smothered by a person of small stature, whom she finally recognized as Patrick before she clawed his eyes out.

Word of the alleged miracle had spread quickly through Upton Arms. The early versions were fairly close to the truth, starring Todd's index finger. Subsequent retellings included an army of demons, heavily armed angels, and a bare-chested Todd hurtling into the fray aboard a white horse, lightning bolts shooting from his eyes.

At one point, an excited Darnell lurched into the room, bounced off the snack machine and knocked over a few chairs, moaning louder than usual. George, a ghoul swearing he was well-versed in zombie speak, indicated that Darnell desperately wanted to speak to Todd "so Todd can make him less dead."

Todd, however, hadn't been seen since the (alleged) miracle. His disappearance only heightened interest in The Touch, which was exactly what Todd wanted, Vlad knew.

Vlad took another sip of his Bloody Mary, still convinced Todd was nothing more than a talented healer with a side of mind-reading. Putting his glass on the bar, he told Luis just that, as if saying it out loud made it true.

"But dude, only someone with some serious powers can suddenly be bathed in a white aura." Luis took the fresh napkin from under his beer, sprouted a misshapen claw and began shredding it methodically. "And how about when the ceiling opened up and a beam of light lit up Beatrice, and as she floated above the bed that bush appeared and spontaneously ignited as a flock of doves flew overhead? That's powerful stuff."

Vlad, in mid-sip, nearly spit into his drink. "What the hell are you talking about?"

"I was bullshitting about the doves, just to fuck with you," Luis said, arranging the shreds into a neat pile. "But the rest is totally true. I heard it from Aiko."

"That weird spirit who crawls on the ceiling and wants to move into the TV?"

"Yup, as if Patrick would let anyone take over the one object that gives him a reason to live, even if that reason is the *Santa Came Down Your What?* Christmas special on Medic Plus."

Vlad put his hand on his friend's shoulder. Not only did he fear his friend's knowledge of obscure streaming channels, but that he could be more gullible than people who believe in the Loch Ness monster, when everyone knows the lake's megalodon killed it hundreds of years ago. "The only two people in the room were Todd and Beatrice, and neither one of them have gone into those kinds of details. But I can promise you I heard no heavenly choruses, nor did I notice any white light glowing from underneath the door. Don't believe everything you hear, especially from a spirit who has no idea how to use a towel."

The vampire motioned to Chet, the only person he trusted at The Tipsy Narwhal, a charming dive bar festooned with thousands of Christmas lights. The place was within walking distance of Upton Arms, and while location played a role in making this the unofficial favorite hangout of aging creatures of questionable origins, Chet's casual acceptance of the unbelievable was also important.

Vlad knew Chet had witnessed levitating beer bottles and disappearing customers. He shared with the vampire that time when one of his most loyal (and decayed) customers attempted to pay a large tab with his arm and leg, Chet embracing the literal translation of the metaphor but still insisting on cash. And on more than one full moon, he had to break out the muzzles to prevent bloodshed.

Vlad never saw Chet bat an eye, always pouring drinks like a pro. The fact he was high ninety-nine percent of the time also helped.

"Chet, another Bloody Mary please," Vlad nodded, holding up his glass.

Chet glanced at Luis.

"I'm good," Luis held up his half-full glass.

"Debatable," Vlad couldn't resist.

Not a minute later, Chet slid a tall glass of thick red liquid in front of Vlad before turning his back to the vampire, ringing up the sale as the vampire added his secret sauce. In the mirror opposite the bar, the glass floated, tilted, and dropped back to the dark wood stained with a thousand spilled drinks. If Chet noticed how Vlad didn't appear in the mirror—and surely he did —he ignored it.

Vlad took another sip before setting Luis straight on the story of The Touch.

"Let me make this perfectly clear," the vampire put his glass on the bar, twirling it slowly with lithe fingers. "No auras, no light beams, and definitely no levitation unless you count Todd's smugness. That is straight from Beatrice right after it all happened."

Vlad had noticed Todd's sly smile as Beatrice awoke, a look of pure confidence. What bothered Vlad was that Todd had the talent to back it up. Even the best healers he'd known measured success like batting averages in baseball: If you were successful one out of three times, you were among the best, especially if you could do it without sacrificing livestock.

"I don't think I've ever seen a successful healing," Luis sighed, draining his glass and plunking it next to the shred pile. "Not counting those evangelical shows that are on in the middle of the night when the paralyzed walk and the blind see, and the preacher's pockets bulge with cash from the gullible. Todd didn't ask for donations, did he?"

"I don't think so."

"Damn, that's the real miracle here." Luis signaled to Chet for another. "Not that Patrick has any cash to spare."

"You might want to keep an eye on Upton's entertainment fund. Patrick would snatch it if he had the chance."

"Nah, it's safe from his grubby little hands. I keep it on a high shelf."

A fresh beer landed in front of Luis. "Thank you, Chet, continue to put it on my friend's tab."

"So, like always," Chet smiled, turning to the register.

Vlad continued his tale, describing the tense moments in Beatrice's room before Todd's arrival, including Patrick's request that Vlad make her a member of the Nocturnal Church of the Everlasting Pale.

"Given the choice, I'd rather be dead," Luis chuckled.

"I'd rather you be dead too, so we can agree on something."

Enter Todd, Vlad continued, all too happy to help. The vampire kept his hallway conversation with Patrick to himself for now, not wanting to fuel Luis's fears. The werewolf wouldn't see it was about a grifter needing a safe haven, but God wanting to keep a close eye on nature's freak show.

Vlad took a thoughtful sip, swirling the dwindling contents. "When Todd let us back in, she seemed fine. Except for extreme grumpiness, not a bad side effect for coming back to life." He finished his Bloody Mary in long swallows, pushing away the glass. "That's the whole story. No special effects. A basic healing."

"Not basic at all."

"Why do you say that?"

"It was successful with, I assume, no lingering effects. She has perfect vision, right? Retains her long-term memory? Hasn't developed a taste for human flesh while having only partial control of motor functions?"

"She's all good."

"Exactly. The only dead I've known to come back to life are zombies. Beatrice displays none of the obvious traits, which means either Todd is more than your typical healer, or Beatrice was faking it."

No, Vlad thought, *Beatrice wasn't faking it*. Nor was she in true danger. Not the way Todd took it all in stride.

"What's your point?" Vlad said.

"Todd is someone, or something, very special."

Vlad resisted nodding, saying only, "I admit to nothing at this point."

"What do we need you to do to get you on board with the idea God is in our midst, and we need to find out why he's here?"

"I have no idea how I can accept the impossible. But after talking to Patrick, I'm open to suggestion."

"Really? And how's that?"

"He actually had a pretty good idea, if indeed Todd is richer than God and we can get him to—"

"Another Bloody Mary?" Chet appeared out of nowhere.

The vampire thought briefly and decided to let the alcohol in his system do the talking. "Yeah, please. Only make it a gin and tonic. Not so stereotypical, you know?"

"Yeah, I do," Chet said before scooping ice into a glass, tipping a bottle of gin for a five-count pour and splashing in some tonic from the soda gun.

"You're cool, Chet," Vlad said, taking a sip since his body could tolerate only a small amount of liquid that was not vein-based. "A keeper. And not in a cage for long-term withdrawals."

"I appreciate that."

Vlad watched Chet walk toward a young woman in a tight red dress flagging him down.

The vampire leaned into Luis, shoulder to shoulder. "There was a time in my life when that sweet young thing would have been on this evening's menu."

"Right, only now we're breaking into blood banks for your fix."

Vlad put his arm around Luis in an unnaturally chummy move. "Speaking of breaking in, I'm giving second thoughts to doing a little 'shopping' at the Victor Breeze estate sale."

"Really? You were dead set against it, emphasis on 'dead.' What changed your mind?"

Vlad had wondered that himself. Beatrice laid her life on the line to save Upton Arms, but she was married to the owner and thus had a stake in the dilemma. Why shouldn't he do the same?

Because it wasn't about Upton Arms. It was about revenge.

"Remember what Patrick said about Victor working on something special?" Vlad prodded. "When Victor and I were seeing one another, he'd get these occasional visits from men far too well dressed for the late hour."

"Mafia," Luis said. "Made guys."

"What? No. More like businessmen."

"Carrying heat. Strapped."

"May I continue?"

"Sure, if you think it's safe."

Vlad shook his head, took a sip he knew he'd pay for later. *Werewolves,* he thought. *So paranoid.* "At least one of them had a briefcase. No, Luis, not filled with cash. Anyway, Victor would excuse himself and be back twenty minutes later or so."

"Dispatching them on hits."

"Fine, dispatching them on hits. Once I got a little curious and peeked into Victor's office during the meeting. They were leaning over the desk, and it looked like they were flipping through—"

"Surveillance photos of their next marks."

"Blueprints."

"Blueprints?" Luis said in a disappointed tone.

"And you know what I think? I think those were plans for Victor's next great invention, that each time there was a change or update, those guys delivered them to Victor. And knowing Victor, he didn't trust anyone else to keep them."

"And you think these plans to the greatest fabric-related invention of all time are still in his house?"

"I do."

"Fine," Luis surrendered. "But it's hardly like breaking into Al Capone's vault, is it?

"Capone's vault was empty."

"There is that. Nowhere to go but up after that, right?"

Wrong.

NINETEEN

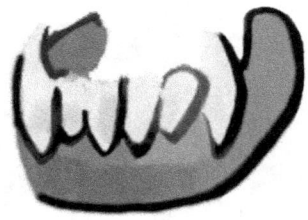

"DROP the controls and get the fuck out of my massage chair before you ruin my perfect ass-grooves," Patrick bellowed, shaking the recliner and its uninvited inhabitant.

"And you need to improve your hospitality skills," Luis sat up, a nearly irresistible impulse to smear the walls with leprechaun building inside.

For the past few days—ever since Vlad admitted the heist was hardly the worst idea since bike shorts and tofu pizza—Luis noticed how Todd had become a common sight at Upton Arms, emboldening Patrick thanks to his friendship with the powerful being. Todd's behavior hovered between a used-car salesman and crooked politician, greeting people and shaking hands as if he truly cared about them. Every smiled demurely, well aware of what the man was capable of and wanting to do nothing that might be mistaken as the least bit rude and thus split in two like a bowling ball. The werewolf would not have been surprised to see Todd hand out hats that said, "Make immortality great again," in his campaign for a spot in Upton Arms.

Until Luis learned why Todd was so determined to live on the island of biological misfits, he would not be holding any community meetings, polls, or votes on the potential resident. That decision led to one very angry leprechaun, who'd made himself scarce lately under a swirling rainbow of rumors and innuendo.

When the werewolf strode into the community room for some informal socialization, the siren call of *Unbelievable Dental Calamities Caught on Tape* told him he was about to find a very angry little man at the end of that particular rainbow. Sure enough, and just minutes after Luis settled front row center, Patrick appeared and demanded the werewolf vacate his rightful spot before, well, what exactly? A firm punch to the privates, most likely, but everyone at Upton Arms was on guard for that.

Even as Patrick rattled the chair, he could not take his eyes of his favorite show to hate-watch.

"Doing a root canal on the wrong tooth is not only believable, but to be expected given the stupidity of people who choose a career where the view never changes," the leprechaun shot a tiny fist at the screen. "It's not even a fucking calamity until the blood starts flowing."

Not one second after Luis clambered out of the chair, Patrick put a palm on the werewolf's knee. "Hold on, President Fuckusover. It occurs to me we need to have a word."

Luis, head down for this could not be good, trailed Patrick to the leprechaun's room. Pity and a desire to roam Upton Arms without looking over his shoulder. Besides, he was curious about what Patrick could possibly want other than charm, wit, and a personality that did not invite spontaneous obscene gestures. Once he entered the lavish apartment, Luis decided that if he was about to face the Irish music, he was going to enjoy a little time in Upton Arms' best (and only) heat-and-massage chair. He sank into its leather cocoon, only to have the leprechaun loom over him. Or, more precisely, Patrick's head peeking over the armrest in an unsettling way.

"Easy there now, Patrick," Luis eased out of the chair as quickly as he had eased in. "You wanted to talk to me, I'm here. I come in peace."

"From what I heard, you haven't come for years."

Luis shook his head because he should have seen that com-... approaching. And while he was hardly a fan of the crotchety Patrick, it was preferable to the lapdog Patrick appeared to be in Todd's wake.

The werewolf moved to the edge of the king-sized bed (the

leprechaun had a penchant for things inversely proportional to him), watched the leprechaun settle into the chair, and waited for the screaming to start. When it died down to an indoor-voice haranguing, Luis offered his side of the Todd situation in plain terms.

"We know almost nothing about him, Patrick. Zero. Certainly not enough to move along his membership."

"Right," Patrick shot back, "like we know so much about the strays you bring here."

"I was a stray too, Patrick, and I haven't—"

"And you need to stay on your leash like a good doggie and not stick your snout where it ain't welcome."

"What did you say?" Luis stood and felt the tingle of fur and claws creeping along his spine, a natural reaction anytime he was compared to canines of the domestic variety. But this was no time for confrontation. He shut his eyes, envisioning a peaceful place. Ramps. Tunnels. Flying tennis balls. Wait, was this a dog park? *Fuck me*, Luis thought. *What have I become?*

He stared down Patrick, daring the leprechaun to say more. Luis finally broke the silence, getting back to the matter at hand and explaining how he couldn't trust Todd based on the prospective tenant's secret background.

New arrivals needed the recommendation of one or more current residents. Luis noted how he'd come to know his "strays," vouching for each and every one of them. On top of that, each candidate had to fill out various forms and submit to an interview.

Even with great recommendations and proven backgrounds, not all candidates were suitable. Like the ghoul caught picking strips of flesh off Darnell for in-between-meal snacks. Or the Yeti who would hoard ice cubes and thus ruin Frozen Daquiri Wednesdays. Todd, however, seemed to have unknown powers far too mysterious to be healthy for anyone. Allow in just one omniscient being and there goes everyone's privacy, Luis reasoned. Until Todd was voted in, the werewolf would remain the most powerful person in the house (politically speaking only, since any number of creatures could kick his aging ass).

Thus, no vote would occur until Luis called one. "By the power vested in me by the board," Luis tilted his chin down to look Patrick in the eye, "fuck off."

"That's it?" Patrick spat. "You're pissed because you can't ask him where he sees himself in five years, especially if it's not halfway up your ass?"

"I mean it, Patrick. Guy comes in here all nonchalant, performs some of the most powerful shit I've ever seen, and no one says boo. But what do we know about him? Really know about him?"

Patrick repeatedly poked Luis's thigh, a gesture not nearly as threatening as the leprechaun likely intended. "I know he's a perfect fit and would be a terrific addition, so don't rock the boat or you'll be out on your ass looking like a shabby 'before' picture in a grooming ad."

"Rock the boat? Whose boat? Yours, I assume?"

"Everyone's boat. We all benefit if Todd becomes a member of our special community."

"We're not even certain he qualifies." *But he does*, Luis thought, and for reasons beyond splitting a bowling ball.

"Please, you've seen what he can do. He's amazing. Maybe the most amazing one here."

"That's just it." Luis began to pace, enjoying the spaciousness not found in his own room. "He's not one of us. He's a step above us. A big step, if you know what I mean. That alone makes him a terrible fit, if not a dangerous threat, for Upton Arms."

Not that Luis knew everything about Upton Arms, but he knew enough. That it was tucked behind an identical retirement home, one for those who didn't suffer from immortality. They also had no idea another Upton Arms existed, though Luis was never clear how their special place had gone undetected all these years. A spell, perhaps, courtesy of Beatrice and her friends.

"You've also been so protective of this place," Luis pointed out, returning to his spot on the bed. "It doesn't make sense you'd jeopardize that by—"

"Jesus H., man, do you not understand?" Patrick sunk down, the chair nearly swallowing him. "Todd is the key to everything. He's got the one thing I need."

Luis slumped, knowing the answer—there was no way to stop Todd from moving in.

"He's got the money," the werewolf said, an observation he knew was slightly more obvious than the sun rising in the east, and that silver bullets fired at point-blank range would have devastating effects on anyone, not just werewolves.

"Indeed he does, and I just need to convince him to part with it in copious amounts."

"What kind of copious amounts do you need?"

"A few hundred thousand should do. More, if he's got it. He likes this place, and I want him to love it. But he won't love it until he gets to know everyone, and that means moving in. At just the right moment, maybe when I hook him up with free broadband—"

"You can do that?" Luis stiffened and pointed accusingly. "I'm still plugging into a phone line."

"You get the internet you deserve. Write a check for six figures, and I will absolutely get you high-speed, even throw in some Netflix. With ads. Double it, and we're in YouTube TV territory. But as I was saying, once Todd's feeling comfortable and happy, I'll do whatever I can to fleece him out of what I need to keep this place open and get a new massage chair, now that you fucked up my imprint."

"Do you hear yourself? You don't have a filter, do you?"

"I'm just doing what needs to be done, unlike the idiots here who still think spells or potions or murderous rampages will get them through the tough times." Patrick cradled the back of his head in his palms. "Look at you, Luis. Sure, you might be able to scare away most rent-a-cops sent to evict you, but when a real deputy arrives with a stun gun, you'd be crawling away with the odor of burnt fur trailing behind you. So do me a favor and get two things: the vote done, and the fuck out of my room."

Luis didn't move. He was not about to be bossed around by the village prick, not when he still remembered what it was like to be the alpha male. Still, the leprechaun had a point about members of law enforcement bearing stun guns. The only worse thing than time in jail was time in kennels. He should know, he'd served time in both. "Patrick, I'm not saying no. I'm saying wait. Let's find out what Todd's really all about. Make sure he is what he appears—"

"Oh, trust me, he's that and more. Just look at what happened to Beatrice when she—" Patrick suddenly went silent, though Luis saw a look of alarm flit across the leprechaun's face.

"When she what, Patrick?" Luis pushed.

"Nothing happened to Beatrice, thanks to Todd," Patrick said, recovering his composure far too quickly.

"You said she cast a money spell and things went wrong."

"Exactly what happened."

A very bad thought scratched at the back of his mind. No, not a thought. A realization.

"It wasn't a money spell, was it, Patrick?" Luis said, knowing the answer.

"'Course it was." The leprechaun's voice had none of the brashness that lifted it a few decibels higher than it needed to be. "Spells go wrong. It happens."

Luis knew his intuition was right. A spell went wrong, but it had nothing to do with money.

"Aw, Patrick, you didn't," Luis pleaded. "Tell me no."

"What are you talking about?"

"Beatrice. That was no money spell, was it? It was more dangerous than that."

"Luis—"

"The lies stop here. Now. If it's any consolation, I know you didn't mean to hurt her."

"You don't know shit," Patrick grunted.

Anger forced Luis off the bed and back to pacing. "Do you think she had a chance in hell to cast a spell over Todd, especially one that attempted to control him, even for a second?"

Patrick threw up his hands in frustration, but Luis took it as surrender.

"Out with it," Luis ordered, pointing a single accusatory finger at the leprechaun. "The whole truth and nothing but the truth. So help you…" Luis paused for effect… "Todd."

Patrick blinked, which Luis had never seen him do. The leprechaun's lips trembled, and was that a tear in the corner of one eye? Was the vociferous leprechaun actually searching for the right words, with none of them profanities?

"First, you need to know…" Patrick swallowed. "I swear it was her idea, not mine. I tried to talk her out of it. I begged and pleaded, but she refused to listen. She was set on saving me, saving Upton Arms. Saving you, you worthless mutt."

Another revelation swept over Luis. "That's why, even though you knew Todd had the power to help, you went to Vlad instead. That had to tear you up inside, asking a vampire for help."

"Had I known what would happen, I would have tried even harder to stop her," Patrick said. "Tied her to a goddamned stake, you know? I never meant for this to happen. I almost lost the only person I care about, and I wouldn't have done that for anything. Even money, Luis. Especially money."

Luis wasn't sure why, but he believed this pathetic creature. Beatrice could be incredibly stubborn. Once her mind was made up, that was that.

And Todd had to know about the spell, probably could even feel it being cast. Made it all that much easier to swoop in the same the day.

It took an exceptional being to show that kind of forgiveness.

Maybe too exceptional.

TWENTY

THE PING-PONG BALL hit thumped off Darnell's chest and bounced along the table, a low moan providing the soundtrack of another lost point. Luis wasn't sure if the zombie was disappointed due to a lack of verbal skills (and display of emotions) among the undead, but the game must go on regardless of the lack of competition.

"It's six-zip," Luis said, preparing to serve to Darnell. "One more point and it's a skunk. Fourth in a row, if I'm not mistaken."

Another grunt. To make sure it wasn't lost in translation, Darnell began to unfurl his middle finger, and it was halfway there when Luis's serve hit him square in the chest again.

"Game," Luis declared, throwing his paddle on the table. "And I hate it when I'm so desperate for distraction, I resort to the undead for entertainment."

Middle finger finally up, Darnell dropped his own paddle for emphasis. Unfortunately for the zombie, the show of defiance collapsed when the prominent finger toppled sideways, like a tree felled in the forest.

Luis retrieved the digit from the table, using his shirt to wipe away the ooze.

"Give me your hand," he told the zombie, holding the displaced finger gently between thumb and forefinger. "No, not that one. The one that's down one finger."

Luis popped it smartly back into place, earning a grudging moan from Darnell.

"No worries my friend, and thanks for the game. At least an attempt at a game."

Life at Upton Arms had fallen into a pleasant lull in the days following Beatrice's miraculous rising from the near-dead. It was as if everyone agreed on a ceasefire when it came to drama, save for the not-so-sudden death of Fred, a mummy who was one of the home's true millennials (he had three millennia under his bandages). At the end of the ceremony, Luis placed the Dustbuster containing Fred's remains onto a shelf as Patrick passed the hat to buy another Dustbuster.

As the home's self-appointed zombie repairman, Luis headed to the shared kitchen to retrieve the staple gun he often used for dismemberment-prone areas until he noticed, out of the corner of his eye, two paddles floating on either end of the ping-pong table. He expected to hear the leveled-up profanities spewed by fairies competing against one another, but there was only silence. If pixies weren't playing, there was only one other explanation.

Ralph the invisible man was back. And he brought friends.

"Ralph," Luis whispered in the vicinity of one of the paddles. "What are you doing?"

"What the hell does it look like?" snapped a decidedly non-Ralph voice.

Luis sidestepped to the other paddle. "Ralph?"

"Dude, in the middle of something here." The paddle zipped past Luis's head, slamming the ball past the opposing paddle. Luis watched it bounce across the floor and roll under the same vending machine that Darnell was bouncing into.

"Looks like you have a minute," Luis said out of the side of his mouth to empty space. "Still living here, I see. Well, not really. You know what I mean."

"Nothing gets past you, Luis."

Jeee-zus, same old Ralph. "Two questions," Luis foraged ahead.

"Who are your companions? And does invisibility make everyone a douchebag?"

"Yes and yes. That it?"

The ball was back in play, paddles dancing in midair.

"No, as a matter of fact. Why are you trying so hard to be noticed? This isn't your style, assuming you're here for the free room and board that comes with being among the visibility challenged."

"Hey 'Neesh, Dom, Paolo—can you give us a sec?"

"Sure thing sweetie," a syrupy voice dripped from the other side of the net.

Paddles paused in midair when the ball hit the net and bounced to a halt. Just a few feet from Luis, a protein bar appeared out of nowhere. The wrapper peeled itself back with a crinkle before a chunk disappeared.

"That's a nice trick," Luis lightly applauded the protein-bar manifestation. "I thought you couldn't make anything invisible but yourself."

Ralph's voice came from behind him. "True until a few months ago. I thought I saw right through the guy, so it was ironic how he didn't see right through me, literally. He shook my hand and taught me a few tricks on the sly, like how to hide small items in my ... well, you get it. I've become a fan."

Luis wasn't sure what to make of that, since he had yet to make up his mind about the newest potential resident. Ignoring it for now, the werewolf swiveled to follow the floating protein bar, another chunk disappearing. "Can you stay in one place? Please? Out of respect?"

To his right. "No."

"God, invisibility really does make you a dick."

"Nah, I was a dick long before invisibility." The voice was in front of Luis now. "Invisibility intensified it."

A thought occurred to Luis when he saw (didn't see) Ralph. The invisible man could play an important part in making Patrick financially whole again, and thus paying off the note against Upton Arms. Then again, would the moral debt of working with a complete jerk be worth paying off the home's debt?

Sure. Why not?

Luis was in no shape to live on the streets again, as he knew that fateful morning when he woke up just as a mom and dad were paying his adoption fee at the animal shelter. He often wondered what that five-year-old would've thought if he knew he was holding a leash to a hungover, half-transformed werewolf rather than the limping mongrel Luis was at the moment. Had that young boy ever gotten over the trauma caused when his forever companion jumped the fence right after dinner (kibble followed by a few bites of under-the-table broccoli)? It wasn't long before Luis was in the comfy confines of Upton Arms, safe from animal control officers everywhere.

"Given your exhibitionism, you must have heard all about Patrick," Luis assumed. "And his, you know, dilemma, which seems to have emboldened you."

"If you mean his stupidity when it comes to money, indeed. Now he's the new invisible man around here out of embarrassment. I've also heard y'all are about to be booted to the street because a leprechaun invested every pot of gold he had in businesses on Forbes' list of top ten 'I Can't Believe You Invested in This' companies."

"So, you have heard."

"Heard and celebrated. Even held a wake for Beatrice's dignity, since it died when everyone found out she was married to that mutant circus imp."

"Good to see you're sympathetic."

A disembodied laugh. "Luis, that's why I've always liked you. That and the fact you keep your door unlocked far too often."

A strong clap on the back nearly sent Luis tumbling. Once he righted himself, he continued. "You're celebrating with an open game of ping-pong?" If this conversation were occurring in public, Luis would hold a phone to explain a conversation with thin air. With such terrible cell reception, Upton Arms was the only place on the planet bystanders would expect an invisible person was involved.

"Indeed, with my good friends, especially Keneesha. She is my very good friend, if you know what I mean."

He did, though Luis tried to figure out how two invisible people had sex. How were you sure what was going where? Or that your partner was enjoying herself? Or himself? If you even were sure of your partner's gender.

"Body paint," Ralph blurted out of nowhere, as if reading Luis's mind.

Or did he read Luis's mind? Did that come with invisibility? The werewolf stopped, banishing all thoughts of mindreading and invisible sex.

"And we're not the only ones crashing here while Patrick gets his shit together," Ralph said, Luis feeling a nudge in his ribs. "You might want to lock your door. All the time."

"Thanks for the heads up. Though I have no idea why in this great visible world, you choose this place to live when you can enter any number of luxurious hotels and couch surf in penthouses around the world."

"Because I'm old, lazy, and like routine. Any other questions?"

"Just one," Luis said, wishing he could look into Ralph's eyes to see his reaction to what he was about to ask. "Any interest in securing your future old age, laziness, and comforting routine at Upton Arms?"

"Nope."

And Luis thought fairies were the biggest dicks.

TWENTY-ONE

LUIS NOTICED the way Beatrice walked into the community room with a flourish and her head characteristically high. She looked good for a woman who was going toward the light a few days ago.

The witch strolled to her favorite recliner, bold strides making it clear she knew every eye on the room was on her. Luis wasn't sure if it was her makeup or a few well-done spells that drew admiration, but the jaws of two zombies literally dropped to the floor, decayed teeth skittering under a vending machine. A water sprite wet herself, not that it was noticeable. And a cue stick floating over the pool table dropped to the felt surface as if even the fairies were entranced by the re-emergence of Upton Arm's unofficial queen (even as fairies had long been banned from billiards as fights among them led to tiny body parts that go in everyone's hair and eyes).

Ever since the Todd incident, Beatrice had been scarce. The rare times she made an appearance, she was untalkative bordering on sullen. That was not the witch Luis knew. Something was bothering her, and Luis was pretty sure he knew what it was. And that's precisely what (who) he wanted to talk about.

The winsome witch settled into the plush recliner, pushed it back, and aimed the remote at the TV. The screen flickered once, twice, a third time. She settled on a show in which people suffered from terminal acne (or at least with skin in such terrible condition, patients may have hoped it was terminal).

The werewolf was torn. On one hand, he needed to talk to her about his Todd-based suspicions and fears generated by a newcomer whose display of powers became bolder, and Beatrice probably knew more about the newcomer than anyone else. On the other hand, he didn't want to be turned into a frog (though he'd transformed into worse) by a woman in need of some quiet time. Luis knew that while Beatrice's powers had diminished over the years—her love potions were more "I find you slightly less annoying" potions—the witch still had some zip in her cauldron.

No time like the present, Luis thought, taking a big breath. *Just be cool.* He slid into the recliner next to hers.

"Hey Beatrice, how's tricks?"

The witch kept her eyes on the screen. "At this point, Luis, it's not worth my time to turn you into something small enough to shove up the nearest intestinal tract since you couldn't be any more pathetic."

"Five minutes, that's all I need."

"I'll give you three because that's how long it will take Patrick to sense your presence in his chair and beg me to turn you into tiny enough—"

"I get it Beatrice. You can zap me into claustrophobic unpleasantness with the snap of a finger. I accept and respect your power and dominance."

"Two minutes."

"Todd."

"Time's up."

"It's life or death," Luis pleaded.

"Look around, Luis. Everything in this place is life or death. Mostly death."

Beatrice was right. Life and/or death wasn't a big deal to creatures who had been around for centuries. Luis switched tactics. "It's about the Upton Arms, its future, and how I think Todd is not what he appears."

"What do you mean, 'not what he appears?'"

"He's even more powerful than he lets on, and I'm worried he thinks our little community here is a threat."

"And?"

"And he may not have the best intentions."

"He saved my life, Luis. Why would he do that if, as you said, he doesn't have the best intentions?"

"That's what I wanted you to tell me because I think you know something we don't."

"Why would you think that?"

Luis took the witch's hand, somewhat surprised she didn't recoil. That's when he knew he was on the right track. "I've gotten to know you pretty well, Beatrice. You've sealed yourself off for most of the last few days, and when you do emerge, you're quiet, even aloof." He paused, searching the witch's eyes for any kind of reaction. "Something is on your mind. Something important. Maybe vital."

Beatrice let go of Luis's hand, plucked the remote from the armrest and aimed it at the TV, its screen going blank. The werewolf was fairly Beatrice's situation was serious but had no idea it was truly grave.

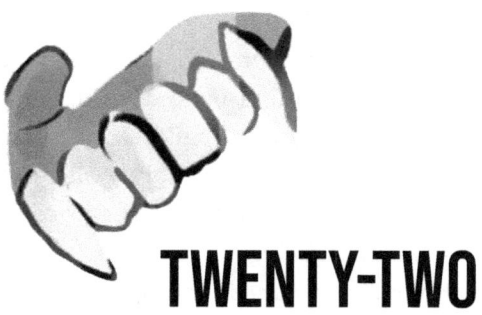

TWENTY-TWO

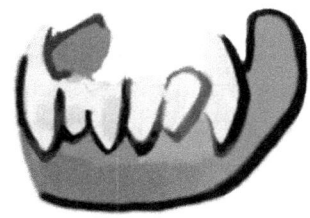

IT STARTED, Beatrice told Luis, with a spell that was unusually complicated, and not just because it required the skin of an oracle.

"Agatha gave me her pumice stone after an aggressive attack on her foot callus," the witch explained, as if that was the kind of information freely shared in civilized societies. Luis offered a look that said, "I didn't need to know that under any circumstance."

Noting Luis's sour look, Beatrice continued. "The rest of the ingredients were easy to obtain. The difficult part was the spell itself. It was a five-hundred-word incantation mixing Latin and Aramaic. No reading aloud, I had to memorize it since I needed a magic more powerful than the being I was attempting to influence. Let me put it in perspective. If I were trying to take over your mind, Luis, a limerick would do."

"Where did that come from?" Luis stammered, but Beatrice went on without missing a beat.

"I didn't need to control Todd's mind, just influence him. You know, steer him in a certain direction, one he wouldn't normally take. Due to his obvious power, such a spell was a significant risk for me, and a huge reward for everyone here."

The witch looked around and lowered her voice before explaining how spells that conjured wealth and power often failed due to their subtle intricacies. Beatrice knew of many conjurers who attempted incantations far above their skill level and wound up in confectionary-built homes deep in the forest, luring children to their deaths. Enchanting a wizard (Todd was at that and possibly more, perhaps even the CEO of time and space) was nearly suicidal, but Beatrice felt she had little choice if Upton Arms were to survive.

"That was all that mattered," she sighed, patting Luis's hand as if to suggest empathy came naturally. "Few residents would survive on their own and there is nothing sadder than a troll living in a freeway underpass." (Or under a playground bridge, Luis added mentally).

Beatrice recalled days and nights spent memorizing the text. When she was ready, Patrick stood by with the written spell in hand to follow along. A mispronunciation here and a wrong word there started a cascade of errors to a point where the witch envisioned a future home requiring load-bearing gumdrops.

As the spell careened out of control, her vision blurred as the wall shimmered and turned translucent. She watched the rest of the spell vanish beyond its liquid borders. Patrick floated into view. "Bea, Bea, darling, what..." and then he vanished into the whiteness that enveloped her.

"All this time, I thought the moment would come where I'd go into the light," she said, recoiling from the memory. "Little did I know it would come to me. The only thing I was sure of was that I had passed onto the next realm, and the next realm was incredibly dull."

She was neither standing nor floating, Beatrice recalled. She was simply there, free to move about with no discernable place to go. It lasted seconds, or hours. Perhaps weeks. She had no sense of time.

Two seconds or two weeks later, she heard a voice. "Beatrice, a pleasure."

She remembered how she seemed to float away from her body, powerless as it swiveled toward that ethereal voice. At first, the source was a bright red smudge at the end of a dazzling white tunnel. It came closer and closer until details emerged.

Luis leaned forward, eyes narrowing. "Todd."

"Indeed," Beatrice nodded. "But he was so...garish. Not in a clownish way, but slightly elegant in a maroon tux with ruffled shirt and top hat. He held a cane in his right hand and made a real show of strutting toward me, taking a deep bow as if about to break out in a song and dance. I got the idea he was about to perform. In a way, he already had, because I got the idea I was in the midst of a miracle."

Beatrice described Todd's close-trimmed beard and mustache, and a full head of hair so white it blended perfectly into the brilliant background. Then there was the charming smile, one that seemed to hide something.

The witch leaned into Luis, putting her hand on his knee. "I spoke to him even though I knew he could read my mind at the moment, that he'd created this place where he and I could have a private conversation. Does that sound stupid?"

"Not at all." Luis gave her hand a gentle squeeze. "Go on."

"I asked him if he could control minds as well as read them. He said no because he believed in free will. Then he denied being a mind reader, just that he picked up on strong emotions."

Bullshit, Luis thought, remaining silent to let Beatrice go on.

"I felt this anger welling up because I knew he was lying. Then he noted I have a lot of anger for someone in the midst of dying. That's when it hit me, that he's here to change the outcome. Because, Luis, that spell should have killed me. I knew it in my heart at that moment."

"You're sure he was there to save you?" Luis questioned. "That he didn't expect anything in return?"

"At first. I felt this overwhelming sense of love and peace, like out of a page in a children's Bible story. It was his gift to me. A gift, not a favor. That was my sense. Then I asked him the only question that seemed to matter at that point."

Luis knew instinctively, blurting it out. "Why."

"It's the one thing we always want to know, isn't it? There isn't always an answer, but this time there was."

Luis wanted to enter that white light with Beatrice right now, wishing he could have heard it firsthand. Was Todd truly about to answer the one question philosophers have debated for centuries, one that every person on Earth has asked at one time or another? The murmurs of nearby conversation, the hum of vending machines, the low whirr of the air conditioning—each noise vanished as Luis focused on Beatrice.

"He said he had a better question. He knew I was in trouble the second I thought the spell could actually work. He said I was underestimating him, one thing those who knew him, or knew of him, never did. While I disappointed him, he was impressed that I was driven by selflessness. That's why he intervened, knowing that even largely immortal beings have limits.

"While he spoke, I could feel myself recovering, getting stronger. It wasn't just a place to talk privately, but to heal. And Luis, don't take this as evidence one way or another, but my soul felt as if it was being fed. I can't think of a better word for that place other than…heavenly."

Luis sat in stunned silence. Had anyone else but Beatrice inferred that Todd was the Alpha and the Omega, especially one wearing a red suit, the werewolf would transform into a laughing hyena. He trusted the witch because it was just as Todd allegedly told her—she was selfless. Luis was wary of the next step, but he had to take it.

"Is he, you think, divine?" He couldn't quite bring himself to say the Almighty.

Her answer only confounded Luis further.

"I hope not. Remember when I said I thought he was giving me a gift?"

Luis nodded.

"It was more of a favor. He wanted something in a return."

"Sacrificing Patrick," Luis smiled. "I think we could get behind that."

"Luis, please. If you only knew that feisty little leprechaun like I do." Beatrice trailed off, folding her hands on her lap. "No, Todd wanted information. On Vlad."

Luis felt his blood go cold. Why would God…no, no, no. Todd. Why would Todd want to know about Vlad?

Beatrice read the expression on Luis's face. "Because Vlad is the—"

She stopped in midsentence, jaw dropping to her chest. Suddenly, her head whipped from left to right before jumping out the recliner. She spun toward Luis. "What the fuck am I doing here?"

"Huh?" Luis leaned forward to push himself up when Beatrice pushed him right back down.

"Did you seriously bring me here when I was sleeping? What the hell is wrong with you? Somebody needs to put you on a leash, and I know just the person to do it."

"Beatrice, I have no idea what just happened because you were telling me about Todd and Vlad, then—"

The witch's nose scrunched, her lips twisted into a grimace. "No idea what you're talking about. And why would Todd want to know about Vlad? If he's who we think he is, he knows all about Vlad. And you. And me. You stupid mutt."

Beatrice spun and stalked off, brushing past a startled Vlad who was still rubbing sleep from his eyes.

"Is it dusk already?" Luis heard the witch grumble..

"Yes," Vlad said, with an odd, vaguely eastern European accent. "Listen to them, the children of the night. What music they make."

"Fuck you," Beatrice said, disappearing down the hallway.

A seemingly unperturbed Vlad plopped himself next to Luis. "What's her problem?"

Luis briefly considered sharing what Beatrice had just told him, but it would either worry his friend or piss him off. More likely the latter. "No idea," the werewolf shrugged. "Good rest?"

"Why is it the only thing my memory foam remembers is how to make my back ache?"

"That's not the mattress, my friend. That's age."

"Well then, you're probably wondering why I'm here."

Luis knew exactly why his friend was here, and did as soon as he heard Vlad's lame Bela Lugosi impression.

"Someone's feeling frisky," Luis said, rolling up his sleeves because he knew what was coming—a night on the town. "That time of the month?"

"Indeed it is," Vlad said with an uncharacteristic clap.

Just as a full moon forced werewolfery upon Luis, his vampire friend got the itch for fresh blood once a month. Vlad enjoyed the hunt every bit as drinking straight from the tap, swearing it kept him young (it didn't) and interesting (nope).

Luis came along to make sure Vlad knew when to say when, ensuring he took a sip and left nothing behind other than a someone who felt as if they'd finished a six-pack of Red Bull and a couple of what appeared to be mosquito bites on the neck. Luis wasn't sure what was in Vlad's saliva, but he wished he could get a few syringes' worth of that performance-enhancing drug.

"Walking or the bus?"

"Uber. I'm feeling good about this one."

"You must be. It's a dangerous way to go if cops check for rideshares in the area."

"Don't worry," Vlad comforted. "I've got this all figured out. Ready?"

"Let's roll. Just make me one promise."

"We won't get caught. But if we do, I'm fine with you changing into whatever and getting out of there, though text me if you wake up in the pound."

Luis walked with Vlad toward the front door, carrying his uneasy feeling about Todd in the pit of his stomach, hoping the T-bone steak in his future would fill it.

It did, though Vlad would be the one paying the price.

TWENTY-THREE

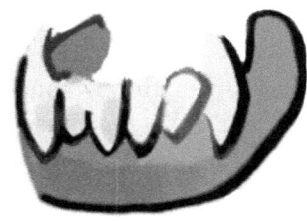

THE HEAT SLAPPED Vlad harder than an offended housewife of New Jersey. It was on evening like this when he felt sorry for his werewolf companion and the fur coat lurking beneath the skin. He could imagine Luis shrugging off a canine-related insult because it was just too damn hot to go mammalian, dignity be damned.

As the two waited outside Upton Arms for their ride, Luis nudged his friend. "Do me a favor," he pleaded. "We play it cool in this fucking heat, OK? Last thing I want to do is get furry."

"I was thinking the same thing," Vlad nodded. Even the vampire had conceded to the weather, wearing a cotton polo, cargo pants and, God forbid, tan Crocs. He had no idea how many generations of vampires were turning in their graves. Well, most of them, since they were just sleeping.

A light breeze felt like a blow dryer set on low. Vlad was not one to sweat, not even under the pressure of pitchfork-bearing villager, but he felt a few beads forming along his widow's peak. Sure, he'd done some nasty things to survive during the plague, but this was bordering on debasement.

"Let me get that for you," Luis offered, dabbing his friend's head with a handkerchief. "Nothing worse than bloodsucker sweat."

"I'd lay fangs on you right now, but these are my good Crocs," Vlad chuckled.

"I'd tear out your throat if you tried, but that would make me pant."

"The only thing unsightlier than a sweating vampire is a panting werewolf."

The only sounds were those of crickets and the occasional car. With a storage facility on one side and a tow yard on the other, Upton Arms was easily overlooked in this dilapidated part of town. Location was an advantage for those needing to stay out of sight, but what did it say about society's treatment of the elderly, tucking them away where they won't be seen or heard? The grounds were pleasant, at least, with expansive lawns, shade trees and a manmade brook bubbling from a squat waterfall.

Vlad crossed his arms, suddenly feeling philosophical. "Have you noticed what Upton Arms says about—"

"Finally, our ride." Luis pointed at the headlights coming their way. "Were you saying something?"

The moment passed. "Nothing important."

"So, the usual," Luis said, waving down the driver.

The werewolf and vampire climbed into the back of the Toyota Prius.

"A vampire and werewolf get into the back of a Toyota Prius," Vlad said, closing the door behind him.

Luis did the same, pulled the shoulder harness and locked the buckle in place with a metallic click. "Yeah, and?"

"I don't know, but there's a joke there somewhere."

"And I'm looking at him."

The driver twisted in his front seat, looked at his passengers. "One of you Stan?" he said, lowering his glasses.

Vlad raised his hand, having used one of his digital aliases to book the ride.

"And you're headed to the Cracker Barrel on Salem?" the driver continued. "'Cause there are two other Cracker Barrels much closer. I thought maybe you got confused with, you know, phone maps. It happens with people your age."

Vlad briefly considered turning his Uber driver into Uber Eats, but hated dashboard dining. "The one I chose, please."

Ignoring the scent of vomit, bleach, and a thousand farts (curse his heightened vampire sense of smell, still sharp after all these centuries)Vlad settled in for the drive and tried to focus on the task ahead. His mind refused to cooperate, drifting back as it often did in times like this, almost as if to punish him.

Memories surfaced, and of course they were the ones he'd tried for centuries to forget. They came back stronger, more vivid each time. Most were from the time he was a brash young vampire wholly deserving of the b-word (bloodsucker). Even though killing had few consequences when he was less than a century old, Vlad still had difficulty accepting past behavior.

For the first half century of his vampire life, he focused on survival, thinking not of his meals as individuals but as bits of a necessary buffet. Hunting was a vital part of living, as necessary as it was to track down a deer or elk to feed the family. The only difference was that Vlad's prey tended to fight back (that and having no urge to mount the head of his prey). In a way, his way of killing was more civil, even compassionate, offering a relatively painless death, like going to sleep and never waking up.

At least that was how he justified it. It was the Dark Ages, emphasis on "dark."

The Black Death in the mid-1300s changed everything. Much of his food supply had been tainted, forcing him to rely on mammals of the four-legged kind. He nearly died of malnutrition since animals contained little of a vampire's recommended daily allowance of nutrients. The Black Death, however, had a silver lining. Vlad became a practitioner of bloodletting, a medically approved procedure that kept him well fed without having to kill. It was a true lightbulb moment long before the lightbulb was invented. He ate well with none of the guilt, even saving a bottle for a pre-dawn snack.

Vlad had no idea how well his patients would respond to the treatment, quickly regaining their pre-Black Death vigor and vitality. Word spread to the point that patients not only stopped complaining about the odd hours but recommended Vlad's unusual techniques to others. It was his golden age of vampire-dom, until scientific enlightenment forced him back into the shadows. At least he took with him the valuable skill of knowing when to say when, drinking just enough so that both parties survived.

Vlad no longer had the stamina to hunt every time he was hungry, but he'd found other ways to drink straight from the tap rather than from plastic bags, seeking those who could use his healing gifts.

As he had for this night.

There was a nudge in his ribs. "Vlad, wake up." Luis's voice. "We're here. And please tell me that what I'm seeing right now is not the reason we're here."

Vlad opened his eyes and looked out the window, his gaze drawn to the colorful Cracker Barrel sign. It illuminated the comforting frontier façade that harkened back to a time of rugged individualism and socially acceptable genocide.

And there, huddled around the entrance, was a mix of wheelchair-bound people and women in scrubs. Vlad peered out the back window to confirm his evening plans, and there it was, a large white van marked Hospice of the Sun.

It was the First Annual Death, Come and Get It Night at the Cracker Barrel.

At least that was Vlad dubbed it two weeks ago when reading about the gathering. He'd been cruising the dark web looking for any interesting vampire meetups, noting it was the usual mix of cosplay enthusiasts wanting to show off their ceramic fangs and handmade silk capes. His next stop was a category that had once sounded so promising, only to be filled with pretenders—"Wanted: Suicide assistants."

There were more than a dozen personal ads requesting an escort for a trip to the afterlife. As usual, most were related to autoerotic asphyxiation, since anything can be made pornographic, even death. The rest were role-play scenarios, all from men likely to have been booted numerous times from Tinder.

One ad caught his eye—"Ending it all at Cracker Barrel." There was even a date and time listed, odd considering the subject matter. The text was long so rather than waste his time on yet another plea to be auto-asphyxiated, he returned to the normal web. Vlad Googled "Cracker Barrel" and "death," scrolled quickly past the many Yelp reviews and noted a story about an unusual event. The story quoted one Olivia Yu, head nurse at Hospice of the Sun. She was looking forward to the agency's event at Cracker Barrel, originally planned as a fundraiser until several patients expressed interest in going.

"There is a real zest for life here, even the end of it," Yu told the reporter. "There aren't a lot of opportunities for the living-challenged to get out, so I thought this would be perfect. A celebration of lives well-lived."

He returned to the personal ad and digested every word.

"The first problems were found when I was seventeen," it read. "Small cysts, removed, but cancer didn't get eviction notice. Two years later, stage four, inoperable, just a matter of time, yet I was a fighter. That started the months of chemo. Tumors shrunk and returned. Different drugs were administered. Again, the tumors seemed to have surrendered, but they had actually been out recruiting bigger, better soldiers.

"Doctors asked to try yet another concoction of drugs designed to kill parts of my body. I was done, but my family was not. I didn't want to let them down—cancer is funny that way—so I let them pump in even more lethal serums. Tumors once again have receded, but I know where this yo-yo is going. I go to bed praying to die, wake up every day wondering when God will add 'mercy' to his resume, because it's clear mercy is one gift He is refusing to bestow.

"I now mark days based on levels of nausea and pain, still alive as if that's a good thing. Last month, cancer's reinforcements arrived. Tumors had invaded territories doctors hoped were impenetrable. Goodbye treatment, hello hospice. My days are spent waiting for the inevitable as my mom and dad try not to cry each time they see me."

The poster added details of the fundraiser and what she'd be wearing, ending it with three words—"Be my hero."

Vlad had been a lot of things in his life, but never a hero. He liked the sound of it. And he was hungry. Win-win.

He typed out his response to "Nancy," short and to the point.

Luis slammed the Prius door and looked at his friend through furrowed brows. "Well, Vlad the powerful, this is pretty low, even for you. Shooting fish in a Cracker Barrel."

"No," Vlad said as the Prius hummed away. "Just one fish in particular. One who asked for my help. Wants me to be her hero."

"What, she called you on the Crisis Hotline? That's supposed to prevent self-harm, you know, not offer to do it."

Vlad scanned the parking lot, a thin trickle of sweat trailing to the bridge of his nose. He pinched the sleeve of his polo to wipe it off. "Trust me, I'm doing her a big favor. She's ready to check out early, and I'm just carrying her bags to the car."

"Damn, pretty flippant for what I assume will be an assisted homicide. Whatever, none of my business, as long as I am nowhere near you when the dinner bell rings. Speaking of that, where's this all going down?"

The lot was filled with the usual suburban gray SUVs and vans. A few pulled up to the front, disgorged their occupants, and returned to the hunt for a space, vultures circling for an opening. Of all the places to sign off from life, doing it here would leave few, if any, regrets.

Sprouting above the fray was a black party bus with tinted windows parked directly under one of the lights scattered about the lot. The vehicle glimmered like a beacon for the reaper. Vlad pointed toward it. "Party bus for the damned."

"Cold even for you," Luis said, pulling a handkerchief to mop his forehead. "If I knew this was waiting for us, no way would I have agreed to come. I prefer your victims have at least a little fight in them."

"She's not a victim."

"Then what is she?"

"A patient."

One that would become yet another memory the vampire wished he could forget.

TWENTY-FOUR

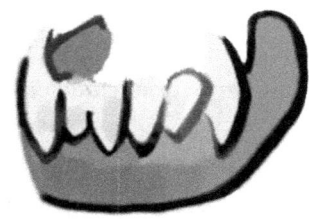

VLAD THREADED through the packed crowd at the restaurant's entrance, jostling patrons without so much as an insincere, "Excuse me."

"Shouldn't you be taking a lower profile?" Luis noted as he followed. "You're collecting a good share of witnesses since you're dining in rather than taking it to go. I mean, you are dining in, right? And somewhere a bit more private than this?"

"Relax," the vampire said. "I have a date with an inviting meal. Literally. Because she—"

"Invited you," Luis finished. "I get it. Still, I'm not of fan of attracting attention."

"Did you see what I'm wearing? I'm as invisible as Ralph in this place."

"You got that right. Funny how the more ridiculous you look, the better you fit in."

The two waded slowly through the crowd, Vlad scanning for a distinctive pink shirt as his hunger began to rise. All he saw were people who perhaps needed to make better dietary choices, but who was he to judge given his atypical nutritional needs?

As he slalomed wordlessly toward the check-in station, he stifled the urge to scream, "Vampire coming through, clear the way or suffer the consequences." Once there, , Vlad engaged the young man behind it, vaguely wondering if the gentleman was at all embarrassed to be wearing a red plaid kerchief around his neck. Vlad reported back to Luis, who had wedged himself between a bench and a shelf jammed with bags of biscuit mix.

"Ninety minutes for a table?" Luis repeated incredulously. "Who waits that long for a table in the seventh circle of dining hell? Gourmet masochists?"

"I need some fresh air," Vlad announced, dancing through the horde with Luis trailing right behind. The two took a seat on the curb, Vlad breathing air anything but fresh. Scents of tobacco and chicken fat floated on an incoming gravy tide, almost ruining Vlad's appetite.

But not quite.

Vlad's eyes drifted over the waiting crowd, picking out those who looked like hospice patients, randomly assigning them terminal diseases.

Cancer, lung. Cancer…pancreas. Heart disease. Heart disease. Parkinson's.

Luis turned to Vlad, casting a glance over his shoulder. "What are you muttering?"

"Uh, oh, nothing," Vlad shook his head.

"No, you were guessing what people were dying from. Cold, man. Even from a guy whose body temperature is a steady seventy degrees."

Vlad was about to defend himself when the hospice group was called inside, a fortunate occurrence because he had no defense. He watched them filter through the front door, wondering which one was Nancy. None of them matched the description.

Maybe she got sick. Maybe she had second thoughts.

Maybe she died.

Luis slapped his thighs. "So, Todd."

"Todd?"

"Todd. We have to deal with the Todd situation sooner or later."

"Oh, so now it's a situation?" Vlad put his hands on his knees, flicking an imaginary bit of lint off his cargo pants. "I thought we were still pretty occupied with the possible sale of the Upton Arms. That's a situation."

"We are," Luis nodded. "But nothing we can do about that now. We can, however, talk about Todd. What better place to discuss God, the meaning of life, and our fates than at a restaurant whose very existence speaks to the mortality of man and the need for an afterlife?"

Luis stood and stretched, his spine cracking audibly. He sat back down with a groan. "Let's just assume Todd is God."

"Big assumption," Vlad said, turning away to stare at the van.

"Assuming two guys sitting outside a Cracker Barrel are a vampire and werewolf is also a big assumption. Yet here we are."

Too exhausted to fight, Vlad sighed and put up his hands in surrender.

"I knew you'd see it my way," the werewolf gloated. "There's only one reason God came to Earth, especially to our little patch of Earth." Luis paused for dramatic effect. "God is retiring."

Luis stopped, waiting for a reaction that never came.

"I'm sure of it no matter how crazy it sounds," he continued. "He needs to find a successor. And I'm pretty sure he came to Upton Arms not just to start collecting Social Security, but to find someone to take over as life's CEO."

Vlad wasn't even sure where to start. First, Todd was a gifted healer, and may well have had a grasp on some nifty mindreading and telekinesis skills. He wouldn't be surprised if Todd had a command of hypnosis as well.

But God? God didn't even exist.

"You going to apply?" Vlad smiled, eyes widening. "You'd look good in flowing hair and beard. You'd even make that white robe look good."

"Fine, make light."

"No, that would be your job. At least on the first day."

"Whatever. But if Todd is God, and granted that's a big 'if,' this will be the most important hire in the history of the world. And I don't think we can ignore it because of the consequences that come with making the wrong decision."

"Don't look at me, I'm not ready to play God yet."

"Really? This coming from a guy who has a dinner date tonight. And by that, I mean a date who is his dinner. You joke about it, but it's a pretty disgusting way to approach ending someone's life."

"What the hell? Where did that come from?"

Luis shrugged. "Most of your life has depended on the suffering, if not untimely demise of, strangers. Correct me if I'm wrong, but unlike tonight, most aren't volunteers. If that isn't playing God, what is?"

Out of the corner of his eye, Vlad noticed a figure by the van. A woman in a wheelchair rolled to the back doors and stopped. She turned her chair toward the Cracker Barrel, and from where Vlad sat, she looked much too young, as he'd feared.

He stood, happy to end the conversation. "Sorry to bring this to a close, but the guest of honor is waiting for me."

At the same time, a woman clad in a long pioneer dress stood in the open doorway, clipboard in hand.

"Wolfington, party of two?" she called out. "Wolfington?"

Luis hoisted Vlad to his feet. "Wolfington? Really?"

"Thought you'd get a kick out of it," Vlad beamed. "What would you have preferred? Blooderheim? Fanginstein? Enjoy your dinner. I'll be in when the appointment's finished."

"Sure," Luis shook his head. "Just one thing, so we're clear."

"What?"

Luis nodded toward the van. "You're not ready to play God unless someone asks you. Right?"

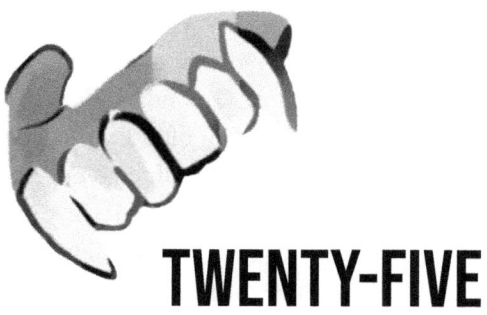

TWENTY-FIVE

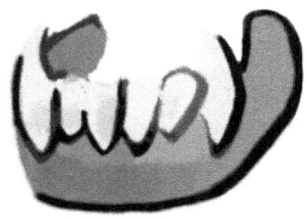

IF VLAD COULD CHANGE one vampire stereotype, it would be the one linking them to bats. These flying rats were blind, dwelled in damp darkness, and subsisted on creatures perched on the lowest rung of the food chain. Vampires were a noble bunch, more like the lioness, queen of the beasts (unlike the contrary sexist view about lions, Vlad knew the females did most of the work while taking little of the credit, just as with humans). The vampire ruled the habitat, facing no suitable competition for prey. The only true enemies were the careless mistakes that could lead the world's apex predator to go into hiding.

But as he strode toward the hospice van, Vlad was not the lioness but a jackal, a lowly beast that hung around the watering hole to pick off the injured or sick. Only this was worse because his prey was a volunteer. He was as much a hunter as a tiger in a zoo being thrown chunks of meat. He was here for nothing more than a bag of Vampire Chow.

It forced Vlad to face his deepest, darkest secret. He hunted not because he had to, but because he should. He was a vampire, after all, a terror of the night. Not some creature picking through a refrigerator for a blood pouch about to expire.

When Vlad confided to Luis that he had to feed off a live victim at least once a month, he didn't share it was for more mental health than physical needs. The monthly forays allowed Vlad to keep up appearances, fooling others even as he tried to fool himself. He was that guy who went to the gym once a month so he could tell others he worked out. Dark alleys may have provided a bland buffet for a hungry vampire, yet Vlad preferred to stay in. He would never admit that to anyone, and at times to himself, as he experienced yet another quiet evening with a blood pouch and Candy Crush. How, then, was drinking from a willing victim any different from popping open a blood sack?

The vampire instinctively crouched when headlights swam across the lot. He remained motionless when he heard the metallic whir of gears, followed by the rasp of metal on metal. The van jostled over so slightly, and Vlad put it all together. Someone, his supper, perhaps, had opened the back door. Vlad, avoiding the lights, crept toward the vehicle for a better look at the menu.

Hiding behind a yellow sedan, a poor choice for camouflage, Vlad eyed the woman in a wheelchair peering into the parking lot, her head swiveling back and forth.

Waiting for her hero, Vlad thought with disgust. He bowed low, putting his hands on the warm pavement, plotting a way back to Cracker Barrel before he was debased even further. Not that such a thing was possible given the best outcome was still dinner at a Cracker Barrel.

"You!"

The voice froze Vlad. He waited a beat before poking his head over the hood.

"What, you think you're invisible?" the woman barked.

"Apparently not," Vlad muttered.

"Maybe don't hide behind the brightest car in the lot when trying to avoid attention."

Vlad stood and instinctually sized her up. Toned but spindly arms emerged from the sleeves of a loose-fitting pink T-shirt. Her thin legs sported just enough definition to suggest a once-athletic lifestyle.

The woman slapped a button to her left, lowering the platform to the asphalt, and landing with a clank. Other details emerged as Vlad approached. Her close-cropped Afro framed a delicate, very pretty girl-next-door face. But it was her smile that riveted his gaze, and Vlad wondered what shocked him most—her welcoming expression as her murderer approached, or the youth that danced in her eyes.

She was no more than thirty, possibly younger. He was expecting bags under sad and weary eyes, a look that made it clear there was no other way out than surrender.

Bending slightly at the waist, and surrendering to fate, Vlad held out his hand.

"Nancy, I presume?" he said in a voice that suggested a first, rather than last, date.

"Yes indeed," the woman responded, taking Vlad's hand in a firm grip. "You must be Steve. Pleased to meet you."

Vlad doubted that, his face giving away his thoughts.

"Yes, *pleased*," she emphasized. "I'm not sure what you think of our meeting, but trust me, this is one of the most amazing gifts I've ever received."

Vlad coughed, though nothing was caught in his throat other than words.

He wasn't sure why as he'd been thinking for quite some time about playing the merciful angel of death. He stumbled across the role shortly after arriving at Upton Arms when he realized his own death was closing in. When that time came, he wanted to check out quickly and with dignity. If he could find another vampire to feed on him, he'd happily die in his clutches.

For now, he could be that vampire for others. Win-win, as they said today. He just had to find willing victims, and it was a zombie who led the way. One quiet night in the common room, Vlad confessed his "death with dignity" plan to Darnell, the only resident who would never reveal a secret because he was incapable of speech. The zombie took Vlad by the hand, led him to the room of the undead, and showed him the dark web. There, amid drug deals, stolen merchandise for sale, and want ads for car thieves, people asked strangers to release them from their mortal bonds. Most of it looked like bullshit, merely thrill-seekers hiding behind lies, but a few seemed legit. Vlad put out what he thought were very good offers, ones that involved relatively painless deaths at an affordable fee.

Nancy, however, was the first to set a time and place. Making his first attempt at the noble calling, Vlad hesitated. Nancy seemed so full of life to want to hand it to him on a silver platter.

"So how're we going to do this, Steve?" Nancy said after a rudimentary yet sincere handshake with her killer. "You promised 'relatively' painless, and I'm going to hold you to that. Not that I'll be in any position to demand my money back if not completely satisfied, am I right?"

"I, uh, yes," Vlad stammered. "Painless. But do you mind if I ask you a personal question?"

"Considering what you're here for, I think we've skipped the getting-to-know-you part and have careened right into the share-our-most-intimate-secrets area. Shoot. Not literally, because that would be the opposite of painless."

There was that smile again, unnerving a man who'd erased countless lives over a few centuries. He got down on one knee, looking at Nancy eye to eye.

"What, you proposing? Because it's way too late for that," she smirked. "Stand the fuck up and don't patronize me. And I apologize for my language, but I've had just about all the pity bullshit I can take."

OK, Vlad thought. *Maybe this won't be as difficult as I thought.*

The roar of a motorcycle rose above the constant hum of traffic, reminding the vampire of their place in a very public space. He glanced around, looking for ubiquitous surveillance cameras. You couldn't do so much as kill someone anymore without it being recorded somewhere.

Nancy placed a hand on each of the armrests and pushed out of the chair.

"Don't worry, hon, I chose this time and this place for a reason," she said, reading Vlad's mind. She glanced back at the van. "Plenty of time since hospice folks rarely get out and are in no hurry to get back to the land of tubes and ventilators."

She reached under the chair. "Where the hell..." she grunted, her hand probing this way and that as various curses escaped motionless lips as if she were a profane ventriloquist. "Ah, here we go." She withdrew a small black box, hit the button in its center, and levitated before Vlad's eyes. "Side door is unlocked," she motioned as the platform rose. "Meet me inside"

This was Vlad's chance to disappear, but the only thing to vanish was his urge to run. It was more his curiosity than a twisted valor to complete the task ahead. The vampire skirted alongside the van as if walking along a cliff, still wary of being seen. He lifted the door handle and slipped inside. Turning sideway, he nudged himself between rows before joining Nancy, now sitting in the back seat.

"I'm sure you noticed the windows," Nancy gestured left and right. "The tinting's darker than the law allows. You play the hospice card, no one gives you shit. We could drive this thing ninety miles per hour downtown and everyone is going to look the other way. It's uncomfortable being around people acting as if they're not dying in the next few weeks. Or days. Or hours."

She reached into the pocket of her shorts and withdrew a small object that shined in what little light was available. She held it up to Vlad, turning it slowly as if it were a rare gem.

"Spare key to the van, giving us access without anyone knowing," she said. "Many Bothans died to bring hospice rebels this plan to escape."

It was Vlad's turn to smile, recognizing the line from the first *Star Wars* movie.

"In this case, a key is better than plans to the Death Star," Vlad said.

"Exactly," Nancy said, turning to hold out a closed fist. Vlad bumped it with his own, Nancy splaying her fingers after contact. "Boom, baby. And may I welcome you to my personal Death Star."

Nancy lifted off the seat to shove the key into her pocket, falling sideways in the process. Vlad caught her, propped her up.

"You've very kind for someone about to take my life. And don't give me that look," Nancy pleaded. "I want to leave the world the way I came in—fucking with people."

Nancy paused and took a breath. Vlad briefly wondered if she had second thoughts about what was about to happen, that maybe dying at the hands of a stranger in cargo pants was not the best way to take her leave. That notion was dispelled when, after another deep breath, it was clear she was struggling to get enough oxygen.

"That's the chemo talking," Nancy said, seeing the concerned look on her would-be-assassin's face. "Took out more than half of my lung function. Anyway…you mentioned a personal question. I'm happy to ask it for you because it's one I've answered a thousand times. Why? Why would someone like me want to die?"

Vlad shifted, unsure of what to say. *The less I know about you the better*, he wanted to tell her, but it would have been lie. He stayed silent.

"I was a vibrant, boy-crazy girl, which is what you should be at seventeen," she narrated as if from a script, causing Vlad to wonder how many times she'd delivered this particular story. "Then I get a persistent stomachache. I kept it to myself for weeks because that's what teens do. Finally, it was too much, and my parents took me to my pediatrician. I'm not going to go into all the particulars, so I'll give you the condensed version, just like I've had to do a thousand times when begging nurses and doctors and well-meaning volunteers to let me go. It was colon cancer, the least glamorous of all the cancers. There were the usual treatments, even a handful of surgeries, and for a few months, I lived with the most beautiful word in the English language—remission. Until cancer took even that away."

She shifted uneasily in the seat, as if fearing to be judged over where her disease ranked on the ladder of slow deaths. She inhaled, held it, let it out slowly, repeated. Her expression softened.

"If I had breast cancer," Nancy went on with a hint of a smile, "I'd be the patient of the month at walks and fun runs and dinners. People would be wearing pink ribbons in my honor, and I'd probably throw out the first pitch somewhere. But colon cancer's not only an aggressive bitch, but one you're actually embarrassed by. Ain't that the shit? Pun intended."

Nancy rubbed her thigh. It came across as absent-minded, but Vlad knew she needed to pause just for a moment, for breath as well as a check on the emotions that threatened to break through her tough-girl façade.

"Cancer took up full-time residency when I was nineteen. I let the doctors do everything, even though my prospects weren't good. More surgery, chemo, meds to help me survive chemo, meds to survive the meds to survive chemo.

"My body finally responded, and the cell count went way down. Until it went up. A chemo adjustment, more meds, down and back up. A decade of this. Imagine ten years of dangling off a cliff, rattlesnakes emerging every few months to bite the shit out of you. There comes a time to let go. And now is that time. I had a great ride for the first seventeen years, better than some get. But it's time to drop because I'd rather land hard than keep struggling."

Vlad resisted the strong urge to wrap his arms around this frail young woman, knowing if he did, he'd walk away and leave Nancy on that cliff, struggling every day. The situation had changed. Each minute with Nancy, hearing her story, made him feel less like an opportunist and more like a—no, not a hero. But he was beginning to understand what she'd meant.

"Motherfucker, I see that doubt in your eye," Nancy glared, leaning forward. "You promised. And look, look here."

She reached into the same pocket that contained the key and pulled out a white envelope.

The vampire's stomach twisted in knots, wishing he could turn back time to a few hours ago when this seemed like a decent idea. Then again, if he could manipulate the universe like that, why not go back ten years to a certain boy-crazy teen, convince her to go to a doctor before she feels any pain?

Hell, he'd be happy going back ten seconds, to tell her to keep that damn envelope.

"That's the two thousand you wanted." Nancy tossed it at his feet. "All of it. Paid in full. You don't hold up your end, I will fucking sue your ass in, in, I don't know, Suicidal People's Court. Judge motherfucking Judy will get up all in your case, make you kill me with a goddamned audience watching."

Vlad looked out the window, toward the sign, the crowd outside, the cars going by. He looked at anything that was not Nancy's eyes. He briefly gave thought to granting her wish, the sweet blood coursing from her neck and down his throat, gulping as waves of pleasure washed over him bringing him to that point—

He squeezed his eyes shut for two seconds, then opened them only to have them land on the envelope that mocked him. Vlad used his Croc to nudge it toward Nancy. With Luis's words ringing in his ear, he'd made his decision.

"I'm no hero," Vlad conceded, finally meeting her gaze. "Not your hero. You're asking me to play God, and I won't do it."

"WHAT!?" Nancy balled a fist and slammed the window. "You want to talk about God? Where was He all those nights when I heard my mom and dad crying themselves to sleep? Where was He when my mom quit her job to take care of me? Where was He when medical bills forced us to move to some shitbox apartment and my little brother got his ass beat time and time again at his new school? Where was this motherfucking prayer-sucker when I was on my knees every night begging for relief? For an end? Huh? Tell me!"

"I just—"

"I'll tell you where. In your fucking imagination. That's where! Because any magical super-being with an ounce of mercy should've reached inside me ten years ago to flick off the lights. Don't you dare talk about God. Don't you fucking dare!"

Vlad shut his eyes again and remembered. The grandmother who cried, believing she'd soon see her husband. The soldier who begged for his life, words flowing faster than his blood. The scores of men and women he watched die, seeing the question in their eyes just before their own lights flicked off.

Why?

Vlad wasn't God, but he'd played Him so many times, he fell easily into the role. Too easily.

But this was his first time playing God as a hero. As the light left her eyes, Vlad had almost convinced himself this was what redemption tasted like. Almost.

TWENTY-SIX

"DUDE, YOU GOT A LITTLE, YOU KNOW," Luis flicked the right corner of his mouth before shoving in a chunk of nearly raw steak.

Vlad stared at Luis's plate, where a T-shaped bone floated in a pool of watered-down blood. The sight had to explain the twist in his stomach.

"Hope your dinner was as good as mine." Luis cleaved another slab of dead cow from the bone and plunged it down his throat. "Who knew you could get a pretty good steak at a place named Cracker Barrel? It's like finding an amazing salad at the Cattle Bunker. Which reminds me, we've got to go back there, and soon."

Luis flicked his lip again, nodding at his vampire friend across the table. "It's still there, and fairly obvious the bit of blood is not steak-related."

Vlad wiped his forearm along his mouth, his long-sleeved black shirt absorbing the mix of blood and saliva. A crumpled napkin hit his chest and landed on his lap.

"Manners, please," Luis urged. "You're making us look bad." He paused, poking his fork in Vlad's direction. "Speaking of which, you don't look too good yourself. Did your meal disagree with you? And by that, I mean she changed her mind."

Vlad nodded, a confused look on his pallid face.

"What the hell is wrong with you?" Luis grilled. "Still hungry after your little hospice appetizer? Can't say I'm surprised, so little meat on the bones of those wiping their feet on death's welcome mat. Maybe you can find someone with a degenerative heart condition for dessert, assuming they've got enough in the pump to make it easy for you. Or maybe a fourth-stage cancer patient—"

"Shut up!" Every plate and glass rattled as Vlad's fist pounded the table. "You have no fucking clue. Absolutely none."

"Jesus, Vlad, keep it down. The goal was not to attract attention, remember?"

The vampire took a deep breath, raising his eyes from the blood-filled plate opposite him. He feared being the object of stares, patrons wondering why this pale, casually dressed man was throwing an absolute fit, interrupting the moment of pure joy they were sharing with their chicken-fried steak and cornbread.

Yet the hum of conversation continued without interruption. Forks stabbed hunks of meatloaf into bites two sizes too big, making those tucked-in napkins a wise choice. Spoons dipped deeply into tapioca pudding, the cups brimming with sugary sodas bearing nothing but DNA by the time diners pushed away from the table.

Thank goodness the hospice had chosen one of the few national chains where people came to eat and didn't give a shit about drama. No amount of family arguments or domestic disputes or screaming free-range toddlers were going to keep customers from consuming their gravy-soaked calories.

Still, Vlad would have welcomed some outside interference. He pushed away thoughts of Nancy, the bus, the taste of her blood. But they kept coming back, entering through the mind's back door, which was impossible to lock without the aid of brain-altering chemicals. The vampire had sworn off self-medication decades before, when he awoke in a remote bar in the middle of the Arizona desert, fleeing before he knew if the dozen bodies sprawled about the dark interior would rise with the sun. He wanted to believe they would, that the only thing they suffered from was the consumption of far too much whiskey. Not that he was going to stick around to find out, fearing the truth when ignorance beckoned him like an oasis in the middle of this godforsaken land.

Unprepared to face Luis or the facts, Vlad dropped his gaze to the table, where it again found Luis's plate. As usual, a side of vegetables remained. Luis always insisted on ordering them, as if their constant appearance one day would convince him to partake of "the Earth's foul offspring," the werewolf's description of any edible once attached to roots.

The bone, of course, had now been picked clean, and Luis was surely doing all he could not to lick up the pooled blood.

Vlad knew exactly how Luis ordered the steak, having witnessed it time after time. He'd start with "Raw" and, when the server balked, would follow with, "Fine, less done than rare." If any hesitation remained, he cleared it up with a quick transformation to were-asshole. "If I could kill the fucking cow myself and dig out my preferred cut, I would. Unfortunately, I've been told that would not only violate health ordinances, but rarely is live beef kept on the premises." The server's reluctance would turn to fear, and she'd return to the kitchen knowing she was in for an argument with the sous chef.

Had Vlad known he would not be up for conversation, or much of anything else, he would have waited outside.

Thoughts of Nancy again barged into his head. He mentally slammed a door on them, picturing himself nailing two-by-fours in place even as he heard these invading memories. He shoved his back against the boarded-up entry, only to have a gnarled hand burst through and wrap around his throat, squeezing the life out of him. A cheer went up among those outside, the crowd rooting for his untimely death.

The applause continued even after the vampire ordered his mind to stop such infernal racket, only the clapping wasn't in his head. It was in the restaurant.

Vlad turned toward the excessive noise, noting a long table where twenty or so people stood clapping. All faced a woman seated at the head of the table, her body dwarfed by a formidable wheelchair that looked as if it could plow through six-foot snowdrifts.

The apparent honoree leaned to one side, her head propped between two large cushions. A screen was affixed to the chair by an L-shaped metal armature. She maintained a blank stare even as everyone cheered.

"Lou Gehrig, dude."

Vlad thought he heard something. And why was he thinking about baseball?

"Well, not Lou Gehrig per se," Luis continued. "The disease. The one he discovered."

Vlad tore his eyes away from the woman in the wheelchair. "What? Did you say 'Lou Gehrig?'"

"Yeah, you know, the 'I'm the luckiest person on the face of the planet' speech guy."

"I remember who he is. Did you say he discovered a disease?"

"That's why they named it after him," Luis emphasized.

"Are you that dense? He didn't discover a disease. He had it."

"Well, that certainly gives it a depressing spin. Thanks, Vlad the dismal."

Vlad was no expert in Lou Gehrig's disease, but he knew it robbed sufferers of their body one muscle at a time. Arms and legs shut down. Pretty soon speech was impossible. The mind remained as sharp as ever, and since they could move their eyes, they communicated with the help of a computer, spelling one word at a time by focusing on the letters on the screen.

None of that explained the cheers, however.

"How do you know what she has?" Vlad glanced at the group and found no clues.

"While you were playing with your food—" Luis stopped when Vlad stiffened. "I mean, when you were out in the parking lot taking mercy upon a poor soul, I chatted with some of the hospice folks. Turns out it's actually a celebration."

"And why would they be celebrating?" Vlad imagined piling furniture against his mind's back door, anything to keep the last half-hour from barging in.

"That woman, the Lou Gehrig lady?" Luis nodded as if Vlad had missed the obvious. "Got her assisted-suicide card yesterday. Been waiting weeks."

Vlad nodded thoughtfully as it began to fall into place. Nancy, her death wish, her insistence it be done tonight. While no doubt happy for the woman approved for a death passport, Nancy was overcome with jealousy. Perhaps she'd been waiting much longer for a legal way out only to be rejected. The final nail in her coffin, so to speak.

"Have to say, those hospice people are a pretty jolly bunch," Luis smiled, putting down his knife and fork for the first time since Vlad joined him. "I hope I can be that resigned to the end when it's my turn. Just don't get any ideas, OK?"

Vlad wasn't paying attention. He again focused on the table, the people laughing, and the woman in the wheelchair who would probably be smiling if her body didn't hold her hostage.

With that, Nancy-thoughts blew through the door he had so carefully boarded up, and Vlad could only hope he'd done the right thing.

TWENTY-SEVEN

A MONTH HAD PASSED since residents found out a certain leprechaun had put their futures at risk. Anger reached a point that if Patrick had stumbled across a pot of gold, they would have put it in a place where rainbows don't shine.

Several tenants moved out, preferring a future chosen by them rather than a wrecking ball. A warlock couple managed to secure a room in the Upton Arms for the non-supernatural, determined to keep a low profile (and resisting the urge to cast spells every time someone microwaved fish or popcorn, but feeling justified if it were both).

A handful of trolls headed for the new pedestrian bridge over the interstate. "No one is going to cross that bitch unless they can answer one very simple question," one troll said as he headed out the door. "What the fuck is it with leprechauns?"

Luis heard a few ghouls landed gigs at a traveling carnival, the werewolf wondering how many patrons would go missing before suspicions fell on the new hires. He pegged the over/under at five, double that if the carnival moved more than three times a month.

Ralph announced he and several invisible people were moving as well, but Luis knew that was bullshit, especially when cans of Old Style beer kept disappearing from his mini-fridge long after their alleged departure.

Most stayed, and Luis had no idea if it was out of hope or delusion, leaning heavily toward the latter. A hastily convened meeting among residents nearly ended in a riot when it was suggested elves could bake cookies to raise funds. Incensed, a lead elf went on and on about how his people were not the tree-dwelling, shoe-cobbling, North-Pole-prisoner workers the media had portrayed, then something mass-merchandised cookies and cultural appropriation. No one was paying any attention by that point.

Finding the mood in the community room to be more depressing than a crowd of social influencers arguing who is more famous for the least valid reason, Luis trudged back to his room, metaphorical (at this point) tail between his legs. He laid down, shut his eyes, and wondered if there might come a time he would have to turn into a terrier just to get a night or two in the local animal shelter.

Something whapped against his chest. "Jesus, what the hell?" He lifted his head, willing his eyes to focus on the shape looming above him.

Vlad stood over him in a cloak, a fashion-backward accessory that was more function than form, protecting the vampire in a sunlit room.

"Vlad, what? Something wrong?"

A long, white, bony finger pointed toward Luis. The werewolf sat up, the thing that slapped his chest sliding to his thighs.

It was a newspaper, an item as mythical as the werewolf himself. He noticed a red, poorly drawn circle in the center.

"It's time." Vlad eyes widened as if going into mesmerism mode.

"Time for what?"

"To save this place."

Luis plucked the newspaper from his lap, the beginnings of a headache pulsing at the back of his skull. He lifted his chin as far as it would go, then tucked it to his chest. The throbbing strengthened.

Shit, what day was it again?

"Thursday," Vlad reminded him.

At first Luis, thought Vlad had read his mind, but at his age, the vampire was lucky to surmise correctly. Besides, everyone knew how often Luis lost track of days until the full moon was near.

"What's up with this relic of the industrial age?" The werewolf picked up the paper and saw a thick black circle around a want ad. Luis hoped his friend wasn't suggesting a job was in order, for either one of them. "Far as I know, not many employers are in the market for someone whose skills include walking on all fours and tearing out throats of small game."

"No, the world has enough politicians," Vlad smirked. "But that's not a job ad. Take a closer look."

The werewolf noted the first line, in big bold letters. "ESTATE SALE." The rest was a blur.

He frisked himself, patted his shirt pocket, then each of his pants pockets in succession.

"Here," Luis heard. "Try mine."

The werewolf snagged the reading glasses out of midair (at least his reflexes maintained a sense of decorum) and snapped them open. Slipping them on, the text cleared.

"Furniture, electronics, housewares, collectibles, and more. 7-bdrm, 4-bth home in Vista del Mar district. Everything as marked. No haggling. 7am-3pm Sat. No early arrivals please. 1487 E Avenida del Paz."

The information, and its meaning, finally pieced through the fog shrouding Luis's still-sleepy brain.

"Wait, I thought that sale was weeks ago," Luis looked up. "Am I losing my mind?"

"Yes to both, but I chalk the latter up to your senility," Vlad winked. "The one Lawster mentioned turned out to be at a Breeze home, but not the Breeze home. Not the one I visited, anyway."

"Just how rich can a guy get on undergarment innovation?"

"Never underestimate the power of comfortable briefs."

Luis folded the paper and tossed it to the floor. "If this is the main home, I'm assuming this is where Victor kept his most valuable possessions, right?"

"Based on the gold-brocaded curtains and Thomas Kinkade paintings that still burn a hole in my not-so-immortal soul, I would say that's a firm yes."

"But those things are less a sign of wealth and more an indication that a sociopathic interior decorator was given free reign. I mean, who does that to a house?"

Luis listened carefully as Vlad regaled him with stories of Victor's terrible taste. It was evident in every room, including one consisting of nothing but black velvet paintings of Elvis, including the singer as Jesus and another of five Elvises playing poker. "In any country but the U.S., injuries would result among buyers racing for the exits," the vampire concluded.

"That's the key, isn't it?" Luis concurred. "We live in a nation with a penchant for the appalling. If it's on sale, someone will buy it. Remember, Kinkade made millions, as depressing as that is."

Luis was sure prospective buyers would strip the Breeze home of everything not bolted down, if not a few items that were. That meant the sale would likely be very crowded, making it easier to blend in.

"I know the house fairly well," Vlad volunteered. "Victor had an office on the second floor, a few doors down from the bedroom. My guess is he'd stash any business-related material there."

"Wait, are you saying you want to do a little, uh, shopping?" Luis mused. "If I remember right, you thought it was a dumb idea."

"I still do. But at this point, we're out of options, and I'm not ready to give this place up quite yet."

"You're in? Really?"

A dull thump got their attention. Luis opened the door to see Darnell standing still, his jaw at his feet.

"Looks like I'm not the only one who's shocked." Luis gathered the chin, taking care not to further damage what little flesh remained, and snapped it in place.

Vlad sighed. "We need a plan, but that shouldn't take us long. How hard can it be to steal from a dead man?"

As it turned out, very hard indeed.

TWENTY-EIGHT

"CHRIST, why do we have to meet so fucking late?" Patrick screeched when he answered the door, ushering the group into his room. The leprechaun poked Darnell's chest. "And you, don't even think about putting your undead ass on my couch. Last thing I need is zombie DNA crawling up my rectal cavity and turning me into another you."

"Uuuugghh," Darnell replied, and no translation was needed to know he meant something along the lines of, "My zombie DNA has better things to do than explore your worthless colon."

Vlad noted that Patrick had set up folding chairs arranged in two neat rows opposite the bed, the massaging recliner was wrapped in yellow caution tape. Vlad took a seat in the front row, watching the rest settle in around him, this ragtag bunch of supernatural misfits who looked as if they'd just stepped out of a Stephanie Meyer story written post-bender.

The vampire's gaze was drawn by the single empty chair. "Ralph," he said, reaching tentatively toward it. "You here?"

No answer. Vlad would have reached out but learned a lesson long ago about trying to touch a naked invisible man. It never ended well.

"Henry," Beatrice whispered to shapeshifter, who was definitely embracing his feminine side for the meeting. "Pat the chair next to you to see if it's truly empty."

Henry leaned and put his hand directly on the seat rather than gently probing much higher. A rookie mistake, Vlad knew. Luckily for Henry, the chair was indeed empty.

"And Henry, stow the boobs if you don't mind," Patrick blurted. "You make them look so ridiculous."

"My body, my change," Henry remarked uncharacteristically, as he rarely defended himself to the surly leprechaun. Everyone knew when Henry felt stressed, his gender-related traits could get away from him.

"Good for you, Henry," Vlad cheered with a golf clap. "Be the man, woman, and everything in between you were meant to be."

"When the hell did we get so fucking sensitive?" Patrick snapped, refusing to back down.

"Some of us don't mind when our humanity shows," Vlad said, tugging on his lapels and feeling like a proper gentleman, at least for the moment. "Besides, you're just jealous because if you could change, you'd be six feet, attractive, and a contributing member of society. In other words, the opposite of what you are now."

Henry laughed so hard, he shifted into what Vlad believed was his traditional self, a Mr. Rogers lookalike in a cardigan sweater, a person that could melt into any background. He often joked that he resembled almost every police sketch he'd ever seen thanks to his generic features.

"Fuck you, Henry," was all Patrick could muster.

"I wish you could change shape," Henry spit out. "That way, you could sprout a vagina and go fuck yourself."

"What did you say, boy-o?" Patrick said.

Henry rose to his full height, back ramrod straight, his gaze locked on Patrick.

"You heard me," Henry said, his voice taut with emotion. "I don't just *change shape*. I transition, actually becoming the person you see. It's not a goddamned parlor trick, it's a meaningful transformation into another being. I am that person, heart and soul."

"As long as that person is a Kardashian, right?"

Vlad saw Henry deflate, his body folding in on itself. It was as if someone had shut off the power to one of those noodle-men posted outside used-car lots. The shapeshifter was empty, not even mentioning how he could change into O.J. Simpson as well, though that was nothing to brag about. Or even mention.

A grin crossed Patrick's face, one so dastardly he would have twirled his handlebar moustache if he had one. "Now that we've established our limitations…"

"And it's because of yours, Patrick, that we're here," Vlad interjected, knowing he had to regain the room. "To save your ass. All of our asses, in fact."

Vlad pulled the newspaper tucked into the small of his back and threw it on the bed. Henry grabbed it, his eyes scanning, before handing it to Beatrice. A few seconds later, she gave it to Luis, who tossed it to Darnell.

Five minutes later, Patrick gripped it, his arms shaking. "Fucking Victor Breeze. That prick. But I thought we missed the sale?"

"We did, for his backup home." Vlad crossed his arms and paused as if about to announce the name of the murderer after a long night at the manor house. "This sale is at his *main residence*. Which means it probably has exactly what we're looking for."

The leprechaun tossed the paper to the side and rolled out of bed. "If I remember right," Patrick nodded toward the vampire, "you thought the idea of an estate-sale invasion was about as smart as a zombie applying for student loans."

Darnell groaned in protest. Luis patted the zombie on the back. "He threw you under the bus, sure," the werewolf said, "but look at you. You've survived worse." As Darnell nodded emphatically, Luis cupped his hand below the zombie's head just in case it toppled off.

Patrick went on. "I am not going to that man's house to see all the shit that should be mine. That kind of thing is beneath me."

Beatrice shot a menacing glance to anyone about to say, "Nothing's beneath you, Patrick, present company excluded of course." The room remained silent for a few beats before Vlad raised his hands in surrender. "Patrick, that's not what we had in mind at all."

"If it doesn't involve arson, I want nothing to do with it," the leprechaun said, opening the door.

Darnell began to stand, so Vlad knew he still had about five minutes to plead his case. He thought back to an incident a few years ago, one that exposed Patrick's Achilles' heel. It was a few days before Christmas. The weather was unseasonably warm, and a bored Vlad suggested an outing he'd come to regret.

———

Each member of their motley supernatural crew beamed at the holiday decorations dripping from the mall's atrium, which appeared to be the epicenter of a glitter and candy cane quake. Each of them was wearing an ugly sweater, both to celebrate the season and to fit in. Patrick, of course, opted out of the celebratory dress code because, "I don't want to be confused with any of those fucking sell-out elves who are nothing more than glorified indentured servants bowing to a fat man who uses his only power to make kids happy. Areshole."

With the pitfalls foremost on his mind, Vlad kept a close eye on the leprechaun, feeling dread dripping from every light and ornament in the mall as he waited for the inevitable.

It arrived minutes after the crew spotted, and were drawn to, Santa's workshop. Henry made the first move, getting in line because he wanted to persuade Santa to move to Upton Arms. "Just for the offseason," Henry explained. "Imagine all the hot chocolate and reindeer games."

Just as Vlad was about to tell Henry that wasn't how Santa worked, his eyes landed on the cutest little girl the vampire had ever seen. Just one problem—she was jumping and clapping with glee when she saw Patrick, the only little person in her vicinity since Santa's helpers were teens in green vests and curly shoes.

No more than three years old, the girl had on an oversized Christmas tree sweater, its abundant glitter dancing in the spotlights. Frosty the snowman smiled from her knit cap. If there were a cartoon speech balloon above her, it would have said, "Norman Rockwell, I'm ready for my close-up."

Vlad, however, paid more attention to the burly lumberjack standing behind the girl, the one who appeared to have a "Violet" tattoo peeking from the collar of his red plaid shirt.

Before anyone knew what was happening, "Violet" ran to Patrick and wrapped her arms around him. "Ooohhhh," the girl squealed. "Daddy, look, it's Santa's little helper. And he's so squishy."

A volcanic spew of profanity hot enough to turn the North Pole into the South Gobi Desert washed over the child whose adult vocabulary grew three sizes that day. The lumberjack emerged from the crowd as if stepping off a paper towel label to clean up this mess. In one of the finest examples of elf-bowling Vlad had ever seen, the loving father launched Patrick into a nearby perfume cart, resulting in broken bottles, splintered wood, and a scent that would linger for months.

Patrick, it turned out, wasn't very squishy at all.

————

The scene dissolved in Vlad's mind, but not before it gave him an idea of how to rope Patrick into the harebrained scheme. All he had to do was appeal to the leprechaun's titan-sized ego.

As everyone began to leave, Vlad held up his hands, begging them to hear him out. As Darnell started to sit, Luis pointed to the vampire and said they'd give him three minutes, the time it would take the zombie to settle.

Vlad clapped in appreciation. "Think of a visit to the estate sale not as trip down memory lane," the vampire said. "but as a first-class ticket to Revenge-Ville without attracting firefighters from five miles away. By the time we're done, Vic the Dick will not only be rolling in his grave but wondering who just cut off his balls."

Patrick took a deep breath.

"I'm listening."

TWENTY-NINE

LUIS DROVE down the quiet street dotted with well-spaced estates, manicured lawns, and an asshole-per-capita that was quadruple the national average.

The small bus sputtered and shook as it headed toward its destination on a day when the weather was on the passengers' side. Thick clouds threatened rain, great news for the complexion-impaired whose skin simmered when exposed to direct sunlight.

Luis checked his watch, noting they were right on schedule. The plan was to arrive an hour before the Breeze estate sale began and stake out a spot near the front of the line. The fewer people – and potential witnesses – the better.

The faulty logic revealed itself several blocks from their destination. A lengthy line of budget-conscious customers (*vultures*, Luis thought) had formed, the line starting outside the locked gates where two nattily dressed men wearing sunglasses stood still with hands folded in front of their groins. So much for a quick in-and-out.

"Do these people have nothing better to do on a Saturday than pick over a dead man's stuff?" Beatrice wondered aloud, her forehead pressed to the tinted window.

The answer to her rhetorical question was clearest when Luis drove past Breeze's mansion. No one was simply waiting. They were reading books and playing cards and playing games on their phones. Others dozed on lawn chairs, and a handful of the maturity-enhanced focused on battery-powered TVs long rendered obsolete by tablets.

"Hey Darnell, looks like all your cousins showed up," Patrick tapped the glass. "Line of the living dead."

As the bus rattled past the gates, Luis marveled at the sprawling estate built in the style of Postmodern Garishness. With its portico columns, layered mansard roofs, and turrets on either side, the pastel mansion was a mix of Spanish Colonial and the Addams Family.

"If Disney ever adds Shoot-Me-Now-land, there's its castle," Beatrice said.

Even Darnell chimed in with a "Mmmm, arrgghh," Luis translated it as, "You got that right, sister."

Patrick slapped the zombie on the back. "You know you've put a stain on humanity when a rotting corpse makes fun of your place."

Luis concerned himself with the line of potential shoppers rather than the great heaping gob of structural phlegm standing as a monument to mankind's eighth deadly sin (tastelessness). The crowd was much too large for his comfort, but at least youth was not on its side. The residents of Upton Arms would blend in quite nicely.

Until they didn't, all part of the plan.

Luis rounded the next corner, slowing for a suitable parking spot that would not block a hydrant or driveway, either of which would result in 9-1-1 calls in this neighborhood. He circled back toward the end of the line, literally and figuratively, and wedged the bus between SUVs whose drivers had allowed plenty of space to pull out. *Well, not anymore*, Luis thought mischievously.

Shutting off the engine, Luis stood and called for everyone to disembark, "Heaven help your souls."

"At least those that still have them," Patrick grinned, staring at Vlad.

Henry was the first out, high stepping it as if to show off an outfit of which he was clearly proud. A fashionable though weather-inappropriate duster hid the little black dress he wore underneath. Beatrice followed, hands clasped in front of her and eyes lowered as if in prayer. Throughout the ride, Luis noticed her lips moving, practicing the spell that would get everything rolling.

"Everything OK?" he said, giving her arm a reassuring squeeze.

"Mostly," She raised her eyes to meet his. "It's just so damn long, and…I'm not infallible, as everyone knows. As long as I stay focused, it should be fine."

"Could you have chosen a shorter spell?"

Beatrice shrugged off his hand. "I don't know, Luis, could you change into a were-horse so instead of eating people every full moon, you could give them a hayride? Spells are just long. It's a thing, no matter what you read in those stupid *Harry Potter* books."

"Got it, thanks," Luis said, not getting it all. As far as he was concerned, the *Harry Potter* books had the right idea.

Darnell was out next, hips swiveling from side to side reminding Luis of an unbalanced toddler. The zombie's role was cut and dried as his skin, a part that came naturally to anyone with a low-functioning cardiovascular system. He was dressed to impress as well as draw attention in a Hollywood-inspired outfit involving a loose-fitting red-and-green-striped sweater and worn brown fedora.

It had the intended effect the second Darnell's brown work boots hit the sidewalk. So startling was his appearance that nearly every shopper in the vicinity whipped out their phones to capture this spitting image of Freddy Krueger, the dream-stalker from *Nightmare on Elm Street*. Even those with walkers carefully balanced themselves for a few shots, and several formed a line for a selfie. Luis just hoped Darnell's appetite wouldn't spoil the effect. One ripped-out throat and it would be all over.

"Great look," a woman marveled, slinging her arm slung over Darnell's shoulder and snapping away. "But that nightmare scent isn't coming from Elm Street, is it?"

Lady, Luis thought, *there's not enough Calvin Klein in the world.*

Vlad eased himself out of his seat and stepped to the door, hesitating when he reached the steps. He scanned the skies for any hints the sun could peek through, but the cloud cover was as solid as their plan.

Just in case, the vampire was dressed for an unexpected turn in the weather, barely recognizable in hoodie, sunglasses, and thick scarf. If only he'd been prepared for a turn in circumstances.

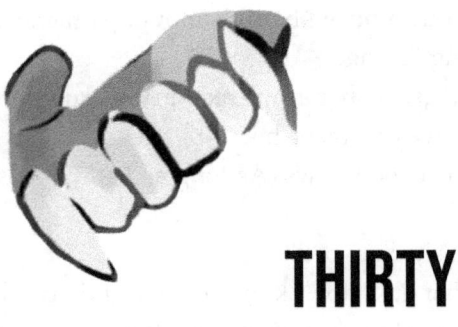

THIRTY

ONCE EVERYONE WAS off the bus, Patrick motioned the group to gather around him. "One thing before we head in," he said, attempting to smile but managing a contorted, and very uncomfortable, rictus. "Beatrice has something everyone needs to stick where the sun don't shine."

The witch, ignoring her husband's creepy look, clarified. "Patrick is talking about your ears." She dug a chewing tobacco tin from her jacket, removed the top and tilted it outward, giving everyone a peek at the scurrying contents.

"Nope," Luis blurted after catching a glimpse. "I got enough problems with fleas and ticks. Not putting that in my ear."

As he watched the insects skitter about, it wasn't so much putting a bug in your ear as it was that bug having a pincer extending from its rear. It was exactly the kind of thing that would lead to a cameo on *You Put What in Where?* orifice.

Beatrice tilted the can for all to see. "These are earwigs. The perfect bug allowing us to remain in contact."

"Because you'll be able to track our screams as that thing burrows into our brains?" Luis shuddered.

Patrick clucked his tongue. "Is it a full moon, because you're transforming into a whiny baby."

"Hold on," Beatrice put up a hand. "These are charmed earwigs. They'll act like tiny audio receivers and microphones, sitting just out of sight. This is the kind of shit the Secret Service can only dream about."

"Nightmare about, more like it," Luis said, ignoring Patrick's sharp look. "Could we just have regular earpieces, the kind that won't set up house in our skulls?"

"Sure." The leprechaun thumped Luis's chest with a stubby finger. "But only if you can scrape together the thousand bucks or so for that kind of tech and fetch it like a good dog."

"I promise you these are safe," Beatrice insisted. "Once they go in, you won't even know they're there."

After a round of sighs, the group formed a line. Beatrice explained all they had to do was place the insect in their ear and the bugs would do the rest. And so they did, the witch watching them into one ear canal after another. After a quick check, everyone was ready to go.

Until everything came to a complete stop.

THIRTY-ONE

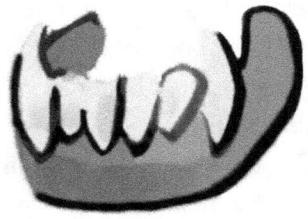

NO ONE NOTICED the weasel skittering amid the bushes in the acreage that was the Breeze backyard, and for that, the weasel was very happy.

Not that it was a weasel, resembling one just enough to be described as such if anyone caught a fleeting glimpse. It was more a half-formed creature with sparse, wiry hair and a pair of disturbingly off-kilter eyes. It also happened to be missing an ear, not the one the creature needed to communicate with the team.

The near-weasel's transceiver clicked to life. "Luis, you in place?" Vlad's electronic voice, filtered through an enchanted earwig, was comically pitchy.

Luis tapped his right ear. "Yeah, for the most part," he responded. While he hadn't been able to go full wolf for quite some time (even the lunar cycle was of little help), he had yearned for something better than were-weasel. He'd focused on squirrel, or at least something cute with a fluffy tail and sharp claws, allowing him to blend in as he traveled among tree limbs that arched gracefully over parts of the mansion.

When he caught his reflection in the backyard pool, an inbred mutant rodent stared back looking as if the product of a mad scientist experiment using DNA contaminated with an extended strand of repulsiveness. And it immediately occurred to him that "Inbred Mutant Rodents" would be an excellent name for a rock band.

Vlad's voice crackled again in the were-weasel's ear. "Do you have eyes on the back of the house?"

"Roger that," Luis replied without thinking. Roger that? When did he drop into a hackneyed caper film?

"Need you to hang on for a bit, little problem."

Luis knew exactly what Vlad meant, since the group always had one little problem. "Patrick," he sighed.

"You got it, Sherlock." Vlad filled Luis on the details since the werewolf had peeled off to the backyard to transform into a creature opposite of cute and fluffy.

The vampire told him things went smoothly at first, the group mingling easily with the crowd of shoppers. They browsed among a plethora of tasteless yet expensive items from tapestries and sculptures. Their only concerns were posed by several yellow-jacketed "hosts" keeping tabs on prospective buyers.

The team split up and went about their assigned tasks, Darnell up first as the main distraction.

"He could make a fortune as a fake Freddy Krueger, as long as he didn't eat his customers," Vlad complimented. The zombie was the perfect crowd sponge, gathering more attention than the shelves lined with Precious Moments figurines. The vampire watched closely as Darnell swept through one room after another, a makeshift entourage in tow. Vlad took special note of the burly men and women in dark suits shadowing Darnell, a security detail that counted eight at this point. It was a number Vlad was sure could be handled.

"Only you were wrong," Luis interrupted. "Because of Patrick."

"Well, yeah," Vlad continued. "Not Patrick, though. Henry."

Luis got a sick feeling in his were-weasel stomach as Vlad described what happened next.

As Henry waited for his cue, Vlad ducked upstairs via an obscure, rarely used back staircase that Breeze forced the vampire to use when visiting. If all had gone according to plan, Luis the were-squirrel would have headed to the roof and looked for Victor's office. Once located, Vlad would summon Beatrice to cast the necessary spells to ease past any suspicious personnel (easy) before divining the combination of the safe (difficult).

Everyone knew Patrick had just one job, to monitor the security team. With everyone in place and the leprechaun giving the all-clear, Vlad would secure whatever treasure Victor had in his safe as Henry went full-blown Kardashian, a distraction that undoubtedly would keep everyone busy downstairs, especially the guards.

And that's where things seemed to be going, Vlad told Luis, until the green giant appeared.

"Wait, what?" Luis said, dividing his attention between the ever-curious update from Vlad and staying out of sight. "We don't have giants."

"Right," Vlad sighed. "Worse, he was far from jolly. Remember the bouncer from the bowling alley?"

"The one who wanted to use Patrick as a human gutter ball?"

"The one and only. I almost didn't recognize him in his green blazer, but he sure as hell recognized Patrick based on the expletive-filled shouts that bruised a lot of ears. By the time I got to the living room, Patrick was refusing to back down, looking that giant straight in the knee."

"Not sure I want to know what happened."

"Here's a clue. While not the most aerodynamic person I know, Patrick's flight was about two seconds long and covered thirteen feet before landing on, and breaking, a coffee table that he now owns."

"We didn't really need Patrick—"

"Unfortunately," Vlad cut him off, "Henry saw what happened and started getting nervous."

"No."

Luis cringed as Vlad detailed, blow by blow, the hectic scene. The real trouble started, as real trouble often does, with voluminous breasts. Luis giggled though, when Vlad stumbled over a description of Henry's spontaneous boob enlargement, repeatedly referring to "ample bosoms," right out of a Victorian romance.

"Big tits, Vlad," Luis encouraged. "You can say it."

He couldn't.

"Beatrice couldn't handle it," Vlad went on. Even as Henry was a third to an as-yet unidentified female Kardashian, the witch disappeared out a side door. That made Henry even more anxious, Luis enduring a flurry of "ample bosoms" in Vlad's telling.

And that is when Darnell went full zombie.

"The Freddy thing was working fine until Henry blew up," Vlad related. "Darnell moaned, then tripped over the carpet, taking a few stumbling steps to catch his balance. Then some woman in a *Walking Dead* T-shirt screams, 'Walker, it's a fucking walker!'"

"So, in the show, a walker is a zombie," Luis mentioned.

"No shit, Luis. Don't were-splain to me. Anyway, Darnell falls into her and may or may not have bitten her. By that time, all hell had broken loose."

"A complete and utter shitshow," Luis summed up, glancing at himself and realizing his part.

"It's down to you and me, Luis," Vlad cautioned. "I just don't think that's going to be enough. It's time to abandon ship."

Luis looked at a tree across the lawn, his eyes following its branches. He told Vlad to hold on. "I have an idea." Scooting out into the open unnoticed (or so he was fairly certain), he jumped onto the trunk and skittered among the branches to the roof, slipping quietly among the eaves. His look may have been awful, but his claw-work was exquisite. Within moments, a small out-of-breath mammal was telling a vampire through enchanted insects that he'd made it to the northwest corner of the second floor. "Say again?" Vlad begged.

"To repeat, I'm on the second floor, northwest corner," Luis gasped.

"How the hell did you get there?"

"Let's just say I decided that if I'm a were-weasel, I'm going to be the best were-weasel on the planet. And one other thing."

"Yes?"

"You need to get here now."

"Why is that?"

"Because," Luis breathed heavily, "the woman listening to a were-weasel talking to himself is getting really freaked out."

"Where are you exactly?" Vlad said, trying to remain calm and failing miserably. "Describe it exactly."

"Based on the overly large desk and the woman freaking out behind it, I'd say Breeze's office."

"Got it, be there as soon as I can."

Luis's earpiece crackled to life again, and he listened to Vlad calling for the rest of the team. He went through the names with no answers. Tried it again with the same result.

The were-weasel imagined the worst. Patrick dangled from a ceiling fan set on low. Photos of half-Kardashian Henry were lighting up AARP's X account. Darnell had commandeered a radio from the security team and was asking for more brains—er, cops. Henry hung from a ceiling fan twirling on low. Henry was besieged by fans.

And here he was, a moving target for a woman armed with a titanium golf club and a desire to whack the head off a mutant rodent. It couldn't get worse.

Could it?

THIRTY-TWO

VLAD HAD JUST two problems to overcome before he could meet Luis. They were, according to their name tags, Alphonse and Tonya, and they stood in front of a staircase that just ten seconds ago was empty.

Worse, they were looking squarely at Vlad, who looked extremely suspicious with not one estate sale item in his hands while heading into a prohibited area.

"Sir, the stairs are off limits to shoppers," Tonya stated in a voice that could have been AI-generated, her stance wide and voice calm.

"Sorry," the vampire muttered, knowing if this had been the early nineteenth century, both would be under his hypnotic sway in seconds. Or he'd simply turn into a bat and fly past them. Instead, he returned to the kitchen wondering if there might be another way. Perhaps a drainpipe or lattice? That's how they did it in action movies and rom-coms.

That's when he noticed an old guy with a screwdriver in his hand and determination in his eyes. The seventy-something stood on the kitchen island and was methodically removing the screws that attached an elaborate brass rack to the ceiling. The pots and pans that once hung from it likely were sold in the first minutes of the sale, not that this fact deterred the handyman.

Vlad turned and raised his arms toward Alphonse and Tonya. "Are you seeing this?" he said, motioning to the man everyone was now staring at.

Alphonse strode forward and tugged on the man's pants cuff. "Sir, that is not for sale," he prodded.

"The hell it ain't," the man said, the rack hanging precariously from its last few screws. "The ad said everything must go. And this is going with me. Give you five bucks for it."

"Sir!" Alphonse shouted, wrapping two hands around the man's ankles and pulling him off the counter, the rack crashing to the ground. A collective gasp went up as the man eked, "OK, ten bucks," as he lay on the floor. Vlad took advantage of the brief disruption in the time-space-sale continuum to head back to the staircase, having an idea of how to get past Tonya. He approached her with a stricken expression.

"I must ask you to return to the sale," she said in a way that let Vlad know it most certainly was not a request.

"Sorry," Vlad stammered, stumbling slightly and using his sickly pallor to his advantage. "Uh, you know, just looking for the bathroom."

"There are portable toilets set up outside for buyers."

"Tried, they're occupied. I really need to go and can't always control it, my enlarged prostate—"

"I am not interested in your medical condition, particularly as it relates to malformed organs peculiar to the male. I must insist you return to the sale."

"But—"

"Sir! I won't ask again. I am forced to disclose I am authorized to use force when necessary." She glanced down at the utility belt wrapped around formidable hips. There were canisters and batons and prods. Vlad half-expected to see a Batarang.

The vampire slapped his hand to his stomach and prepared to go full-fake diarrhea attack when something very odd caught his eyes. Tonya's utility belt inexplicably shifted, as if someone gave it a slight tug. A small black box disengaged from the belt and floated upward like a spaceship awaiting to dock. It paused less than an inch from Tonya's neck, the guard so focused on Vlad she didn't notice. Until a tiny electrical arc flashed between the device and the guard's skin. Tonya crumpled in a heap.

"Ralph," Vlad muttered.

"Vlad," the invisible man answered.

"Thanks."

"Sure. And thank *you* for throwing such an entertaining, ass-backward, fuckery of a heist. The least I could do was Taser a self-important security guard, knocking that off my bucket list. Again. Never gets old."

The Taser dropped to the ground.

"Ralph? You still there? We could really use you right now."

Nothing. Vlad bounded up the stairs, tapping his ear. "Luis, almost there."

"Hurry!" Luis yelled, before there was a slam and the sorrowful "yip" of an injured animal.

THIRTY-THREE

VLAD LOOKED at the woman's golf club, eying it as a caddy might. "What is that, a driver? I'm thinking this particular hole needs an iron."

The "hole" objected. "Really, Vlad?" the Luis/creature said. "She's ready to bash my head in, and you're making weapons recommendations?"

"Shut up, just shut up," the woman shouted, waggling the club in Vlad's direction as the vampire closed the office door, hoping security was still busy below and that the widow Breeze's voice didn't carry far enough to alert them to any trouble.

Vlad needed all of three seconds to judge the woman based solely upon her looks, and she certainly did not disappoint. Had he not known Victor Breeze so well, the vampire might have been able to consider any merits she might have, which at this time was limited to her inability to correctly hold a golf club. But he did know Breeze, intimately. Here was his perfect trophy wife, with a lithe athletic body and an exquisite face marked by high cheekbones and piercing blue eyes. An ample bosom, of course. The fact she was blonde completed the image that had been in Vlad's mind ever since he discovered he'd married. Dressed as if she just came off the tennis court, the woman waggled a golf club as if it were a baseball bat, a vast mahogany desk between her and her uninvited guests.

"I can understand why you're upset given the, uh..." Vlad shot a look at the nearly hairless, heretofore unclassified mammal trembling in the corner. "Circumstances. However, trust me when I say we mean no harm."

"It's pretty clear the only one who means harm is the one holding the club," the small mammal squeaked, an observation followed by the loud bang of metal on wood as the presumptive Mrs. Breeze slammed the club on the desk. Vlad put his hands over his head as if the driver, again pointing at him, were loaded. "I know this probably all seems pretty strange," he said in a voice half comforting, half threatening. "But there's a reasonable explanation."

"Really," the woman argued, moving the club toward a cowering Luis. "You're telling me that having a horrible, twisted creature—"

"Hey," Luis protested. "Uncalled for."

"—who can talk like a fucking mutant Mr. Ed is totally reasonable because you have an explanation. Are you fucking for real?"

"Funny you should ask that because a fair amount of people don't think I'm real. But I most assuredly am." Vlad paused and bowed with an unnecessary flourish. "My friends and I are here to collect on a debt incurred years ago by your late husband."

"Not my concern," she barked. "The only thing you and the freak of nature need to do is get the fuck out or the next debt incurred will be your caved-in forehead."

"Fine." Vlad kept his hands steady in front of him, workable as a defensive posture or sign of surrender, whichever would be needed. "But again, we mean you no harm."

"That's what an alien invading force would say," the woman countered.

"You think we're...?" Vlad trailed off, realizing if he was going to surrender to anything, it was to this woman's lunatic beliefs. He glanced around the room looking for, well, he didn't know exactly. But somehow, he had to take control of the situation without hurting, maybe even killing, the very upset Mrs. Breeze.

Luis remained huddled in the far corner, his size making him useless in any fight in which he couldn't out-ugly his opponent. Mrs. Breeze, on the other hand, not only wielded a weapon but was shielded by a desk whose dimensions likely compensated for the buyer's shortcomings in other areas. To Vlad's left was a closet, its door cracked open just enough to reveal a teetering stack of file boxes as well as a golf bag, explaining the widow's weapon of choice.

"Look, Mrs. Breeze..." Vlad begged, struggling to find the words that could comfort a woman facing a pale, gaunt man and a creature out of a Walt Disney nightmare.

"Wait," she interrupted, her eyes going from Luis to Vlad. "How do you know who I am?"

"Uh...Instagram?"

Her face flashed pleasant surprise before returning to its natural, and enraged, state. "Fine, but who are you and what are you doing here? And how is it you're a fucking Dr. Doolittle to the world's ugliest animals?"

"Excuse me, but Dr. Doolittle was the only one who could talk to animals," Luis interjected. "I actually talk."

"Not the point, Luis," Vlad pointed out.

"That thing has a name?" Mrs. Breeze asked, brows furrowed in confusion. "And it's Luis?"

Vlad cleared his throat. "Maybe if we did this one question at a time. "

"Fine. Who in the exact fuck are you?"

"Good, OK. I'm an old friend of your husband's. Er, your late husband. We met years ago and let me say how sorry I am for your loss, you must be devastated after just, what was it? Eight months of marriage?"

"Oh please," Mrs. Breeze sighed. "You don't mean that any more than anyone else who's said the exact same thing."

"No, I don't," Vlad agreed. "He was an asshole."

"Yes he was, which is why as soon as I sell the house and all the crap in it, I'm gone. You understand why I'm not letting anyone get in the way, especially a pasty-faced asshole and the Creature from the Ass-Crack Lagoon."

"Such a way with words," Luis muttered.

"How about we all go back to the sale and forget this happened?" Vlad suggested. He may not have been able to hypnotize anyone, but he could stall with the best of them.

"Too late," Mrs. Breeze said, Vlad followed her eyes to the portable radio on the corner of the desk. It was within snagging reach of the club, and Vlad knew he wasn't quick enough to get there first. He tapped his ear to wake the earwig, which had fallen silent. "Beatrice, if you can hear me, we need your help ASAP."

Mrs. Breeze stiffened, Vlad sure she was about to make her move. A glance at Luis revealed a creature losing what little fur it had, falling off in clumps.

"Luis," Vlad muttered from the side of his mouth, "this is a good time to turn into something useful."

"I'm freaking trying," Luis stammered as another patch of fur peeled away.

The high-pitched squeal of a door long in need of oil was followed by the appearance of Beatrice. Vlad exhaled with relief. "Beatrice, thank God."

The witch looked from Vlad to the were-weasel to the woman who appeared ready for the driving range. "In the flesh, more than I can say about Darnell and, well, let's just say there are a few fewer fans of zombie movies."

"What—" Vlad started, but Beatrice cut him off. "Now is not the time as we seem to be in the middle of something with this woman wearing far too much makeup and holding a, what is that, a three-wood?"

"Driver," Vlad corrected.

"Too much club," he and Beatrice said at the same time.

"And just who the fuck is this old hag?" Mrs. Breeze yapped, waving the club for emphasis. "You know, forget it, doesn't matter. This will all be over soon, and you asswipes will be getting a free Uber directly to jail."

Vlad had no idea what Mrs. Breeze was saying because he was focused on Beatrice, specifically that the witch's eyes were closed as her lips moved. Was it too much to hope it was a spell to turn the golf club into a snake? And if there were no spells for that, why not?

"A lockbox," Beatrice intuited, arms rising at her side like divining rods. "In this room. But I couldn't quite find it in her booze-soaked mind. Going to need another ten minutes or so."

The alarm in Mrs. Breeze's eyes told Vlad that Beatrice was right on track. But he also was sure they didn't have two minutes, let alone ten.

"Shut up!" Mrs. Breeze shouted, bringing the club down once again for emphasis. That was when the were-weasel made his move.

Luis leapt for the club head, wrapping his pink body around the business end and hanging on for dear life as Mrs. Breeze waved it over her heads. She brought it down once, twice on the desk, the vampire wincing with the soft thump of mammalian hellspawn striking oak.

She swept the club in a broad arc, crashing into the monitors and sweeping all three onto the floor in a tidal wave of glass and plastic.

"Vlad, a little help!" Luis cried as Mrs. Breeze paused briefly on her backswing, looking to hurl the club through the window.

Vlad lunged, grabbing the driver and wresting it away from Mrs. Breeze, though not in time to keep Luis the flying were-weasel from slamming into a garish Kinkade portrait of a lighthouse, sending both artistic and biological tragedies to the ground.

Revealing a small safe.

"Fuck me," the vampire, the witch, and the widow said in perfect synch and different tones.

With the club safely in his hands, Vlad backed away from a stunned Mrs. Breeze, who slumped into the office chair in defeat. He peeked toward the floor at the creature who may or may not have seen better days.

Vlad stumbled to the weasel-thing's side. "Luis? You OK?" The creature didn't stir. Vlad took that as an, "I've been better." The vampire reached for Luis when a sharp rap at the door got everyone's attention.

"Mrs. Breeze," came a voice on the other side. "Everything OK in there?"

"No," she said, her voice reenergized. She leaned forward for emphasis. "Get in here and take care of these assholes." A very smug Mrs. Breeze turned her attention to Vlad. "You're fucked now," she seethed. The vampire had no time to agree as the door burst open in a spray of splinters, followed quickly by three burly, well-dressed men stumbling in with Tasers at the ready.

"Jesus, did you even try the door before kicking it open?" Mrs. Breeze said, voice still dripping with venom in a way that convinced Vlad it was her resting bitch tone. "It was unlocked. That shit is coming out of your paycheck."

OK, Vlad thought, *stalling is no longer a valid option. These guys are itching to Tase someone.*

He tapped his enchanted earpiece. "Beatrice?" he whispered. "Could use a spell right now. Maybe a *hocus-don't-fuck-with-us?* Or *abra-cadaver-these-assholes?* Not picky right now."

Beatrice shot the vampire a side-eye. "Really?" she exclaimed so everyone could hear. "You're going to throw magical stereotypes in my face right now?"

The head guard, or so Vlad assumed based on his larger utility belt and roll of zip ties, nodded toward his employer. "Ms. Breeze, you OK?" Without waiting for an answer, he requested permission to take care of the situation "using extreme but non-lethal means."

"Make it lethal, I don't give a shit," she said with a smugness remarkable even for a trophy wife. "As long as I can watch."

Vlad thought he heard the tinkling of glass. He looked down toward the unfortunate blend of picture, glass and Luis, and noticed two things —the were-weasel was conscious, and it wasn't a were-weasel anymore. It was more a schnauzer mixed with a lab accident, and it was getting larger.

"Uh, boys?" Mrs. Breeze jumped from the office chair and pointed toward the mammal-thing. "Do something."

The second guard stepped forward, raised his Taser and shot Luis, the spikes embedding themselves in the animal's flank. The crackle of static mixed with the scent of burned flesh.

"Bad move, chief," Vlad observed. "You just pissed him off."

The vampire stepped back, knowing what came next. Within seconds, Luis grew to respectable werewolf dimensions, saliva dripping from razor-sharp fangs that lined a formidable snout.

"You guys are going to need bigger stun guns," Vlad said to Mrs. Breeze. "It's a great show and will get even better if I authorize lethal means."

"Shut up, Vlad," Luis chastised before he stood erect, putting his snout to the vampire's ear. "Not sure how long I can hold this. You need to get into that safe."

The guard dropped his Taser without a word, the other two following his lead.

Vlad turned to Beatrice. "Might you be able to worm the combination out of our friend?"

The witch closed her eyes. "Give me just a bit."

Between Luis struggling with full-on werewolf and Mrs. Breeze looking for any opportunity to run, Vlad knew they didn't have a bit. He wasn't worried about the rent-a-cops, one of which had pissed his pants. He feared the commotion would draw others, perhaps even the police. There would be much explaining to do.

"Thirty-six," Beatrice uttered.

Vlad went to the safe and turned the knob right to thirty-six.

Silence as the world stood still.

"Twenty-four."

No, Vlad thought. It couldn't be that easy.

"Oh my god, seriously?" Beatrice said, eyes wide.

"Don't tell me. Thirty-six?" Vlad said, rotating the knob to thirty-six. He yanked on handle.

Nothing.

"Vlad, there's a fourth," Beatrice divined. "She's thinking of a digit, but I can't see it. It's a blur. And, for some reason, red."

It had been a long time since Vlad needed his sensitive vampire touch to crack a safe. Late eighteen hundreds, a bunch of crazies who called themselves the Hole in the Wall Gang. They paid well and never asked questions, two attributes that—

"Vlad, the safe?" Beatrice reminded.

The vampire snapped back to the present. "Sorry, right. If you could just knock everyone out…"

"You're a very demanding vampire." Beatrice looked at Mrs. Breeze as if for a reaction, of which there most definitely was. The witch reached into her pocket, threw some dust in the air, and mumbled a few words. With that, Mrs. Breeze and the guards collapsed on the floor. "That'll last at least ten minutes and when they wake up, they won't remember much."

Vlad patted Luis on the back. "And you, my friend, need to return to a form that won't lead to posts with the hashtag 'I told you they existed' I'll have this safe cracked in a moment or two."

Already, Luis's fur was beginning to retreat, revealing human flesh. Still, a naked man was going to attract nearly as much attention as a werewolf. Vlad peeked inside the closet, noting how the guards had already become glassy-eyed. He snagged wool slacks, a cardigan, and slippers. Seemed Vic the Dick liked to get his Mister Rogers on when in the office.

"Vlad, you sure you've got this?" Beatrice said with a note of doubt that hit the vampire where it hurt.

The vampire thought of the years ahead if Upton Arms closed. Would he have to hunt again? Kill? Would instincts drive him to do anything it took to survive, rather than live out his days peacefully and accept death when it was near?

What about Luis and Darnell and Henry and Ralph and Beatrice?

Or Patrick? *Nah,* Vlad thought. *Fuck Patrick.*

"I said I've got this," he repeated, hoping it didn't sound as angry as he felt. "Seriously, it won't take very long. We've come all this way. Can't give up now."

As soon as his cohorts left, Vlad checked on the nearest guard, whose eyes began to flutter.

"Ten minutes my ass," Vlad whined More like five, given Beatrice's waning powers. He had to work fast.

THIRTY-FOUR

VLAD PLACED his ear above the safe's dial, only because that's how he'd seen it done in the movies. After entering the first three numbers, he would listen for a telltale click, the last tumbler falling into place. How difficult could it be?

After more than twenty attempts, Vlad had the answer— exceptionally difficult. He was running out of patience and, more importantly, time. He took a deep breath and took a step back to think even as he envisioned an hourglass with the last few grains dropping toward "You're screwed up." He again studied the safe, a basic version with combination dial and handle. Was Victor Breeze the type of man who settled on ordinary, especially when guarding his most cherished secret?

Not at all.

Vlad leaned in close, rubbing a pale finger over its surface, circling the dial once, twice, then under the handle.

There. Amid the powdered metallic gray paint, a smooth spot. He leaned in closer and saw a small square reflecting the light. At the same time, he flashed back to Beatrice's words. She said she sensed a "digit." Was it significant that it was "digit" instead of "number"?

That's when his own tumblers fell into place. Vlad didn't need a final *number.* He needed a *digit,* one to place over what he was sure was a biometric sensor, the final piece of the safe puzzle. But where was he going to get—

Shouts erupted from downstairs. Rapid footsteps. A slamming door. It was now or never. "Sorry, Mrs. Breeze," only he wasn't, not at all. He hunched over her still unconscious body and focused on her carotid artery, noting its slow and sensual pulse. He imagined the sumptuous flow of life just beneath the flesh, the ecstasy it would deliver. He felt his fangs slide into place and lock, then used them to slice off her right index finger at the second knuckle, a surgical separation. He took a handkerchief from his back pocket and tightly wrapped it the wound.

Vlad returned to the safe, twirled the three numbers and touched the fingertip to the reader. After a faint beep and satisfying click, Vlad twisted the handle and swung the door open to reveal papers, envelopes, and binders. Vlad brushed them aside and saw the lockbox in the back, just as Beatrice had conjured.

"Got you, you beautiful son of a bitch." Vlad gripped the treasure, tucked it under his left arm, and eased open the office door. Peering out, he counted at least five members of the security team heading toward him. The vampire locked the door and went over his options. He could hide and cower or summon his supernatural strength and attack. The latter would require a time machine and going back to 1922 when he still had supernatural strength. The thought of turning into a bat flitted through his head, but he knew that would result in a more pitiful version of Luis's were-weasel.

The window, perhaps? Not optimal but based on his options, the best of the worst.

Vlad lifted the window sash and squeezed onto a narrow ledge. He felt his fortune change for the good when he noticed a drainpipe just two steps away, and it led to the angled tile roof.

It beats a trellis, he thought as he made his way to the escape route. He tossed the lockbox up to the roof and froze, hoping it wouldn't come sliding down. He counted to five and, with the box secure, gripped the pipe and knew immediately why Crocs are best for lounging rather than climbing. The first Croc tumbled to the bushes below as soon as he tried his first step up the wall. Vlad abandoned the second Croc, peeled off his socks, and scaled the pipe to the roof. The skulking brought joy to his heart, reminding him of hunts in Victorian England when he wore, well, he didn't quite remember the details. Except that Crocs were not involved.

Once safely on the roof, Vlad tiptoed across the tiles, surveying the crowd below. Toting furniture, paintings, porcelain figurines, and other booty from the sale, they streamed toward the front gate. He could find another drainpipe, maybe even a trellis, to slip down and blend in with the other shoppers. It was the perfect plan.

Until he noticed how some patrons were walking fast. Others began running. Then the screaming started.

"Shit," Vlad whispered, until he realized it would be easier to escape among a fleeing horde. The chaos was a stroke of luck.

Moments later, Vlad saw it was a stroke of Darnell. He watched in admiration as the zombie lurched amid the crazed shoppers in a dead-on impersonation of a flesh-eating zombie (learning later it was no impersonation due to temporary insanity).

"Darnell!!" Vlad yelled.

The zombie took a few stumbling steps, stopped, and turned in a slow circle.

"Up here!"

Darnell looked up, his head wobbling as if about to fall from its delicate perch. Vlad flashed a thumbs-up, Darnell responding with a lopsided index finger in a "We're Number One" gesture. And when that finger was knocked off by a fleeing patron, Darnell's plaintive moan filled the air.

"Hold on!" Vlad screamed over the din, patting his pockets. He withdrew, and tossed the finger to Darnell, figuring the red polish would bring out the zombie's eyes.

Darnell snatched it out of the air and plugged it in. It may not have been a perfect fit, but the zombie moaned happily and lurched along with the terrified public, a pep in his undead step.

So far, so good, a very pleased Vlad thought as he remained undetected and not a security guard in sight. He put one foot in front of another, creeping slowly since he was fairly certain his body would react poorly to a twenty-five-foot fall. When he noticed the large oak growing at the corner of the house, he thought his body was up for a five-foot leap to the safety of a sturdy branch. A quick shimmy down the tree, and he'd be out safely with lockbox tucked under his arm.

He picked up his pace, since a running start was the only way he was going to make that jump-

"Sir!"

Vlad stopped and turned toward the shout. A guard leaned out of one of the garish turrets. "I need you stop and put your hands up!"

It wasn't so much the guard that froze Vlad, but the stun gun leveled toward him.

The rent-a-sentry beckoned with his non-stun-gun hand. "Come inside and let's sort this out." He thrust the Taser toward Vlad. "Or I can let fifty thousand volts decide for you."

Vlad weighed the options. He wondered what was in the lockbox, if it was really something that could have saved Upton Arms. He was about ten feet from the tree, fifteen if you counted leaping distance. When Vlad did the math, it came down to two things, the quality of the guard's aim and the quality of the vampire's stamina.

His equation ended with the realization he didn't have a choice. Vampires don't do well in prison, especially when it comes to afternoons in the exercise yard.

"Sir," the guard implored. "I'm authorized to let you know that based on unusual reports in and about the premises, I've been allowed to use lethal force." Vlad heard a distinctive click. Had the guy really traded his Taser for a handgun? That was a risk Vlad wasn't willing to take. A bullet could seriously damage him far beyond his ability to heal.

"OK." The vampire lifted the lockbox above his head in surrender. He took a step toward the guard when he heard a shout above the screaming. It was not one of fright, but genuine excitement.

"Holy shit, it's OJ!"

Even the guard turned to see where it was coming from.

Sure enough, OJ Simpson (actually, the Henry version of the youthful OJ, a thankful Vlad knew) burst from around the corner. The shapeshifter had gone way off script, fitting in well with the way the day had gone.

The ad-lib gave Vlad one more idea. He took a step toward the roof's edge. "Henry! Henry!!"

The OJ figure came to a quick stop, legs running in place. Once Henry as OJ got going, there was no stopping him.

"Henry! I mean, OJ! Catch!!"

Like an arthritic John Elway, Vlad hurled the lockbox toward Henry, who snagged it with both hands before cradling it in his right arm. He shot his left out in front of him, straight-arming three would-be tacklers before hurdling over a suitcase dropped by shopper.

"Go, OJ, go!!" someone screamed.

The move inspired Vlad to give his own escape one more try, reaching deep into himself for the vampire of old. With the guard riveted by OJ, Vlad raced toward the oak.

One foot after the other, pushing off the tile roof with a power he hadn't felt in years. The tree hurtling toward him. Three more steps. Two. One. He braced for the leap, having no idea if that loud crack was the branch snapping, his skull fracturing, or a gun firing. No matter which one, it wasn't welcome news.

THIRTY-FIVE

"THE GOOD NEWS," announced a voice from the heavens, "is that you are alive."

"The bad news?" Vlad struggled to say confirming his lip, tongue, and vocal cords were among the functioning parts of his body, even if just at fifty percent.

"It's going to leave a mark. Several, in fact. But only one I'm worried about."

The unearthly blur floating over Vlad refused to come into focus as the vampire performed a check of his extremities. Toes flexed and knees bent, his below-the-waist area giving an all clear. Fingers dug into what felt like wet grass. Good. Arms responded as well, lifting enough to let Vlad know they were still attached. But the intense pain spreading from the base of his spine, that was concerning.

He switched his attention to the floating smudge, an ethereal cloud that shifted, pulsed, and eventually coalesced into a mouth, nose, eyes. If he didn't know better, Vlad would have sworn it was a face. That made sense, didn't it?

"Who..." The vampire lifted to his elbows, then reality began to swim around him, forcing him back to earth.

The face spoke again. "I'd strongly suggest you get up before things get worse."

That voice. The face. Vlad knew them both, grasping at a name when the world finally came into focus. "Lawster?"

The attorney, the one representing…Patrick? Or Todd? He was at the bowling alley. Mr. McLegalton, that was it. How could anyone forget such a stupid name?

"In the flesh," Lawster replied, taking a seated bow.

Vlad took in his surroundings, the oak towering above. It all came back. The estate sale, the widow, the lockbox. "Shit," he moaned, sitting up.

"That was quite a fall," the lawyer said. "I thought you people could fly."

You people? Vlad thought. *Really?*

"I also thought you wore shoes," Vlad heard, the statement prompting him to look at his feet. They were indeed bare.

"I was wearing shoes," the vampire insisted. "Uh, Crocs."

"Never admit that unless under oath," Lawster commented.

Before he could defend his footwear, Vlad was jerked to his feet like a rag doll. Pain rolled through him like a tsunami, the hand gripping his bicep keeping him upright. He heard a sharp slap and a split second later, the hand released him, Vlad struggling to stay upright.

"Touch my client again," Lawster threatened, "and I guarantee that by this evening, your new roomies won't be impressed that you're a rent-a-cop."

"I have no idea what you're talking about," a man in a dark suit said, standing erect and recrossing his arms as if to assert his authority. A similarly dressed man stood next to him, and both looked grim. Vlad sensed that, unlike their yellow-jacketed counterparts, these men knew what they were doing.

"I'm talking being arrested for assault and seeing what it's like on the wrong side of a jail door," Lawster said. "Unless you're carrying a badge and some official authority to manhandle innocent people."

Vlad took a deep breath, glad things were coming back into focus, including the pain throbbing along his spine. Once upon a time, a broken back would have been an inconvenience, an injury unworthy of aspirin's healing power. Now he worried he might come apart at the hip, an unfortunate, and convincing, Darnell impersonation.

"If you're suggesting we call police, go right ahead," the other guard said, repeatedly poking the air for...emphasis? Vlad didn't see the point.

"I'll fire up nine-one-one, but not for police," Lawster retorted. "For an ambulance to treat my client before he bleeds out. Then we can call the cops who will want to know why you shot my client in the back."

"What?" Vlad blurted, embarrassed by the alarm in his voice. He reached around and felt a dampness on his lower back. He examined his hand that now had blood dripping from splayed fingers. For the first time in decades, it was his own. How odd.

"Sir," the first guard turned to Vlad, the vampire detecting a flustered tone. "You were—are—a suspect in a theft at the Breeze residence. Appropriate action had to be taken."

"I believe the police will disagree with your reaction to a non-violent offense," Lawster intoned solemnly, Vlad happy his attorney had no idea of the four-fingered Mrs. Breeze. "But for now, I'm taking my client to the hospital."

"Based on your client's condition and the fact he is ambulatory," the security man shot back, "I believe that wound is not from a gunshot, but from hitting the tree."

"Are you serious?" Vlad turned to show them the wound, no doubt a gaping, life-threatening wound "Does that look a scratch to you?" Vlad watched as the guards conferred.

The second spoke. "We would like to conduct a quick search of your person in a way to either confirm or disprove your insistence you've done nothing that would violate the laws of this state."

Lawster rolled between Vlad and the guard. "Son, I can tell by the way you talk that you probably didn't finish the online 'Be a Security Guard in Your Spare Time' course. You have no right to place your hands on my client."

Vlad put his hand on Lawster's shoulder, giving it a reassuring squeeze. "Hold on." He then looked the guard square in the eye. "Go ahead and search."

The attorney rolled forward to intervene, leveling a finger at the guard. "I think my client has suffered enough here, and I will not allow you to put a wooden stake into the heart of the Fourth Amendment too."

Vlad couldn't help but laugh, both at Lawster's vampire reference and the fact that the rent-a-cop had no idea what the Fourth Amendment entailed.

Radios on the guards' belts erupted spontaneously and a screaming Mrs. Breeze filled the airwaves. "Where is my finger? What the fuck happened to my fucking finger?"

"And I think that's our cue," Lawster said as the two guards ran toward the house. "Normally I wouldn't ask, but for expedience, I could use a push."

Vlad grabbed the handles of Lawster's wheelchair and the two rumbled steadily across the lawn, not a person in sight. "How long was I out?"

"Not that long, maybe five minutes or so," Lawster said. "People clear out pretty fast when they think their brains are being targeted by a member of the walking dead."

The image of a lumbering Darnell came to Vlad's mind, the fog dissipating. "What about Luis? Beatrice?"

"No worries, everyone made it back to the bus."

The two raced down the Breeze driveway, the exit in sight and, thank God, the gate was open. Vlad gradually picked up speed, the pain subsiding. He could almost feel the injury healing, reminding him he hadn't lost all his powers.

"Take a left outside the gate," Lawster pointed. "My van isn't far away."

Vlad slowed, snagged by a question that burst through all the confusion. "Lawster, what exactly are you doing here?"

"Right now? Saving your ass. Any other questions?"

"Not what I meant, and you know it. You're not the kind of a guy who would hit an estate sale for collectible plates from the Franklin Mint, or spoons from all fifty states. Again, what are you doing here?"

A moped chugged by, a couple of candelabras strapped to its rear.

"If you remember, hitting the estate sale *was* my idea," Lawster gloated a bit too huffily for Vlad's taste.

The vampire stopped and bent over Lawster in a way meant to be slightly threatening. "True. But not *this* estate sale. How did you know we were even here?"

Lawster broke eye contact for a split second, telling Vlad that whatever came next was probably going to be a lie.

"Yeah, Patrick called."

"No," Vlad cut him off, narrowing his eyes. It was all he could do to keep his fangs sheathed. "He didn't. He doesn't trust you nearly as much as you seem to think he does."

"You guys were already at the sale when he rang. He called from inside a bush or something, saying he needed me to come and get him, that he was in trouble, so here I am."

Vlad may have lost most of his vampire senses over the years, but he was sure Lawster was lying. Still, he let it go knowing this was neither the time nor place. He stalked off, listening to the rattle of wheels as he imagined Lawster rolling to catch up.

Which he did within a minute. Advanced age had even stunted Vlad's stalking-off speed.

"I can help you," the attorney pleaded.

"How?" Vlad whipped around. "As an opportunity for a little day-drinking?"

"Maybe police are on their way. You could use a good lawyer."

"Great. Can you recommend one?"

Lawster stopped abruptly, spun a one-eighty, and headed in the opposite direction. It was a blatant ploy to inspire a change of heart.

It also worked.

"You really think police are on their way?" he shouted to the departing attorney.

Lawster came to a halt, spun, and rolled back.

That was easy, Vlad thought.

"No, I do not think police are on their way," Lawster said calmly. "Cops tend not to take zombie sightings too seriously. Besides, they have a long history with Victor Breeze and his family, all of it unpleasant."

"Really? Like what?"

"Drugs. Prostitution. Rampant biting. My guess is no one is calling—"

"Wait, what? Biting?"

Lawster pushed his wheelchair forward and Vlad joined him.

"This was a few years ago," Lawster related, "when a cop friend was telling me this crazy story about how Breeze kept biting people. It wasn't a Hannibal Lecter thing since Breeze never even broke the skin, not for lack of trying. Still, he and his detective buddies made out pretty well for keeping it quiet."

A few years ago, Vlad thought. Could have lined up with his last visit with Breeze, the tycoon believing he'd been turned into a vampire. The thought brought a smile to Vlad's lips, his first pleasant memory involving Breeze since that fateful night.

"You know, not going to ask," Lawster said, noticing the grin. "But as I was saying, I'm positive we won't be hearing from the police. It would take a gangland slaying to get them to the Breeze home."

"What about a finger-napping?"

"What are you talking about? Nope, let's add that to the 'Don't want to know' bucket. The van is just up here."

As Vlad walked along silently, it sank in that they'd done it. Despite the missteps along the way, damned if they didn't get what they were after. They'd saved Upton Arms.

The flare in his back reminded him of his wound.

"Might you be able to drop me at the hospital? My powers don't include bullet expulsion. At least I don't think so. I've been on the wrong end of torches and pitchforks many times, but I've never been shot."

Lawster chuckled. "Please, Vlad, if you'd been shot where several vital organs hang out, do you really think you'd be able to stand, let alone run while pushing a wheelchair?"

Hell yeah, Vlad thought, *because I'm a badass vampire, bitch*. But he wasn't a badass vampire, not if he couldn't make a five-foot leap to a branch. He should need a wheelchair, not be able to push one.

Lawster reached into his sportscoat and withdrew a pencil, its very sharp tip crusted with dried blood. "I got the idea when that young man fired and missed, the bullet hitting the same branch you grabbed. It snapped, you fell, and I needed to make it look like they'd messed up bigtime, shooting someone in the back."

"You stabbed me?"

"No, it was a spontaneous puncturing to save you. Don't be so dramatic. It's not like it was a wooden stake. You don't need a doctor, just some Neosporin. Ah, my van."

Vlad was torn between clapping Lawster on the back or stabbing it with the same pencil. Figuring the attorney may yet be of use, discretion and laziness won out.

When they turned a corner, Lawster punched a button on his key fob. Vlad heard hissing as the driver's door opened, and a metal platform lowered to the asphalt.

"Need any help?" Vlad offered as Lawster wheeled himself onto the grate.

"Do I look like I do? Hop in the other side and let's get out of here."

Vlad settled in for the twenty-minute ride back to his place, unable to shake his growing suspicions of Lawster. The attorney seemed to know far more about the workings of Upton Arms than he let on. It wasn't just his involvement in the retirement home's finances, or his representation of an angry client with a short temper (emphasis on short). How could a mortal so easily accept the existence of creatures in a world built to refute such miracles? And what was Lawster's relationship with Todd? He was more than a go-between. Wasn't he?

"OK, we're home."

Vlad looked out the window to see the familiar, and welcome, sight of home. The passenger side door slipped open with a whisper. Gripping a rail and lifting himself to his feet, Vlad stopped. "Just one question," he said, keeping his eyes on Lawster.

"Shoot," Lawster smiled. "Wait, too soon?"

Vlad ignored the crack. "Just to be clear, where were you when Patrick called? From inside the bush."

Another split-second break in eye contact.

"I happened to—"

"Do not lie to me again," Vlad growled in his "don't screw with an angry vampire" voice.

Vlad noticed Lawster's knuckles go white as he squeezed the steering wheel. Silence, and the strain, mounted one second at a time. No matter. The vampire could wait all day if it meant an ounce of the truth.

"Just keeping an eye on you," Lawster relented.

"Why?" Vlad considered that question for a moment, then thought of a better one. "For whom?"

"Sorry, I'm not at liberty to disclose my client. Good luck with the lockbox."

The van jerked forward, the door shutting in front of Vlad before Lawster gunned the engine and sped off with a screech.

It didn't matter that Lawster refused to answer. Vlad could find the answer from his pre-vampire days, the days when he was a believer.

Todd was always watching. But why in the hell did he need to do it through another pair of prying eyes?

THIRTY-SIX

OBTAINING the lockbox was one thing, opening it was quite another.

"Luis, for the umpteenth time, no, I did not see a key," Vlad insisted with a loud exhale, his headache intensifying. "At the time, I was more focused on getting out of there after severing a woman's finger and tossing it to a zombie in need."

Darnell moaned his appreciation, raising the finger in question, the red polish faded and chipped. Definitely a little worse for zombie wear.

Once back at Upton Arms thanks to the chauffeur services of one Lawster McLegalton, Vlad followed a rhythmic banging he found to be coming from Patrick's room. The noise was being made by Patrick himself, who was attacking the lockbox with a hammer nearly as big as him as the rest of the Breeze Seven (assuming Ralph was there) looked on. The second Vlad opened the door, Luis asked him for the key.

When Vlad explained that keeping the key with the box was expedient, it wasn't very smart when it came to securing the contents. Still, Luis asked Vlad to check his pockets, and after the vampire and turned them all inside-out revealing nothing but lint and lip balm, the werewolf wondered if the key hadn't fallen into Vlad's shoes, reminding Luis how his nocturnal friend had left the house wearing the most ridiculous footwear he'd ever seen.

That was the one that sent Vlad over the edge.

"Enough with the key and the Crocs," Vlad screamed, feeling a fang-on coming.

"Fine," Luis harrumphed, telling Patrick to carry on. No one said a word as the one-man wrecking crew that was Patrick went from hammer to chisel to hacksaw. Only Vlad cried, "Enough!" when Patrick dragged a sledgehammer out of his closet, the vampire wondering why the leprechaun owned a tool he couldn't even lift. Then again, he didn't want to know the answer since it likely involved criminal intent. He'd had enough lawbreaking for one day.

Patrick tossed the box to Vlad, who spun it in his hands as if it were a puzzle rather than a surprisingly impenetrable container.

"This is where you use your super vampire strength to get what you want," Patrick grinned. "Oh wait, it's a locked box, not an octogenarian wishing you a great Walmart day."

Vlad ignored the leprechaun's cackle, turning the box over a few more times, his faux rumination a stalling tactic. How many times over the centuries had he figured his way out of impossible situations involving a trail of corpses, angry town folk, and the inevitable dead end? He discovered that his best thinking came when cornered. He found a solution every time. Then again, all of them involved abilities Father Time had since stolen.

Vlad snatched the hammer from the bed and slammed the lock once, twice, three times. Not just to open the box, but to release his anger. His efforts failed on both counts.

Luis cleared his throat. "Maybe the key fell out when you tossed it to Henry, and if we went back—"

"Enough with the goddamn key!" Vlad roared, hurling the box at Luis who shocked everyone, including himself, when he caught it inches from his nose.

"Fine. No key. Now what?"

Vlad's shoulders drooped, his spirit at the breaking point. He slumped onto the bed and tried to remember a time he'd been this exhausted.

Maybe it was that time he'd had to outrun fifty or so villagers who'd recently upgraded from torches and pitchforks to muskets. The invention of gunpowder made fleeing so much more difficult. Only this was a different kind of exhaustion, one so debilitating he felt he could find a quiet place to hang upside-down and sleep forever. No more running and hiding—not just from those who meant him harm, but from the person he was. Was he smiling at the thought? Perhaps, if only he could see a reflection to show his true self.

A hand landed on his shoulder, snapping Vlad out of his trance.

"Hon," Beatrice said, massaging the vampire's muscles between fingers and thumb. "You look pale. I mean, even paler that usual, as crazy as that sounds."

"We should put him through concussion protocol," Luis suggested. "You know, test him for possible brain damage. Like in the NFL, only we take it seriously."

The werewolf leaned toward Vlad holding up his right hand. "Vlad, how many fingers am I holding up?"

"Three, but it will be two if you keep this up."

"He seems fine to me."

Vlad pushed Luis away, tired of this game. Tired of everything. But the one thing he was not was a quitter. He motioned for the box, which Luis tossed with a sigh. Again, the vampire twirled it in his hands as if the secret would reveal itself under scrutiny. He kept his eyes glued to the box, its featureless metal hypnotizing him to the point he never heard Patrick mutter, "Fuck this," before opening the closet.

Shouted protests and a flickering orange flame definitely got Vlad's attention.

"Unlike the rest of you tools, this is the right one," Patrick said, holding a metal nozzle connected to a black hose trailing from a tank in the closet.

This, thought Vlad, *is not going to turn out well.*

It didn't.

THIRTY-SEVEN

EVEN AS PATRICK demanded the lockbox while waving a flickering orange flame like a flag at a political rally, Vlad wondered which of Upton Arms' numerous rules allowed the personal use of an acetylene torch. Several paragraphs outlined the prohibition of loud music past six p.m.. More than one page was devoted to the ban of all personal electric appliances used for the storage and/or preparation of food. There was even a section listing all genera and species were not allowed to visit, and oddly specific way of forbidding any visitors at all. Yet he could not for the life of him recall anything that explicitly restricted the use of an acetylene torch.

He knew that at that moment, it was an unfortunate oversight.

"Patrick, if residents aren't allowed to have toasters in their rooms, pretty sure we can't have blowtorches either," Luis remarked from the far corner, as if reading Vlad's mind.

"That's for residents," Patrick hissed, his eyes sparkling in the light of the flame. "I'm the fucking owner, the unelected president of this place. Lord of the manor. No need to change rules because they don't apply to me. Now give me the lockbox and let's end this thing."

With a twist of a knob, the orange flame transformed into a

whooshing blue jet of pure cutting power. Everyone in the room instinctively backed up, giving the flame a wide berth.

Everyone except Vlad, who remained seated on the bed, lockbox on his lap. He had to disarm Patrick before the situation headed into territory requiring a call to nine-one-one.

By the looks of it, the torch would chew right through the lockbox, as it would flesh. The healing power in the room was a fraction of what would be required if Patrick were allowed to complete his task.

The leprechaun turned his attention from the flame to Vlad, specifically to the box on the vampire's lap.

"Vlad, my boy, you can't survive a tan let alone projectile fire," Patrick said as he twisted the knob one more time, the flame sprouting another few inches. "Drop and step away from the box or you may find out how a marshmallow feels at a s'mores party."

Beatrice stepped between Vlad and her husband. "Hon," she appealed, palms up. "We can all agree you've had some terrible ideas in the past. Remember Douche Hats, the baseball caps with sunglasses permanently attached to the top of the bill? Or Gayprons, aprons for men with a hole in the crotch? That wasn't just horrible, but offensive and homophobic. Yet both of those combined aren't as stupid as using a blowtorch in a residential building because Douche Hats and Gayprons won't kill anyone."

"How else are we going to get inside that damn box?" Patrick insisted, the flame dangerously close to a plethora of flammable objects, not the least of which was Vlad.

"Here's the thing," the witch remarked calmly, putting her hand on her husband's non-torch-wielding arm. "If that box burns, melts, whatever...anything inside will be destroyed. And all of this will have been for nothing."

Patrick's bushy red eyebrows turned from angry spikes to confused arches, his expression softening. With a twist of the nozzle, the flame returned to an orange flicker.

Henry shook his head. "You didn't realize that until just now? Did you skip basic science in leprechaun school, or was it all about the benefits of wearing curly boots as they relate to finding the terminus of droplet-refracted light?"

Vlad read the room and everyone in the place thought the same thing. "Oh shit."

Patrick's eyebrows returned to their natural pissed-off position. Finger curled again around the knob, turning clockwise. The flame came back to life a second at a time, Patrick's sneer widening along with it. He twisted again, the spout of razor-sharp reaching six inches. "Size matters," he grinned.

Vlad shot Henry an angry glance to let the shapeshifter know you don't piss into the wind, step on Bigfoot's toes, or insult a leprechaun known to overreact as a way to compensate for perceived shortcomings. Henry noticed the vampire's disapproval based on a body halfway to a Kardashian. Kim, perhaps?

Patrick tilted the flame toward Henry. "Remind me what you said again? Something about boots and rainbows."

As Henry backed toward the door, Vlad took advantage of the distraction. "Luis," the vampire called. "Catch!"

The lockbox arced over Patrick's head, Luis snagging it at chest level. It was a perfect pass. Now all Luis had to do was push Henry out of the way and make his escape with a box that surely could be opened without the use of tools of mass destruction.

Except Luis panicked as Patrick charged the werewolf, flame bobbing. Luis tossed the box right back to Vlad, who froze until the leprechaun swiped at him with the torch. A look of disbelief crossed the vampire's face as he felt a searing burn across his stomach, the familiar scent of scorched flesh in the air as he flipped the box to Beatrice before doubling over in pain.

Even as the box flew around the room, a hollow metallic thud sounding with each catch, Vlad focused on the black stripe scratched across his stomach. Bits of shirt still burned red and yellow along the edges. In the vampire's prime, a burn like this would already be stitching itself back together. His only concern would be the shirt. But this? It was going to leave a mark. With his left hand, Vlad tamped out the cotton and polyester embers. He hesitated to examine his stomach, not sure he was ready to face reality.

The box bounced from Luis to Henry to Beatrice and back again. Darnell's plaintive moans (for being excluded, Vlad believed) were drowned out by Patrick's colorful stream of curse words that formed a rainbow of profanity.

After several minutes, Patrick stopped his chase and leaned against the bed, all eyes on the potentially lethal yet mesmerizing blue jet. "Fine, fuck all of you," the leprechaun growled, holding the torch above his head. "Keep your goddamned box. But you may want to put on your running shoes."

Patrick gave the nozzle one more twist, the flame geyser spouting another three inches, the flame bringing a new light to the leprechaun's eyes.

"Patrick? Love?" Beatrice took a tentative step toward her husband. "What are you doing?"

"Beatrice, dear," Patrick soothed in a patronizing tone. "Have I thanked you recently for keeping up with all the insurance payments on this dump? It means the world." He tapped his chin in thought. "I was going to ask you for one more favor, a spell to tell everyone they might want to move out before flames make the decision moot. But you know what? If you're a supernatural creature who can't outrun a little fire, your days are done. Consider this me doing you a favor."

With that, he tossed the flaming nozzle to the base of the curtains, a wondrous bloom of yellow sprouting along their gauzy length.

Luis stood rooted to the ground, a werewolf in the headlights even as Vlad screamed for everyone to get out. None waited for Vlad's exhortations, having fled the second the flames hit the curtains. Even Darnell reacted quickly, going from shuffle to ramble in less than three seconds.

Luis, however, hadn't budged an inch even as the fire licked at the ceiling.

"Luis, time to go," Vlad implored. "Now."

"No."

Vlad barely heard it above the growing whisper of flames.

"Luis—"

"NO," the werewolf shouted, more defiant than angry. "This is all I've got. This is all a lot of us have. If this place is lost, I'm lost too."

"If you stay here, you're worse than lost. You're dead."

"Exactly." Luis remained riveted by the spreading flames. "Which is why it's time I finally did something to save myself."

Vlad could only watch as fur sprung from Luis's now-bulging forearms. The werewolf stuck his hands into the middle of the flames and pulled. A shimmering veil of fire floated downward and onto Patrick's beloved recliner, which began to glow.

Luis bellowed as cinders caught on his shirt and fur, smoke and the scent of burnt flesh filling the room. The werewolf snatched the still-burning torch from the corner and tossed it onto the recliner. He grasped the bottom of that leather chair soaked with years of leprechaun oil and sweat, a volatile mix upon which flames eagerly fed.

Vlad leapt into the fiery fray, grasping the other side of the recliner and lifting, the blaze spreading to his own flesh.

"Window," Vlad gasped, though Luis had already taken steps in that direction.

It was too late to consider the ramifications of a flaming vampire hitting the rays of sunlight now breaking through the clouds. Vlad fought through suffocating heat as he did the one thing vampires should never do—head toward the light. With his last ounce of strength, Vlad hurled the recliner/firebomb through the windows. Shards of glass sliced his forearms, pain masked by the third-degree burns that turned his skin into a well-done steak.

Vlad looked at Luis, visible now without the recliner between them. His friend was already returning to his former state. "We did it," Vlad would have said had Luis not stared at him with a look that was between relief and horror, the edge going to horror.

Another thing struck the vampire. If the mass of burning curtains and recliner was safely outside, why was his face on fire?

For the second time that day, Vlad passed out.

THIRTY-EIGHT

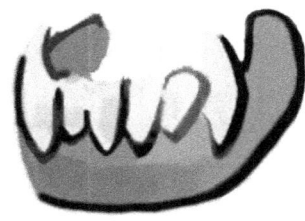

"BE HONEST," Vlad sighed, knowing it couldn't possibly look worse than he felt.

"You look like someone put a fire out on your face with a hot poker," Luis observed, sitting beside Vlad on the vampire's bed. The lamp on the nightstand provided a sickly glow that made everything look worse. "On a scale of one to ten, with one being able to walk into a room and have only half the people faint at the sight, and ten being four out of five funeral directors blaming a lackadaisical cremation, well, you're not even on the scale."

"So it does look worse than I feel," Vlad complained, voice dripping with disappointment.

"Let's just say somebody would definitely swipe left if they saw you on zombie Grindr."

For once, Vlad felt fortunate vampires didn't appear in mirrors, though it would be nice to see himself when checking for things between his fangs. Even as Vlad's seared stomach throbbed, the pain from his inflamed face overwhelmed him, reminding him how having flammable skin was a distinct disadvantage.

"I need some time alone, Luis. If you don't mind."

"Not at all. Only thing worse than watching paint dry is watching a vampire heal. And the paint is a better conversationalist than a whiny vampire."

"Appreciate your support. Please turn off the light on your way out."

Without another word, Luis hit the switch and slipped out, leaving Vlad in the dark. The vampire looked at the glowing dial of the clock, doing some quick math in his head. He'd been out fifteen hours. In his younger days, he would have returned to normal in no more than an hour. Adversaries could throw their worst at him—crosses, holy water, and the most annoying (and common) of all, pepper spray—and he'd be back as strong as ever. Now a measly little fire put him on the sidelines for, well, who knew how long. He was nothing more than a LOV, a Loser Old Vampire. In human terms, he was the elderly guy in cargo shorts and tucked-in polo going to Costco every week to graze the free samples. How he'd fallen from the top of the food chain. He'd settled into no higher than the third tier, with those who drank vegetable smoothies as if nature had ever intended blenders to be used in food preparation.

Vlad knew he wasn't the only one in jeopardy. Before acting as a vampiric mirror, Luis had filled him in on what happened after the werewolf carried an unconscious Vlad back to his room.

As Luis made his way back to Patrick's room to make sure damage from the flaming recliner was contained, sirens approached, no surprise since open flames were a cause of concern at a retirement home. Luis, Beatrice, and Henry ran to the front of the "real" Upton Arms to meet first responders. Even as they insisted everything was fine, that a cooking fire had been contained, the captain remained stubbornly focused on safety and ordered them to take her to the source. The three did so reluctantly, leading her through a maze of corridors impossible to follow without an experienced guide.

"It was all I could do to keep Beatrice from turning the captain into a frog," Luis related. "My mistake was telling Beatrice specifically not to do that, and she went on some harangue about witch stereotypes. Like at her age she could turn someone into anything else, which is just what I told her when—"

"Luis," Vlad was forced to interrupt. "What happened next?"

The werewolf continued, describing the scene as the captain examined the damage, asking if anyone knew the last time the building had been inspected. She had recalled several visits to the main building but said she didn't recognize this area.

Vlad was not surprised. When residents of a supernatural persuasion moved in, they learned how this part of Upton Arms didn't exist on any deeds, maps, or tax rolls. That was thanks to various manipulations of people through bribes, threats, or spells, depending on what worked best. On the rare occasion Upton Arms' most sensitive parts were exposed, first responders were treated to complimentary doughnuts imbued with a very special hex that erased their will (temporarily) and memories of the visit (permanently).

As the captain surveyed the damage, Luis noticed Beatrice holding a cinnamon and sugar Pop Tart (no time to whip up doughnuts) and assumed it contained the necessary ingredients for the required hex. The captain was happy for the treat and was escorted out in a daze.

"We asked Darnell to board up the window because no one knows boarded-up windows like a zombie," Luis mentioned. "He moaned and groaned, probably something about zombie stereotypes. When did legendary creatures get so damn sensitive?"

"And what of the lockbox?" Vlad had asked Luis.

Luis bent and reached under the bed. He put the box on the nightstand, saying all agreed to make a second attempt only when Vlad had fully recovered.

And that was a problem because Vlad knew at once he'd never recover. Not fully, anyway.

THIRTY-NINE

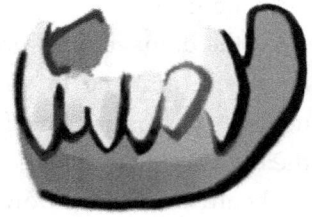

AS HE ROCKED in a chair conducive to napping, it hit Vlad how close he was to the end of this particular road.

He was tired of hiding. Tired of feeding. Tired of bursting into flame.

He wondered what it was like on a beach with the sun high in the sky. Luis had described it once. The cool breeze carried the salt-tinged air over burning sand. Kids raced into the waves, frothy water knocking them back, only to have them bounce right back and try again. Large white birds sailed overhead, their cries echoing off cliffs that rose to protect this idyllic land like a fortress.

Not that idyllic beauty reigned wherever the sand stretched. Luis also spoke of men who overestimated their level of attractiveness, cavorting in bathing suits that suggested they came from a land where mirrors had yet to be invented. Floral Lycra trunks were hardly a match for untethered flesh that constantly threatened to breach containment. But maybe those descriptions were just Luis being a dick. The werewolf had his own untethered flesh to worry about.

To complete what seemed like a fairytale to a man forever imprisoned by the darkness, Luis placed a brightly colored tube under Vlad's nose and flipped up the cap. "And that," he said after breathing in the contents, "is the smell of a hot summer day."

Vlad inhaled as well, scenting flowers and honey and, yes, there it was, even sunlight. That tube now rested in his top drawer, in a handkerchief that belonged to the only man he'd truly cared for.

Vlad found it ironic the substance was called "sunblock," as if that were even possible.

In his mind, he reached for that tube now, popping the cap to remind himself of what humanity smelled like. He marveled at those who lived life in light and dark, how crossing an impenetrable boundary for him was as simple for them as watching a sunrise.

The norms had no idea how good they had it. Even more depressing was the realization that ninety-nine percent of them would choose immortality no matter the cost. It was a debt Vlad would owe forever, and he was ready to make the final payment.

But now, he just wanted to go to the beach, to smell the flowers and honey and sunlight that did not derive from paste in a tube. It might even erase the disappointment that was inside a lockbox that should have remained a mystery because at least it meant there was still hope.

Four or five days after the fire—Vlad had not lost track of time, just felt no need to track it at all—he had been in Beatrice's room as the witch sprang the lock using a lockpick and, according to the witch, "A few clever runes that can also steal elections, but enough about that."

There were indeed detailed plans of Victor Breeze's latest fashion development, making it very obvious why Breeze kept them locked up. It was not out of fear of theft, but of embarrassment.

"From what I make of it," Beatrice said, spreading the prints on her desk, "he'd developed polo shirts with elastic hems for easy tucking."

"And simple emasculation," Luis added.

The heist, the escape, the fire—it had all been for nothing.

That was the one thing Vlad could identify with.

FORTY

EVEN AS BEATRICE was breaking the unwelcome news to Patrick—that Victor Breeze's last fashion "do" was a fashion "don't" —Vlad regretted the team's decision not to restrain the leprechaun prior to releasing the unwelcome news. The vampire noted the many breakable objects within reach as the involved parties had approached Patrick in the community room.

The idea of elastic-hem polo shirts did not sink in right away. Upon the revelation, Patrick broke into the kind of jig rarely seen outside commercials for a certain cereal. He shared his vision of a string of stores selling stay-tucked shirts with a sales pitch involving the term "from nuts to butts." Even after Beatrice calmly explained that no man over the age of ten would wear such a shirt—tucking, after all, was an easily learned skill—Patrick remained enthused. Until Luis showed him a site on Etsy that sold such shirts, with models that appeared to be no older than six. And the models looked to be very embarrassed.

That's when Patrick hurled Luis's laptop across the room before storming out. The werewolf now was on his knees gathering glass shards into a small pile and lamenting the loss of his life's work.

"Writing was my way of escaping this place, this life," Luis fretted. "Now it's gone, just like that. Like everything else."

Vlad was torn between offering a comforting shoulder to issuing a swift kick to the ass. "Are you saying you didn't save anything to the cloud?"

"Never trusted it. You put something there and suddenly you have the National Park cops at your door asking about a series of mysterious wolf attacks back in 1963."

Vlad stifled a laugh and refrained from commenting on his friend's crazy conspiracy theories, in no mood to start an unending debate about alternative facts and fake news. Let sleeping werewolves lie. Instead, he plucked the damaged-beyond-repair laptop from the floor. "Did you print out anything?"

"A bit." Luis brushed the carpet with the whisk broom absentmindedly, the swishing slowly putting the vampire to sleep. "But not much. Couple of poems. A short story or two."

Vlad put the computer on the ping-pong table. "The hard drive might still be good. You could take it to a guy, have him hook a couple of wires or whatever, transfer it to a disk or something."

"A disk? You mean a floppy disk, the kind we can get after time-traveling to the mid-1970s when you could store as many as twenty photos on a single magnetic circle just three inches across? And it only took five minutes to download an entire book?"

"You know I mean a compact disc. You can be such a were-dick sometimes."

"Oh, a CD. That zips us back to the 1980s. But no, I'm not letting some strangers feel up my hard drive. I'll figure something out."

Luis wedged a blue dustpan under the pyramid of shards. With the broom, he pushed the pile onto the pan, leaving behind a thin line of glass particles reflecting the light.

Vlad reached out and took the pan from Luis. He walked across the room to the trash can and pushed the pedal. The lid flipped up to release the familiar scent of ointment and vomit, with a hint of eucalyptus that Vlad knew was fairy dust. If you piss off a fairy—bring up Tinkerbell, for example, known as a "Pursey," gold on the outside, money on the inside, thus a fairy sellout —and you'd get a light sprinkle of magic causing instant projectile vomiting.

Vlad held his breath as he emptied the glass into the trash, lifting his foot from the pedal.

"Jesus, I can smell it from here," Luis sniffed. "Somebody must've mentioned Tinkerbell again. You'd think people would learn."

The werewolf got to his feet and plodded to the storage closet, returning without broom and dustpan. Back at the scene of the laptop homicide, Luis ran his tennis shoe across the floor, scattering the last tiny bit of glass.

"That'll do it," he sighed. "I should've made the fucking 'chaun do the work."

"It was time to cut your losses." Vlad settled into a recliner with a groan. "I know I'm nocturnal, but I could use a nap."

"It's been a long goddamned day." Luis plopped next to Vlad.

"So, you're a writer, huh?"

"I dabble."

"In what, exactly?"

"Writing, remember? Is your memory that bad?"

"Fine," Vlad said, leaning back and closing his eyes. "I forgot how sensitive authors can be."

"I'm hardly an author."

"No kidding." Vlad silently counted, waiting for the obvious response. He didn't make it past two.

"Fuck you, you have no idea."

Vlad smiled. Werewolves were so temperamental, if not predictable.

"Promise you won't laugh?" Luis put his hands behind his head and closed his eyes.

"No, but I will do my best to suppress my initial response should it tend toward mockery."

"Good enough." Luis inhaled, let it out slowly. "Werewolf erotica."

"What!?" Vlad opened his eyes, fangs glistening in a broad smile. "Are you kidding? There's such a thing?"

"Thanks for suppressing your mockery. Much appreciated."

"Sorry, really, I was just surprised. I've never heard of werewolf porn."

"It's not porn, goddammit. It's more than sex. There are feelings. Relationships. Tough breakups. Self-realization."

"Then sex?"

"Then sex." Luis turned toward Vlad. "Hot werewolf sex. Middle-of-the-change sex. And since I know what you're thinking, yes, *everything* gets larger."

Noting Vlad's eyes widen, Luis quickly added, "In my stories. Not in real life."

The vampire's expression remained the same.

"Seriously, Vlad, you want to know what happens in real life? Sorry, that one I'm keeping to myself."

The vampire sat back again, all sorts of pictures in his head. He shut his eyes. "Luis, do you ever get tired?"

"Tired of dealing with assholes? All the time."

"You know what I mean. In general. We've both lived such a long time..."

"And for the most part, it's been great. The things we've seen, Vlad, the amazing progress that's been made. I'll admit I miss the clean air and the forests that went on forever, but overall, it's been a helluva ride."

Vlad sunk his finger into a puff of fluff erupting from a small hole in the tattered chair. He tucked it back into place. "We've been on this planet hundreds of years. We've seen wars, pestilence, famine, a goddamned man on the goddamned moon. And here we are, with all of that behind us, and it's gotten us nothing but, what, seniority? What exactly is the point? Or is there one? Is the joke on us?"

"The point right now is I am far too exhausted to get into a deep philosophical discussion. I'm going to hit the hay and start all over again tomorrow. Well, later today. Because life goes on, right?"

"Life goes on," Vlad echoed. And that was the problem.

FORTY-ONE

VLAD THOUGHT back to the last time he'd been fed up with life, as one might tend to be after living a dozen lifetimes. This overwhelming tiredness—if not deep depression—struck him every eighty to ninety years, as if the human body were programmed for a certain expiration date. He'd seal himself in a dark room for weeks at a time wondering if it was time to push his way through life's exit door.

The first time it happened had nothing to do with age but morality. It was the second anniversary of his turning, three weeks into his latest vampire residency in a small Slavic village. He fed as little as possible, practicing an intermittent fasting diet centuries ahead of its time. Still, the bodies piled up even as he cut his meals to one every four or five days. Vlad dwelled on a fate that death was necessary for life. Specifically, his life.

On that fateful day, a starving Vlad was fangs-deep in a young teenage boy who was taking flowers to his beloved. He carried a letter professing his eternal love, a letter Vlad could not stop reading as his moral consciousness rose from the dead. Returning to his lair—that's what it always had been, after all, a sanctuary of malevolence, no matter if it was a medieval fortress or, later, a condo in a gated community— Vlad was determined to take himself out of life's equation. It was too late, perhaps, to balance the scales, but this act of selflessness just might balance them. Or if not balanced, make them less weighted toward evil.

With a sense of irony every bit as sharp as the silver cross he carried with him everywhere, Vlad knew it was time to embrace the one thing that led him to destroy lives. Holding the cross out at arm's length, its glittering tip poised over his heart, he plunged it deeply into his chest. He prepared for a torrent of blood, an ebbing of his life force.

Instead, he felt little more than a tingle. He tried again. And again. Perhaps a dozen times, wondering how he could possibly miss his heart. Worn out, he threw the cross into the corner, a ruined shirt the only evidence of his good-faith attempt to spare the world his presence.

At the time, Vlad believed God was behind his failed attempt, forcing him to live an undesired life as a way to pay for his multitude sins. Never mind that this blind faith was encouraged by a youthful stupidity convincing him an omnipotent being watched over humanity, guiding (if not manipulating) from afar.

His powers, and not God, provided the ingredients for his survival. Vlad's detailed examination of (rapidly healing) wounds proved it was his subconscious drive for survival, since each stab missed a vital organ, heart included. Good thing because a few days later, he was back to his old ways, convinced by his resolute immortality that he was too young, too powerful to willingly depart a world full of those waiting to be conquered.

Such was the start of a consistent lifecycle, the vampire surviving cyclical depressions by self-medicating, his spirit temporarily lifted after sipping from those under the influence. For decades he would live well, going from village to village, from victim to victim. No ties, no complications. No thoughts afforded to those left behind as he fled into the shadows, their blood providing him the life he had taken from them. Still, he hit those periods of intense sadness and regret when he felt compelled to again test his immortality. If he truly had to fight for his life by placing himself in danger, and he survived, then he deserved a place among the living.

Or so he had convinced himself over the lifetimes of killing.

Only in his darkest moments would Vlad accept the truth, that he didn't want to die because no one would grieve for him.

The times he thought he was finally ready to surrender, when it was time to tempt death once again, he did so through various, and unsuccessful, means. Initially he tried conventional means, including drowning and asphyxiation. Then it was by inflicting mortal wounds, and finally by sunlight. Each time he blacked out before the deed was done, his body's survival mechanisms kicked in to deliver him to safety. He would wake up safe, sore, and extremely hungry.

There was one method he would not submit to—the wooden stake to the heart. No doubt he could have made himself available to any number of angry villagers, particularly those with a basic knowledge of the human body. If he were to surrender his life, it would not be to a demeaning trope. If he were able to die, it would be with dignity.

That's when the thought—the possibilities—finally struck him.

In decades past, his vitality played a role in unsuccessful attempts. Even as his body and mind had the strength to fight back, his resolve to complete the task was less than adequate. But this body and mind, caught in a losing battle with Father Time, was ready to be shed. It just had to be on Vlad's terms.

So it would be, this time.

He opened his top dresser drawer and pulled out the business card of the one man who knew enough about his situation to be extremely useful, even if not wholly trustworthy. Perhaps Vlad would be able to check out for the last time with a little help from a guy who knew how to pull strings.

When it was done, he could also send invitations to the people Vlad was pretty sure would show up for a vampire funeral.

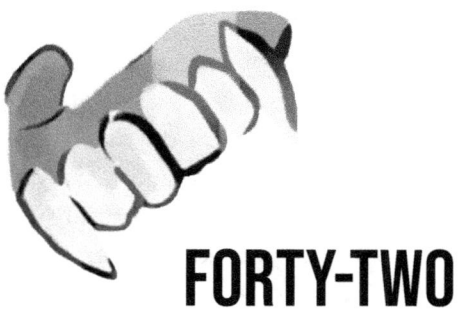

FORTY-TWO

AFTER A FEW HOURS of quality time with Google, Vlad determined the answer to his timely demise wasn't so much physical as it was legal. He happened to live in one of the few states that was fine with self-inflicted euthanization as long as a physician agreed with two things: (1) that the patient's mental and physical condition warranted a dignified death and, (2) would thus oversee a humane departure. If the method was good enough for generations of aging canines, Vlad decided, it was good enough for a vampire on his last wings.

More importantly, as death-by-choice was a legal proceeding, it provided attorney-client privilege. Everything remained confidential, allowing Vlad to slip from this mortal coil with little (OK, no) fuss. It would be as simple as convincing a doctor he had a terminal disease, for which he'd need a few fake medical records and, more importantly, a legal representative willing to break a few rules.

The vampire knew exactly who to call to get his future death rolling.

He punched in the number on the card, almost hanging up when a robotic voice answered. After a warning to listen to the entire message because options had recently changed, Vlad punched three for "Make an appointment" (and knowing he'd chosen the right guy thanks to option five, "File a complaint with the state bar"). At the beep, he stated his preferred date and time, sure that the appointment would be accepted given a likely lack of clients.

The next day, he was dressed in his usual daytime outfit of wide-brimmed hat, long cloak, and dark sunglasses, taking a twenty-minute rideshare to what turned out to be a rundown industrial park, just like the one Vlad had pictured for a guy named Lawster McLegalton. A chime announced his entrance into a small wood-paneled room with a lamp, couch, and coffee table, a look that appeared to be carefully curated from the Goodwill Collection. He'd taken two steps inside when the door on the opposite wall swung open.

"Come on in, my thieving friend," a voice called from the next room. Only then did Vlad notice the cameras in each corner before it struck him that he didn't show up, not even under ultraviolet light, since he had the same heat signature as any inanimate object.

"I know you're there, Vlad," Lawster beckoned. "Only one person I know who is invisible to the best technology. That and the fact you're right on time."

The vampire stepped through the doorway to see a familiar, and well-dressed, figure seated behind a nicked, scratched, and faded desk that fit right into the design theme. Lawster McLegalton shifted in his wheelchair, closed his laptop, and offered a broad smile to his visitor. "Can't say I expected to see you again. This is a business call, right? Kind of counting on still being alive when our time is up."

Vlad laughed because he knew Lawster was only half kidding. "Relax," the vampire said, palms up as if a vampire would need a weapon. "Not only will you survive, but probably even make your standard fee."

"Then by all means, take a seat."

Vlad settled into the chair opposite the attorney, the vinyl squeaking under the his weight. "Before we get started, mind if I ask you a personal question?"

"Not at all, since it's probably one of the two that everyone asks."

"It's not about the wheelchair."

"Damn, because that's the easiest one to answer, though I appreciate your embrace of my privacy. That means you wonder how Mr. and Mrs. Legalton were so prescient, if unmindful to future bullying, to call me Lawster."

"If you don't mind."

"You may be shocked to discover it's not my birth name."

"What!" Vlad shouted in mock surprise. "And it was all so perfect unless you went into auto repair."

"Then I'd be Fixit McTuneup, which has a better ring to it," Lawster smiled. "No, my current moniker stems from an unfortunate collision between parent-focused spite and a daylong, alcohol-imbued celebration of my law license. That morning, I woke up as P. Addison Waverly, a member of the pretentious Waverly family who for centuries birthed either attorneys or losers. By the time my head hit the pillow, I was the unknown and soon-to-be regretful Lawster McLegalton. I could blame the tenth shot of Fireball as well as the clerk who knew of and despised the Waverlys, thus happy to overlook my suspect condition when I applied for the name change. But I blame myself. Besides, I've come to embrace the fine McLegalton name, at least until I have a child, at which point my partner's name will take over for further generations."

"What if that other name is McTuneup?" Vlad said, unable to let go of the ridiculousness of it (and nothing more than further stalling, he knew).

"I have yet to come across any names as unusual as mine in all my time on dating apps. By the way, I'll bet you didn't know you can't change your name again for five years."

"No I didn't," Vlad agreed.

"Neither did I. And that brings us to you." Lawster eyed Vlad up and down. "I'm just as curious about your name. Did your parents know you were going to grow up to be a vampire?"

"That or a Russian dictator. Not that I can remember them, my parents. It was centuries ago. There are times I've convinced myself I was born a vampire." That was a lie, something easier to face than the truth, but Vlad went on. "I wish I had a more interesting tale to tell but I've been Vlad going on five hundred years, maybe longer. *Much* longer." He took a deep breath. "Which is why I'm here."

"Let me guess. You need a legal ID to collect Social Security? You came to the right guy."

"Not exactly."

"Then for Medicare to ensure many healthy years ahead."

Vlad fidgeted impatiently. "The opposite, in fact. More like Kevorkian-care."

FORTY-THREE

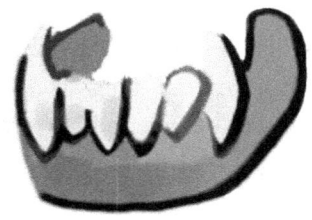

AFTER EXPLAINING the reason behind the visit, Vlad waited for Lawster to say something, anything, even if it were, "Sorry, can't help you" (not that Vlad could imagine Lawster telling anyone that). The attorney rolled out from behind his desk pulled next to Vlad, staring into the vampire's eyes.

"Are you really trying to tell me immortality is a bitch?" the attorney scoffed. "Because people would kill for that. Literally kill. Did you know that eight out of ten people would end a stranger's life if it gave them thirty more years? No? That's only because no one has asked. But if there were such a poll…"

Lawster stopped midway, Vlad seeing that it just dawned on the attorney that the vampire had indeed killed for the privilege.

"Well, I mean, immortality isn't something to throw away just like that," Lawster finished.

Vlad had prepared for just that reaction because Lawster, like damn near everyone else, had not lived long enough to know each day was not a precious gift. In fact, it can be agony. Without a word, the vampire stood and asked Lawster to follow him to the waiting room. "Please. I'll make it worth your time."

The vampire threw open the tinted front door, a rectangle of sunshine glowing on the worn carpet. Vlad removed a glove and put his hands into the rays. Tendrils of black smoke rose from the exposed skin, his flesh starting to bubble. The scent of roasted meat mingled with the office's refrigerated air. He turned the hand over as if flipping a burger, burning the other side. Vlad thrust the hand toward Lawster so the attorney could get a better look.

"I'm supposed to pity you?" Lawster ignored the hand and raised an eyebrow. "There are people with certain skin conditions who can't bear sunlight. Put on a hat. Wear long-sleeved shirts. Sorry, but if that's a price for immortality, I can't imagine anyone who wouldn't pay it."

Anticipating just that reaction, Vlad focused on Lawster's throbbing carotid artery. His body reacted, fangs sliding at the ready. Approaching the attorney from behind, he grasped Lawster's shoulders, pinning them in place.

"What the hell are you doing?" the attorney squealed as he squirmed under Vlad's viselike grip. "Let me go before I sue your ass from—"

Vlad's head was a blur as it plunged to Lawster's throat. The vampire stopped when his fangs touched flesh, pursing his lips and giving Lawster a quick peck on the throat.

"I could have easily taken your life," Vlad said with an eerie calm. He led Lawster back to the inner office and settled back into the chair. "There was a time I wouldn't have hesitated to erase you from existence, and not just because my life depended upon it. Sure, that was centuries ago when the only consequence was my own conscience, thus no consequences at all. I've evolved since then, each and every death weighing on my soul. Just another price of immortality, right, Lawster?"

The attorney's eyes remained wide as he gripped the wheels and gave them a push, saying nothing as he returned to his spot behind his desk with Vlad seated opposite, re-establishing the more comfortable, and far safer, attorney-client relationship.

"Well?" Vlad broke the silence.

"Something to consider."

"Something to consider? Building your life on a pile of bodies is something to consider." Vlad dared him to respond. Hearing nothing, he went "Fine, Lawster, let's pretend I'm the victim. Imagine falling in love and each time forced to watch that person, not just lovers, but everyone from close acquaintances to dear friends slowly fade away as you remain as strong and vibrant as ever."

Vlad's eyes looked right through the attorney. He knew what was coming next, the same thing the vampire heard in those rare times he revealed his innermost, and most destructive, thoughts.

"Couldn't you, you know…" Lawster stammered.

"Couldn't I what?"

"Turn them all into vampires."

Vlad was accustomed to such hesitancy in suggesting something that surely any vampire had tried at some point. If only they would think a moment about the dire consequences of such a replicating ability. Vlad repressed the urge to blurt, "Oh my god, I should just fire up the old vampire photocopier, how did I not think of that these last five hundred years?" He was in no mood for sarcasm, however, and instead leaned into logic.

"We'd have ourselves a bit of a bloodsucking apocalypse. Not to worry, Lawster, it can't happen," Vlad lied, knowing fang-duplication could happen, but only under unique circumstances, as with his own turning. "Erase any thoughts of a vampire assembly line."

"That's probably a good thing."

"A very good thing, both on personal and planetary levels." Vlad leaned back, his long sigh covered by the chair's mournful squeak. "If you'll allow me to go back to playing victim again, remember what I said about remaining strong and vibrant forever? Turns out that's immortality's greatest falsehood. It only stretches out the inevitable decline over decades. Death will take me in its own sweet time. Meanwhile, I slowly fall apart one power, one brain cell, one aching joint at a time."

"Damn," Lawster pondered, realization settling in. "Never thought I'd say it out loud, but I would not want to be a vampire."

"Not a real one," Vlad said. "Just the one you are now."

"Ouch, where did that come from?"

"Kidding. You know, banter. To make this thing comfortable again. Attorney-client, not vampire-victim."

Lawster laughed. "Got it."

"You want to know the most annoying thing about being a vampire? Do you have a mirror?"

Lawster reached behind him. Vlad heard a rip of Velcro before the attorney produced a black satchel. He reached in and withdrew a small mirror. "Need to look good when in court," he explained. "Comes in handy."

Vlad stood, motioning for Lawster to stay where he was. The vampire positioned himself next to the wheelchair and took a knee. "Put me in the mirror and tell me what you see."

"I think I already know what's going to be there. Everything but you."

Lawster swiveled the mirror back and forth. Vlad reached out with his good hand and steadied it, tilting the mirror to center on the attorney's face. According to the glass, the vampire didn't exist. He returned to his seat and continued.

"My life," Vlad said solemnly, finger arched in front of his face, "has depended on being that man in the mirror."

"The one no one can see." Lawster nodded, understanding in his eyes.

"Exactly." Vlad leaned forward, fingers now pressed in a triangle below his chin. "If I did appear, you would see the pale skin and the sharp teeth. The reflection of a monster. Instead, you see nothing of who I really am. While I may complain how it makes it difficult to even my sideburns, I've usually preferred not seeing who I was."

Lawster remained silent as he leaned forward, waiting for the vampire to continue.

"Imagine that life. One without reflection, to be lived in the dark, sustained only by the sacrifice of others. While I was able to find ways to, well, dampen the consequences suffered by those who met me, I've killed. Many times. Quickly. Invisibly. I am a drop in a pond, melding in, disappearing. Yet the ripples I've caused have devastating effects."

"But you're a vampire," Lawster argued. "That's what you do. It's not a moral choice."

"When lions take down a zebra, it's not a moral choice, it's survival," Vlad agreed. "That's how I saw myself at first. No more. It *is* a moral choice, especially if I make it one."

"I get it. But from what I understand, you're no longer killing people. You're not, right?"

Memories and faces surfaced from a dark well. "I don't kill..." Vlad paused, listening to the pleading voice in the back of a van parked outside a Cracker Barrel. "...just so I can keep living."

"Good, good, OK, perfect."

Vlad noticed Lawster still held the mirror, its polished surface pointed toward the vampire. Shifting to the left, then to the right, Vlad saw only the door directly behind him. In the mirror's world, he doesn't exist and never did.

But now he wanted to gaze upon the vampire in the mirror, curious to see who it was peering back.

FORTY-FOUR

AFTER ANOTHER HOUR of explanation and debate, Lawster McLegalton finally accepted the "why." It was time to address the "how."

"I heard a wooden stake through the heart had an efficacy of one hundred percent when it came to ceasing all vital signs, vampire or otherwise," the attorney noted matter-of-factly. "Four out of five Van Helsings recommend it for their vampires who want to die. And the fifth was killed before answering the poll question."

"Funny, and not a chance," Vlad said instinctively. "Simply and very offensively put, imagine killing a terminally ill Black man by lynching him."

"Yeah, that is incredibly offensive. The comparison, not the manner of vampire death."

"Understood, but I had to dumb it down so we don't waste any more time on wooden stakes."

"Let's move on," Lawster agreed, still shaken.

Even as Vlad considered the best way to drop his key at the front desk of life, he couldn't stave off thoughts of his past and what he was truly surrendering. Vlad loved the thought of immortality when he first started living *la vida* nocturnal. Thoughts of power consumed him. To live forever meant time enough to establish dominion over people and places. By his second century, or maybe his third, immortality's complexities came into focus. Now and then he was forced to take a life, particularly when superstitious villagers became suspicious of this recent arrival who claimed to be a doctor. For example, why did he refuse to make house calls between sunrise and sunset? And when caught sipping the drained blood directly from the tube, how could that possibly be for research purposes? That's when the pitchforks came out and Vlad was forced to find sustenance, and employment, elsewhere. But an even worse consequence was watching those he truly cared about die. Despite a will strengthened over the years to refrain from love, it always found him even when he isolated himself in the most forbidding castles or deepest caves. Incapable of facing death not brought by his own hands, Vlad would vanish as his partner suffered time's ravages. Escape was always the answer, a new life awaiting somewhere.

Not anymore. Vlad was tired of running, even if he could. His body betrayed him with aching joints and sagging skin. How does one accept a fate of slow decay when immortality was promised?

One doesn't.

"So," Lawster said, snapping Vlad back to the present, "if not the W.S—"

"W-S?" the vampire interrupted.

"Wooden stake? I don't want to offend you again."

"The words don't offend me, the practice of driving it through my heart does."

"Well…" Lawster paused, pushing back from his desk to balance on two wheels. "It's not like vampires are upstanding citizens."

"True, but to clear things up a bit, I've fed off real bad *hombres*. I know that doesn't make it right, but it makes me less reprehensible. However, I didn't come to you to justify my life. Just my death."

Lawster lowered his front wheels and spun once, twice in place. "Helps me think," he said as he twirled.

He stopped spinning and rolled to a small bookcase in the far corner. Running his fingers along identical bindings, he hooked the top of one with his index finger and tilted it from its place. Lawster riffled through the pages. "Why me?" he asked Vlad without looking up.

Vlad turned his chair to face the attorney, who kept his focus on the text. "I'd think my choice is pretty obvious given your knowledge of my, um, proclivities. Imagine me going to a lawyer who didn't believe in vampires. I'd convince him, of course, and a few minutes later there'd be a SWAT team outside the door."

"Agreed, then why the legal system at all?"

"Because it's proven to be extremely effective at killing people when it wants to. It doesn't stop until the job is done, and I need this job to be done."

"I'd say all you need to do is confess in a state that has the death penalty—"

"—and hang around another twenty years going through mandatory appeals. No thanks. Upton Arms is bad enough, but at least I'm allowed outside."

"Got it," Lawster noted, pulling another book. Placing the hefty tome on his desk, he flipped quickly through the pages as his eyes darted left to right. "Give me a few minutes."

Vlad had surprised himself when he called the attorney to make an appointment. If he had any guts at all, he'd keep attempting suicide until it stuck. Another bullet to the brain. Another slash across the throat. Another long walk on a sunny day.

The problem was he was even more tired of the pain. Not just physically, but mentally. Vlad wasn't sure he could handle the emotional devastation of continued existence.

He was, down deep, a complete chickenshit. That's why Vlad needed assurance that once the process of death began, it would be completed to its legally binding end. No better way to bring the final *adios* than under the watchful eye of an attorney being paid good money to ensure results.

"OK, here we go," Lawster said, his index finger pinned to the middle of a page. "Even in the relatively short life of this particular right-to-die law, there's a ton of legalese and even a few court decisions, so let me boil it down for you in plain language. You're fucked."

FORTY-FIVE

VLAD WAS angry enough that his body conspired against him as it broke down slowly and refused to die. But now the legal establishment was in on it as well?

The vampire had prepared himself for the challenges of his euthanization. Given the moral obligations of the medical community, he expected a litany of hoops to leap through, each formed of red tape dripping in bureaucracy. In a perfect world, he'd be dead just as Upton Arms went into financial flatline, bleeding residents over the next year before its new owners turned it into a hotel or condominiums or a multi-level parking structure.

This finding e news from Lawster was the figurative wooden stake to his heart that put an end to his hope for an ending, happy or otherwise.

The attorney forcefully reshelved each of the books in a way that punctuated his frustration. "Unfortunately" (slam) "you're not suffering from a medically approved terminal disease" (wham) "nor do you have the benefit of a physically debilitating condition that makes death a welcome experience." (whap) "You're not lucky enough to be so incapacitated with pain" (bam) "that death would be sweet relief."

With books back in place, Lawster spun to face Vlad, a disconsolate look on his face. "I feel for you. Your burden of relatively good health is too much to bear."

Vlad slapped the armrest in frustration and pointed to the bookshelf, moving his index finger to the left, right, and back again. "There has to be something in those pages that lets a person wave a white flag when it comes to life."

"There are and the problem is you don't qualify for any of them," Lawster said much too flippantly for Vlad's taste.

The vampire stood and leaned over the desk, putting on his best "Don't make me fang you" glare. "Can't you at least file papers? Give this thing a shot?"

"No. The court would throw it out. "

"There must be something. Let me testify. Put me on the stand."

"Vlad, if there was any way to—"

"JUST KILL ME ALREADY!" Vlad screamed, slamming his palms on the desk, which shuddered under the impact. Lawster moved as far away as he could, his chair against the wall, and remained still. Vlad stared at him, knowing the lawyer had just added, "Provoking a vampire" to his list of things one should never do.

Fear, however, was hardly the best motivator in this situation. Vlad relaxed his arms and eased back into the chair. *Keep it together*, he thought. *This isn't you.*

And it wasn't. He'd long tamed such rashness. Even in those rare times when he had to kill to survive, it was never done with an anger that would turn feeding into a contemptuous act.

Ah, Vlad, there you go again, rationalizing immoral deeds when you have no justification to do so, he thought, *and don't give me your "it was about survival" bullshit.*

He squeezed his eyes shut and focused on slowing his rapid heartbeat until he heard a telltale squeak. He opened them in time to see Lawster heading for the door. Vlad put his hand out about to grip the wheelchair's armrest until he noticed the look in the attorney's eyes. It begged, "Please don't kill me."

"Hey, sorry, sorry." Vlad clasped his hands in front of him. "I wasn't thinking."

Lawster stopped, turned toward his once-potential client and put his palm out, motioning for Vlad to chill out.

"I'm rarely intimidated, and I've represented short-tempered, two-hundred-and-eighty-pound bikers who took everything personally," the attorney fretted. "But none of them saw me as lunch. Have to tell you, it's a little unnerving to share personal space with a vampire. No offense."

Shoulders slumped, Vlad shook his head. "I'm sorry, I really am. I thought you could do something for me."

"Vlad, I'm sorry. I get it."

"Do you?"

"Yes," Lawster exhaled. "I thought immortality would be life's greatest gift, but you made me see the...*sun*light."

Vlad could not help but smile. "Saw what you did there."

"All I can do is give you the truth. And the truth is there is nothing I can do. Maybe you just need to pray on it."

"What?"

"Ask God for answers. I'm not a deeply religious man, but I've prayed a time or two and it's always helped."

"God? If he existed, do you think I would?"

"I've never seen a scientific or evolutionary explanation for vampires. The way I see it, how could you exist without God?"

Vlad had to admit that in the times he'd pondered his own existence, he never considered God a part of the equation.

Maybe that's why things never added up.

FORTY-SIX

VLAD FOUND himself in a searing whiteness, a void pressing in from all sides. He floated and yet wasn't floating, affixed in time and space.

His clothing stood in stark contrast to the surroundings. He wore a finely tailored black suit, complete with black shirt and black leather shoes. A red tie glowed like an open wound.

A voice came from above. "What makes you think you're better than them? Why do you get to live, and they do not?"

Without thinking, Vlad answered with a defiance that surprised him. "Because I'm stronger. Because this is how I choose to be."

"You chose this life? Do you really believe you have that kind of power?"

"Not power. Self-determination. If not fate."

"Fate? There is no such thing as fate."

Vlad looked up, shielding his eyes as he looked for the source of a voice that came from nowhere and everywhere. It might have been Him, uppercase and all. The white light and deep voice met the standards for a heavenly stereotype.

"You want a stereotype?" the voice boomed. "I'll show you a stereotype."

The whiteness dimmed to a dull gray as particles of light coalesced to form a gold frame a few feet away. Blacks and reds swirled and shaped an imposing figure within the frame. He wore a high-collared cape the color of midnight. A white ruffled shirt peeked from beneath a blood-red vest. Black pants and glossy black shoes completed the familiar picture. Atop the neck, an oblong mist took shape, two black dots bobbing to the surface like chunks of coal in snow. Below that, a slash of crimson bent into a smile, a hint of white fangs protruding from the corners. It was the face of a vampire.

Vlad stared at the figure, which was more caricature than creature. Was it supposed to be him?

"It is how the world sees you," the voice said. "That and nothing more."

Vlad peered deeply into the mirror. No, not a mirror. The thing in the frame was three-dimensional, painted in hues of blood and darkness.

A hand shot from the mirror, grasping Vlad's wrist and pulling the vampire closer. The pseudo-Vlad leaned forward, an unmistakable click of fangs sliding into place. Hot breath pulsed against Vlad's vulnerable neck.

"This," whispered Vlad 2.0, "is your true self. The monster you embraced when you first discovered the powers it brought. The one you've since tried to hide from everyone, even yourself. The monster you've been all along."

Vlad shook loose, pushing the figure back into the frame. "No, times have changed," he told himself. "Methods have changed. I've changed."

The room darkened further, the whiteness leaking away at the edges. The mirror disappeared, replaced by a pulsating red light that came from below. Vlad looked down to find himself on a precipice, the glow coming from a fiery pit though he felt only an icy coldness. His attention was drawn to the crackling above, like the fracturing of glass. He saw the frame, now bobbing as if on a calm sea. A spiderweb of cracks spread across the surface, shattered yet still in one piece. One by one each fracture receded, the glass healing itself. Another picture came into view, one so vivid Vlad could not turn away even when that was the only thing he wanted to do.

He stood upon a pile of bodies. Dozens. Hundreds. More, so many more. Eyes open and lifeless. Mouths gaping in silent screams. Blood bubbling from a thousand necks.

"This is what you have built your life upon," the voice whispered. "Your weeks, your months, your years. Each time you chose to live, another died."

"No," Vlad lied.

"These are the results of each decision you've made," the voice continued. "It's the life you longed for. Choosing to end it makes no difference. It will never change who you were. Who you *are*."

"If I had to make that choice again…" Vlad trailed off.

"Nothing would change. Because if you hadn't become *this*," the voice hissed, "you would have been nothing at all."

No, not true, Vlad thought. He would have led a quiet life. So very peaceful. So very—

"Ordinary? Is that what you want to be, Vlad?"

Vlad felt a hand gripping his ankle. An arm from the mass of flesh reached for him. The summit of this grisly mountain crumbled, and Vlad fell, putting his hands to his ears to stop the screams, the cries, the pounding and pounding and pounding…

FORTY-SEVEN

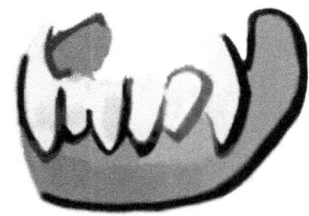

"STOP THE DAMN POUNDING!"

Vlad, hands clapped over his ears, kicked off the covers. He was bathed in sweat and cloaked in a bad mood. The dream remained vivid, and if there was one thing that annoyed Vlad more than old people digging for the right change at the market, it was meaningful nightmares.

More pounding. Vlad threw on the ratty gray robe that was a welcome antithesis to the sleek vampire cape. "Hold on, I'm coming." He flung open the door and was rewarded with pain shooting from his kneecap.

"What the holy goddamn, Jee-zus," he groaned, grasping his right leg, the knee already turning a supernatural shade of purple. Vlad's attacker, still in the doorway with hammer in hand, screamed at him.

"Close the fucking door, you nocturnal douchebag, so I can finish," Patrick sneered, waving the tool.

"Finish what?" Vlad said, still rubbing his knee.

"Putting up your 'Time to fuck off' notice, what else?" The leprechaun nodded toward the front of the door, Vlad peeked around to see a sheet of paper nailed two feet off the ground (and diplomatically ignoring the shortcomings of placing a notice far below eye level of those blessed with typical stature).

The vampire saw nothing but the two bold words at the top. "Eviction Notice."

"What the hell, Patrick," Vlad groaned. "You're evicting me?"

"What a shrewd deduction based on the phrase 'eviction notice.' You're a true fucking genius, that's what you are."

"What's going on? I'm paid through the end of the year."

"If you'd bothered to attend my 'You Need to Get the Fuck Out' meeting a while ago, you'd know. Or maybe all you had to do was show your pasty face every now and then, someone could've told you about how the new owner is tearing this place down to build a casino."

"What? You can't build a casino here. I mean, it's probably zoned class-three shithole."

"You can if you're on a reservation. Turns out this place is built on an ancient Indian burial ground. Ain't that something? Talk about a pot of gold at the end of the fucking rainbow."

"A cemetery?" Vlad questioned. "That makes no sense."

"Or maybe it makes a lot of sense. Think about it. But not now because you barely have enough time to pack your coffin and move on."

Vlad was about to flip Patrick some fang until the leprechaun stepped forward and offered an expression that hinted at sympathy, with a side of disdain.

"Turns out no amount of money could have saved this place, boy-o." Parick shook his head, perhaps with regret if he were capable of such a feeling. "Whatever government bureau is involved in such things has transferred these many acres back to whatever tribe claimed ownership. A casino is going up and to be honest with you, I'm not even sure anybody is going to dig for bodies first. But it does make you wonder, doesn't it? Is it coincidence we all wound up here, or some cosmic fucking joke to make us feel safe, if only temporarily?"

Patrick stepped back, the familiar sneer returning to remind Vlad who was in charge. In a voice loud enough to be heard several doors down, the leprechaun boiled it down like a potato in an Irish stew. "What that means for you and everyone else is that you need to be gone. Like, yesterday."

Vlad pulled his robe tight. "How long do I have?" He would have been happier posing that question to a hospice nurse rather than to of an irritable, hammer-wielding leprechaun who was also the landlord.

"As I told everyone else when I announced the news, five weeks ago," the leprechaun said. "Except that was around a month ago. I would've been happy to inform you via wrecking ball, but Beatrice insisted I offer the more personal touch, thus the eviction notice since Hallmark doesn't sell '*Do* let the door hit you in the ass on the way out' cards."

For the past—what's it been now, four weeks, perhaps more? —Vlad had been on a bender, vampire style. He slipped into a drug-testing lab, downing vials of tainted blood as if they were tiny bottles of liquor from the minibar. Wearing a white lab coat bearing the nametag of "Devin," he worked a couple of night shifts at the blood bank, sipping from bags even as donors filled them. He hit rock bottom when he found himself lapping at the gutters in a slaughterhouse like a horse drinking from a trough.

He'd suffered through worse, as when he dove fangs-deep into the death pits filled by the plague. But those memories were slowly slipping away, the traumas that shaped him blurring as if whipped in a blender set on "Puree."

Ironic, then, that one of the most painful experiences was the one as sharp as his incisors used to be. He could still hear Nancy, the colon cancer patient, begging him to take her life before she lost even the ability to speak. He entered her life just as he was accused of playing God, a truth he'd been able to keep at bay until that night.

And he did play God, but not the one he hoped to be. He didn't even try.

He'd slunk home a few days earlier, hiding in his room as he slept off a junk-blood binge. He wasn't even sure *how* he got home. Did he hitchhike? Call a taxi? No, wait, it was forming. He saw Luis behind the wheel of the Upton Arms' bus. Then the werewolf carrying him inside, putting him on the bed.

Another bang on the door, Patrick pounding the last nail in Vlad's metaphoric coffin.

"You've been officially served," the leprechaun announced,

smoothing out the eviction notice. "Feel free to hang around as long as you'd like, of course. Won't be long until you'll have a place with an open floor plan and plenty of sunlight."

Patrick turned on his booted heel and danced a jig down the hallway. It was as if the leprechaun had finally found his pot at the end of the rainbow, and it was filled with the despair of others.

For the first time, Vlad wondered what Patrick would taste like. Whiskey-soaked corned beef hash? Was that racist?

Probably.

FORTY-EIGHT

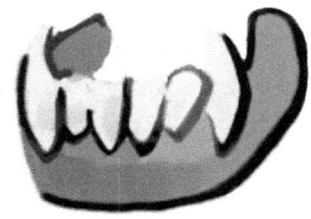

AS WITH ITS RESIDENTS, UPTON ARMS' community room had been stripped of its dignity, the bare rug boasting only the floor plan outlined in crumbs, mouse droppings, and expansive colonies of dust bunnies. Vlad was saddened to see everything had been removed, save for a vending machine and the king that had ruled them all, the TV. The only sound was the rhythmic thump of Darnell bouncing against that machine, as if it were his last friend on earth.

A bang of metal on concrete lured Vlad to a window. Rubbing the sleep from his eyes and then carefully evading any stray rays of sunlight, he peeked through the blinds and saw a large box truck parked outside. Two burly men in yellow jumpsuits thudded down the metal ramp bridging the gap between the truck and sidewalk. They burst into the community room and unceremoniously dethroned the TV, whisking it to the truck.

"This is how it ends," Vlad mumbled to no one. "Not with a bang, but with a zombie hitting a snack dispenser."

With his few possessions packed, including the first vial of holy water ever hurled toward him to thwart an attack (water was circa fifteenth century, the attack unthwarted), Vlad considered his limited housing options. He had enough cash for a few months in an extended-stay hotel, but cash was not his greatest concern at this point. He might rouse the suspicions of the housekeeping crew when he replaced the Toblerones with blood bags in the minibar. Perhaps, then, he should return to eastern Europe, taking up residence in a small castle and living out his life ironically. With his species trending positively in pop culture, he might host a "Medieval Legends" tour. He could hear the guide: "Two hundred years ago, villagers claim they were hunted by a creature of the night, one who feasted on blood. Yes, a vampire! Look, there he is at the window. Is that a rat on which he's feasting? It is! Wave, everyone." Why not license the idea and open up a string of dark-ages-style accommodations, calling it VampAirBNB?

As bleak as Vlad's future appeared, Darnell's was as grim as the reaper's. The zombie could not possibly have the option of physician-assisted suicide, what with Darnell lacking the necessary vital signs that would qualify him for non-deadness.

Vlad had long wondered just how one became a zombie. Hollywood insisted it was as easy as being bitten by one of the infected, a viral chain caused by military-grade bioweapons, radioactive waste or, Vlad's favorite, a virus that jumped from bats. Not that there were a ton of zombies around, but there were enough. The vampire recalled a small town from his past where residents swore there was a zombie attending a local middle school, not that the vampire bought such a ridiculous tale.

If nothing else, Darnell was blessed with a blissful ignorance of the current situation, if not of life's challenges in general. He was in a world of his own, bouncing off the vending machine without a care.

"Hey Darnell," Vlad strode to the zombie.

Darnell didn't look up, shuffling two steps forward, hitting the machine, stumbling two steps back, repeat.

"Buddy, hey." Vlad deftly slid between the zombie and the machine, forcing Darnell to stop. The zombie met Vlad's gaze with a fretful "Mmnn."

"Bite me," Vlad ordered, rolling up his sleeve.

"Mmrrrnn?" Darnell tilted his head like an inquisitive golden retriever.

"Take a chunk out." Vlad pointed to his forearm. "Right here. Free meat."

Darnell examined the patch of skin and leaned in for a sniff. His lips parted to reveal rotted teeth, some worn to a nasty point.

If I can't have death, Vlad thought, *I'll take eternal incomprehension.*

A drop of saliva hit the landing zone, leaving a trail of ooze as it slid to the side. Another drop followed the same path.

Vlad closed his eyes, hoping this crazy scheme would work. Knowing his luck, it—

"No thanks," came a deep voice.

The vampire's eyes widened in shock. He swiveled his head from side to side, looking for the voice's origin. But there was only Darnell, dead eyes staring into Vlad's.

"Vampires taste terrible." The zombie's jaw and lips moved in a way to strongly suggest he was indeed the speaker, yet Vlad had a tough time believing it.

"You can talk?" Vlad said hesitantly, thinking the voice was more likely to be in his head than from Darnell.

"Of course," Darnell answered, his voice slow and ponderous as if taking great pains to be understood. "I'm dead, not brain dead."

Vlad had a million questions, the main one having to do with Darnell's refusal of a quick bite. "Is it the way I'll taste?" But he couldn't get it out, his brain too busy wrestling with this new reality.

"If you'll excuse me," Darnell said, walking and bound for who knew where. No shuffling, no lurching. The zombie stepped smartly across the floor, disappearing into the hallway and leaving the vampire dumbfounded, if not disappointed. Vlad would have accepted a life lacking a sense of reflection, if not embracing it.

FORTY-NINE

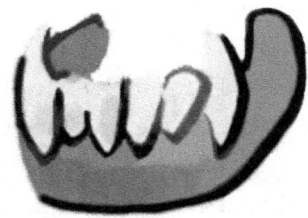

AS DARNELL'S FOOTSTEPS RECEDED, Vlad heard more approaching.

"One of the greatest 'What the fuck' moments of all time, am I right?"

Vlad turned to Luis who wore a smile as if he'd just been laid by the hottest wolf in the pack.

"You knew?" Vlad gasped. "This whole time?"

"Most of this whole time."

"And you kept it to yourself?"

"Yup."

"Even though we all looked like idiots?"

"That was the best part."

Vlad tried to absorb the revelation. According to legend and Hollywood scripts, zombies moaned rather than talked and feasted upon flesh and brains. While Darnell apparently bit someone at the estate sale, it was more out of stress than hunger. Come to think of it, the vampire had never seen Darnell eat anyone, and Upton Arms was full of slow-moving prey (and those plastic containers in the community fridge labeled "Darnell" actually belonged to Patrick, using a clever and effective theft deterrent). Like so many others seeking a quiet life at the retirement home, Darnell broke the stereotypes.

"Two things I never thought I'd see—a polite fairy and a talking zombie," Vlad shook his head. "Still waiting for a polite fairy, or even a tolerable one. How long have you known about Darnell?"

"I had a good idea when he arrived without an apocalypse behind him," Luis offered. "A solitary zombie challenged all my beliefs about the end of the world. I asked him about it. He answered."

"And you didn't think that maybe we'd want to know he wasn't brain-dead?"

"Of course you wanted to know. Darnell, however, preferred you didn't. He's very shy."

"He spent most of his time bouncing against a vending machine."

"He's also easily entertained."

"Jesus, Luis, if we'd known he could talk, he could have been one of us. Debate the news or play rummy or make fun of Patrick. Instead he's, he's…"

"Dead to the world?" Luis completed the sentence. "He may have been, and he was cool with that. Still is. You know, he still feels guilty for crashing through my window so many years ago."

"He what?"

"Crashed through my window," Luis said, shaking his head. "He was very apologetic, and even paid for damages. At the time, he was still adjusting to being undead and hadn't figured out front doors. Or knocking. He just needed a place where people weren't always trying to shoot him in the head. And you know what? He didn't bat an eye when I told him eating residents was strictly prohibited. I'm pretty sure he was insulted at the mere mention of dining on others. I knew then he'd fit in well."

Vlad half-heartedly swatted at a fly buzzing around his ears. "Why the silent treatment? Especially once he found out he was among like-minded people."

"We don't all fit into neat little packages," Luis noted, shooting a fist within inches of Vlad's head, the vampire not even flinching. Luis uncurled his fingers, releasing the fly. "Still got it."

"Darnell's an observer, not a participant," the werewolf continued. "As far as I knew, he'd always been happy here. Or at least content. You also must remember death has a traumatic effect on the brain. Maybe

Darnell's operates at less than its original capacity. Doesn't matter because he lived life the way he wanted to. I envy him for that."

"That doesn't seem enough. It's a waste."

"Not your call."

Vlad knew Luis was right. The vampire was in no place to judge, especially since his days were consumed by the time, place, and manner of his own death. Darnell was a step ahead in that department.

Vlad wondered how Luis would make his exit if he could choose.

"I'd go out as a wolf," Luis declared, Vlad unsure if he'd wondered aloud or it was merely coincidence. "I'm running with the pack chasing down a zebra, one we've separated from the herd. I'm the first to leap, latching onto the neck. Then bam, my heart stops, and I die with zebra on my last breath.

Vlad couldn't help but laugh, and it felt wonderful. "Sounds like you've given it a lot of thought."

"Most of that was off the top of my head. Not about those PETA assholes, though. Fuck them." Luis exhaled, a louder-than-necessary sigh at the end. "We've all dealt with our semi-immortality in our own ways. Even when I thought I was immortal, as in feeling like a twenty-something until shot in the head with a silver bullet, I wasn't sure I wanted to live forever. Once I was a hundred years or so into this werewolf thing, I was already pretty tired. Not tired enough to call it quits, even though aging's been a much bigger bitch than I'd ever thought. The way I see it, I'm still playing with house money and not ready to cash in. Nor will I double down when my time comes, I'll play that hand when it comes."

"Those are some decent poker metaphors," Vlad interjected.

"It's this app I can't stop playing," Luis explained. "Pretty sure it's not real money. I hope. Anyway, the only thing I fear about death now is that it comes in my sleep. Dying normally after such an abnormal life."

The community room door burst open again. The moving men entered, one pushing a dolly. They brushed past Vlad and Luis as if the vampire and werewolf didn't exist rather than shouldn't exist. Strapping the vending machine to the dolly, the burly men tilted it back and guided it toward the door. It thumped over the threshold and was gone.

"Going to miss the cinnamon sugar Pop-Tarts most of all," Luis muttered. "Nothing like devouring them fresh out of the wrapper."

"You don't toast them?" Vlad raised a disapproving eyebrow.

"I like my pastries like my prey, *au natural*."

"That's just wrong. What do you think the 'Pop' refers to? You have no respect for non-nutritional foods."

"This from a man who subsists largely on a liquid diet. You should refrain from topics you know nothing of."

"You think I've never popped a tart? Why sir, I've popped more tarts than, than..."

The two burst out laughing, no longer able to continue their feigned anger.

"Damn, Vlad. I'm going to miss you."

"I'll definitely miss you, Luis. At least until I get hungry."

"You'll have to catch and overpower me first."

"I'll do just that, then force you into the nearest toaster so I can have you warmed, as intended."

Vlad couldn't remember the last time he hugged someone motivated by affection rather than appetite. Years. Decades.

Far too long ago to remember. He didn't want to let go. He did anyway.

"Where you off to?" Vlad prodded.

"The Moonlight Hotel. Thought it fitting. Just three hundred bucks a week. Housekeeping every other week. Hot- and cold-running divorced dads. Mostly cold."

"That sounds perfect," Vlad said in a flat voice implying no thought was given to the reply.

"Not as perfect as the fairies, from what I hear."

"What are they up to?"

"Apparently," Luis leaned forward and lowered his voice, "they're not going anywhere. Flitting around during construction and then taking up residence in the casino."

"Why would they do that? Can't they go back to the forest and live among the sprites or whatever?"

"Their powers aren't up to independent living. The casino will provide unlimited food and drink. Who's going to notice a fairy in a Mai

Tai? They're also going to spread around a little fairy dust while they still have it. Charm people so they win. Then cut them off and watch them lose it all and then some."

"Fairies are such dicks."

"Right?" Another sigh, softer this time. "What about you. Any plans?"

There was the question Vlad had been expecting earlier. At least this time, the subject was much easier to address.

"Not sure," he lied, too embarrassed to admit the truth about his future digs. "I don't even know what I'm going to have for dinner."

"Don't you mean 'who?'"

"Funny."

"Fucking with you because I love you. But seriously, if you need a place to crash for a while as you figure things out, the Moonlight awaits." Luis's eyes roamed around the empty room. "Time's running out. So is Patrick's patience."

"I know. Nothing worse than a stern lecture from a leprechaun."

Luis snapped his fingers. "Reminds me. About an hour ago, I heard Patrick screaming at Todd, dropping nuclear f-bombs. Just as the shit is starting to get real crazy, it stopped. I opened my door to see Patrick race by, hands on his throat, his mouth moving like a fish gasping for air. I look down the hall and there's Todd, huge grin on his face. Weird, huh? Like he shut Patrick up, all omnipotent like."

Vlad shook his head, feeling a familiar ache starting behind his eyes. Todd had arrived a few weeks ago, moving in without an official community vote. Still, the kindly gentleman endeared himself to most residents thanks largely to his power to change channels without the remote, making him the Alexa of the common room—"Todd, switch to *I Can't Believe It's Benign: World's Largest Tumors.*

"The point is," Luis continued, "Todd asked me where you were. He wanted to speak with you."

"And you didn't tell him to ask me himself?"

"Who am I to question his word? Todd works in mysterious ways."

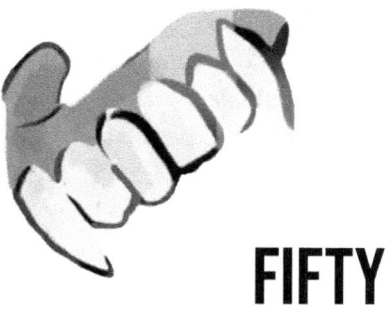

FIFTY

VLAD GAVE the empty room one last look, going through the checklist one more time. He had his black loafers, his three favorite Lands' End polos, a couple of pairs of wool slacks, and his favorite pajamas featuring a Valentine's Day pattern of blood-red hearts. The usual complement of toiletries, underwear, and socks filled his suitcase, reminding the vampire of his inconvenient ties to humanity. A cooler held two months' worth of meals, and he silently thanked Luis for suggesting he stash some away for hard times.

Vlad had found a decent Airbnb a few miles away, and he briefly thought about driving nights with Lyft to pick up a few bucks until he realized that would necessitate a driver's license and dozens of uncomfortable questions (starting with his date of birth).

As he hefted his worldly belongings, his mind produced a fleeting thought of Todd, as well as the disappointment he would never know the truth about the mysterious stranger.

I can die with that, he thought to himself.

The air shifted, Vlad's hands suddenly empty. His room was gone, replaced by a dingy hallway where a light flickered above his head. He faced a white door, one so unblemished it didn't belong.

"Come in," pronounced a voice on the other side.

Vlad knew that voice all too well, and how impossible it was to resist the invitation. He succumbed to the inevitable.

While the vampire wasn't sure what to expect when he opened the door, he found the room's ordinariness disappointing. An oak dresser occupied the far wall and, in the center, a leather recliner and wooden rocking chair faced one another. A larger-than-necessary TV was bolted to another wall, completing a design with strong Post-Leprechaun influences. The opposite wall boasted only a tattered, dog-eared calendar with a photo of a rocky seashore, and foamy waves crashing over boulders and pillars. Vlad couldn't swear to it since his eyesight wasn't what it used to be, but he thought the month read "July 1231."

"Vlad, good to see you," Todd grinned, easing back in the recliner that was empty a second ago. "Thanks for coming by, I appreciate it."

"As if I had a choice," Vlad hissed through gritted teeth.

"We all make choices, sometimes whether we know it or not." Todd gestured to the rocking chair. "Have a seat. Please."

Like an out-of-body experience, Vlad watched himself settle into the chair, elbows on the carved armrests. He opened his mouth, but nothing came out. He stared at Todd, knowing he'd underestimated the psychic's ability as well as Todd's willingness to control others.

Vlad was sure of only one thing. He'd never encountered anyone like Todd before.

"No, you haven't," Todd agreed. "And honestly, I've met very few like you. And that's the problem."

The vampire cleared his throat, largely to see if his voice had returned. "What exactly are you trying to say?" Vlad croaked.

"The problem is that while you don't believe in me, I believe in you. And it is a very big problem indeed."

Vlad threw up his hands. "No idea what you're saying."

"It's simple," Todd said. "You exist."

Vlad patted himself down as if looking for something. "Seems so, unless this is a simulation, and we're all inside a computer in Albuquerque, New Mexico."

"If only it were so simple." Todd stood and walked slowly around the rocking chair, Vlad keeping his eyes straight ahead. "Things were going according to plan for the first few thousand years after I orchestrated the appearance of hominids."

"Wait, what? *You*." Vlad stood to face Todd. "You're telling me *you*, um, 'orchestrated' the creation of human beings."

"Vlad, you're testing my patience. I've gone millennia with a simple rule when it comes to faith. I don't have to prove anything. The irony here is that you, the ultimate exception, require an exception to that rule. Fine."

Todd snapped his fingers. Again the air shifted, an electrical current running through it. Todd pointed to the TV, only there was no TV. It was a photo of a sunny day taken from Vlad's window.

"Take a close look," Todd suggested. No, *ordered*.

Vlad saw Beatrice and Luis on a bench, turned toward one another as if in deep conversation. Henry sat at the base of the aging, twisted pine at the center of the lawn. A headless set of clothes—Ralph—stood twenty feet from Darnell, the two facing one another. Just another afternoon in the quiet courtyard of Upton Arms.

No, there was something more. The scene had unnatural depth, more of a tableau than a photograph.

This wasn't an image sealed behind glass. This was a window, an outside moment frozen in time. Vlad could even make out the red slash of a Frisbee hovering between Ralph and Darnell.

"How, what…" Vlad stammered.

"You wanted proof," Todd stated with an authoritative tone. "I can stop time. It's not just pretty damn convincing, but very damn cool."

"No, this is something else," Vlad insisted, eyes scanning for any movement. "Mind control. Or I'm drugged."

Another snap and Vlad was outside. He instinctively curled to shield himself from deadly sunlight, but his flesh felt nothing but the warmth of a winter fire.

"You're safe," Todd assured, throwing an arm over the vampire's shoulder. "No drugs, no mind control. Just an insignificant, and somewhat embarrassing, display of omnipotence." He removed his arm, gripped Vlad's biceps, and got nose-to-nose with the vampire. "We are about to have an important, life-changing conversation. It will be much easier for both of us if you believe."

Vlad nodded, his gaze at something just over Todd's left shoulder. It was a tiny creature, its wings spread and motionless, its middle finger thrust toward Vlad.

"I believe, yes, I believe," Vlad said, not only in Todd, but the notion that fairies were such dicks.

FIFTY-ONE

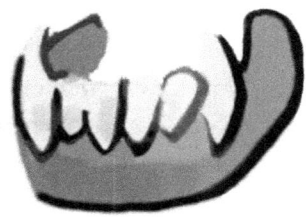

VLAD FELT as if he were in a snow globe minus the snow, imagining a dome high above that sealed them off from reality. Everything was too perfect, from the temperature (a breezeless seventy-two degrees, if the vampire was correct), to the saturated colors all around him. The only cloud in the sky was so billowy and cartoonish, Vlad almost expected to see eyes and a beaming smile.

"Is the rest of the planet like this?" Vlad wondered aloud, shifting on a bench that didn't wobble in the slightest. Nor did the blades of grass, which had remained stiffly at attention as he and Todd walked across the lawn before taking a seat.

"It's complicated," Todd said.

"I can imagine."

"To put it in terms where your mind can say, 'Cool, I get it,' I've removed us from the timeline. Not just to prove I can, but I wanted to have a conversation for which I need your full attention."

"And you thought freezing time was a good way to get me to focus."

Todd released the long, exasperated sigh, the kind reserved for parents discovering a disastrous diaper breach after handing the toddler to friends. "Actually, yes. No distractions."

Vlad shut his eyes and tried to accept what was happening to him.

Was he really talking to the universe's top deity, creator of all things? Or was it another mind game, that he was not here shooting the shit with God on a park bench but still in his room, lying motionless with saliva sliding down his chin?

One thing was clear—he had nothing to lose. And if Todd were the divine one, he could grant Vlad's only wish like a genie in a bottle. That possibility alone was worth riding this out.

Vlad opened his eyes and met Todd's stare. "I'm listening."

"Finally," Todd exclaimed, breaking eye contact and leaning back, putting his hands behind his head. "Did you happen to notice that calendar in my room? Or anything strange about it?"

"I had no idea Hallmark was making calendars several hundred years ago, and that they were as cliched then as they are now. Looks like it was from the 'Relaxing Seascapes' collection."

"I do love a relaxing seascape. However, I keep that calendar more for its significance than the photo." Todd leaned forward and clasped his hands on his lap. "You see, the year 1231 is when the Spanish Inquisition started, a real stain on my record. Innocents tortured and slaughtered by people invoking my name, not that they had any right to. It was a heinous example of the dark side—the *evil* side—of free will. It was the closest I came to intervention on a mass scale."

Intervention, Vlad thought. *What the hell did that mean?*

"I'll tell you," Todd continued without missing a beat. "First, you need to know that I dabble with little miracles here and there. It happens when people or circumstances so delight me, I deign to reward them. I dabble, adding tiny brushstrokes here and there to remind the faithful of the goodness in the world. That coin has a flip side, of course, keeping the whole good and evil balance. Truly intolerable actions, like killing innocents in my name, deserve retribution. Pestilence, perhaps. Or something more localized. Drought or diseased crops. Angry polar bears."

"What?"

"Truth be told, I did toy with angry polar bears out of curiosity because if any animal deserves to be angry, it's polar bears. Point is, I haven't interfered in a way that would have deep, perhaps cruel effects on certain sectors. Not during the Inquisition, not when the Nazis swept across Europe. Nor have I been tempted. "

Todd stopped, eyes boring into Vlad.

"Until you."

Vlad smirked. "Don't tell me I'm not one of God's creatures. I'd be crushed."

"You were, as you say, one of my creatures," Todd said. "That changed in your twenty-third year."

"You mean when I became who I am today? Because I was twenty-five. Maybe you're not so perfect after all."

"Exactly, Vlad. Hit that nail right on the head. Let's walk, shall we?"

The two crossed the grass, weaving between Ralph and Darnell. Vlad grabbed the flying disc and tugged, but it remained stubbornly in the sky as if encased in Lucite. He giggled when he lifted his feet and began swinging, feeling as if he were ten years old. He kicked out, mistimed the landing, and fell right on his ass. The giggle turned into a boisterous laugh, and he could not remember a time he'd felt so carefree. Perhaps he never had.

Vlad hopped up and brushed non-existent grass from the seat of his pants. He joined a patient Todd on a leisurely lap around the lawn, the vampire drinking in the sunny day with every sense. He'd forgotten what it was like to be in the light without having to pat out flames. It was like roaming in a postcard, so much so he looked up expecting to see "Greetings from Upton Arms" in dazzling yellow script.

After fifteen minutes (or so Vlad guessed, since time was frozen), they plunked down onto the lawn and stretched out. Vlad hesitated at first, seeing those erect grass blades as a thousand tiny knife blades, but it was rather cushy. He could definitely fall asleep with the sun on his face, even as he pictured himself back in his otherwise empty room suffering a stroke. Maybe this scene was a gift of his own death. If it was, he'd take it.

Just one problem—this felt too real. The things that could have spoiled the frozen-in-time illusion—a light breeze, the chirp of birds, a movement of shadows cast by the statue-people—did not exist, preserving the effect. No, this was happening. Todd was no pretender, a thought that terrified Vlad. Only one thought terrified him more.

What did Todd want from him?

Vlad sat up, his timeless companion doing the same thing at that precise moment, as if mirroring him. They exchanged glances.

"You're wondering why you're here," Todd stated the obvious. "To be honest, I'm wondering the same thing."

Todd's words—one in particular—flicked a switch at the back of Vlad's brain. He'd never been the religious type, having brief flings with various sects to break up the boredom. While such groups all had their own twists when it came to biblical interpretations, they united in the belief that God knows all and sees all. No exceptions.

So why, and how, could God possibly "wonder" about anything?

That's when it hit Vlad like a ton of Bibles.

"Oh... my..." Vlad stuttered.

"God?" Todd completed.

"It's not you," Vlad bobbed his head in a slow nod. "It's me. I'm the exception to life's rule."

"Come again?"

"Humans are an open book to you, life proceeding with absolutely no variation. A civil conflict here, a world war there, a host of natural disasters...it all goes as expected. There are no surprises." A smile slid across Vlad's face, fangs exposed. "Except me. Or should I say us, the good residents of Upton Arms who are life's outliers, those who for reasons even you may not know, possess talents that don't check the usual boxes."

"Let's not get ahead of ourselves," Todd warned.

"See? Even now you're not sure where this conversation is going. You may be able to read my mind, poke around my thoughts, but you have no idea what my future holds. I'm, I don't know, a *mystery* to you."

Todd plucked a blade of grass, put it to his lips and blew. It took off like a bullet, zipping past Vlad's ear with a muffled whoosh.

"Not a complete mystery," Todd corrected. "You're still human. Mostly. But that other part of you, that creature-of-the-night thing, doesn't fit. Not in this world."

"You're telling me I'm a mistake?"

"Not a mistake. God doesn't make mistakes."

"I think I saw that on a T-shirt once."

"You did. In fact, there are two hundred and seventy-three versions of that T-shirt in the western hemisphere alone. I wasn't aware of that statistic until you mentioned it, so I did a little cosmic Googling and found it in a few nanoseconds. I used to say the world's an open book to me. Now I say the roughly seven billion people make up my personal internet, and I know each and every website revealing all. But your site is a little buggy. The server connects me most of the time, but it will crash for no reason and there goes the connection. It can stay that way even after I reboot. And that doesn't just happen with you."

It was coming into focus. God could follow anyone, anytime. Always knowing. Always seeing. Like Facebook and Instagram with privacy controls off.

But Vlad and his supernatural allies faded in and out as if there was some cosmic interference screwing with the stream.

"I can see by your face certain realizations are becoming apparent," Todd mused. "You're right. The vampires and witches and werewolves...the magical types. Supernatural. Paranormal. Even dicks, as you obsessively refer to the small winged creatures among you. Call them whatever you want. They don't fit. *You* don't fit."

"Aren't *you* to blame?"

Todd sighed, Vlad feeling the warm breath of a supreme being on his cheeks.

"Perhaps," Todd confessed. "But life and its tenacity still surprises me in a way. Did you know there are creatures that live near deep-sea volcanic vents spewing toxins lethal in most solar systems? Yet these fish and worms romp happily amid gardens of poison. Go figure."

Vlad hugged his knees to his chest. "I assume you don't like life taking unexpected paths."

"Don't mind at all, it's a bit thrilling to see your creations stumble into uncharted territories, as long as I see it coming. And I have for millennia. But you, Vlad, you and the others go into uncharted *and* prohibited territories."

"Why did you let it happen?"

"That's just it. I didn't. I had no idea what was going on until it was too late. Look, I've always been about free will. I was willing to see where you and your friends took us. Until everything went off the rails."

"You mean when *we* went off the rails."

"Yes, that's exactly what I mean. It's time to rein you in."

Vlad hated the sound of that. As many times as he hated himself, should he be punished for his very nature? Should Luis and Beatrice and Patrick and the rest as well?

And what did Todd mean by rein in?

More importantly, why now?

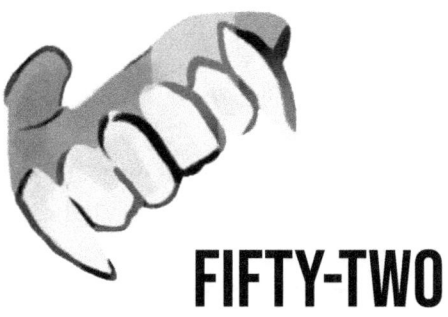

FIFTY-TWO

AT THE MOMENT Vlad felt a tickle at the back of his head, more unnerving than uncomfortable, he found himself back in Todd's room, seated again in the rocking chair with a tingle in his hands and feet. *So this is what teleportation feels like,* the vampire thought. *Cool.*

But in that split second before the temporal travel, he felt he wasn't alone in his mind. Vlad sensed a nosy visitor poking around, checking the books on his shelves and opening the medicine cabinet.

"Find anything of use?" Vlad inquired of the elderly gentleman now seated opposite,

"Didn't find much of anything," Todd chuckled. "That's not true, of course, but I'd expected to find much more. People are encyclopedias to me. You're a brochure. Still, I see a giant neon sign blinking over your head and it says, 'Why now?' My answer is wholly unoriginal. Why *not* now?"

Vlad drew himself up, quickly tiring of the runaround. Unlike Todd, he didn't have eternity to figure it out. "Please, then, get to the point."

Todd clapped his knees. "You're right. Enough of the chatter since we've both got better things to do, especially me with that Sargon 7 cult uprising."

Vlad's eyes widened, but before he could ask the obvious, Todd put his hand out. "Nah, messing with you. Or am I?"

"Fine. Let's start again. What's all this about? And if you can keep it to our galaxy, I'd appreciate it."

Todd pulled the handle on his chair to elevate his feet, giving Vlad a look at the spotless soles of his shoes. "Simply put, Vlad, you're a risk. I've worked pretty hard to make this world work, and in just a few centuries—an imperceptible moment, a fraction of nothing—you've unbalanced the timeline. It means little now, but over the next few centuries, the mistake will compound itself. That makes me nervous given I can't quite see where you're going."

Vlad shifted uncomfortably, crossing his left leg over his right and folding his hands on his lap. He thought back to his church days and the lessons preached from the pulpit. What did he really know about God? Enough to make an argument for himself? Or at least engage in conversation until a better idea comes along?

The vampire hadn't given up the notion this was occurring in his mind and nowhere else. If so, this was such a waste of time. He hoped that wasn't the case because Todd/God had some explaining to do.

"Why does God let bad things happen to good people?" Vlad asked thoughtfully.

"What does that have to do with anything? And who are you to question God?"

"Remember, I didn't ask for a face-to-deity meeting. You did. If you're going to take us, *me*, out with a cosmic delete button, I was hoping you'd at least answer a few questions. It's not like you do as much talking as you did in the Old Testament."

"Because I was misquoted so often. Fake news. These millennia, my heavenly silence is more a courtesy since anyone who says they talk to God is judged mentally unbalanced to the point where they almost can't buy a gun."

"I get that," Vlad agreed. "But if you'll indulge—"

"Why do I let bad things happen to good people, right? Because bad things happen to everyone. I am the word and the light, and I love all my children equally. I'm not going to play favorites. The consequences of free will, my most precious gift to you."

"Do you ever give people more than they can handle? Do you answer every prayer? Does everything happen for a reason?"

"Not going to play your parlor games, Vlad. Sorry. Life is what it is and no matter how hard anyone prays, I'm not helping your team win or steer the winning lottery numbers your way. Let's go back to your first question, since I wasn't entirely truthful. Why now?"

There was that tickle in Vlad's mind again. For some reason, he knew the answer to this question. He just needed a moment to think. What was different now than four hundred years ago, or a hundred years ago? Maybe just a decade ago, or even yesterday.

That's when it lit up in those neon letters Todd had mentioned.

"Upton Arms. It's closing. And…and…"

"Yes?"

"We're leaving. No, not just leaving. Scattering."

"Keep going."

"And like bad cell signals, we fade in and out. That's why you can't track us."

Something else, though. Another thought coalesced, one that was more important, even nefarious.

"You're warm bordering on combustible," Todd smiled. "No offense."

Vlad ignored the weak dig. "It's about tracking us. You had to do something to make that possible."

Upton Arms blazed in the vampire's mind, letters fifty feet high. "It's not a retirement home," it dawned on Vlad. "It's a collection jar. You're very own supernatural creatures under glass."

"Winner winner chicken dinner," Todd exclaimed, throwing his arms over his head. "While not every bit of paranormal flotsam and jetsam is here, there are enough to effectively wipe out the lines and put an end to your peculiar branch of randomness. Or at least make you of no concern for another five thousand years, and by that time, nothing will be of any consequence. Spoiler alert, by the way."

The answer inspired another question, one Vlad hesitated to ask because no matter the explanation, he knew he'd been suckered, as had every resident at Upton Arms. How did a deity conduct earthly business? Wouldn't red tape be enough to foil someone capable of miracles? Especially if that someone was determined not to use his powers to interfere.

Vlad's curiosity won out over his pride. "How did you do it?"

"Create the world?"

"No. Create Upton Arms."

"Let me just say that creating the world was a lot easier. Far less red tape."

Knew it, Vlad thought, high-fiving himself.

"I had help, of course," Todd grinned. The divine one, as Vlad was starting to see Him, related how it was an inside job (as Vlad had suspected, at least for the last few minutes). Todd admitted he couldn't always track supernatural creatures, let alone gather them in one spot. He needed a scout, someone who could gently steer the enhanced to Upton Arms.

The vampire's conspiracy-based thoughts immediately went to the fairies. They had the means (fairy dust could convince anyone to do anything) and the motives (they were dicks). But no, that was too obvious, like Colonel Mustard in the library with the pipe.

Speaking of the obvious, a thought occurred to Vlad that would crush his soul if it were true. Who had ushered Vlad and so many others to Upton Arms? Who made it his mission to "rescue" the aging and escort them to the secure confines of a place designed not as a refuge, but a trap?

And why hadn't Vlad seen it coming?

"Just kill me now." Vlad's chin dropped to his chest, any hope squeezed out like water from a sponge when all traitorous signs pointed to Luis.

Todd leaned over and patted Vlad's knee. "You're wrong, Vlad. It's not quite the butler who did it, but pretty close."

Vlad took a deep breath as anger displaced anguish because everything fell into place.

"Patrick," Vlad snarled.

"Who else?" Todd shrugged.

Todd was right about how this was the closest thing to the butler doing it. Patrick was the cardboard-cutout villain they all should have expected, shaped precisely as the missing piece of this particular puzzle.

Patrick was so tightly packed with rage, the density of his anger collapsed in on itself creating a black hole of desperation. It was true that every now and then, a particle of genuine concern escaped, a reminder that a sliver of humanity existed deep within Patrick. When Vlad witnessed the leprechaun's love for Beatrice, it was like finding the oarsman of the River Styx dressed like a Disneyland princess before sailing off to "It's a Small World". Though the attraction's damnable song was a sure sign of hell.

"Sorry if the ending was more Encyclopedia Brown than M. Night Shyamalan," Todd said. "You may think you know everything about Patrick, but there is much to our rainbow-pursuing friend. I'm happy to fill you in."

Vlad settled in for the tale, firm in the belief there would be no happy ending unless a massage table suddenly appeared.

FIFTY-THREE

PATRICK'S POWER, "if you could call it that," Todd chided, was that when it came to games of chance, the leprechaun couldn't lose. With the luck of the Irish behind him, he'd consistently win at just about everything, whether it was investments, games of chance, or betting on the horses. The apparent power, the manipulation of luck, came at a cost. Patrick's pot of gold at the end of a dark rainbow came on the back of those who lost.

"He was such a minor player in the supernatural game, I paid him no attention," Todd noted. "Then came 1919, when I had a little luck of my own."

The leprechaun was losing one bet, the one with Father Time over whether or not he'd live forever. Realizing his fate, and that both his luck and life were temporary, Patrick decided to take a more proactive stance. Todd was ready.

Vlad snapped his fingers. "I know why 1919 seems so familiar. That was the Black Sox scandal, right? Chicago threw the World Series."

"Patrick was the mastermind, beginning to end," Todd nodded. "His luck had run out, and this was proof. He ran up the white flag in surrender, but I saw it as red. It was my chance because suddenly, everything changed."

"How can something change for someone who knows all and sees all?"

"Vlad, let's pretend you can't keep up rather than aren't listening. Your kind is risky, if not dangerous, precisely because your mere existence changed things. Life, death, wealth retention. The good thing was that this time, the change was in my favor. A different timeline, one with a rather unique retirement home, came into focus. He was like a beacon in the night, a constant dot on my radar. I stood by as Patrick evolved from can't lose gambler to moderately successful businessman. Ahead, however, were financial blunders that, if not corrected by a higher power, threatened my plan to fund and build a certain supernatural melting pot."

"Without Patrick, then," Vlad concluded, "no Upton Arms."

Todd paused when a muffled shout penetrated the room's relative silence. Vlad recognized the angry voice, Patrick no doubt screaming at someone to get their shit together and vacate before they were penetrated with some blunt object placed uncomfortably in one of the body's more sensitive orifices.

Todd placed folded hands on his lap. "Close, Vlad. He was a key figure but, as you know, our leprechaun friend tends toward the volatile side, especially when a modicum of patience is required. He had to be, let's say 'domesticated' for lack of a better word, if he was to be my front man in the mortal plane. I could snap my fingers and make it so, but that would be cheating, especially with my strong belief in free will. What I really needed was stability in future dealings, a dealmaker behind the scenes. A real insider, one who wouldn't attract undue attention."

It fell into place for Vlad, the last piece in a Normal Rockwell jigsaw puzzle suitable for framing. He felt like an idiot that it took this long to put together.

"All this time I thought he was working for Patrick," Vlad said sheepishly.

Todd beamed as if rubbing it in. "Mr. McLegalton was happy to help. Even better, he cozied up to Patrick with his slick personality and discount fees, forming a solid business relationship. Patrick got what he thought was a rare sycophant, and I got a guy who was my eyes when things flickered. And you people, Vlad, you flicker all the time."

"He didn't get any call from Patrick. You're the one who sent him to the Breeze mansion."

"Yes, and other places. Have you seen those *Family Circus* cartoons where a frenetic dotted line traces little Billy's steps all over the neighborhood? Lawster was my dotted line." Todd clapped suddenly like an excited child. "You're going to *love* this last little detail, my friend."

Vlad waited, tired of being played.

"For reasons previously mentioned, I couldn't mold Patrick into the perfect dupe, one who would carry out my bidding without question. I knew he'd always try to pull a fast one. Unless he thought there was far more to me than I showed, with something he could exploit."

"Your 'performance' at the bowling alley," Vlad relented. "You let everyone know you're not just another rich white guy, but someone with impressive powers. And with power comes Patrick's responsibility to himself to use, or abuse, those powers to his benefit."

"Don't forget the parting of the red bowling ball." A smug Todd rubbed his hands together. "It's one thing to know and see all, another to send a subtle message clad in wit. Lawster needed something more to convince him, so I froze time for a bit, which was why he and I just seemed to appear out of nowhere at the back of the bowling alley. Nothing like stopping time to convince someone you're ethereal, and very powerful."

"Wait, I'm not the first?"

"Sorry Vlad, I've been stopping time for as long as it's existed. First time was between the fourth and fifth day of creation because I needed a little break. Funny thing about Lawster was how he wasn't nearly as impressed with that maneuver as I'd hoped. Even with the world around him in a dead stop, he still felt the need to negotiate, though eventually agreeing to terms for a reasonable price."

"That he'd be able to walk again?"

"What?" Todd blurted as if shocked. "No, of course not, he's very happy with the body he has, and it makes him the man he is today. Why would you assume otherwise?"

Vlad mumbled a very humble apology before Todd continued.

"It was money, Vlad. Legal tender for all debts public and private. Soon the deal was in place to build, fund, and operate Upton Arms. Owned and operated by Patrick, just another supernatural creature, albeit one whose power had faded a century ago. The perfect gathering spot."

"Internment camp," Vlad interjected.

"Oh please, you all came of free will, perhaps the first few with spells necessary to get off the ground. You've also had a comfortable life here."

"Looks like everything came together save for one very important detail," Vlad said, allowing a thin smile to cross his face because it was about to be check and mate for this pawn. "How in the world did you allow Upton Arms to close?"

"Finally, we get to the point why we're here Vlad. Right here, right now…"

"You're pausing for effect."

"I am."

"Fine. I'm in no hurry."

Todd huffed his disappointment. "This is where your timeline, and those of your friends, had come to an end. I didn't know if it was because you were all eventually destroyed, or you disappeared from view. The bad news for you, Vlad, is that I must rely on the former so that the latter does not occur."

Vlad let that sink in. He was ready for his timeline to end, even yearned for it. But the right to make that choice belonged to each and every one of his friends. His fingers curled into a fist, fangs sliding into place as he felt an energy he hadn't experienced in a hundred years.

"Don't get your cape in a bunch," Todd exclaimed, holding up his hands. "I don't want to zap everyone out of existence. The fact I didn't see the home's demise coming is another nail in your figurative, not literal, coffin."

"What are you saying?"

"That I am a just and caring deity. It may be you and your friends are ready for humanity's scrap heap, keeping the Cro-Magnons and Neanderthals company. But there's one thing I need to do. While things don't always happen for a reason, they certainly will now."

After several more minutes of conversation, God snapped his fingers, transporting Vlad back to the moment it all started, a moment that stalked the vampire all his life, wondering if could have made a different choice. A wiser choice.

He was about to find out.

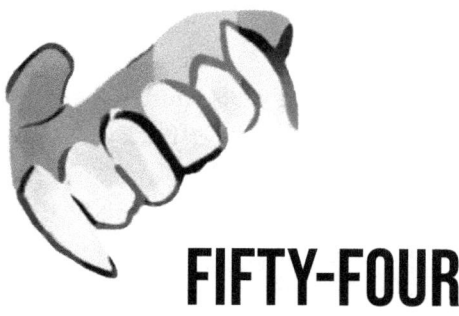

FIFTY-FOUR

VLAD TILTED his head back and stared at the sun with his eyes closed. The daylight felt so good, he wanted to stand here forever inside a body he barely remembered, its age measured in years rather than centuries. Even without powers, it felt powerful.

He didn't need to open his eyes to see the small peasant house on the hill, surrounded by a rickety wooden fence built to keep goats and chickens long since gone. It was where he and his older brother Pietor grew up knowing only a life of hard work and poverty. Behind the house, a narrow footpath led to their Romanian village two miles away. It was the same trail taken by the wayward soldiers who killed their parents for sport when Vlad was eleven and Pietor fourteen. It forced Pietor to become mother and father, mentor and protector—roles that would wear on him for more than a decade.

That fact alone made every bit of this journey back in time so regrettable. Vlad had precisely conjured this scene as heavenly fingers snapped, his memories strengthening even as his physical became mortal. While this day could pass as any in the twelfth-century Romanian countryside, it was *the* day. Vlad's rebirth.

Vlad was hardly a naïve waif on this summer day. He was, after all, twenty-five years old and working six days a week at two jobs. When he wasn't at the inn serving and cleaning up after visitors, he traveled among the farms that required his skills as a butcher. Pietor was just as busy, spending twelve hours a day as a blacksmith. Over the years, the job sculpted his body as if a flawless statue, thick chest and sloping shoulders. Pietor's intimidating shadow was cast not just by his imposing his stature, but his reputation as a brawler. Most steered clear and those that didn't made sure to say nothing that might ignite his short fuse. His brother enjoyed his ranking in the village, embracing it as his revenge for years being largely ignored.

Over the past few months, however, Pietor's routines and demeanor had drastically changed. It wasn't just his odd sleeping habits, refusing to stir while the sun was up, or the way Pietor had boarded the home's windows over Vlad's protests. Most bothersome was the way his older brother vanished every evening, returning in a shirt spattered with blood. Pietor offered no explanation other than a random quip, typically "You should see the other guy."

But this was the day, Vlad knew all too well, when the local prophet had first warned of a nearby *vampir*. Word of the danger spread quickly, gossip moving even faster than the latest virus (as this was a time when "going viral" meant a lot of people were dying). The revelation soon reached Vlad, and he knew his brother was in danger. It was only a matter of time before villagers made their way along that narrow path, sharp tools and sharpened stakes in hand. Vlad narrowed their options down to three—Pietor must flee, Vlad must kill Pietor, or they could both wait for angry villagers to set things right.

It would be this night, then, that Vlad would confront Pietor, a God-given second chance to make everything right.

Vlad remembered each moment of this day since he'd relived it thousands of times. The memory started just after sunset when Vlad confronted Pietor as his brother tried to leave the house. In no uncertain terms, he told Pietor he'd been outed, quickly offering their only choices under the circumstances. Harsh words and blows followed. Before Vlad knew it, fangs were buried deep into his neck and his vision began to fade. Suddenly, a surge of energy overcame Vlad, a power he'd never felt (having no idea at the time he'd experienced his first few seconds as a vampire, reasoning centuries later it wasn't just the bite, but the shared

DNA). He pushed Pietor with a force that launched his brother across the room and onto deer antlers jutting over the mantle, a three-pronged horn bursting from his chest. As the light in Pietor's eyes dimmed, Vlad wrenched the bloody body from the wall in time for each brother to whisper, "Sorry."

Now he was given something so few people are privileged to have— a second chance.

Vlad shielded his eyes and looked west, the evening sun shining brightly. He turned toward the house, knowing he had minutes before his brother awoke. Suddenly there was a heaviness in his hands, fists wrapped tightly around what felt like sticks. He looked down to find a hefty mallet with a large head made of iron in his right hand. In his left hand, a wooden stake roughly ten inches long, perhaps three inches around, one end sharpened to a point.

Todd had called this a test, but Vlad knew that with the tools he held, he'd been given the answer, if not the only way to save himself and his friends. "I leave it in your hands," Todd had said as he snapped his fingers, meaning it literally.

Vlad hefted the weapons and marched toward the all-too-familiar home amid lengthening shadows. He threw open the front door with unnecessary force, took a sharp left and stood over his brother, who slept peacefully under a wool blanket that rose and fell with each breath.

While still gripping the stake, Vlad pinched the top of the blanket with thumb and forefinger and peeled it back to reveal his brother's muscular, pale chest. He focused on the left side of the rib cage until he convinced himself he could see the rhythmic pulse of Pietor's evil heart. Vlad placed the stake's point over that spot, recalling the many horror movies where this would be the time the vampire's eyes snapped open. But no, Pietor slept peacefully even as the wooden point touched skin.

Vlad raised the mallet swiftly, confidently. With one strike, his nightmare would be over. He would live his life normally, tending goats, even finding a wife because that's what life dictated. He would have children, tend more goats, until he rested, and his children would tend goats. And he would die peacefully. No Patrick. No Victor Breeze. No Ralph or Henry or Beatrice or…or …

Luis.

Mallet still poised, one more word came to him.

"Easy," Vlad heard.

Where had that come from? And why?

He lowered the mallet and thought.

Easy.

He let that sink in.

It came to him. Not just easy.

Too easy.

Vlad thought back to the conversation with Todd in the moments before the deity snapped his fingers and sent Vlad back through the centuries. He'd asked Vlad if the vampire had any regrets.

Of course he had regrets, Vlad answered. Who didn't?

"I don't," Todd said. "That's a side effect of omnipotence, but also my decision to let the world spin without interference, save for the careful sprinkling of minor miracles."

Todd paused, raised an eyebrow, and pressed his lips together, an expression that suggested puzzlement, the one expression one would never expect to see on someone claiming to be omniscient. He continued. "That's not completely honest. I often interfered as civilization began to ramp up, when it needed reminders of who was in charge. Since then, I've been hands-off. Well, until now.

"I'm resisting a very strong urge to wipe out your kind once and for all, going against all I've stood for, the whole live-and-let-live thing. But what's happened at Upton Arms over the years has been very curious indeed. You've been friends and lovers and trespassers and betrayers. You've come to the aid of one another while at the same time harboring grudges that would destroy lesser beings." Another pause as Todd scratched his chin. "Your humanity is beguiling."

"Um, thanks?" Vlad said, slightly baffled.

"You've evolved, leaving behind some of your worst traits and adapting in ways that are less threatening to your fellow man," Todd judged. "But what's to say you won't fall back on old habits? It's a flip of a coin at this point, and I need one more bit of evidence."

God stood, folded his arms, stood on his tiptoes, and settled back on his heels. He was a deity in deep thought.

"This is what we're going to do," Todd proclaimed. "For most of your life, you've played God with other's lives. Only makes sense I let you play God for real. I'm granting you temporary use of a very limited range of omnipotent powers to change one moment in your life." He pointed squarely at Vlad's heart. "Show me your humanity."

Vlad liked the idea of so much power, even if it was a small slice. But with omnipotence came great responsibility. It also seemed extremely complicated.

"Don't worry," Todd said, dipping into Vlad's mind. "I'm sending your subconscious a user's manual, one that is way easier to follow than instructions for an Ikea bookcase."

That made Vlad feel even less confident.

"I'm giving you a slight push to the natural starting point of your journey," Todd said, holding up a glowing hand. "As decisions are made, the coin will fall. Heads, your life goes on as I remain behind the curtain. Tails, it will be like none of you ever existed. Because none of you will have ever existed."

Then the snap of fingers, a sound that sent Vlad on a mission to defend his life and those of his friends. As he stood over his brother, stake and mallet poised to take the path most frequently traveled, he paused. He was to live a normal life, but what was that exactly? Could it really be this easy?

There it was again.

"Too easy." This time the words, from a voice deep inside him, felt like a slap across his face.

If he were to subtract his vampire side, would the repercussions spread to the rest of his community? Would Todd then subtract the werewolf and the witch and the leprechaun? Or would they cease to exist altogether, left on the celestial cutting-room floor like inessential scenes? Todd had that power, perhaps the right, to do just that. But did Vlad?

Vlad stepped back, literally and figuratively, to see his life wasn't just his own. Even as the tools of death grew heavy in his hands, he tilted his head back and closed his eyes. Suddenly, he saw his face staring back at him, the one waiting for him hundreds of years from now. Instead of a mallet, he held a pebble, which he dropped, creating a series of ripples that made him unrecognizable.

The solution—his solution—was not here. Not with Pietor.

Todd had mentioned humanity, wondering if Vlad possessed so much as a spark of it.

To answer that question, Vlad needed to travel to another time and place. But first he would enjoy the last of the day's light before he bid goodbye to it forever.

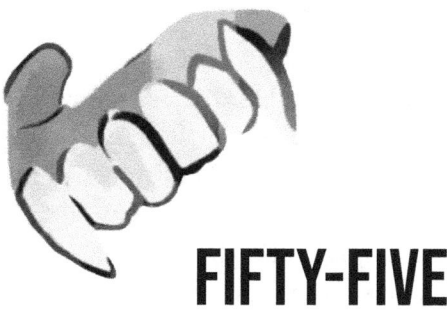

FIFTY-FIVE

VLAD LISTENED THIS TIME, really listened when he returned to a van that had seemed so much larger on his first visit. The cramped interior seemed to collapse on him, the dense and hot air taking away his breath. A curtain of sweat bathed his forehead, and for a second he wondered if he'd made the right choice.

But just for a second.

The rest was familiar, even faintly comforting. Vlad noted the faint glow of a Cracker Barrel sign through the tinted windows, detecting the unconstrained scent of fried food. Further memories of that night flowed into his mind, bringing with them the emotions he'd locked away.

His eyes adjusted to the dim cabin, and he took in the details that matched his recollections of a night that haunted him. The hospice van was parked in the same space, not far from the restaurant where dozens celebrated a legally approved death. Across from him sat the woman far too young for her fate. She stared at him through narrowed eyes, her body shaking with…tension? Anger?

When her mouth opened wide and screams poured forth, Vlad went with the latter. Before her words started to make sense, he noted a rectangle of white laying at his feet. Shame overwhelmed him when he realized it was the same envelope that had crushed his soul.

This time he left it where it lay.

"You want to talk about God?" Nancy continued, the words finally coalescing in Vlad's mind. "Where was He all those nights when I heard my mom and dad crying themselves to sleep? Where was He when my mom quit her job to take care of me? Where was He when medical bills forced us to move to some shitbox apartment and my little brother got his ass beat repeatedly at his new school? Where was this motherfucking prayer-sucker when I was on my knees every night begging for relief? For an end? Huh? Tell me!"

So much pain, too much for the world to carry. Vlad knew it this time.

He remained silent.

"I'll tell you where," she went on. "In your fucking imagination. That's where! Because any magical super-being with an ounce of mercy is going to reach inside me and flick off the lights. Don't you dare talk about God. Don't you fucking dare!"

Vlad knew this was where he should be if he was going to do the right thing.

No, not just the right thing. The most impactful thing. The one thing that would actually make a difference in this world.

His mind flipped through the user's manual one more time, God's simple instructions for the use of limited Almighty powers. He was right, it was much easier to understand than anything packed in an Ikea box. He couldn't find exactly what he was looking for, so he was ready to improvise when the time came.

And Nancy would let him know when it was time.

For now, she shook with anger and fear and grief. Vlad hardly needed a side of omniscience to know that. He listened to her ragged breathing via lungs nearly destroyed by chemotherapy, part of the scorched-earth policy necessary to attack cancer.

Vlad knew what was about to happen thanks to memories that refused to give him peace. He was about to lean in, mouth open, fangs at the ready to bring her the only thing she wanted.

Mercy.

He would put his upper lip to her neck, feeling the feathery pulse of her carotid artery. She, in turn, tilted her head to welcome relief, remaining still even as an incisor sliced through flesh like a scalpel, Vlad relishing the first drops of warm, rich liquid as a man dying of thirst enjoyed his first taste of water in days. The moment had brought the vampire a measure of guilt, enjoying pleasures from a willing victim rather than prey.

"Yes," he'd heard her whisper. "Yes."

That's when reality struck him like a stake through his heart. He was no hitman selling his talents like a grim-reaping prostitute. Vlad pushed her away, blood still in the corner of his mouth, more streaming from the wound. The rest was a blur, save for the seconds he needed to snatch the envelope before jumping out of the van.

How many times had these moments run through his mind, summoned when his subconscious felt the need to punish him? Too many.

But that was then.

This was now.

He was going to set things right thanks to his God-given skills.

He crawled out of his own mind and faced down the moment.

"Well," Nancy said, her face softening from anger to pleading, her voice wrung of all emotion. "Are you going to do this or not?"

Vlad knew what to do. What had to be done. All those yesterdays when the vampire played God, now he was going to do it for real.

"I know you don't believe in God," he whispered softly.

"Damn right," Nancy agreed, squeezing her fists as tendons jutted from her forearms like cables. "If God did exist, and assuming he was a decent guy for a supreme being, he'd at least give me the courage to swallow a bottle of pills or put a gun to my head before it was too late with nurses and parents and assorted fucking caregivers hovering all the time."

"I get it," Vlad agreed, a rare bit of honesty given the death he'd delivered over the years. "I get your anger too." He paused. "So does God. He's listening right now."

"Great, I want to die, and you give me fucking platitudes."

But it was hardly a platitude, Vlad knew. He could feel God looking over his shoulder, curious enough to let this play out. But would he give Vlad enough line to make this right? He was about to find out.

"There's no way you could know or understand," Vlad explained, his hand tenderly cradling the back of her neck. "But trust me, God is watching."

"I need a mercy-motivated killer, and I get a tele-evangelist trying to talk me out of death," Nancy spat. "Save the 'God wants the best for you' pro-life bullshit for the pregnant seventeen-year-old carrying their rapist's baby."

Nancy let go of the armrest, shoulders slumping, pushing him away. "Get out. Just get the fuck out. Leave the envelope but be sure to take God with you."

"Give me a minute," Vlad pleaded, waiting for the moment he felt— that he knew—he had the power to do what he wanted.

"You had your minute and more. Can't tell you how much I'm looking forward to the next days and weeks and months of agony. Fuck you, fuck God, and fuck life in general. Get out before I start screaming bloody murder." She laughed. "How ironic is that?"

Now or never, Vlad thought. He reached deep, summoning what he needed from his partial omnipotence. Only it remained stubbornly out of reach.

He did the next best thing.

He bowed his head.

He prayed.

And it was answered.

"Thanks, big guy," Vlad murmured. To Nancy, he said, "Let's do it your way."

He leaned toward her, mouth open, fangs ready. Closing his eyes, he was ready to bring her the mercy she so eagerly sought. He put his lips to her neck, feeling the feathery pulse of her carotid artery. She leaned in, her chin up, welcoming his touch.

The first incisor cut through flesh like a scalpel, the first drops of warm, rich liquid touching Vlad's tongue, sinking in, sending strong signals to his brain's pleasure spots.

As he felt the power drain from him, he couldn't remember being so happy.

FIFTY-SIX

VLAD SLUMPED INTO THE CHAIR, exhausted. He'd gone off-script, wondering how Todd—God? —was going to react. The best thing to do now was play it cool.

"Surprised?" the vampire said, crossing his legs casually to suggest his world, and that of his friends, did not hang in the balance.

Todd rubbed his chin. "I will confess that I did not see that one coming. And remember, this is from a guy who knew where single-cell organisms were headed. See why I'm worried?"

Vlad's eyes wandered, double-checking where he was. Same room, same furnishings. He wondered if he'd return to the same time, or his actions had changed things for the worse. By all appearances, he had returned to Upton Arms—or a gulag deep in Todd's mind.

Vlad felt slightly better when he heard Beatrice screaming at Patrick to quit selling all their stuff on eBay. "That cauldron is a keepsake handed down since Salem!" she yelled.

"Sounds like all is well," the vampire said, more a suggestion than an observation since he had no clue if anything was well.

"For the most part," Todd informed the vampire, news hardly meant to comfort Vlad. "You want to know what will happen with the miraculously cured Nancy?"

"Not really," Vlad lied, though he did have a light fear of a horror-movie outcome when death was cheated. Last thing he wanted to hear was how Nancy would be killed by a runaway logging truck, or something as meaningless as choking on a peanut.

"I get that," Todd agreed. "Suffice to say one of her grandkids will con a half-dozen small businesses out of several million dollars because, you know, no good deed and so forth."

"Awesome."

"Yeah, awesome."

"But she will devise an effective treatment for colon cancer that adds three months to the lifespan of Stage Four patients, so you've got that going for you."

"Especially if I develop colon cancer," Vlad mentioned offhandedly, still stressed as to where all this was going.

At this point, however, all he wanted to do was sleep. He tilted his head back and closed his eyes. A fifty-year snooze should make him right again. Omnipotence was draining.

"Before you drift off," Todd interrupted, "would you like to hear what you've won?"

"Nope," Vlad lied again. He was dying to know, well aware the knowledge may involve his death and he kind of wanted to stick around a little longer.

Maybe a lot longer. "Are you sure?" Todd pushed. "It involves your continued existence, as well as that of your friends."

"Then…" Vlad wanted to say yes, or nod his head, or maybe just open his eyes. He couldn't summon the energy to do any of that, drifting off for hours, years, centuries…

Until the moment he felt a tap on his forehead and a jolt of electricity running down his spine.

"Damn, a simple alarm would have done," the vampire complained, his back still tingling but the cobwebs gone.

"No, it wouldn't," Todd argued. "Believe me, I know how changing time and space takes it out of you. You know how I took the seventh day off? It was more like a million years, not that I missed anything."

Vlad's eyes began to close as Todd rambled on about supermassive volcanoes and planetary collisions and plate tectonics. "The Bible makes it sound so easy, creating a livable environment for intelligent beings. Like I just snapped my fingers. You know how hard it is to communicate by burning bushes and stone tablets. If I'd thought to install the internet then, things would be different. Anyway…Vlad? VLAD!"

"Sorry, I'm back, please no more lightning bolts down my spine."

"Getting to the point…" Todd slapped his knees and glanced briefly at the door, which only slightly muffled the argument between Beatrice and Patrick. "I enjoyed your choice, the way you saw the tree through the forest. You showed sympathy and selflessness, with a dash of sacrifice given the physical pain inherent in that particular power. It was humanity at its best and in this world, and I don't take that for granted."

"I wasn't sure it was going to work," Vlad admitted. The scene replayed itself in the vampire's mind. Leaning over Nancy, fangs surgically slicing through flesh. Calling on an extraordinary ability he knew was his, if only just for this moment. His body seizing, contracting in a war with an adversary that was more than a match for miracles. Pain and pressure filled his head, a feeling so agonizing that Vlad nearly wished (prayed) for it to explode.

Then it was over as quickly as it started. A deep serenity washed over him, its pleasure as intense as the love he now felt for Nancy. His Nancy, whose faith in him was so strong he swore he could see it, silver strands between them. Vlad knew the connection could not be severed, even as he landed back in the rocking chair.

"Is it always like that?" Vlad grinned, the memory washing over him in warm and gentle waves. "The afterglow?"

"Not so much that I would ever take it for granted," Todd said. "It always reminds me why I did what I did. Creation and such." Todd leaned forward, patting Vlad's thigh. "Now, before you get too full of yourself, there's a loose string that needs attention."

Vlad sighed. "Do I have a choice?"

"Always."

After Todd laid out the next journey, the choice was obvious.

FIFTY-SEVEN

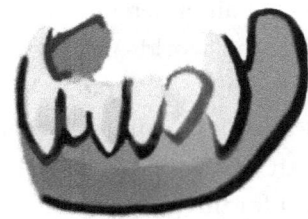

STANDING unseen in the corner of a small office, Vlad felt like the Ghost of Christmas Past. While it was discomforting to be a stalker (a feeling apparently unknown to Ralph the invisible man), watching things unfold in person was much better than viewing grainy footage from a surveillance camera. No doubt the CIA would jump at the chance to upgrade to magical technology.

Vlad eyed Victor Breeze with as much contempt as he could for a man whose future was not nearly as rosy as he believed at this moment. Breeze oversaw the meeting behind a desk covered in brightly colored fabric. Vlad's future ex stood rigid and upright, a position proving the stick up his ass was there years before Vlad had ever met him.

The vampire had no idea where he was on Victor's timeline, but given the ramshackle environment and mediocre quality of the sparse furniture, Victor had yet to make it big. It wasn't until Vlad heard the traffic noises outside the narrow window that he knew this must be Victor's first office in New York's garment district when he was a struggling designer.

"This is a can't-lose proposition," Victor insisted, leaning back with unearned confidence. "If you don't get in now, don't blame me in a year when everyone is rocking Monet on their asses, and you're still wearing old-timey shorts with too many pockets."

"Jesus fuck, Victor, how do you come up with this shit?" An inexplicably excited Patrick rotated the shorts, admiring how the bridge over lilies arched gracefully over the zipper. "It's like going to a museum every time you put on your pants."

Patrick put down the Monet and ran his hand over the other designs spread in front of him. He "ooohed" over Picasso's cubist stylings, and "ahhed" while admiring the broad and colorful strokes of Van Gogh. He lifted a pair that featured Edvard Munch's "The Scream," its elongated face centered over the groin.

"When I wear these, it'll be the ladies who'll be screaming, am I right?" Patrick said with a crassness Vlad knew was not unusual for the time. While the world would change, Patrick's immaturity would be frozen in time.

"They'll be screaming alright, in fear," Beatrice cackled.

Good to know some things won't change, Vlad thought.

"You're just jealous, woman," Patrick shot back, a dangerous thing to say to a witch. Sure enough, Vlad instinctively stepped back as Beatrice screwed her face into a tight spiral, a sign a harmful spell was coming on. But the look vanished as quickly as it appeared, indicating the witch had a thing for the leprechaun long before Vlad would have guessed.

Patrick picked up a Salvador Dali and modeled it, asking if it brought out his eyes. "Or maybe Monet would make a better impression?"

Beatrice didn't even have the energy to groan.

Patrick examined each of the dozen or so samples overlapping one another on the desk. "How many works do you plan on bringing to market?"

"Aiming for twenty-five in the initial rollout, each painting an instantly recognizable classic," Victor said. "I haven't even told you the best part." Vlad recognized the well-timed pause because Victor loved the drama. "To appeal to our younger customers who want to wear contemporary art, check this out." From a drawer, Victor pulled a pair of shorts emblazoned with a loosely painted skull filled with colliding colors.

Patrick shook his head. "Imagine a woman going down, and she sees a dick poking out of the scary thing. Gives a new meaning to skull-fucking, and not in a good way."

"OK, it's your money," Victor sighed. "But Mr. Basquiat is going to be very disappointed." Breeze stuffed the shorts back into the drawer.

"Don't worry about it because the rest of the line is going to make a fortune. Victor, you've outdone yourself this time. What was it you called these again?"

"Shorts with art," Victor said. "Sharts."

This time Vlad groaned, even though he knew it was coming.

"I'm amazed no one thought of this before," Patrick said.

Considering Victor's many fashion fails, Sharts were up there with Tirts (ties sewn into shirts) and Shankies (dress shirts housing handkerchiefs up each sleeve). Then there were the ludicrous shapeless rubber loafers that sacrificed self-respect for comfort. Who knew Victor was just way ahead of his time and that one day millions of people would wear such shoes even if it made them look like preschoolers from the ankle down? (Nor would Vlad recommend them for capers of any kind).

"Sharts, Jesus," Vlad ranted, wishing they could hear him. He knew what would happen next since this was the deal that put Patrick in the hole for the first time, the first domino in the line that one day would topple Upton Arms.

"Let's talk about what you need from me to get this thing rolling," Patrick urged.

Vlad strolled to the window not to see an endless line of taxis crawl, but to step into the shaft of sunlight in all its glory.

It was good being God. Or at least his tool.

Vlad closed his eyes and raised his left hand. He imagined an old-fashioned traffic light in the middle of a busy intersection, jalopies cruising by at a hectic pace. A bell sounds and a red stop sign flips up, traffic coming to an immediate halt.

Vlad opened his eyes to see everything frozen in place, with Victor looking more mannequin than usual. As much as the vampire wanted to enjoy his handiwork, he'd been warned his time and powers were fleeting. And he was already feeling very rundown.

Vlad conjured another vision and snapped his fingers. He felt a wave go through him, as well as the kind of tiredness that only came with weeks of blood starvation.

The traffic sign switched back to "Go."

Patrick was no longer smiling. Instead, he had a look of concern as he shuffled through the contract that suddenly appeared in his hands.

"Before I sign, I'm going to have my lawyer take a look," the leprechaun said. "Just to make sure everything is in order." Patrick opened the office door and beckoned with his index finger. "We're ready for you."

In rolled a young P. Addison Waverly, his muscular body and awkward handling of the wheelchair suggesting whatever had put him in it occurred recently.

"I'm sorry, where did you come from?" Victor suspiciously eyed Addison and the battered briefcase on his lap. "Representation really isn't necessary, is it, Patrick?"

Up until a moment ago, and before Vlad changed the timeline, Patrick would have agreed. But thanks to the vampire's interference, the leprechaun had the kind of levelheaded representation necessary to save him from financial disaster.

Patrick stood at attention as he addressed Victor's challenge. "I never do business without Mr. Waverly. If that's a problem—"

"No no, not at all," Victor agreed reluctantly. "Let's go on."

Addison spun toward Victor. "As I said, a moment with my client."

Patrick followed the lawyer into the hallway. Vlad slipped through the wall to join them. Awesome.

"Patrick, I overheard everything I needed to hear." Addison struggled to keep his voice down. "Sharts? What the fuck?"

"They can't miss," Patrick insisted. "Put these on, and you're not just someone in leisurewear, you're a walking art gallery. People will stop and stare in admiration."

"They'll stop and stare in disbelief that someone would wear the Mona Lisa on their crotch."

"It's less pretentious that way. Even approachable."

"Paintings are designed for walls, not butts. It's a terrible deal, Patrick, and that's before we get to licensing."

Patrick took off his green derby and scratched his balding head. "Licensing? This is famous art. It belongs to the people."

"Sure, up to the point you're making a buck off them. First, some of those works are not in the public domain, and you will hear from estate lawyers as soon as the paintings turn up on someone's ass. Then there's the name. You don't need to walk away. You need to run."

Patrick's shoulders slumped. "Damn, maybe you're right."

It was Vlad's turn again. He leaned into Addison's ear with a suggestion.

FIFTY-EIGHT

"LET ME GET THIS STRAIGHT," Victor reiterated. "You want to invest a quarter million dollars."

"Absolutely," Patrick said, fingers thrumming on the armrests.

For the first time, Beatrice spoke up in protest. "Babe, you know I trust you, but I'm not so sure about this."

Patrick put his arm around her knees and gave them a squeeze. "This is going to make us rich. We're not so much investing in sharts as we are in our brilliant fashion designer here."

Victor beamed at the compliment. "I appreciate your confidence as much as your investment. You said you wanted an opportunity to invest in any future products I may devise?"

"That's right," Patrick nodded.

"Correction," Addison interrupted. "Any *fabric-related* invention."

Vlad smiled. While Victor's tagless underwear was still a few years away and would change the way people chose their undergarments, other inventions would have little chance. The vampire thought specifically of Victor's Breeze, a line of fans with a fatal flaw causing them to catch fire and shoot flames at anyone hoping to cool off. No one died, but it took a chunk from his tagless licensing deals.

"Sure, any fabric-based invention," Victor agreed. "Because I'll have a ton of ideas. At some point. Maybe even better than sharts."

"Yeah?" Patrick said, leaning forward.

"Can't really say at this point, trade secrets and all. But sure, yes, you'll get the first shot at investment."

Addison snapped open his briefcase. "We'll want thirty percent of the business, and that includes future licensing deals."

Vlad saw Victor's mind light up in a way that could be seen in space, yet his ex's voice remained calm and steady as if he wasn't convinced he'd just rigged the lottery. "I can do fifteen percent."

Vlad shook his head, wondering what he ever saw in Victor, even if it was the briefest of flings. A thought flitted through his mind—*Enjoy your tanning-salon memberships while you can, asshole.*

"That seems a little short," Patrick argued.

Victor stifled a laugh. "It's negotiable, of course."

"No," Addison chimed in, "fifteen percent is fine."

Because fifteen percent would be more than enough, Vlad knew. He had shared his insider information with Addison earlier, the attorney not even bothering to question its source. Vlad wasn't sure if by this time Todd had introduced himself to the future Lawster McLegalton. Nor did it matter, as long as the attorney was eager to make a deal.

"If it's settled, I took the opportunity to draw up the papers before we arrived," Addison said, placing a sheaf of documents on the desk.

"You did?" Patrick and Victor chimed.

"I mean, no, I asked him to," Patrick corrected. "Of course. That's how much I love sharts. And whatever else comes out of that brilliant mind of yours."

"I already have a few ideas." Victor eyes sparkled. "Imagine pants that come with an adjustable waist so you can let them out if you gain weight. Or pants you can wear without a belt. Without a belt! It will change the fashion industry forever while bringing an end to the belt-industrial complex."

Patrick glanced at Addison, who was shaking his head. "Sure, Victor," the leprechaun said in an overly patronizing tone. "Sounds great."

Two pens landed on the stack of paper. "Gentlemen," Addison announced, backing away from the desk, "let's get some signatures and do this deal."

FIFTY-NINE

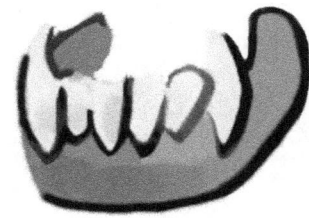

THERE WAS no whoosh of air or flash of light. Nothing that would suggest Vlad even moved, let alone jumped decades into the future. But there he was, facing the Almighty.

"Hey God."

"Vlad."

The room, however, was different yet familiar. The bed, the clothes strewn across bed. His favorite chair. Definitely his room, but hadn't he packed? Then there was the spacious walk-in closet packed with khakis, jeans, and short-sleeved plaid shirts. That was new. When he poked his head into the bathroom, he was shocked to find a separate bathtub and shower stall. And was that a bidet seat on the toilet?

"What the hell?" Vlad wondered aloud, ignoring God's sly smile.

The vampire crossed the room, skirting a king-size bed, another upgrade. Opening the door to the hallway, he found instead a cozy room with a loveseat, coffee table and, wait, was that a seventy-inch TV hanging on the wall? He scooped the remote control from the coffee table and pressed the red power button, the screen powering up with an electronic chime. Every streaming service he'd ever heard of, and a few more he hadn't, were displayed on the home screen. He clicked on the one he knew had both live TV and streaming shows, expecting to get a message urging him to sign up for a free one-week trial. Instead, the TV grid popped up with sports, cooking shows, local channels and, yes, an outlet dedicated to nothing but medical mysteries. He fired up *How Did This Not Show Up on the X-ray?* and was mesmerized for a few moments before putting down the remote. Wait, was that an ad for—

A knock at the door, rapid and insistent. Vlad turned off the TV and started to turn the knob when he noticed the peephole. Was this still Upton Arms? What had happened when he was gone?

Peering through, he saw Luis. But in full werewolf mode. Something was definitely off. He felt something he hadn't in decades, two fangs sliding instinctively, even blissfully, in place.

"Were-Eats with a delivery," his friend growled from the other side of the door. "Open up."

"You're not going to kill me, are you?"

"What are you talking about? I have your monthly shipment. I can just take it back, no skin off my nose."

"I mean, you're a werewolf." Vlad stared at the monster in disbelief. "As in teeth and claws and seriously huge. Did I do something to piss you off? If it's what I said about you to Todd—"

"Who the fuck is Todd?" Luis interrupted with a growl. "Look, if you don't want to eat for the next thirty days I'll go back, but make up your mind because we have somewhere to be in five minutes. This is one meeting we can't miss."

Many things had changed but Luis remained as stubborn as ever, which was somewhat comforting. Vlad ushered him inside, his friend plopping down a large Styrofoam container even as fur receded, the elongated jaw returning to its normal dimensions. "Better?"

"It's not often I see you go full werewolf because I know you have trouble..." Vlad trailed off with a sheepish look. He wasn't sure how to address Luis's were-performance issues without sounding insensitive.

"What the hell are you talking about? Not that it's any of your business, but I'm meeting everyone at the local watering hole later tonight and felt like getting in the mood a little early. Had I known you'd be offended—"

"Watering hole? You mean Chili's?"

"Chili's? What the hell is a Chili's? I mean the Were-Bar. Yeah, I know you look down on national chains, but it's still pretty damn good."

"I guess it's not where you're going, but that you're going as a werewolf."

"Vlad, please," Luis exhaled. "Not you too. We're not flesh-ists. Anyone is welcome, fur or no fur. Some of my best friends are hairless. We prefer our alternate state because we got it, and we want to flaunt it. Anyway, good talk. Here's your stuff."

For the first time, Vlad noticed the bold red cross on either side of the container, wrapped tightly in cellophane.

"Need help putting it away or you think you can take it from here?" Luis said in a tone that made it clear Vlad's only answer was the latter. "By the way, you're welcome to come as always. I know this acceptance is relatively new, especially to those of us who had to spend most of our lives hiding who we were. Who knew gay weddings would one day be outdone by gay werewolf weddings? Speaking of that, any luck on RamPire?"

Vlad had nothing to offer but a perplexed look.

"I get it, Vlad. Dating by app takes a while to get used to, especially one with such a crappy name. Anyway, we're going to be late if you don't put that stuff away." Luis nodded toward a doorway Vlad hadn't noticed. As the vampire hefted the cooler, he spied the words, "Must be refrigerated." That could be a problem because this was not going to fit in the mini-fridge.

Only it wasn't a problem because the doorway led to a fully appointed kitchen with glass-top stove, convection oven, and massive French-door refrigerator. Placing the cooler on the granite counter, he opened the fridge to find two of its six shelves lined with blood pouches.

He picked one up and read the label.

"Type B-positive. Seven percent human blood. Vampire grade."

Vlad popped the cap on the plastic tube extending in inch from the top. A bit of plastic emerged from the top. Vlad pulled.

A straw. It was a vampire sippy pouch. He tasted it. It didn't have the rich copper taste he preferred, but it wasn't bad.

"Dude, you done?" Luis called from the other room.

"Hold on."

"The meeting includes the final three contractors presenting their bids on the gym addition. We don't want to be late because you know Patrick will choose the cheapest, and we don't want to cut corners. Residents want quality locker rooms with enough showers and a sauna. We're also choosing equipment for the free-weight room. I want my exercise equipment to be like my favorite music—heavy metal. No hurry, but hurry."

Some things never change, Vlad thought with some comfort. "Just a sec," he said, storing each pouch with label to the front, noting the expiration dates were months from now.

"No way you expected this, right?"

Vlad spun toward the voice.

God sat on the counter, wearing a white T-shirt, cargo shorts, and flip-flops.

"This is why I had my reservations." He wagged his legs like a three-year-old. "But I thought what could it hurt? Let you have a little reward for your work and faith. Because I like you."

God hopped off the counter. "No use in crying over spilt blood, right? If the shit gets really crazy, I can just wipe the planet clean and start over again."

"I thought you promised never to do that again after the flood," Vlad reminded Him.

"I did promise that, didn't I? I'll find a loophole if I have to. Shouldn't be hard with religious dogma."

"You'd wipe us out just like that?"

"Why not? It's just one timeline."

Vlad felt each pouch slip through his hands, his chin dropping as well. "You wouldn't. You couldn't."

"Man, I'm just messing with you, again." God said with an impish grin. "In all honesty, I've tried making some huge alterations to timelines, and more often than not it backfires. Stuff always happens. Maybe one day I'll tell you about the universe where Earth's most popular movie series is *Planet of the Humans*."

Luis's voice again. "Vlad, let's go, or Patrick's going to refuse to resurface the basketball court as well."

"But—" Vlad stopped, unable to take it all in. He remained silent as he stored the last of the pouches before turning to speak to, wait, wasn't someone there? An old guy wearing shorts? Or...

"Vlad, it's time," Luis called. "Shake a wing."

Vlad met Luis in the living room, resisting an urge for one last glance into the kitchen because he could have sworn...

"Alright, let's go."

Luis moved his left hand in a pendulum swing. "After you."

Vlad headed to the front door and put his hand on the knob.

"Uh, you forgetting we're playing pickleball after the meeting?" Luis prodded. "We're in the semis against Darnell and that douche Ralph and his fucking floating paddle. Get your 'screen."

"My what?"

"Jesus, dude, what is wrong with you today?"

Luis ducked into Vlad's bathroom and emerged with a white and yellow plastic bottle. He tossed it toward Vlad, who snatched it with reflexes he thought he'd lost years ago.

Vlad looked at the label: **Vampire grade. SPF 34K. Reapply every two hours to prevent charring.**

"It's a brave new world," Vlad muttered.

"No shit," Luis said with a wink. "And a much better one at that. By the way, wanted to show you something."

Luis took a phone out of his back pocket, tapped the screen twice then swiped once, twice, three times. A smile spread over his face, one broader than Vlad had ever seen. He flipped the screen toward Vlad showing a photo of two young girls, each around six years old, both in hospital gowns. The girl on the right wore a baseball cap that didn't hide the fact her head was smooth as a bowling ball. Between them was the most beautiful golden retriever Vlad had ever seen, no doubt the source of the beaming smiles on either side of it.

"Yeah, nice," Vlad said, unsure of what he was looking at. "Friends of yours?"

"Funny stuff," Luis said, making it clear it wasn't funny at all. "This was from our visit to the children's hospital Sunday. Have to say, I never thought becoming anything but a wolf could be so rewarding. But being a therapy animal has changed my life."

Vlad held his hand out for the phone. He brought the screen closer, focusing on the golden retriever. He looked at Luis, then the golden, back to Luis. Sure enough, there it was. In the eyes. Both were indeed his old friend.

He handed the phone back to Luis, resisting the urge to pat him on his big werewolf head. "Good dog," Vlad said.

"Right?" Luis said, taking one more look at the photo before stowing the phone back in his pocket. "God, I love my life. Anyway, we've got to get going."

As Vlad followed Luis out the door, he stopped, just for a moment, to check his reflection in the small mirror hanging by the door. A few more gray hairs, a few more wrinkles, but damn, not bad for a guy up there in centuries.

A movement behind him caught his eye. He swiveled quickly, swearing he could have seen some old guy in shorts. But no, nothing there. The buzzing in his ear, however, was no illusion. He swatted at it, noticing a gold speck hovering out of the corner of his eye.

"Shut the door before it gets in," Luis warned.

Vlad did just that, hearing the latch click home.

"Better safe than sorry, what with the FCE policies instituted by the new administration," Luis said.

"FCE?"

"Vlad, you cannot miss any more meals, it makes your brain foggy. Fairy Control and Enforcement, the agency that deals with all tiny, wing-enhanced magical creatures charged or convicted for crimes." Luis cleared his throat and spoke as if quoting the FCE manual. "Such crimes include but are not limited to unlawful surveillance, unauthorized sales of fairy dust, and public urination in food and drink. Ever since word came down that FCE is sending fairy-sniffing dogs to Upton, those dust-snorting pests have been sneaking into rooms to hide out for a while."

Vlad thought about it for a moment.

"About time they're cracking down," he nodded.

"Yeah," Luis agreed. "Fairies are such dicks."

———

Thank you for reading! Did you enjoy? Please add your review because nothing helps an author more and encourages readers to take a chance on a book than a review.

Discover more from Scott Craven at www.authorscottcraven.com

And find your next read, HELL'S HERESIES, by Kat D. Coffin. Turn the page for a sneak peek!

You can also sign up for the City Owl Press newsletter to receive notice of all book releases!

SNEAK PEEK OF HELL'S HERESIES
BY KAT D. COFFIN

Something snatched Emerie's ankle and yanked her off the bed.

At first, she assumed she'd rolled the wrong way and sat up, trying to figure out why her bed was so hard and cold. She blinked owlishly at the leaning tower of laundry across from her. She registered that one of her windows was open, which accounted for how cold her bedroom was. But before she could center herself and fully realize she was no longer on her ebony sleigh bed, an invisible force grabbed her leg and pulled her out the open bedroom door. She snatched desperately at the door jamb, but it slipped through her fingers. She heard it vibrate ominously as she was towed along.

"*Hey!*"

Her head hit several boxes as she careened down the hallway. Emerie attempted to seize the wall, but only succeeded in slamming her body back and forth against the plaster like a pinball. She kicked her free leg fiercely at the imperceptible aggressor. She felt something icy-cold, as though she plunged a bare foot in slush—but she was released.

Emerie scrambled to her feet and punched the air wildly. She was at the tail end of their long hallway, almost in the upstairs parlor. Monsters crouched in the darkness until her eyes adjusted and they became unpacked boxes strewn across the room. She squinted and steadied her breathing. There was nothing there. As usual.

Dylan poked his head out of their bedroom. His eyes narrowed.

"Emerie?" His clicked his teeth. "Did it happen again?"

"No," Emerie said. "I just—went to get a glass of water. Tripped on a box."

Dylan snorted audibly. But Emerie knew three a.m. was too late for this particular fight for her early bird boyfriend. He retreated into their bedroom and she sighed with relief. This wasn't the first time she had been forcibly jerked out of bed and dragged down the hallway. She considered herself lucky it always pulled her into the parlor, rather than making a sharp right turn at the end of the hall to push her down the stairs. These unfortunate instances were just one of the many examples Dylan had of why they *should not have moved into this house.* But Emerie refused to accept that kind of negative thinking about their home renovation plans.

She started to follow him back to bed and bit back an angry squawk —she stepped in a paint roller tray. Creamy-cold goop covered her foot.

Her lip curled and she carefully removed her bare foot, resisting the urge to kick the roller tray against the wall. This was getting ridiculous.

She took care to walk on the plastic sheeting which covered the floor and detoured into the bathroom to wash off the paint in the clawfoot tub. She loved that tub, with its strange taloned feet and a showerhead faucet combination styled like an old-fashioned telephone. It was one of the reasons she moved in—along with the huge kitchen overflowing with cabinet space, three extra bedrooms, and wraparound porch. She exhaled as she flicked the light—they'd been having electricity problems since the move. Thankfully, it buzzed on.

"Are you kidding me?!"

The doors of the medicine cabinet were flung open. Their collective toiletries littered the floor. Her Spider-Man toothbrush floated sadly in the toilet over Dylan's electric toothbrush head. She stared at the mess, balancing on one foot. Dylan would be furious. His assortment of hair products far outnumbered her own and he had organized them *so carefully*. She scooped them up and haphazardly stuffed them back into the medicine cabinet. Gingerly, she reached inside the toilet and threw both toothbrushes away. She eyed the shower curtain, which had been torn down for good measure.

Scowling, Emerie hopped on one foot to the tub. She twisted the knob and hissed as the icy water blasted the paint off her foot. She had not been getting much sleep since they moved in. Their first night here, booming explosions of thunder woke them up repeatedly through the night—but the skies were completely clear. After making sure there was no hidden bowling alley in the attic, she blamed the neighbor's pickup truck.

The following night a high-pitched scream interrupted them while they tried to unpack the dining room boxes, shattering a crystal tea set. Emerie didn't much care for the gaudy collection, so she made an offhand comment about the squeaky pipes in the basement and pretended she had dropped the tea set. At this point, Dylan began to grow suspicious.

After a week, Emerie started feeling cold pokes and prods, like someone slipped ice cubes down her shirt. Of course, this eventually evolved into chilly hands that wrenched her out of bed and towed her down the hallway. Terrifying the first time, scary the second, and then painfully annoying the rest—not that the experience wasn't frightening. But an awful case of carpet burn converted fear into deep irritation.

Not to mention, different rooms kept getting trashed—like their bathroom. The longer they stayed, the more the activity seemed to increase.

Emerie stepped away from the tub, shaking her foot dry. An ice-cold draft enveloped her body and she shivered. She noticed with alarm the water in the toilet bowl had frozen. She wrapped her arms around herself as the mirror fogged over. Words started to appear on the condensation.

Emerie squinted. "LLIK...Lick? Wait, are you trying to write 'kill'?"

The words halted.

"It's a mirror." Emerie placed her hands on her hips. "Are you on the other side of the mirror? Then you'll have to write words backwards."

The mirror fogged over again and new words appeared. **KCUF**

"Yeah, well, kcuf you too!" Emerie yelled at the mirror. She stalked out of the bathroom and climbed into bed. Dylan mumbled something at her presence but she ignored him. After hijacking the majority of the pillows, she nested comfortably. Just as she started to drift off, a loud blast of organ music shook the entire house.

Bach's Fantasia in G minor.

"Where is that coming from?!" Dylan demanded into his single pillow. *"We don't have an organ!"*

"You're dreaming!" Emerie yelled over the organ music as she buried herself in the rest of the pillows. "I don't hear anything!"

———

Of course, Emerie *had* heard the organ music. She was also quite aware their new house was, in all likelihood, haunted. Emerie Fox and her boyfriend moved to Milton, Massachusetts about three weeks ago. She'd fallen in love with the fixer upper with a bright red door, an outdoor upstairs balcony, and a large varnished back porch that overlooked a small patch of forest. It was within walking distance of the library and fifteen minutes away from I-95. Aside from the supernatural pest problem—the house was perfect.

Unfortunately, the real estate agent had not been forthcoming about the paranormal infestation.

Her boyfriend had been less than enthusiastic about the purchase of the house with or without hauntings. He claimed they were the only people their age in the world who were buying houses and what's more, he wanted to live in Boston, not Milton.

Dylan didn't like Milton. He had an aversion to small towns and did not share Emerie's love of the obscurely historical. His family hailed from Chicago; he was used to having his home be a touring spot for his favorite bands and twenty-four-hour conveniences. There was not much to *do* in Milton, unless you enjoyed early American history or taverns that Washington Irving drank in. No concert venues, no clubs, no Broadway shows or any sort of night life. Instead there were churches, houses that dated back to the 1700s, a quaint Main Street, a pleasant forest preserve…and even more churches.

Worse still, Dylan's hour-long commute to his job in Boston was aggravating—Emerie understood this, but as she'd pointed out several times, it was too expensive to live there.

He didn't understand, of course. Probably because the high cost of living was a motivator, not a detractor. Dylan had never had to worry about things like if a paycheck would cover rent and groceries. If he fell in love with an apartment out of their budget, he would simply go to his parents for assistance. (His father was a high-profile politician and his mother ran a lifestyle web series where she explained which thousand-dollar table setting was the most striking.)

Emerie could not conceive of asking her parents for help. Once she had moved out, that meant she was *done*. It was now up to her to take care of her family, not the other way around! Her mother was getting older and her father had just retired. That needed to factor into Emerie and Dylan's budget.

Of course, his usual rejoinder was the restorations on their new house were far more costly than a high rent. Emerie would finish the conversation (he claimed it was an argument, she insisted it was a conversation) by declaring their house was *an investment* in their life together. Dylan would generally give up at that point.

The poltergeist was his latest gripe, a technically understandable irritation, but frankly, Emerie wasn't about to let a little thing like a haunting stop her home makeover plans. Which was why she tried her best to ignore the entity.

This was easier said than done. Particularly since the poltergeist was becoming bolder with its antics with each passing day.

After managing to get a few scrapes of sleep, Emerie awoke and trudged downstairs for her morning fix, the found that her coffeemaker was missing.

Emerie had unpacked the coffeemaker the first day and they had been enjoying steamed lattes every morning since. Their love for all things caffeinated bonded them as a couple and neither one of them were particularly pleasant until their second cup. It simply wasn't possible for the machine to have been lost in the move. After she checked every single cupboard twice, Emerie was forced to deliver the bad news to Dylan.

"This is the last straw, Emerie!" Dylan stormed into the kitchen. He was already dressed, in camel-colored slacks and a salmon dress shirt. He had forgotten to iron his dress shirt, which gave him a somewhat rumpled appearance. Emerie toyed with letting him know but ultimately chose to allow him to continue his rant.

"What are we supposed to do? Drink *tea*?!" Dylan's tone suggested that forcing him to drink tea could lead to unemployment, disenfranchisement, and homelessness in one fell swoop.

"I like tea," Emerie said mildly. She was seated cross legged on the counter, still in her dinosaur-patterned pajamas. To prove this point, she took an exaggerated sip of herbal tea out of a mug shaped like Edgar Allan Poe's head.

"The thumps and thuds are one thing." He snatched the box of Froot Loops and poured them into a Star Trek mug. (The bowls were not yet unpacked). "It's an old house. We could chalk it up to faulty construction or boxes falling over or—whatever."

Emerie nodded earnestly.

"The organ music at three a.m.—we could live with that, it makes us more cultured," Dylan continued, setting down his mug. His fingers tangled in his white and blue striped tie. He was trying and failing to tie it round his neck, but only succeeded in making a noose.

"But stealing our *coffeemaker*?!" He then took a large gulp from his mug of Froot Loops. Ordinarily, Dylan was fairly finicky in his breakfast tastes, preferring egg white omelets with skim milk, perhaps some Greek yogurt and fruit. But desperate times—being late for work, not having proper groceries yet, their kitchen not fully unpacked, a haunt terrorizing them—led him to fall back into college habits and subsist purely on cereal.

"Nothing has stolen our coffeemaker," Emerie assured him as she grabbed a small pot and filled it with cereal herself. Unlike Dylan, Emerie had no stress-related qualms about eating breakfast cereal.

"We have just misplaced Norman. We will find him."

"Stop naming our appliances!" Dylan nearly garroted himself with his necktie. Emerie hopped off the counter.

"You used to think it was cute." She tied a Windsor knot easily and took a step back.

"This is all your fault." Dylan accidentally tripped over the garbage can. "*You*

encouraged it."

"What are you talking about?!" Emerie said, stung.

"The offering! When the lights started flickering, you set out a tray of mochi and salt water like the damn thing was a visiting neighbor!"

Well, that was unfair. That was how you dealt with spirits in Japan. You appeased them with a food offering, everyone knew that. And in her defense, the spirit *had* taken the food—the tray was empty the following day—although its activity increased.

Dylan would not let up. "How do you misplace a two-hundred dollar coffeemaker? It's a Keurig! It's priceless!"

"Well, it's not priceless." Emerie pointed out reasonably. "You just said the price. Two hundreds."

Dylan's face went purple. He was generally a handsome man, with a somewhat roguish look—high cheekbones, prominent brows, classically handsome. Emerie thought he looked a bit like Errol Flynn on a good day. But the purple somewhat ruined his countenance.

"I cannot live in this town, much less this house, without coffee!"

Emerie sighed. Dylan's repulsion to the house had some valid points —she could admit it was a trifle unfair they lived so close to her work and so far from his. The ever-present fear of purchasing a money pit was legitimate. The house needed a *lot* of repairs and the moving/renovating process was constantly hampered by ghostly pranks and burglaries.

Emerie took a deep breath. "It's garage sale season. I'm sure I could find a Mr. Coffee for a reasonable—"

"*I want my Keurig.*"

"All right, all right." Emerie munched her Froot Loops. "I'll find it. Norman's around here somewhere."

Dylan rolled his eyes at her refusal to stop calling their MIA coffeemaker Norman and exited the kitchen for a moment. He returned with his phone and handed it to her. He'd Googled the address—and apparently came upon some poorly designed websites. Emerie's brow furrowed.

"I'm pretty sure *this* is why we got the house so cheap," Dylan said as she scrolled with her thumb.

"Hm." Emerie handed the phone back to him. "I did tell you the house had a colorful history."

Dylan coughed. "*Colorful?* Apparently all manner of occult practice and ritual went on here. Spiritualist clubs came from all over the world to conjure and perform the darkest spells...did you know about this?!"

"The entire town of Milton is built on ghost stories." Emerie explained patiently. "It's part of the tourist trade."

That was the other side of Milton. Unfortunately, neither Nathanial Hawthorne nor Washington Irving ever wrote any short stories about the town, but Milton was still resolutely proud of its haunted woods, local goblins that apparently terrorized farmers in the 1970s, and their documented persecution of witches in the 1600s. A few B-movie horror films had been shot in town—nothing of true notoriety, but enough to warrant the occasional cult status. Emerie thought of Milton as a sort of less renowned Salem.

But it seemed Dylan's opinion of the town's supernatural folklore had shifted. "This house has a historical marker for the Lucifer Club. A crazy bunch of old biddies that summoned demons for laughs!"

"Did you know that in New Orleans they have little signs outside their properties that say if it's haunted or not haunted?" Emerie asked conversationally. "It's part of the allure. But none of it's real."

"How can you say that?" Dylan raked his fingers through his hair. "You have been dragged off your bed and down the hall three times this week!"

"I'm going to the doctor next week." Emerie slurped the milk out of her pot. "I bet it's a sleep disorder."

"And the organ music?!"

"You know, we live near several churches. Maybe we're in, like, a sound wave Bermuda triangle kind of area and we just *absorb* all of the churches' sound waves—"

"Emerie!" Dylan held up his hands. "Stop. Listen to yourself. You sound like a lunatic."

The lunatic line was an old favorite of Dylan's. He used it when she first found the house and excitedly pointed out the magenta living room and the possibly broken beyond repair antique oven in the attic. But while Emerie would concede her home décor taste was less than usual, being called a lunatic in this context annoyed her.

"You're the one talking about ghosts and haunted houses." Emerie placed her drained pot in the sink. "Just because I don't believe in the boogeyman doesn't make me a lunatic. Stop being condescending."

"I'm not being condescending." He poured the rest of his breakfast into the sink in disgust. "I'm being realistic—I'm being an adult. We can't live in this house!"

Emerie placed her hands on her hips. "*You're* being an adult?! You're the one who wants to abandon our house without even giving it a fair shot! Who's being the immature one?"

It was perhaps not the best idea to get into a "who's more of an adult" argument while she was clad in dinosaur-patterned pajamas—Dylan's suit shook the foundation of her point. But she stared at him resolutely, not giving an inch.

"Maybe we have different ideas of what constitutes adulthood," Dylan said finally.

"Maybe," Emerie agreed, "but I'm not *quitting*, Dylan. I'm sticking it out—I have to! I bought the house, I made the commitment, and I am *not* wasting the money Ji-Ji left me. This house is mine. I hope you'll make it yours too."

She had brought up the big guns. Dylan *knew* how devastated she'd been upon her grandfather's death. It had been his idea to use the money from her inheritance to purchase a small home, but hers to refurbish an old home—just like her Ji-Ji had done back in Hokkaido. The idea had shortly turned into an obsession, whether Dylan liked it or not.

There was an awkward pause as Dylan avoided her gaze and absorbed his surroundings—the piles of unpacked boxes, the stacked paint cans, the ratty curtains. The kitchen certainly wasn't looking its best. The window overlooking the sink revealed a daunting jungle of wild hedges and giant trees that littered leaves all over their front lawn. Those trees did an excellent job of blocking light into the kitchen, which gave the room a very gloomy atmosphere. Some of the black-and-white floor tiles were missing, the wallpaper was peeling, and the light fixtures were dingy. Like everything else in the house, it could do with a complete overhaul.

"I have to go," Dylan said finally. "My flight's in an hour. Emerie, if this haunting shit doesn't let up, *we are leaving*. We are not sticking around to become the next Amityville!"

Still stung by the "lunatic" comment, she folded her arms. "I will say this one more time. There is nothing wrong with this house. We are not going anywhere. Is that clear?"

Before he could respond, there was a mighty *CRASH*—all the pots and pans hanging over the kitchen island fell to the floor. The mini-egg skillet ricocheted off Dylan's forehead.

Emerie glanced upwards. "I will get that fixed by the time you return."

———

Dylan was attending a "Pioneers in Digital Marketing" conference in New York. The conference only lasted a week, but he had sworn he would spend an additional two weeks taking a detour in Boston to look for reasonably priced apartments, no matter what Emerie said.

They hadn't even been living together for that long yet it seemed they were fighting constantly. She kept hoping he would see her side of things and join in on the project with gusto...but everything he did to help seemed to be done only to appease her, not because he understood or even cared about her feelings for the house.

It was unfortunate Dylan left right after a fight. But by late afternoon, Emerie felt energized and motivated. She ripped the rest of the magenta wallpaper from the living room, she sanded down the floors, she swept, she scrubbed the kitchen, she replaced tile, and she contemplated paint colors. Projects were healing. Sweat provided a sense of Zen towards her situation. Tasks distracted her from thinking too hard about her boyfriend's dampening attitude. She wondered if he really *would* find an apartment in Boston. He'd agreed to move in with her—after all, the house was in her name, not his. Dylan came to Milton for her...he didn't have as much riding on the house as she did.

It would be easy for him to call it quits. The entity was especially hard on Dylan, who seemed to carry the brunt of the haunts—not counting it occasionally dragging Emerie down the hallway. All of his left socks disappeared in one night, along with his boater shoes, and his Netflix queue was abruptly deleted. He complained of the drafts more than Emerie and constantly whined something was *watching* him.

Emerie sighed. She opened the fridge (named Midge) and helped herself to some cold pizza—they had pretty much been subsisting on Chinese food and pizza. She retrieved another Guinness and walked into the living room, ready to settle in on the couch for an early dinner.

She froze and nearly dropped her pizza. There was large, graffiti-like writing on the wall where she'd intended to hang her flat screen.

HE'S A JERK, EMERIE. DUMP HIM.

She continued to stare. The words were a bloodish color and faintly glistened in the light. It was recent.

It was one thing to receive condensation mirror messages at three-a.m. on her bathroom mirror—she could chalk up to being half-asleep if she were feeling particularly rational. But this…?

Emerie set her dinner down, turned on her heel, ran out of the living room into the foyer and raced up to her bedroom to retrieve her large wooden bokuto—a Japanese wooden training sword—from the closet.

Emerie's mother's side of the family came from Hokkaido, Japan. Emerie spent most of her summer holidays there, staying with her Ji-Ji and Ba-chan. When Emerie was ten, she became enchanted by a Japanese swordsmanship demonstration at a Tanabata festival. Upon her return, her father had signed her up for kendo, much to the delight of her mother.

This phase hadn't lasted long, as the bokuto was her approximate height, which made wielding it a difficult affair. Her instructor insisted over and over that her diminutive size would have no bearing on her skill, as long as she practiced regularly. Unfortunately, Emerie wasn't exactly diligent and the wooden sword constantly fell from her fingers when she raised it over her head. Her kendo obsession lasted about as long as her ice-skating interest.

Still, Emerie had kept the weapon. Now she patrolled the house and looked for signs of…anything.

Nothing. All the doors were locked. All the windows were snapped shut. No signs of forced entry.

Emerie exhaled deeply.

"This is getting ridiculous," she muttered, retreating to the living room. "I will not live with a ghost! Especially a ghost that dispenses relationship advice! I have girlfriends for that job!"

Nothing responded.

Furiously, she stormed upstairs to her bedroom. She was going to figure out a way to de-haunt her house before Dylan returned.

————

Don't stop now. Keep reading with your copy of find your next read, HELL'S HERESIES, by Kat D. Coffin.

Discover more from Scott Craven at www.authorscottcraven.com

And then, find your next read, HELL'S HERESIES, by Kat D. Coffin.

———

Emerie Fox's New Home Comes with Unwanted Surprises...

Leaky pipes, moldy basements—and a mischievous demon poltergeist who's redecorating her home, stealing her stuff, and leaving blood-soaked messages on the mirror. Sure, the messages are helpful (like reminders to buy milk or grab an umbrella), but Emerie is not the kind of person who tolerates vermin—supernatural or otherwise.

When DIY Exorcism Goes Wrong...

In a desperate attempt to rid herself of the supernatural nuisance, Emerie accidentally rips open a rift between worlds, unleashing the forces of Hell onto her quiet New England town. Now, with a sarcastic witch, a no-nonsense priest, and a dangerously attractive (and seriously irritated) demon named Samael by her side, Emerie has no choice but to track down and exorcise every demon before the portal to Hell consumes everything.

But as things spiral out of control, Emerie begins to wonder: is this just a simple case of demon extermination, or is something far darker—and much more personal—at play?

Perfect for fans of dark humor, supernatural adventure, and steamy demon romance, this fast-paced, laugh-out-loud paranormal romp will keep you hooked until the very last page!

All reviews are **welcome** and **appreciated**. Please consider leaving one on your favorite social media and book buying sites.

Escape Your World. Get Lost in Ours! City Owl Press at www.cityowlpress.com.

ACKNOWLEDGMENTS

No author is an island, though it seems like much of the writing occurs there. Thank you to Jenn B., whose editing skills turned my scattershot story into an arrow of plotting, character development, and redemption.

I'm indebted to the amazing people at City Owl Press who believed mythical creatures could age and do stupid stuff unbefitting of their years. Thank you, Danielle DeVor, for your fine-tuned editing skills that brought everything into focus.

I'd also like to apologize to my big brother Gary, who read a very early draft and was brutally honest in a way you'd think we weren't related. Even as I simmered, I knew he was right and made several changes based on his review. Not that I ever told him that.

Most of my gratitude goes to you, fine readers, who gave this book a shot. When I told people I was writing about a retirement home for supernatural creatures, a few said, "That's completely unrealistic." I never mentioned the irony of criticizing a book about fictional creatures as "unrealistic," but for everyone else, thanks for stretching your limits of believability.

ABOUT THE AUTHOR

SCOTT CRAVEN is a retired journalist with more than 40 years in the newspaper business. Much of his career was spent as an award-winning feature writer for The Arizona Republic in Phoenix. He's had numerous short stories published in online magazines and journals.

He's the author of the middle-grade trilogy, "Dead Jed: Adventures of a Middle School Zombie," available online, in print and on Audible.

He lives with his wife Melissa and their three dogs in tiny homes in a small Oregon town. While he can still take care of himself, Craven will be fine with moving to an unassisted-living home as long as it has pickleball.

authorscottcraven.com

f facebook.com/authorScottCraven
X x.com/authorscottcraven
instagram.com/authorscottcraven

ABOUT THE PUBLISHER

City Owl Press is a cutting edge indie publishing company, bringing the world of romance and speculative fiction to discerning readers.

Escape Your World. Get Lost in Ours!

www.cityowlpress.com

facebook.com/CityOwlPress
x.com/cityowlpress
instagram.com/cityowlbooks
pinterest.com/cityowlpress
tiktok.com/@cityowlpress